Also by Andrey Biely
ST. PETERSBURG

Other books written, translated or edited
by George Reavey

DEAD SOULS by Nicolai Gogol
FATHERS AND SONS by Ivan Turgenev
THE POETRY OF BORIS PASTERNAK
THE LAST SUMMER by Boris Pasternak
A SKY-BLUE LIFE AND SELECTED STORIES by Maxim Gorky
THE MEANING OF HISTORY *and* SOLITUDE AND SOCIETY
by N. Berdyaev
THE NEW RUSSIAN POETS
THE EGYPTIAN DOVE *and* AGAINST THE CURRENT by K. Leontiev
SOVIET LITERATURE TODAY
COLOURS OF MEMORY: Poems

The Silver Dove

The Silver Dove

ANDREY BIELY

Translated from the Russian
and with an introduction
by George Reavey

Preface by Harrison E. Salisbury

Grove Press, Inc.   New York

ISBN: 0–394–17859–9
Grove Press ISBN: 0–8021–0046–5
Library of Congress Catalog Number: 73–21039

First Evergreen Edition
Second Printing
Manufactured in the United States of America
Distributed by Random House, Inc.

GROVE PRESS, INC.
53 East 11th Street, New York, N.Y. 10003

~~~*~~~ Preface ~~~*~~~

Nearly twenty years after writing *The Silver Dove*, Andrey Biely looked back on his work in wonderment and even awe. It was, he clearly understood, an unsuccessful novel in many ways. It revealed his own confused spiritual and psychological state in the period of its creation: the shattering days after the Russian revolution of 1905. Technically, it was not a success. He had tried too much, written too rapidly in those few weeks which he spent in the remote village of Bobrovka, far from the maelstrom of Moscow. He had poured everything into it—his mystical imaginings, his effort to give Russian literature a new vocabulary, his secret (and not so secret) attraction to the Cabbala, the terrible and conflicting pull of his own complex relationships with the Bloks (the poet, Alexander, but more specifically his wife, Lubov), the agonizing not-to-be-understood power which was wielded over him by Anna Rudolfevna Minstsleva, as strange a siren as the decadent salons of Petersburg had ever seen.

All of that went into *Serebryanyi Golub, The Silver Dove*. But had that been all, the novel would have remained a literary curiosity, long abandoned, unread except by a small band of specialists examining the confused Russian literary experiments of the first decade of the century, sifting the ashes for omens which would serve to point the way to the brilliant explosion in Russian creative life just getting underway.

Except for one thing—something which lay within the novel, something which, indeed, is its very core and heart, the prophetic allegory which it contains: the allegory of the fate which even then loomed over Russia.

What Biely had done—and this he did not realize until long after, not until the events had actually occurred and the path that Russia would take had been firmly fixed by the revolution, by Lenin and all that happened in the early years thereafter—was to create a psychic vision of Russia's future. He painted a picture of a young intellectual, such as himself or any other of the young intellectuals then struggling over a spiritual and intellectual solution for Russian backwardness, Russian darkness, Russian evil, falling into the grasp of the very forces which he was striving to overcome—those dark elemental earth forces which lie at the base of the Russian ethos.

Biely's young man, Daryalsky, is a sophisticated university graduate, a writer, an educated Russian *intelligent,* such a man as Biely himself. His fiancée is Katya, a beautiful, innocent girl straight out of Turgenev, a girl of pure heart, open blue eyes, unable to comprehend the power of dark forces, on the one hand, or of Daryalsky's "scientific" theories of Marx, Lasalle, and the other rational gods who were to lead mankind out of the ignorance of the nineteenth century into the bright new world of the twentieth, which, in a sense, Daryalsky symbolizes.

But, as in the case of so many Russian intellectuals, science and theory were not enough. Something ate at Daryalsky's being. He drank—occasionally too much—in the dreary village tavern, and he craved what he could not imagine.

And in this "something" lay the fatal weakness of Daryalsky's twentieth-century image. He found himself powerfully, irresistibly attracted to the earth mother Matryona, a pock-marked peasant woman, dirty, shameless, whose body swallowed him in its robust passion. Matryona was the wife of Mitry Kudeyarov, a crippled carpenter, leader of a sect called the "Doves," one of the countless mystical sects, like the *khlysti*, that have flourished since remote time in the gray Russian villages, flourished despite the crusades of the Orthodox Patriarchs, the repression of the Czar's police, or the propaganda of the Bolsheviks. Kudeyarov, a man with a face like a gnawed bone and a grasp of black magic and village poisons, uses his woman to draw Daryalsky into the sect.

Quickly, despite his veneer of twentieth-century sophistication, Daryalsky enters the inner circle of the Doves and comes to believe that here he has discovered the secret of Russia—and perhaps he has.

"The Russian earth knows the secret. So does the Russian forest," writes Biely. "In the West there are many books; in Russia there are many unspoken words. There is that in Russia which destroys books and smashes buildings and puts life into the fire; and on that day when the West comes to Russia it will be totally consumed by fire; all will burn that can be burned because only from the ashes of death does the Zhar-Ptitsa, the Firebird, fly to heaven."

A feeble effort—she has no real strength—is made by Katya to rescue her fiancé. But her powers, and even those of an intellectual friend of Daryalsky's and of her uncle, a symbol of bureaucratic Russia, cannot cope with the elemental force of the true children of the Russian soil. Daryalsky is lost in the black pit of Russian ignorance, superstition, hatred, and evil. So Russian intelligence, Russian creativity, the spirit of its poets and artists, is extinguished by the black force of the earth and the forest.

The discovery which Biely made so long after writing his book was that he had created an allegory of the tragedy which was waiting in the wings for Russia. Daryalsky represented the intellectuals who strove to create the revolution—the intelligentsia. Katya represented the pure ideal of Russian dreams, untainted either by sophistication or superstition. Matryona was the Russian soil, the earth tradition of the great country. And Kudeyarov was Rasputin, the crafty peasant, the member of the Doves, who matched wit and cunning against the aristocrats, the bureaucrats, and the revolutionaries, and who, in the end, won out, breathing his spirit and not that of the scientific-social theories into the new regime which was to take over—destroying not only the Czar but Lenin, and placing in their stead on the Russian throne a man of the same blood, crafty, cruel, superstitious, earthy, evil, a true Dove—Stalin.

"*The Silver Dove*," Biely said, "was unsuccessful in many ways but it was successful in one. It pointed a finger to a still empty place. But soon this place would be occupied by Rasputin."

William Irwin Thompson has evolved a theory that poets and great creative artists live "at the edge of history," that, in effect, they prevision what is to come; that we can better see what lies beyond the rim of today by turning to the poet than to the futurologist.

To read *The Silver Dove* is not always easy. Much of Biely's language is almost literally untranslatable. But it compels reading, for no better example can be found of the soundness of Thompson's theory. *The Silver Dove* lacks the form and unity of Biely's great *Petersburg*, forever a monument to the mystery and drama of that richest and most complex city, half-Russian, half-European, half-ancient, half-contemporary—an unrepeatable mixture of the Russian past and the Russian dream. But contained in the feverish, cloudy, nightmare, haunting pages of *The Silver Dove* can be found not only the blueprint for Russia's twentieth century, but a reliable index to her past and an almanac which gives us the clues to her future centuries.

—Harrison E. Salisbury

⚜️ Translator's Note ⚜️

Astonishingly, while finishing my translation of *The Silver Dove*, I found a long lost letter from Samuel Beckett addressed to me in February, 1937. Among other things, Beckett told me he had heard a lecture in Dresden on "Belji" by "Prof. Fedor Stepun." Evidently impressed, Beckett wrote: "Why don't you translate *The Silver Dove* . . . ?" I was already involved with Biely, but the oncoming 1939 war postponed what is now being realized in the 1970s.

Andrey Biely completed his first novel, *The Silver Dove* (*Serebryanyi Golub*), in the winter of 1909. It was a novel of about five hundred pages and sensational in every way. It broke with the realist Turgenev–Tolstoy tradition and revived that of Gogol's *Dead Souls;* it introduced many twentieth-century innovations parallel in some ways to those of James Joyce.

To begin with, *The Silver Dove* was first printed serially in Moscow in 1909 in the last issues of the literary review *Vesy* (*Scales*), the central organ of the Russian Symbolists. It was then issued in book form under the imprint of *Skorpion* (Moscow, 1910). In 1917, it was reprinted in Moscow by the publisher Pasukanis; and then, after the Revolution, it appeared in 1922 in a Russian edition by *Epokha* in Berlin, where a great many Russian authors, including Boris Pasternak, were also published at that time owing to paper shortage and censorship in post-civil-war Soviet Union. Since then, *The Silver Dove* has been reprinted in Russian by Wilhelm

Fink Verlag in Munich in 1967. The Grove Press edition of *The Silver Dove*, published in New York in 1974, is therefore the first English-language edition, based on the 1922 Russian *Epokha* edition, which I was lucky enough to find in Paris in the early 1930s.

Thus, *The Silver Dove*, one of the great novels of this century, has so far never been reprinted in the Soviet Union as distinct from Tsarist Russia. Of course we must realize that, since 1932 under Stalin, "Socialist Realism" had become the official literary theory. Andrey Biely's vision and style, love of satire and the grotesque, were radically different from this political realism, though they have influenced many Soviet writers in the 1920s and some in the 1960s.

The nonpublication of *The Silver Dove* does not imply that Andrey Biely, up to 1934, did not write or publish anything during this Soviet period. On the contrary, he wrote and published quite a number of important works—critical, autobiographical, and fictional. Among them were *Reminiscences of Blok* (1922–23), *The Beginning of the Century* (1933), *Between Two Revolutions* (1934), *The Jottings of an Eccentric*, and *Moscow* (a novel in four volumes). But only one prose work of Biely's, a critical study—*The Art of Gogol*—appeared posthumously in 1935. Significantly, it was Nicolai Gogol, with his novel *Dead Souls*, his *Mirgorod*, and other tales, who had exercised such a vital influence on Biely's prose and vision of character. I must add that another volume, *The Correspondence of A. A. Blok and Andrey Biely (1903–1919)*, a correspondence between the two leading Russian Symbolists, was also published in Moscow in 1940. Even though the bulk of Andrey Biely's prose has not been reprinted in the U.S.S.R. since his death—just as none of Pasternak's prose has been—the poetry of both these writers was reprinted in collected editions in the mid-1960s.

A word about Biely's original conception. In 1909 he had planned a trilogy under the general title of *East or West*. *The Silver Dove* was Volume I. The other two volumes were tentatively titled *The Traveling Companions*, or, later,

The Lacquered Carriage; and *The Invisible City.* Although the theme of *East or West* still predominated, Biely lost touch with the unifying plot and characters. As a result, his second great novel, *Petersburg* (serial, 1913; book, 1916), was unrelated, except in theme, to his first novel. As to the third novel, *The Invisible City,* not a trace of it remains. Actually, his third turned out to be *Kotik Letayev.* Written in 1915–16 in Switzerland, it was first published serially in *The Scythians* (1918), and then as a book in Berlin in 1922. This novel is autobiographical and has no thematic relation to his previous two. It is about a child's life in the womb and up to the age of five. Rich in irony, sarcasm, and character analysis of the parents, it is extremely experimental in structure and language.

To quote a few critical opinions about Biely's *The Silver Dove.* Prince D. S. Mirsky, in his *Contemporary Russian Literature* (London, 1926), writes: "This remarkable work . . . was soon to have such an enormous influence on the history of Russian prose. . . ." "He was, together with Blok and Gorky . . . the biggest figure in Russian literature, and far more influential than they." "The novel is written in splendid, sustainedly beautiful prose." "*The Silver Dove* . . . is one of the works of Russian literature that are most full of the most various riches." K. Mochulsky, another noted emigré critic, and biographer of Biely, whom I met in Paris, says: "No other Russian writer undertook such fearless experiments with the word as Andrey Biely." "*The Silver Dove* is constructed on the antithesis of the 'people' and the 'intelligentsia,' on the theme of 'love–hate,' which is the foundation of Russian historical tragedy."

A word about my personal involvement with Andrey Biely. At Cambridge University I became interested in Pasternak and Biely, but Biely's texts were more difficult to acquire. I established a correspondence with Pasternak in 1931 and met him in Paris in 1935 and in Moscow in 1943–1945. Andrey Biely died too early for me to meet him, although by 1931–32 I had already written about him and published an excerpt of his *Kotik Letayev* in *The New Review* (Paris), edited by Samuel Putnam. I also included some of Biely's prose and poetry in *Soviet Literature*, which I edited with Marc Slonim in 1933. After the war, in October of 1948, I gave a talk on Andrey Biely at the Russian Society at Oxford University. Then, in March 1951, the French review *Roman* No. 2 published my article "Le Mot et le Monde d'André Biely et de James Joyce," an article originally accepted by Ruth Stefan for *Tiger's Eye*, a New York review which folded before the article appeared. I next brought Biely to the attention of Grove Press in 1955, which led to my translating *The Silver Dove* in the next year or two (first draft), and to the appearance of *Petersburg* in 1959 with a preface by me. In the later 1950s and the 1960s I became so involved with Pasternak and various other authors that I neglected Biely, except for the appearance of his "The Gropings of Cosmoses" in my anthology *Modern Soviet Short Stories* in 1961. Moreover, I have translated the whole of *Kotik Letayev* and some of his other works.

I must comment on the difficulties of translating Biely. Unlike most authors, Biely composes rather than writes; that is, according to him, he structures his sentences rhythmically in his head while walking in the country. His prose is therefore essentially rhythmical. The translator's first task is to grasp that rhythm—the general rhythm and the variations within it. Another peculiarity of Biely's style is his extensive use of the colon and the semicolon, sometimes extending throughout a long paragraph. Biely has also deeply researched the nature and the dynamism of the word, which his article "The Magic of Words" (1909) illustrates. He also plunged into esoteric studies which are reflected in *The Silver Dove*. His vision of the word and character, stemming largely, but in an even more exaggerated form, from Gogol, is that of an unstable universe poised on the brink of disaster. Grimace, gesture, and sound effects figure systematically in his depiction of character. I must add I have been prevailed upon to diminish some of the verbal sound effects possibly perplexing to the reader.

Lastly, a few words about the pronunciation of Biely's name. Andrey Biely is a pseudonym; his real name is Boris Bugáyev. In the catalogues of the New York Public Library, for example, we come across "Bugáyev" and "Bely." If I have spelled him "Biely" since the early 1930s it is because of the soft sound ("ie" or "ye") of the "e" in "Bely," which means "white." If Boris Bugáyev had been an English or American writer, he would have been known as Andrew White.

I should like to thank my wife, Jean Reavey, for her help in typing the manuscript and correcting the proofs.

—George Reavey,
New York, 1974

Table of Contents

Part Two

·:ン· Introduction ·ン·

Andrey Biely: Childhood and Education

Andrey Biely (1880–1934) was born on October 14 in Moscow, some fifteen months before James Joyce and less than a year before the assassination of Tsar Alexander II. Andrey Biely was not his real name, but a pseudonym assumed after he began writing in the early 1900s and when he published his first book, *Symphony (Second, Dramatic)*, in Moscow in April, 1902. This was to be the first of four *Symphonies* (1902–1908), which were full of irony, satire, and musically discontinuous prose. It certainly created a sensation at the time, especially in those academic circles which Biely frequented. In anticipation of the "scandal" and the label "decadent" his work would provoke, Biely decided on a nom de plume. However, it was a friend of his, Serezha Soloviev, who suggested "Andrey Biely."

The real family name was Bugáyev, and his Christian name was Boris; he was the son of Nikolai Vasilievich Bugáyev, an internationally known mathematician and professor at Moscow University, who is described as unusually ugly, clever, and eccentric; a man of humor, grotesque imagery, and verbal puns. His mother, Alexandra Dmitrievna, was a beautiful society lady, fond of music and piano-playing, in temperament, very different from her husband. She tended to be hysterical and highly strung. She was also very possessive of her child. The differences in temperament between the parents often led to tension and conflict in the home, and this affected the future writer as a child and later played an important part in the mature novelist's dramatic and nightmarish view of the world, which he was to conceive as perpetually on the brink of disaster and collapse. Early on, Biely sensed that their household was somehow destined symbolically to illustrate the collapse of a whole cultural order. To escape from this nightmarish presentiment, he attempted to found a new verbal world of understanding. In his third work, a short novel entitled *Kotik Letayev* (he was his mother's "kotik"—"pussycat"), finally published in 1922, Biely treats of his childhood, family life, and social environment up to the age of five in a most extraordinary verbal and symbolic way.

His father, Nikolai Bugáyev, did not confine himself to purely academic circles. He was a friend of Michael Soloviev, the brother of Vladimir Soloviev, the famous religious and Symbolist philosopher, who was to exercise a great influence on Biely and whom Biely met shortly before he died in 1900. For a time, Michael Soloviev and his family actually lived in the same house as the Bugáyevs, and Andrey Biely became great friends with Serezha Soloviev, the philosopher's nephew. By early 1904, through the Solovievs, Biely was to meet Alexander Blok (1880–1921), the great Russian Symbolist poet, whose life and writings were also to become very involved with Biely's. Their correspondence alone throws much light on the age. Leo Tolstoy was also a visitor to the house, and in *Kotik Letayev* Biely describes how he once sat on Tolstoy's knee. In 1896, his mother took Andrey to France, Germany, Switzerland, and Paris, where he met Paul Boyer, just as later, in 1906–07, he was to have frequent meetings in Paris with Jean Jaurés, the French socialist leader. By 1910, at the age of thirty, Biely was not only prominent in Russian literature but also knew practically everyone of note in Russia in the literary and philosophical fields. Among this group were the Merezhkovskys, Vyachis-

lav Ivanov, Valery Bryusov, Boris Pasternak, Anna Akhmatova, Nikolai Berdyaev, Maxim Gorky, Marina Tsvetayeva,
to mention only a few. He was also deeply involved in
Symbolism, the great movement in the first decade of the
twentieth century in Russia, and he attempted to raise Symbolism to a greater ecumenical height and to set it on
religious foundations. This, of course, led to polemics and
much shifting of positions as well as violent disputes. At one
point, Biely was challenged to a duel; at another he challenged Blok.

Andrey Biely's first ten years were spent at home under
the guidance of his mother and two successive governesses. It
was his mother who introduced him to music, and once,
when he was ill, to Gogol's *Dead Souls* as read by her. In
1891, he entered Polivanov's Gymnasium (the Russian
equivalent of high school), where he remained until he attended Moscow University in 1899. At the University he
studied science as well as literature, ending as a philologist.
He began writing and publishing while still at the University.
Up to 1909, apart from the *Symphonies* and several books
of verse, he devoted himself mainly to Symbolism and criti-
cism. In his critical five-hundred-page volume, *Arabesques*,
covering the years 1904–09, which finally appeared in 1911,
he has written on Nietzsche, Dostoyevsky, Ibsen, Baudelaire,
and many other literary and philosophical subjects. The
scope of Biely's critical essays makes it clear that he was a
writer eager to shape the destiny of art and of the world. But
he was certainly not actively involved in political activities.
Alexander Blok wrote in his essay "Intelligentsia and Revolution" (January, 1918):

> I am speaking of writers, for instance, who, if they are con-
> cerned with politics, sin against themselves for they "run
> with the hare and hunt with the hounds." They will fall be-
> tween two stools. They will not succeed in becoming politi-
> cians and they will lose the authentic voice of the artist. I
> maintain that it is not only their privilege but their duty to

be inexpedient, "indelicate," in listening to the great music of the future whose sounds fill the air, and not in searching for separate, shrill and false notes in the majestic roar and ringing of the world orchestra.

The music of the future was certainly something Biely understood, and from 1909 he was soon to reach a climax in his creative work.

The Silver Dove and Petersburg (1909–1913)

In the winter of 1909, Andrey Biely entered into his most creative period. Urged by M. O. Gershenzon, a biographer and historian, he isolated himself in the country to start writing a magnum opus, a trilogy of novels under the general title of *East or West*. At the same time he began putting in order his essays and lectures which were soon to appear under the titles of *Symbolism* and *Arabesques*. He also began to delve into the occult arts—astrology, magic, the Cabbala, alchemy—and into sectarian beliefs such as those of the *Khlysti*, a seventeenth-century sect of flagellants. About this time he met Assya Turgenev, who had been studying engraving in Brussels and who was related to the then already deceased famous writer. Within a year or so Biely was destined to marry Assya and travel with her to Europe and the Middle East.

The Silver Dove turned out to be the first volume of the intended trilogy. The setting of this first novel is the countryside, that is, a noble's estate, fields, forests, villages, and provincial towns. The main village is Tzelebeyevo, and the local town is Likhov. The Russian peasant, the tiller of the soil, does not really figure in the novel. The principal characters are landowners, merchants, priests, servants, handicraftsmen, and intellectuals. The hero Daryalsky is a poet and writer spending his summer in the country. The heroines are drastic opposites: Katya, the granddaughter of the Baroness Todrabe-Graaben and Daryalsky's fiancée; and Matryona, a

pock-marked wench, the wife of the carpenter Kudeyarov.
Owing to various circumstances, Daryalsky abandons Katya
for Matryona. But this is no simple betrayal. It turns out that
Kudeyarov, the carpenter, is the head of a secret sect known
as "The Doves," which has its own rituals and magic ceremonies. The carpenter is actually planning to have his wife
made pregnant by an outside spirit so as to engender a new
Savior. To begin with, Daryalsky fulfills this role and, having abandoned the Baroness's estate, he stays with the carpenter and Matryona, and even works as a carpenter himself.
However, the situation becomes complicated, for no young
Savior seems to be forthcoming. The carpenter begins plot-
ting against Daryalsky, and the latter, sensing this, tries to
escape to Moscow, but is waylaid and murdered.

The Silver Dove is of course much more complex than
this simple outline suggests. It is rich in characters, in varied
language, in rhythmical prose, and in character contrasts of
men and women, and social strata. It is full of amazing
descriptions of nature and magic rituals. It is replete with
mysterious allusions. It has an astrologer in the person of
Schmidt, a friend of Daryalsky's. It also has an underground theme, that of *East or West*. The fate of Russia
is at stake. Russia is menaced by aggressive "panmongolism." There is a scene of a Japanese man driving through
a village in an automobile—an unexpected picture in a
Russian landscape of 1909. The idea of menacing "panmongolism" was already present in the work of Vladimir
Soloviev. Events in China and Japan, and the Russo–Japanese
War (1904–06), had no doubt given rise to the idea of "The
Yellow Peril." At this stage, Andrey Biely even identified
"Mongolism" with the encroaching threat of communism
and terrorism. After 1918 he changed his mind about this and
sided with Ivan Razumnik's "Scythian" theories, namely that
the revolution was of Russian origin. But in 1909 Daryalsky
was also engulfed and destroyed by a secretly spreading sect.
An intellectual's attempt to unite with the "people" brought
only disaster. Daryalsky, now in boots and a red shirt, had

turned from West to East. And Kudeyarov, the carpenter,
seemed to be a premonition of Rasputin and his damaging
erotic and political influence. Biely himself realized this later
when he wrote in *Between Two Revolutions:*

> In Bobrovka I sat down finally to write my first novel. I
> heard the Rasputin spirit before Rasputin arrived on the
> scene. . . . I fantasized him in the person of my carpenter:
> it was Rasputin's village past. The nature of my carpenter
> was composed from a series of natures (a carpenter I saw
> plus Merezhkovsky and others). Matryona's nature from a
> certain peasant woman plus (L. D. Blok*), plus . . . and
> so on. The novel also reflected a personal note, tormenting
> me throughout my illness: the unhealthy sensation of "per-
> secution," a feeling of snares and an expectation of destruc-
> tion: it is there—in the fable of *The Dove.*"

It is indeed true that Biely fell sick from time to time, and
seemed possessed by the "persecution mania"—especially so
in 1916 when he left Rudolf Steiner and Dornach.

The Silver Dove appeared serially late in 1909, and as a
book in 1910, the year Leo Tolstoy died. Alexander Blok
called it "a novel of genius." For a while, as he began working on his second novel, Biely thought of it as a continuation
of *The Dove.* By 1913, the title had been changed most ap-
propriately to *Petersburg* (called *St. Petersburg* in the American edition), for the novel covering three days reveals to us
many aspects of that city just as James Joyce's *Ulysses* did
so for Dublin in one day. *Petersburg* was finally brought out
in book form in 1916. Except for the East or West theme,
Petersburg was in no sense a continuation of *The Silver
Dove.* There were no characters in common. It is a great and
extraordinary novel in many ways, and portrays the life of
the city as a sort of phantasmagoria. A chief character in the
novel, Ableukhov, is of Mongolian descent and an arch-
bureaucrat. His son is a radical and a terrorist. It is interesting

---

* Lubov Dmitrievna Blok (1881–1939), born Mendeleyev, the wife
of Alexander Blok, with whom Biely was in love at one time.

that Biely revised this novel at least five times. The final *Epokha* version of 1922 had been cut by almost a quarter. This was mostly as a result of a post-revolutionary transformation in Biely's view of the world, of anthroposophy and "panmongolism" in particular. The third part of the trilogy, provisionally entitled *The Invisible City*, has never been found.

Andrey Biely and Rudolf Steiner

As we have seen, Andrey Biely, somewhat like W. B. Yeats, was attracted to theosophy and the occult. But by 1910–11 his interest shifted to Rudolf Steiner and his system of anthroposophy, and this interest finally led him, in 1914, to Dornach, in Switzerland.

But before going to Dornach, where he spent almost three years, Biely completed *The Silver Dove* and, after marrying Assya Turgenev, set out on what might be called a honeymoon trip to Palermo, Tunis, Kerouane, Cairo, and Jerusalem, returning to Russia in April, 1911. During all that time, Biely kept up his correspondence with Blok. In the summer of 1912, Biely and Assya went to Norway and then sailed from Bergen to Newcastle, visited London and Paris, then Switzerland and Germany. In Leipzig they attended some lectures given by Rudolf Steiner and went to the grave of Nietzsche, who had greatly influenced Biely in his earlier years. There he had an ecstatic experience, which developed into "fits of incredible illness." By February 1, 1914, they arrived at the Anthroposophical Center in Dornach, where Steiner was constructing a temple, which they helped to build. While in Switzerland, he got the idea of writing a cycle entitled *My Life*. The cycle was never completed, but the first volume turned out to be the remarkable *Kotik Letayev*, which we shall return to later on. Then the First World War broke out and Biely was very much cut off from Russia. He began to have bouts of a strange malady—a return of his "persecution mania." He also began to react against anthroposophy and Rudolf Steiner. In the summer of 1916 Biely received notice that he was being called for military service. He decided to leave Dornach and return to Russia via France, England, and Norway. But his wife Assya refused to return with him, and, like Daryalsky and Katya, they were never destined to reunite. During his trip, Biely imagined he was being followed everywhere. In August he finally set foot on Russian soil and felt better. Very soon he was involved in the Russian Revolution.

Biely's next and last stay outside Russia was from November, 1921, to October, 1923. He spent most of those years in Berlin, at that time full of Russian writers who were busy publishing their works there. It was here that Biely republished both *The Silver Dove, Petersburg,* and *Kotik Letayev,* among other works.

Andrey Biely and James Joyce

Andrey Biely can with justice be regarded as one of the "peaks" of the modernist school. He can take his place beside James Joyce as an innovator, an artist of vision, a writer who has attempted to construct a new system of reality in the domain of the moribund novel and flagging prose. Of his work it can be said, as T. S. Eliot has said of Joyce's, that, "It is, I seriously believe, a step towards making the modern world possible in art." Biely's energies were devoted to making a new synthesis of the modern discoveries in the spheres of thought, human consciousness, literary form, and language. Like Joyce, Biely was acutely aware of the "flux," and laid an almost disproportionate stress on evolving a new medium of expression—a new language to express a new age sensed in all its extreme possibilities.

Andrey Biely may be described as the Russian contemporary of James Joyce. But, whereas Joyce continues to have his commentators, Biely, for political reasons, no longer has his outspoken commentators or disciples in the Soviet Union.

Moreover, as the author of an original system of writing, he is not always easily decipherable and has not so far made an impact on the West. Here, I shall not point out all the analogies between the Russian and the Irish writer. My main concern is with Biely's innovations in language and the form of the novel. That an affinity exists between the two writers will emerge from concrete examples. There are many points of difference, too—in vision, esthetic, and technique. But there are also enough points of similarity to justify a parallel. To emphasize the latter may also help to rescue Biely from his present oblivion. In any case, it is time that Western critics attempted to assess his work and consider it as a related part of the creative effort of the first forty years of this century that embraced Russia as well as Western Europe.

It may be argued that Biely failed to concentrate his energies in a few stupendous works as Joyce did; that he perhaps theorized too much; that he was more limited in confining himself exclusively to the Russian language, never attempting a work of the scope of *Finnegans Wake*, "that letter self-penned to one's another, that neverperfect everplanned"; that his symbolism was less purely esthetic; and that, finally, his background lacked the vast and systematic cultural sweep of the "Catholic" writer, who attempted "the totality of human experience on a simultaneous plane, to synchronize past, present and future in the timelessness of a millennium." But, even if Biely is less monumental, the aims and intentions of the two writers are in many respects qualitatively similar.

Biely and Joyce certainly shared an esthetic background—that of the European Symbolist movement; and this largely explains the affinity of their aims and achievements. The multiple effects, the international ramifications, the interpenetration of media, the dominance of music as the ideal condition of the arts, the consequent revolution in vision, structure, and language, resulting from the Symbolist ethos, and its influence also on the esthetic systems of Joyce and Biely, have perhaps not yet been adequately investigated.

Biely is certainly a new link for a broader assessment of the Symbolist movement as a whole and its impact on Russia. Indeed, in its wider manifestations, the Symbolist movement may be interpreted as a sort of modern Renaissance—one followed by a reformation, the politico–religious debate and strife that have predominated since the 1930s and driven the esthetic vision very much underground.

Andrey Biely was a prophet of the word, of the medium as its own raison d'être, the essential matter and material, a matter charged with an energy of its own, requiring no justification in terms of objective reality; for the assumption became that significance lay deeper, in the roots, in the latent potentialities and the interrelation of phenomena. Thus, at an earlier stage, and independently of Joyce, Biely began to arrive at the root conception of the word as the chief esthetic and dynamic source of the transformations he set out to depict. In his philosophy, the dynamic of the word coincided with a Heraclitean vision of the world in flux. As with Joyce, after successive experiments and an increasingly consistent application of the newly discovered principle, the new vision and the new technique became blended into an unmistakably novel system of expression.

By 1910–11, the year of *The Silver Dove*, Andrey Biely had published a book of essays entitled *Arabesques* and another critical book entitled *Symbolism*. Some of the essays in *Symbolism* were written as far back as 1903. From them we can extract the essence of his esthetic theory. Biely was no narrow esthetician of the "ivory tower" branch of the Symbolists: he was very much preoccupied with the vast problem of the "crisis of culture"; and faced with this crisis, he attempted to make of Symbolism a new "world view." As the chief theoretician and one of the leaders of the Russian Symbolist Movement, he identified himself more with that label than did Joyce, who absorbed, used, and developed the possibilities of the Symbolist esthetic without parading the label. And yet if we consider Joyce's statement of 1918, as quoted by Frank Budgeon, "But I want the reader to under-

stand always through suggestion rather than direct statement"; and if we connect it with George Moore's reaction
to Mallarmé's first reading of the *L'Après-midi d'un Faune*,
"But what is Symbolism? Vulgarly speaking, the opposite of
what you mean. For example, you want to say that music,
which is the new art, is replacing the old art, which is
poetry. . . ."; and then remember Poe's statement, "I know
that indefiniteness is an element of the true music of poetry
. . . a *suggestive* indefiniteness of vague and therefore spiritual in effect. . . ."; Baudelaire's "*Les parfums, les couleurs
et les sons*" and his "*forêt pleine de symboles*"; Verlaine's
"*rien que la musique*"; and many other such affirmations
stressing the symbol, music, and the suggestive rather than
the logical use of words, we should not underestimate the
Symbolist ethos in Joyce's work. Indeed, in its musical conception and structure, in its very symbolism and historical
awareness, *Finnegans Wake* can be regarded as the greatest
and ultimate product of the Symbolist esthetic. But already
in January 1903, Alexander Blok, the great Russian poet, in
a letter to Biely, wrote: "I have just read your article *Forms
of Art*. . . . It is the 'song of a system' I have long been
waiting for. . . . 'The depth of music and the absence in it
of external reality suggest the idea of the noumenal character
of music, explaining the mystery of movement, the mystery
of life. . . .' I can see that you wish to hear the music of the
future. . . ." Biely was in the habit of expounding his theories more than Joyce, as can be seen from his *Symbolism*
and other critical works or Prefaces. Here are some statements Biely made between 1904 and 1910:

> We "decadents" are convinced that we are the final link in
> an endless chain of experiences—that central station from
> which new paths will lead.
>
> —*Criticism and Symbolism*, 1904

> Such ages are characterized by the intrusion of poetry into
> the sphere of terminology, the intrusion into poetry of the
> spirit of music. The musical force of sound will be revived
> once more in the word.

The word creates a new third world—the world of verbal symbols by means of which can be illumined the mysteries of the world outside me and also the mysteries of the world inside me. . . . In the word, and only in the word, can I create for myself what is both outside and inside. "I" am the word. . . .

> —*The Magic of Words*, 1909

The really new in Symbolism is the attempt to illumine the deepest contradictions of contemporary culture seen through the prism of various cultures; we are now experiencing, as it were, the whole of the past: India, Persia, Egypt, Greece . . . pass before us . . . just as a man on the point of death may see the whole of his life in an instant. . . . An important hour has struck for humanity. We are indeed attempting something new but the old has to be taken into account; there is a novelty in the plenitude of the past. . . . Therefore Symbolism in literature attempts to sum up the individual statements of artists about their art and attitudes. . . .

> —*The Emblem of Meaning*, 1909

Symbolism is for me . . . a certain religious creed, having its own dogma. . . . *This dogma is the Verb become Flesh.* . . .

The symbol is an image taken from nature and transfigured by creation. . . .

The Symbolist school merely unifies the statements of artists and poets to the effect that the significance of beauty lies in the artistic image and not merely in the emotion which that image rouses in us; and certainly *not* in the analytical discussion of that image. The Symbol cannot be split up into emotions or debates: it is what it is.

> —Preface to *Symbolism*, 1910

In order to emerge from the bewitched circle of contradictions we must stop talking even about art, knowledge and life. We must forget the present: we must re-create everything anew: to do so we must first create ourselves. The only height we can scale is ourselves. . . This is the artist's reply: if he wishes to remain an artist, without ceasing to be a human being, he must become his own artistic form. Only that form of creation promises any salvation. There lies the future of art.

—The Future of Art, 1907

Andrey Biely believed that he was living in an age of death and rebirth, of transformation, of "the crisis of culture." "Reality is like a diamond, a prism, the play of light, simultaneity. . . .", he wrote. Biely's "simultaneity" suggests the "totality of experience" of Joyce, just as his "prism of various cultures" evokes the reintegrated worlds of Joyce and Picasso. The "crisis of culture" was also the crisis of the theory of knowledge, and Biely argued that metaphysics must disappear and give place to a theory of creation. "In the confusion of the modern world, the symbol (i.e., the word) must serve as the means of unity." For Biely the word was symbol, a unity of two incomprehensible substances: space and time. He maintained that both time and space could be expressed and objectified in *sound*. In analyzing the sound effect of the word *grom* (thunder) he reduced it to its basic "growl"— *grrrr*. The root sound became a key to Biely's verbal system: he used it to characterize individual phenomena. Sense limited, sound interpenetrated and unified: the word must throw off its slavery to sense and serve sound. Biely concentrated on the "hidden significance of words," their creative nature, and their latent power of creating new worlds. Logic and terminology, classical or scientific concepts implying as they did differentiation, failed in themselves to explain the complex modern world. The prelude to a new renaissance lay in the "healthy barbarism" of new words, in the exploration of their multiple meanings, in the autonomy of the verb. "The Verb become Flesh"; this became Biely's active principle, one that he discovered, applied, and developed. Biely identified his creative esthetic with the principle of "transformation": his ultimate aim was "to re-create the personality in more perfect forms," as he defined his objective in *The Problem of Culture* (1909). As he was later to reaffirm in his

book *Rhythm as a Dialectic* (1929), "This is a fact of trans-
formism: a fact of the third dialectical stage, the fact of the
search for a principle and its departure from nomenclature.
In this sense, my very interpretation of rhythm is a symbolic
divorce from the Aristotelian scholasticism: rhythm—x, y,
z—call it what you will; but: you will not be able to discover
it in present-day terms, in the formal definitions of metre,
until you can establish a correspondence between a variety
of exceptions. . . . I call the principle of rhythm the principle of *metamorphosis*. . . ."

From "the crisis of culture" Biely derived the awareness
that, "At present in art we are experiencing again all ages and
all cultures" (1910). His range of references was ency-
clopedic but not as systematically "Western" or "Catholic"
as Joyce's. He was already groping in the subconscious:
"The biology of the dream has not yet been learned; its
demands have not yet been understood: it enters into us with
bacilli, it is swallowed with water—and vodka" (1910). In his
novel *Petersburg*, a character, Apolon Apolonovich Ableukhov, has a secret of his own: "a world of curves, palpita-
tions, sensations—a universe of strange things." Biely's critical
thought as well as his creative work reveal an acute sensitivity
to a "fluid or crumbling world." He faced the problem of
the accumulation of knowledge in all spheres: history, philosophy, psychology, esthetics, ethnology, science, and especially physics—in 1904 he had already referred to the
quantum theory. He began to see knowledge, untransformed
by creativity, as merely "an abyss of problems." "The problem of art, of life, is more serious than we think: the abyss,
over which we are hanging, is deeper and gloomier than we
imagine. . . ." (*The Future of Art*, 1907).

The specter of this abyss haunts his creative work. His
characters are frequently to be found walking on the edge
of some engulfing experience, over some floor that will
crumble, or past some wall that will collapse.

> Still sleeping? The awakening will come: the floor of the
> study will fall away; still sitting in an armchair you will

find yourself hanging over the abysses of the night: then
you will see the moon cropping, an expanding globe of
stone, flying straight at you: that will be an illusion: you
will fall into a chasm; and the house, from which you have
dropped, will vanish, turning into an empty wrapper. . . .

—The Crisis of Culture (1912–18)

In this work, Biely contrasts two sorts of writers: the
writer who faces the elements ("the real rhythm of the age")
and the writer who shuts himself up in his study, "the cube
of culture." But there is no real safety or escape in the
cube; the elements will invade it; it is not uncommon in Biely
to have a parquet floor washed away by a flood. The free
creative individuality was Biely's only answer to the problems of the day: "The dogmas of our culture are becoming
incarnated in mankind, winding spirally into a single point;
that point is the 'I'; the free 'I'—the peak of a vast cone." In
Biely's view, man was now assuming a perpendicular attitude
in relation to history. The old images, even the traditional
image of man himself, were disintegrating. A fragmented
world could only be rebuilt by the creative power of words,
to produce new associations, a new order out of chaos. Biely
never created a symphonic polyphony of the order of *Finnegans Wake*, but from his *Glossalogia*, "a poem on sound"
(1917), we gather that he had reached the stage of thinking
in terms of a new universal language in the later and larger
Joycean sense: "Hail to the brotherhood of peoples: the language of languages . . . will break up the languages. . . ."
A strange coincidence: like Joyce, whom he never met,
Biely also spent some of the war years in Switzerland, and
there he must have been affected by the babel of wartime
tongues. In *Glossalogia*, he attempted methodically to arrive
at a unifying symbolical, phonetic principle behind words in
many different languages: *ero, ira, ire, terra, earth, airtha,
Erde*. In his creative work he never applied this vocabulary
of international verbal association; but clearly he had grasped
the principle.

Biely's creative development can be studied in his four

Symphonies (1902–8), *The Silver Dove* (1909–10), *Petersburg* (1913), *Kotik Letayev* (1915–16), and *Moscow* (1926–1934), to name only his major prose "compositions." Biely did not practice his method on a small scale; most of his works are solid and extensive: *The Silver Dove* is a novel of over four hundred pages, and *Moscow* was planned in four volumes.

The scintillating verbal edifice Biely raised was an organic expression of his esthetic as it evolved and grew more complex. It is not easy to render its "multiple meaning," its brilliance, in another language. As in the case of James Joyce, his works raise many problems for the translator—those of alliteration, allusion, verbal association and symbolism, poetic rhythm, ellipsis, onomatopoeia, the transferred image, puns, the symbolism of proper names, ambiguities, a cyclic order, the interpenetration of reality and myth, musical refrains and motifs, structure, punctuation, and what might be called the "autonomous dialectic" of the verb.

In *The Silver Dove*, Biely was still partly traditional in the narrative structure of the novel; but the lyrical, colorful texture, the devices of alliteration and refrain, the symbolism of the characters, were new ingredients destined to change the character, feeling, and structure of the Russian novel. Biely had undertaken to replace "objective realistic description" by a symbolical and symphonic pattern of movement: both his objects and characters were alive with sound. His second novel, *Petersburg* marked a further stage in the disruption of conventional reality: the world of this novel is phantasmagoria, a tense, nerve-racked, delirious abstraction of reality; the crowd in the Nevsky Prospect is seen as sort of an anonymous "many-footed monster." This is already the world of metamorphosis, and Biely was to plunge deeper into this universe when he wrote his third novel, *Kotik Letayev*. Biely showed his awareness of the new region into which he had penetrated when he wrote:

> The consciousness of self, like a babe within me, has opened wide its eyes and has broken up everything—down

to the first flicker of consciousness; the ice was broken—of
words, concepts and meanings; the multiplicity of debatable
truths sprouted through and was clasped in rhythms; the
architectonic of rhythms defined itself and shook my former
meanings as so many dead leaves; meaning was now life,
my life; expressed in the rhythm of the time: in gesticulation, in the mime of momentary events; the word had become mime, dance, smile.

Concepts were now as the spray of a fountain: they were
in the ceaseless ebullience, in the refraction of meanings
which builds a rainbow of the world thrown up by them;
explanation was the rainbow it lay in the dance of meanings; in the dance of words; in meaning itself, as in a drop
of spray, there was no rainbow. . . .

This is one of the main propositions in Biely's esthetic
theory and practice. A word, a concept, has no meaning, no
significance in static isolation or in conventional pattern.
Significance derives from a momentary play or association
of words, likened to a dance, the spray of a fountain, a
fleeting rainbow. Significance lies in the play of the whole,
not in any one "drop of spray." Meaning springs out of
motion. "Spray," "refraction," "rainbow," are all essentially
Heraclitean images: they are dynamic. Biely's world, his
characters and objects, are therefore never static. His is a
world of perpetual ebullience, of the interpenetration of men
and objects, of ceaseless surge, of storms, noises, cascades,
flowing water, mirrors—of endless refraction. "An old Heraclitean—I visioned the universe metamorphosed in the flaming hurricanes of the flowing present; and very definitely I
realized: what today was nanny's head had once been the
aperture of a kerosene lamp. . . . Daddy spurted like a vol-
cano. . . ." (From *Kotik Letayev*.)

The reference to Heraclitus is not incidental: when Biely's
world dissolved into phantasmagoria (*Petersburg*), the image
of Heraclitus began to recur symbolically as though to emphasize that the author was consciously associating his esthetic of dynamic disintegration-and-integration with the
Heraclitean idea of the universe as fluid matter: water and

fire. The association persists, and in the novel *Masks* (1932), the second volume of the cycle *Moscow*, we can find a passage entitled Heraclitus:

> His eye drank in the sun like a goblet of wine; the sky was a blaze of flames; he stood on the steps, his beard silvering into the luminous frost, a fold of his fur coat flapping open, and then he slipped and fell on his back, his nose leaping into the sky.
>
> He saw an inert sky, a bluebell sky at its zenith—a bow bent tautly into infinity, on the peak of which—
>
> —he seemed
>
> to be standing.
>
> At that instant he felt: linear time, history, bent tautly in a bow, were in the process of becoming—spiral time: everything was in motion, topsy-turvy: the past reflected had transformed all the projections of the future into a linear past: this past began to move, outstripping itself . . .
>
> He understood: now no one would be able to grasp anything: the age of clear Aristotle was over.
>
> Heraclitus has risen!

Biely's world is indeed Heraclitean: it has no point of rest. If the alliterative, associative pattern of this passage is not quite rendered, its rhythm and the devices employed in it are conveyed: the pattern of composition, the use of the colon for intonational effect, the substitution of the part for the whole (beard, nose, etc.)—a major device in Biely's system of symbolical realism—the rhythmic gesture, as in "his beard started to move, rushing up in white combs," and the alternation between abstract statement and concrete image. The image of gesture and the rhythm of movement play a considerable part in this vision of reality. Biely was bent on breaking with the automatism of reading. His insistence on a visual pattern, his punctuational breaks and pauses, his emphasis on sound effects, were largely aimed at awakening in the reader a sense of the dynamic subject. "I am an author who speaks rather than writes," he says in the Preface to his novel *Masks*. "I make my voice felt by means of verbal sounds and phrase construction. I pay great attention to speech, the lines, the pauses, the emphases, and especially the intonation. In order to make the reader take note of my phrase, I split it up in some such way as this:

> Ting-a-ling—
>   the glasses ring . . ."

Biely claimed that his method was a deeper reflection of reality, corresponding more closely to the actual world in which gesture and intonation play a preponderant part.

His revolutionary vision can perhaps be studied best in *Kotik Letayev*. In this work, Biely attempted an extraordinary feat: the depiction of the metamorphosis of a child's impressions from a stage of prenatal sensations to that of a later conceptual clarification. The structure of the work suggests a symbolical plan. A child's vision in the process of formation was a theme that provided Biely with the opportunity "to break the ice of concepts." Thus he set out to split the atom of the word. His technique has a certain mathematical precision about it: "The consciousness of self was a pulse; wordless, I thought in the pulse; the words beat in the pulse; and I had to smelt each word into a currency of movements: into gesticulation, into mime; understanding was in the mime . . . and the sense of the sound of the words split up. . . ."

A further passage of the child's impressions reveals the type of verbal associations Biely practiced:

> . . . the sound of the word Kremlin surprised me: Kremlin —what was it? I had already tasted *crême-brulé;* that was a sweet; it has been served up to me as a mold—with escarpments; this Kremlin I had been shown in Savostyan's pastry shop; it was built of sugar candy escarpments (of the Kremlin, the cream and the crenel), and: the m, the *mlin,* represented softness, mellifluousness; and later, from a window on the back stairs . . . I was shown: the Kremlin turrets soaring in an azure horizon: rosy, crenellated, mellif-

luous . . . for me those turrets were the quickflowing
sounds of words. . . .

This associative play on the word "Kremlin" suggests the
principle also discovered by James Joyce when he linked
"ivory" and "ivy" in _Portrait of the Artist as a Young Man._
This wordplay is typical of Biely, who practiced it independently of the Irish writer. _Kotik Letayev_ abounds in such
examples. The scribbled formulae of the child's father, a
mathematician—the x's, y's, z's, the p's and r's—are suddenly
associated in the child's mind, first, with "ants" and later,
when out in the streets, with "terriers." In depicting Pompoul, a comic rotund character who assumes various shapes
in the infant imagination, a number of associations are
worked out with a pot-bellied, striped sideboard and then a
landau.

As in _Finnegans Wake_, there is a great deal of humor in
Biely's work, and this sense of comedy must be kept in mind
in our appreciation of the verbal juggling of this virtuoso of
the word. The sudden metamorphosis of characters often
produces humorous effects: "A very elongated reptile, Uncle
Vassya, would come crawling out behind my back: serpent-
footed, moustachioed, he afterwards split himself in two;
one end of him would drop in for dinner at the house, the
other I came across later: on the jacket of a very handy
book—_Extinct Monsters;_ there he was called a 'dinosaur.'"

The pun is another recurrent device in this humorous
universe. It is made use of in a passage about Leo Tolstoy:
"I had no idea what Tolstoy or 'stoutness' meant: [In
Russian, "Tolstoy" means "stout."]—It might have been a
calling like that of a prelate, priest or mathematician;
and wherever prelates are to be found, there stoutness
abounds. . . ."

In the process of metamorphosis, the grownup characters
that impinge upon the child's consciousness assume various
guises, mythological or objective. A whole scheme of my-
thology is involved in the work: the growing child passes
through various stages of prehistoric and historic life. The

child's father is associated with fire and is symbolically equated with Vulcan, Vesuvius, vulcano, thunder, lightning, and electricity; he is invariably associated with "rumbling" noises: "the Daddy-passage, the thunder-passage. . . ." The uncle, as we have seen, become a "reptile" and a "dinosaur."

In certain respects, Biely's technique is reminiscent of Gogol's in *Dead Souls*. Indeed, Biely claims to have derived his "ornamented" language from Gogol. An analogy could also be made between some of their character descriptions; between Pompoul in *Kotik Letayev*, for example, and Sobakievich, that bear-like landowner surrounded with awkward, bear-like furniture in *Dead Souls*. But Biely's identification of the character with the object is more radical, more phantasmagoric, his pattern more abstract, and his verbal images and symbolism more revolutionary. He carried the process of disintegration and recomposition much further.

Biely died in the Soviet Union on January 8, 1934. His death was the result of a sunstroke in July 1933. He left behind him an imposing body of both theoretical and creative work, which is very little known outside Russia. And even there, especially since 1935, his work has been shelved. Except for his correspondence with Alexander Blok, published in 1940, none of his works has been reprinted. In 1946, Zhdanov, attacking Akhmatova, Pasternak, and Zoshchenko, also made some slighting references to Biely. Naturally, Biely's esthetic, like Joyce's, is not easily intelligible to the masses; and since the era of Socialist Realism has established "mass intelligibility" as a criterion, it is not difficult to understand this present neglect. I find it surprising that Biely's works were actually being published as late as 1935. To have had so original a writer continue his experimentation and propound his theories right through the period of the first two Five Year Plans is a fact that most people in the West ignore. At his death, Biely was still working on the later volumes of his novel, *Moscow*. In 1932, in the Preface to *Masks*, Biely published a restatement of his credo. The emphasis had somewhat changed: there is nothing there about Symbolism nor much about dialectics; but, in essence, the esthetic principle remained the same. Biely in no way opposed his esthetic to the dynamic of the revolution. On the contrary, he maintained that his "verbal dialectic" was a parallel phenomenon: the revolution of the word went hand in hand with the revolution in other spheres; in 1929, he also published a theoretical work entitled *Rhythm as Dialectic*. He did not realize perhaps that he was on very dangerous ground, for such "parallel phenomena" were to prove inadmissible to the exponents of Socialist Realism, who were to insist upon the strict interrelation of all social phenomena and on the subordination of literature to the over-all Party Plan. By 1937, classical nineteenth-century prose—Pushkin's or Tolstoy's—became again the model, and the verbal fireworks of the "comedian" Biely, as he was often labeled, however dialectical they may have been, began to look very remote and strange to the new progeny of social directors. The era of experiment, of a new reality created by the autonomous word, was over in Russia. But that need not prevent us from rediscovering Andrey Biely and attempting to assess his contribution, a very original and memorable one. As Biely himself wrote:

> It is not for me to know whether I have succeeded in achieving new colors—only the future can decide that. . . . My fault is that I do not buy ready-made words but prepare my own. . . . What may be unusual today may become a commonplace tomorrow. . . . My prose is really a poem in verse printed as prose for economy. I usually compose my lines when out walking and never sitting at a desk. Therefore *Masks* is really a big epic poem, written as prose for the sake of economizing paper. I am a poet.

The author who could write this in the Soviet Union in 1932 will grow rather than diminish in stature.

—George Reavey

PART ONE

CHAPTER ONE

The Village of Tzelebeyevo

☙ Our Village ☙

Again, and yet again, the belfry of Tzelebeyevo plunged its sonorous peals into the blue abyss of day, full of cruel and sultry gleams. In the air above the belfry martins flitted back and forth. Stifling in sweet odors, Trinity Day showered light pink sweetbrier upon the bushes. The heat lay heavy on the breast; and, in the sultry air, wings of dragonfly flashed glassily over the surface of the pond, soaring into the heat, into the blue abyss of day—higher, into the azure stillness of desolate space. With a sweaty sleeve, a perspiring villager was assiduously wiping the dust from his face as he dragged himself to the top of the belfry in order to start the brass clapper of the big bell swinging, and to sweat there for a while, applying himself to the greater glory of God. And again, and yet again, the belfry of Tzelebeyevo pealed into the blue abyss of day; and above it, in formations of eight, the martins darted and wheeled, twittering as they did so.

Tzelebeyevo was a fine village, and close enough to town; it spread among meadows and hillocks; its little cottages stood scattered here and there, richly adorned with fretwork like the face of a typical curly-headed lady of fashion, adorned with small brightly painted tin cockerels, with gaudy flowers and angels; it was finely ornamented with wattle hedges, little gardens and even currant bushes, as well as with whole rows of starling coops projecting at dawn from crooked broom handles. A fine village this! Just ask

the priest's wife: whenever the priest came back from
Voroniye (for the past ten years his father-in-law had been
in charge of the diocese there), this is what happened: he
would return from Voroniye, pull off his vestments, embrace and kiss his full-fleshed wife, adjust his cassock and
immediately blurt out: "Heat up a little samovar, my soul."
And then perspiring over the samovar, he never failed to
become sentimental. "A fine village ours!" he would exclaim every time. As the proverb says, a priest has always a
text handy; but this priest was not that sort: he would never
lie.

In the village of Tzelebeyevo the little houses were
scattered here and there, and there: the clear pupil of a one-
eyed house would squint at the daylight, squint evilly with
its pupil from out of a scanty shrubbery; there, it would
thrust forward its tin roof—no roof at all, but a proud
maiden thrusting forth her green headdress; and yonder out
of a gully, a hut would peep out shyly—and go on peeping
till the evening wrapped it coolly in the mist of its dewy
veil.

From hut to hut, from hillock to hillock; from a hillock
into a gully, and then into the bushes: the further, the more
there was; and as you gazed, a murmuring forest would
already be showering drowsiness upon you; and there was
no escaping from it.

In the center of the village stretched a large meadow; it
was so very green: there was space here for walking out,
for folk dancing and for plaintive maiden song; and there
was place for the accordion too. Not like any ordinary
town promenade: you could not spit it all thick with sunflower seeds, nor trample it all down underfoot. And when
the village dancers began to weave their steps, when all the
rouged maidens, in silks and beads, appeared and their shrill
voices rose and their feet began to tread, then a wave of
grass went scudding forward and an evening breeze came
whooping along—giddy and strange; and very soon you had
lost your bearings, everything seemed strange, even this

merriment. . . . And the grasses scudded forward, scudded on; running in alarm down the highway, they finally broke in a wavering splash; and then some bush by the roadside sobbed out and the bedraggled dust bounded up. If, of an evening, you were to kneel down and put your ear to the ground, you might hear the grasses growing, you might hear the big yellow moon rising over Tzelebeyevo and the cart of some belated freeholder creaking stridently along.

The white highway, the dusty highway: it ran on and on, grinning wryly; it should have been dug up again, but the authorization to do so was being held back: a few days ago the priest, in person, had explained the reason for this delay. . . . "I'd not be against it myself," he had said, "but the local authorities . . ." And so the highway was still there and no one was digging it up. But, in days past, the peasants themselves used to come out with spades. . . .

Clever people, staring tranquilly into their beards, would relate that folk had lived in these parts from time immemorial; then the highway had been constructed and, of their own accord, peasant feet had tramped off along it; the village lads had loafed about for a time, loafed about shelling sunflower seeds, and it had looked all right at first; but then they began going off down the road to return no more; that is the way things stood.

With a wry smile the highway cut across the large, green Tzelebeyevo common. Some unknown power was driving a sundry crowd of folk past the village—wagons, carts and transports loaded with wooden cases of bottled vodka for the "state liquor shops"; transports, carts, trudging peasants—they all went streaming by: the town worker, the pilgrim and the "socialist" with a wallet, the cossack sergeant and the gentleman in his troika; all these folk came surging past. The huts of Tzelebeyevo had crowded down to the edge of the highway—those that were the ugliest and the dirtiest, with roofs awry like some band of drunken louts with caps askew; here stood the inn and the tavern there, where a fierce scarecrow clownishly stuck out its arms and thrust a dirty broom from under its rags—yes, there; and a crow was perched upon it cawing. Further on, a pole jutted out of the ground, and way beyond it stretched a large empty field. And through that field a white, dusty track ran on, ran on, scowling at the open spaces all around—ran on toward other fields, toward other villages, toward the fine town of Likhov, from where sundry folk came wandering along, a band of them at times so merry that the Lord preserve us from them; some of them on machines—a town Miss in a hat of sorts with a petty official, or icon painters the worse for drink in fancy shirts and in the company of some mister "shtewdent" (who he was, the devil alone knew!). And they made their way at once to the tavern and then the fun would start; the Tzelebeyevo lads would come sidling up to them and, ah! how they would begin to bawl: "Y-e-e-a-a-r-s on y-e-e-a-a-r-s g-o-o- by, g-o-o by . . . Y-o-o-u-n-g a-a-s I a-m, I a-am d-o-o-ne f-o-o-r, d-o-o-ne f-o-o-r n-n-n-o-ow f-o-o-r-e-e-v-e-r. . . ."

⤜⤛ Daryalsky ⤜⤛

On the golden morning of Trinity Day, Daryalsky strode along the road to the village. Daryalsky had been spending the summer as a guest of the grandmother of the young Miss Gugolevo. The young lady was of most attractive appearance and even more attractive disposition; she was by way of being Daryalsky's fiancée. Drenched in heat and light, Daryalsky strode along recalling the previous day, which he had spent very cosily with his young lady and her grandmother; with honeyed phrases he had entertained the old lady that day, spinning tales of old times about the unforgettable hussars and other such sundries, which old ladies find such delight in remembering; he had likewise diverted himself by taking a stroll with his fiancée through the oak groves of the Gugolevo estate; and picking flowers had brought him even greater enjoyment. But neither the old lady, nor the hussars of never-to-be-forgotten memory, nor even that stroll, so pleasing to his heart, through the oak groves with his young lady who was dearer to him than ever, seemed to rouse any sweet remembrances in his mind this particular morning: the heat of Trinity Day crushed him and stifled his soul. Nor, indeed, had his favorite volume of Martial tempted him earlier as it lay open— slightly spotted by flies—on a table.

Daryalsky—that is the name of my hero. Do you not find it noteworthy? Why, listen, this is Daryalsky—the same who, for two summers running, had, with a friend, rented

Fyodorov's cottage. Wounded by a maiden's eyes, he had for two successive summers sought the best means of meeting the young lady of his heart here among the meadows of Tzelebeyevo and the oak groves of Gugolevo. In his design he so outsmarted everyone that when the third summer came he had moved, baggage and all, to Gugolevo, the estate of the Baroness Todrabe-Graaben. The frail old lady held some very decided opinions as to her granddaughter's match with a young man who, according to her, had a draught not only in his head but also—and that was worse—in his pockets.

Since his early youth Daryalsky had passed as a simpleton, an orphan, and a man without private means. "A rolling stone gathers no moss," was what solid folk had snorted into their mustaches; but the young lady herself was of different mind; and so it came about that, after a lengthy argument with her grandmother, in the course of which the cunning old woman had dug her toes in more than once as she sat back in her armchair sipping fruit waters, our beautiful Katya took the plunge and blurted directly to the daughter of the Tzelebeyevo priest that she was now engaged; after that, Daryalsky had moved into the imposing manor house with park, hothouses, roses, and marble cupids covered with mold. Thus, the young beauty had succeeded in convincing the frail old lady of the agreeable qualities possessed by the young man whom she had so casually encountered.

As a young man, Daryalsky had been considered odd. It was said that he had attended an educational establishment in which, year in, year out, a dozen or so of the canniest students were pleased to construe verse of a most indecent kind in heaven knows what languages rather than to apply their talents to serious study—and that's the truth! Daryalsky was a great amateur of that sort of verse, and a deft hand at it himself; he wrote about everything: about the *white lily heel*, the *myrrh of lips*, and even—the *polychrism of nostrils*. Yes, just think of it: he had published a book of many pages with the image of a fig leaf on the cover; and in it the youthful bard had rhapsodized about the "lily heel" and about the young Gugolevo lady in the guise of a young goddess—nude, of course, and the daughters of the Tzele-beyevo priest were loud in their praises—much to the priest's vexation. The priest swore that Daryalsky wrote only about naked women; Daryalsky's friend defended him (this friend, Schmidt, still rented a cottage in Tzelebe-yevo), yes, he defended him: it was the fruit of a poet's inspiration, he argued, and the women in question were not just naked women, but goddesses. . . . But, may I ask, what is the difference between a goddess and a woman? A goddess or a woman, it is all one. Who were those goddesses of antiquity if not women? They were women without a doubt, and of a dubious quality besides.

Daryalsky's friend was extremely modest: he had a non-Russian name and spent his days and nights reading books of philosophy; although he rejected God, he was still in the habit of dropping in to have a chat with the priest; the priest was not a bad fellow; and the authorities were also not so bad; and he was really quite orthodox, only his name was Schmidt and he did not believe in God. . . .

As he approached the church, Daryalsky shook himself out of his reverie; he was passing by the pond just then and his reflection lay in the deep blue water; he shook himself out of his reverie and then plunged back into it again.

When clear of clouds, the lofty sky, so high and pro-found, looked fresh and taut; the surging wave of a meadow embraced the clear, glassy, crystal pond where serious ducks swam about; and how they swam! They would swim for a while, make for dry land to pluck at the grass, wag their tails, and then go waddling off primly, very primly, in the wake of the quacking drake, pursuing all the time their incomprehensible chatter; there was a hollow birch tree stooping over the pond, suspended there these many dec-ades with its ragged arms outstretched, preserving the secret of all it had witnessed. Daryalsky longed to throw himself down under the birch tree and stare, stare into the depths, through the branches, through the scintillating cobweb spread taut on high there—where a greedy spider, after his fill of flies, looked as though he were spread-eagled in the air, apparently a denizen of the sky. And as for the sky? The air of it was pale at first sight but, when scrutinized closely, it looked utterly black, that air. . . . A shudder crept over Daryalsky as though some mysterious danger threatened him from that quarter, as it had threatened him more than once in the past, as though the terrifying mysteries, which had from time immemorial been confined to the skies, were now calling him secretly, and he said to himself: "Ah, don't be frightened, you're not up in the air—just look at the water mournfully lapping against those wooden planks."

On some planks nearby a pair of sturdy legs protruded from beneath a red skirt which had been tucked up over the knees, and a pair of busy hands were rinsing out some washing; but who it was washing could not be seen: an old crone, a peasant woman, or a maiden? Daryalsky kept staring and though it was daylight and the festive bell was pealing in a clear sky, he thought the planks looked depressingly gray. A clear sunny day it was, and clear sunny water, all azure; when you gazed into it, it was hard to tell the water from the sky. "Hey, lad, you'll turn giddy. You'd better step aside!"

And stepping aside, Daryalsky strode away from the pond toward the village, toward the shining church, wondering at the yearning which had invaded his soul as it used to do in childhood, looming out of the unknown, overwhelming and seducing; and, at such times, people had called him an eccentric when, unawares, he had gone on talking at random to himself, making people smile and shake their heads at his talk.

Daryalsky strode on, reflecting: "What the devil do I really need? Is my bride not good enough for me? Does she not love me? Was I not chasing after her for the past two years? I found her at last . . . Oh, go away, you magic thoughts, go away! . . ." Only three days had passed since his engagement to his beloved; he remembered the luck that had come his way at that stupid gathering, where he had dazzled the beauteous young lady with a smile and a witty phrase; and afterwards he had gone in pursuit of her; and it was not at once that the beauty had yielded to him; then finally he had arrived at her white hand; that was her gold ring on his finger and he had not yet grown accustomed to its pressure. "Darling Katya, my bright one," he whispered; and then he realized that it was not the tender maiden's image on his soul, but something else—some kind of a separation.

With these thoughts on his mind he entered the church; the smell of incense mingling with the fragrance of birch branches, the sweaty smell of numerous peasants in grease-blacked boots, the smell of wax and ever-obtrusive fustian pleasurably assailed his nostrils; he had already disposed himself to listen to Alexander Nikolaievich, the sacristan, who, from the left wing of the choir, had already drummed out a tattoo, when, suddenly, in a far corner of the church, there was a flutter of a red-and-white-spotted kerchief worn above a red satin dress; a peasant woman was staring fixedly at him; and he was about to say, "Ah, what a woman!," to heave a sigh, and put on an air of dignity so that he might begin forgetting it all, to pay his devotions to the Queen of Heaven, but . . . he did not heave a sigh, he did not put on an air of dignity, and he did not pay his devotions. A sweet wave of inexplicable pain scorched his breast and he was not even aware that he had turned pale and was barely able to stand on his feet. The woman's face, browless and pock-marked, was fixed on him with a look of avid emotion. What that face was communicating to him, what echo it roused in his depths, he could not tell; he was only conscious of the flutter of that red-and-white-spotted kerchief. When Daryalsky eventually recovered himself, Alexander Nikolaievich, the sacristan, had already finished drumming out his bass tattoo from the left wing of the

choir; and Father Vukol had already appeared more than
once at the altar and a beam of sunshine had hopped several
times over his reddish hair and silver vestments patched
with blue bouquets; the priest was now genuflecting inside
the open door which revealed the altar; the choir had
already chanted the *"dori nosima chinmi"** ; and the landowner Utkin's five daughters—this one and that—had already in succession turned their round turnip faces toward
him and stood there capriciously pouting their lips to the
point almost of indecency, while the sixth daughter (an old
maid) with a branch of cherries on her hat, bit her lips
morosely.

The mass was over; the priest, holding a cross in front of
him, came out among the congregation to bestow plump
wafers upon Madame Utkin and her six mature daughters,
and upon those of the peasants who were the most prosperous and important, those who wore the newest coats and
creaking boots, those who in their wisdom had built themselves prosperous cottages and had saved sufficient money
by the illicit sale of liquor and deals of all kinds—in short,
those whose characters were the strongest and most exacting. These peasants approached the honest cross pompously
and decorously, bending not without dignity their bearded
faces and heads of hair that had been cut in the shape of
brackets and exuded a smell of wood oil; and when these
notable villagers had walked away from the altar, the priest
began to wave the cross very emphatically at the noses of
the common herd (no wonder the village "teacher" had
hissingly complained that the priest had knocked her, Shkurenkova, on the teeth with the cross and that her teeth had
been sore for a long time after). Daryalsky was on the point
of kissing the cross, which the priest was already holding
out to him with one hand while, with the other, he was
about to pick up a wafer, when he suddenly felt himself
scorched again by the gaze of that prodigious peasant

_____

* A liturgical chant in Church Slavonic implying ascension.

woman; her red lips had parted in a smile and quivered slightly as though drinking freely of his soul; and, as a result, he could hardly remember kissing the cross or how the priest had invited him to partake of cabbage pie or what he had replied: he could only remember that the peasant woman had claimed him. Summoning in his mind the image of Katya, he repeated in vain, "A good bride, my good bride!" But the image of his beloved was now mere chalk on a blackboard: an arbitrary hand had wiped that image clean with a duster and, in its place, there was nothing now but a yawning void.

The pock-marked woman, a hawk with browless eyes, was no tender flower germinating in the depths of his soul, no dream this, no rosy dawn, no honeyed grass, but a storm cloud, a female tiger, and she entered him like a werewolf and called him imperiously; her soft smiling lips intoxicated and confused him with a langorous sense of sadness and joy that banished all shame; and thus, revealed for an instant, the gaping jaws of a millennium now resurrected the memory of what had never been part of his personal experience, awakening the unknown face which was terrifyingly familiar only in dreams; and that face was now embodied in the image of an incredible and yet existent childhood. So that is your face, pock-marked wench!

So thought Daryalsky—or, rather, did not think; because his thoughts were involuntarily taking place in his soul and she had already walked out of the church and Kudeyarov, the carpenter, with sickly face, dragged himself after her; as he passed Daryalsky, he gave him a shove and stared at him for an instant: for some reason, his stare excited a vague tremor in Daryalsky. Daryalsky hardly remembered how he reached the porch; neither did he hear the Tzelebeyevo belfry plunging in sonorous peals, nor the twittering martins as they flitted above it. Trinity Day glared in a shower of light pink sweetbrier, and swarms of flies, like so many buzzing emeralds, settled on the backs of the peasants' sunfaded coats.

A peasant lad went by, hugging an accordion to his belly and kicking up noiseless puffs of dust; as he walked down the road the lad bawled out something like a song; a convoy of laden carts filled the highway and the cartwheels, which had not been oiled for a long time, creaked and grated; the tin roofs of the peasant cottages and their flame-angered windows (those of them that were not stuffed with pillows) deflected the glittering beams of the sun. Full-bodied maidens, with green, blue, canary and golden sashes around their plump waists, were out walking in pairs; they were wearing blunt-nosed boots that looked like sawed-off logs and strutted about like peahens. The slender branches of plaintive birch trees stirred now and then above the graveyard. Someone was whistling and making the bushes ring. Domna Yakovlevna, an old maid and daughter of the lately deceased Tzelebeyevo priest, prayed over her father's grave; the church warden emerged from behind some currant bushes and, shading his eyes, stared at the old maid from a distance; since he was on bad terms with her he growled loudly into space and yet so that Domna Yakovlevna could hear him, "They ought to dig up the bones and purify this place; it's too crowded as it is, and yet we must preserve these bones . . ." Then, approaching her, he pulled off his cap ingratiatingly and jestingly remarked, "So you have come to visit your papa? What's there to visit? They've rotted no doubt, the remains . . ."

"Fie! What the devil!" Daryalsky thought and rubbed his eyes. Had he fallen asleep in the church? Had he been seeing visions? Nonsense. He must have been drowsy—it was not a good thing to dream at noon. No wonder the Scriptures said: "May the midday devil not tempt us."

And Daryalsky, twirling his mustaches, set off to visit the priest. On the way he deliberately evoked in his mind the image of Katya and then quoted his favorite verses from Martial; but he did not succeed in evoking Katya and, instead of the verses from Martial, he unexpectedly began to whistle: "Y-e-e-a-a-r-s on y-e-e-a-a-r-s g-o-o

by, g-o-o by . . . Y-o-o-u-n-g a-a-s I a-am, I a-am
d-o-o-ne f-o-o-r, d-o-o-ne f-o-o-r n-n-n-o-ow f-o-o-r-e
e-v-e-r. . . ."

Such, for Daryalsky, was the unexpected prelude to that
day. From this day, too, we shall begin our story.

⁓⁂ Cabbage Pie ⁂⁓

"Pfu!"

The priest grunted, downing another snifter together with Alexander Nikolaievich, the sacristan, and then tasting some mushrooms picked in the autumn by the priest's virtuous wife and a numerous progeny each smaller than the other.

The priest's wife had finished three classes of Likhov high school and she liked to remind her guests of this; on the broken piano she also used to play a waltz, "Times Without Return"; she was buxom, stout, with purple lips, green-brown, cherry-like eyes on her tender, almost sugary face dotted with yellowish freckles, and she already had a double chin. Here she was now cracking jokes about the priestly life, the clownish homespun coats, about Likhov, fussing around the steaming pie and cutting slices of enormous size with immensely thick crust and a very thin lining of cabbage. "Anna Yermolaiyevna, eat some more pie! Varvara Yermolaiyevna, why so little?" Thus she addressed in turn the six ripe daughters of the landowner Utkin, who formed a pleasant flowerbed round the tidily set table; a birdlike warbling issued from the six open pink mouths and there was much twittering about all the new events occuring in the neighborhood; the handy priest's wife hardly had time to serve the pie, at times slapping a priestling who inadvertently got in her way, messily chewing a crust and with a dirty nose; and at the same time she chattered more than all the rest.

"Have you heard, Mother, what the village constable was saying, that these very socialists have turned up not far from *Likhov* and started spreading their vile leaflets; looks like they want to go against the Tsar, in order to take charge of the "Monopoly" and thus get the nation drunk; the Tsar, they say, has sent out edicts everywhere printed in gold letters, calling upon the Orthodox Christians to defend the Holy Church: seems like "proletarians, unite!"; it is said the Likhov archbishop is waiting to receive the Tsar's edict any day so that he can send it out all over the district . . ." Thus Alexander Nikolaievich, the sacristan, unexpectedly blurted out, twitching his rowanberry nose, and then fell into confusion when six maidenly heads fixed him with an expression of utter contempt. . . .

"Pfu!" the priest cracked, pouring a helping for Alexander Nikolaievich. "And are you aware, brother, what the proletariat is?!!" And noticing how that place on the sacristan's forehead where his eyebrows should have been (the sacristan did not wear any brows), formed an arc, the priest added expressively: "That's it, brother: the proletariat is he who will prolapse to all points, that is, will fly out of a chimney . . ."

"Well, enough of that Father Vukol!" whispered his wife as she passed, referring not to the pleasant and at the same time jesting sense of the priest's clarification, but to the rowanberry liqueur to which her lord and master had helped himself more than once; in answer the priest blurted out "Pfu!" and downed yet another round with Alexander Nikolaievich, the sacristan; then they both sampled the mushrooms.

At a corner of the table Daryalsky smoked in silence, constantly sipping the rowanberry liqueur; he was already tipsy, but tipsiness did not disperse his strange thoughts; although he had come to taste the pie, because he had no

desire just then to return to Gugolevo, he was so morose
that they all stopped talking to him; in vain the young
Utkin ladies tried to converse with him; in vain they turned
their languorous looks upon him, with obvious coquettishness fanning themselves with their lace handkerchiefs: with
obvious coquettishness they rearranged their décolleté or
transparently enough alluded to Daryalsky's heart and play-
boy Cupid, who has pierced it; Daryalsky either did not
respond or merely grunted to no purpose, or patently
approved the young ladies' hints as to the state of his heart,
discarding all playfulness; and he altogether ceased to pay
attention to the maidens' eyes and, even less, to the
maidenly décolleté showing attractively rosy from under
their gaping muslin. For two years Daryalsky had dawdled
in the neighborhood and nobody could tell for what purpose; business people supposed at first that he had a purpose,
that there must be a purpose, and that this purpose was
antigovernmental; there were to be found curious observers
who loved to whisper, and, if need be, to denounce (the
deaf and dumb Sidor, the best slanderer in the district, who
could not pronounce a single word except his senseless *"apa-
apa,"* but who could sensibly explain himself with gestures,
was the man most interested in Daryalsky). So it was. But
neither Sidor nor anyone else discovered anything dangerous in Daryalsky's conduct; they decided then that his
presence in the neighborhood had another reason and that it
had to do with matrimony; thereupon every maiden in the
neighborhood imagined that she was the object of those
amorous sighs; this was also imagined by all the six Utkin
daughters; and though each of them named aloud one of her
sisters as the object of Daryalsky's attention, she arrived at a
different conclusion about herself; and therefore they were
all struck as by thunder at the news of his betrothal to
Katya Gugolevo, the very rich granddaughter of the
Baroness; no one imagined that, to be frank, a coarse snout
could have insinuated itself into such a situation. I must
stipulate that they used the expression "coarse snout" in a

special sense: for that part of the body vulgarly termed "snout," to put it simply, with your permission, was not at all coarse but, so to speak, "velvety": the sheen of his black eyes, the tanned face with a prominent nose, the thin crimson lips, trimmed with mustaches, and a cap of ashen curls formed the object of the secret desires of more than one young lady, maiden, or young widow, and even of a married woman . . . or, to be blunt, even of the priest's wife herself. They expressed surprise, gasped, but soon grew accustomed; Daryalsky's sojourn in our neighborhood became self-defined; they stopped spying on him, for to spy on him was difficult: not everyone had entry into the Baroness's country estate. In truth, there were other people here who understood better what my hero needed (Was it love, and something else?), where the nostalgic gaze of his velvet eyes was directed, how passionately he gazed ahead of him when there was not a single maiden ahead, not even on the horizon, whereas the horizon flamed and shone in the evening sunset; they understood many other things about Daryalsky and, so to speak, encircled him with an invisible net of observation for reasons no one could fathom: these were simple folk, entirely non-educated; well, about them, let us only say this: *such folk did exist;* let us likewise say that, if they had understood the subtleties of poetic beauties, if they had read what was hidden under the fig leaf sketched on the cover of Daryalsky's book—yes, they would have smiled, ah! what a smile! They would have said, "He's one of us" . . . Well, it is not time at all for this now; it is time, however, to introduce the most notable of the Tzelebeyevo folk.

So be it.

The Inhabitants of the Village Tzelebeyevo

Distinguished people, do not disdain our village! Often enough the likes of you have come here, and nothing amazes us in the end. Do not turn up your noses, nothing good will come of that. If you hurry too much, you will only make a laughing stock of yourselves. The peasants will ridicule you and go off in a bunch, blowing their noses with their fingers: on the common they will leave you alone with the ducks. "Walk about alone," they will say, "pick flowers, amaze the ducks. Maybe you will meet the woman teacher; but what's a teacher? A nasty creature, in truth."

Nothing truly surprises the villagers. As soon as you arrive, they will greet you as their guest; they will treat you to all kinds of pies—they will not let you go away hungry; they will feed your horse oats, serve your coachman a snifter of vodka. Live and be healthy, grow fat; if you don't want to, God be your judge: the Tzelebeyevo folk will manage to live their own life without you.

When a chatterbox of a woman begins at times to count on her fingers the distinguished visitors, she will not miss very many: the merchant Yeropegin, the very rich Likhov miller, the serene Father from Voroniye, and the Baron Todrabe-Graaben, a General of consequence (the son of the old lady Graaben who lives in Gugolevo), and guests from Moscow. These guests called on the priest's daughters, the daughters of the late priest of Tzelebeyevo, worthy girls of whom there is much to tell: after their father's

death, they had acquired a house here—Agrafena Yakov-
lena, Domna Yakovlevna and Varvara Yakovlevna; so then:
students and writers used to visit them, yes: once a song
writer appeared in our midst: he induced them to sing, to
lead girls' choirs, and he jotted everything down in a little
book. "That song writer, be he a *stubent* or a striker?" the
good folk asked. "Most likely a striker." After he left, the
village lads here for a long time used to yell out: "Rise and
revolt, ye working people!" . . . Once a glib woman begins to count on her fingers, it may strike you that the
Russian people have but one occupation: to live in or visit
Tzelebeyevo. If she had enough fingers the woman would
account for all the visitors: fixing the ground with her eyes,
a look of carefree authority on her face, she will seem to
say: "We also have whiskers. . . ."

So just try and turn up your nose!

Staid folk live in Tzelebeyevo: first of all, Ivan Stepanov
has kept a shop here for many years—he traded in textiles;
there's no contradicting that he will skin you in a thrice,
strip you of your trousers, dishonor your wife; they'll burn
his property one day; and his race and tribe will lose their
heads: his relatives, fathers-in-law, sons-in-law, will all pay
for it; but there he is, a God-fearing peasant, standing in the
church at the counter, clinking copper coins; in appearance
well-made, he has a beard like a spade, his hair in curls,
boots bottle-shaped with a fringe, creaking, always oiled
with tar, and he wears a brass watch.

In the second place, Father Vukol Golokrestovsky, the
priest, and his wife. A notable priest. You will not meet
another such priest in the district though you may travel
forty miles around! A diligent priest, strict, and fond of
prayer.

But as soon as he had drunk of wine, he immediately
made his wife sit down and tinkle on the guitar (they had a
real guitar: eight years ago they had come to the village and
the priest's wife had brought the guitar with her: true, the
guitar had a busted string, but that is what a priest's wife is

for, to play, unabashed, on only three strings—for that she
had graduated through three classes in the Likhov high
school!). Yes: he would sit his wife down to strum on the
guitar: "Play the 'Persian March' now, Masha!" His face
glowed, became spotted with yellow freckles, and his eyes
sparkled in the direction of the palisade: "Play, Masha, play,
and forget all your everyday chores." The priest's wife
would burst into tears, "Father Vukol, you had better go to
bed." And priest Golokrestovsky would have gone to bed
had it not been for the sacristan: that's what a sacristan is
for, to egg on the priest. Well, he'd turn stubborn: play, go
on, play. Shedding tears, the priest's wife would tinkle on
the guitar, and the priest would at once adopt an attitude:
he would roll up his sleeves and imagine aloud—for his own
satisfaction and the sacristan's instruction—the capture of
the mighty fortress of Kars;* he would give free rein to
his fancy, while he still had the strength to imagine, until
the piercing martins began to twitter above the church
spire, until the cold drops of dew like clusters of transparent berries hung from the currant bushes of the priest's
palisade, until their fiery dawn began to splash its red velvet
over the edge of the cottage. Then Father Golokrestovsky
would toss up his beard at the sunrise, shake his curly hair,
tap with his feet, and move his palms smoothly now from
left to right, now from right to left: "Listen, the drum is
beating: the enemy forces are crossing the bridge: the
machine guns are blazing . . . Aha, let us note that!"

And in the dawn, at dawn, the guitar "tinkles-tinkles,"
spilling out; and over the guitar the priest's wife spills out
too, swallowing salt tears, but not daring to cast aside the
guitar. Alexander Nikolaievich, the sacristan, sees to this;
the priest himself would not have noticed it, but Alexander
Nikolaievich would have immediately drawn his attention

---

* Fortified city and capital of the Transcaucasion province of Kars.
Under Turkish domination till the Russo-Turkish War of 1877–78
when the Russians captured it.

to it: the sacristan, though tipsy, remembers everything: he sits over the rowanberry cordial, twitches his rowanberry nose and wonders at the priest; but the priest is living his fancy; he will shrink, his head will sink into his shoulders and with a scraping of feet he'll vanish into the bushes: what he's doing there, God alone knows, but, on emerging from the bushes, he'll shout: "Hurrah, we have won!" (he had imagination, that priest). As soon as he shouts, "We have won," the priest's wife will put the guitar aside: she knows that Father Vukol will imagine no more: he will retire to sleep till late morning; and the sacristan will quiet down too and intoning a psalm of King David he will stumble off to his wife who will give him what for. Awakening later that morning, the priest will run off very dutifully to Ivan Stepanov's shop for some mint ginger-bread (fifteen kopecks a pound) and with them treat his corpulent half; and so the matter will end.

But the folk already knew all about it: as soon as the guitar began tinkling in the priest's currant bush garden, it meant the priest was tipsy and was imagining the capture of the fortress of Kars by a brave warrior and the cruel defeat of the Turks; they'd gather in the bushes: the priest has a lively imagination; they gaped, shelled sunflower seeds, giggled, squeezed the girls and, when the girls squealed at last, they all scampered away. The priest had a lively imagi-nation; but in previous times there had been nothing of the sort: he'd been exacting, correct, domestic; and he'd often found fault with the sacristan.

Such was the priest in Tzelebeyevo: a fine priest—you would not find such another; another would not attain to all this, no, he wouldn't! Such then is our village, such the people inhabiting it. A fine village, a fine lot of people!

But nowhere is it true that fine neighbors live in amity with each other, that they equally exchange bows, affection, gifts and other such kindlinesses; one will knead his cap and stoop at the sight of a neighbor's wealth, of his gleaming, creaking boots, and that not because he himself on that occasion had failed to don his suit, but just out of sheer amiability, while his neighbor will turn up his nose, keep his hands in his pockets; it hurts: the heart burns, points to means of defense: no grand personage: master of his own cottage, he sits in his own attractive corner beneath the icons, in no one else's; thus one neighbor begins to harm another, defending his honor; he will scrawl an obscene word on his neighbor's fence or offer a neighbor's dog a piece of meat with a needle stuck in it; the dog will perish— that's all, but the neighbors will quarrel, spy on and provoke each other, send in denunciations: as you watch, each of them will scatter the other's ashes upon the wind.

What of it!

Folk were also amazed that Father Golokrestovsky should hold Ivan Stepanov so firmly by the hand; well, he'd not betray the priest, he'd be subservient before him and when looking at the priest his eyes no longer flashed lightning, but were just so-so—fishy and muddled. . . . They coaxed each other.

On days when the priest's wife had baked a cabbage pie, the priest would send to ask Stepanov to please come and taste something hot, or he would begin fussing himself: how was the pie baking, and by applying his nose to the crust, he would keep testing whether the dough had baked properly; then he himself would select the plumpest portion and send it off by a worker to Stepanov's shop. Nor did Stepanov remain under obligation to the priest: he used to send the priest's wife a length of decaying satin (for a blouse), presented her with stale sweets in curled wrappers, dried out gingerbreads and other such desserts. So there was never a shortage of sweet things in the priest's house; and, because of that, flies multiplied ruinously.

The shopkeeper had contributed no mean assistance toward the repair of the church. The church was an ancient one; the icons in it were of old handicraft—austere, black, gloomy images: the prelate Mikola, and the wisest of pagans —Plato, as he was called—and the Ethiopian Saint with the dog's head, one of the Arabs (evidently in ancient times they painted according to euchology*)—gloomy, gloomy images: simply to look at them gave no joy; but when the icon painters came from town, the first thing they did was to scrape those images—they scraped them off, white-washed the walls, and on a fresh background painted gay, smiling Saints (more fashionable and mannered) after the model of the Likhov cathedral; how much more alluring! But that's where history went out!

For your information, the icon painters got a fixed notion into their heads of extracting some "extras" from that skin-flint of a shopkeeper, but there was no way of approaching him: he was a shopkeeper all right: so the wily icon painters took it upon themselves to paint the likeness of Ivan Stepa-nov, representing a certain man: in his left hand this man holds a five-headed little church as if it were a wafer, and in his punishing right hand he is pleased to raise a sharp, heavy sword—this is Ivan Stepanov. . . . Only he is all in brocade, with an omophorium, and a circle of gold leaf with ecclesi-astical letters round his head; and his eyes threaten storms, keeping vigil, exactly like at the shopkeeper's (especially if the shopkeeper should plan to put an enemy and adversary to the torch!). Yes, and this also: are you about to smile? If you visit the temple, I'll show you that man at once: to this day this righteous man is depicted there to the right of the iconostasis (you can see him for yourself). Well, you'll believe it in any case!

Since that time Ivan Stepanov has taken to standing by the icon during mass to impress the probability of it on the congregation. Look and compare, he seems to say. Some-times, while crossing himself furiously, he keeps staring round him: are they comparing? There's whispering all round . . . Turina, a woman landowner, came to Stepanich

---

* The book which contains the ritual of the Greek church for the celebration of the Eucharist and other sacraments, and for all eccle-siastical ceremonies.

in his shop and smiled at him; Utkin came before Trinity Day, stared at him superciliously and asked him directly, "Well, what?" And he answered him back: "Yes, what: nothing, we are scraping along." The bandy-legged carpenter kept going to church, and could bear it no longer; he went straight to the priest. "It's so and so, Father—a shameful thing." But the priest did not blink an eyelid: "You must prove," he said, "that the likeness was intentional and not just a coincidence of faces: Stepanich is a God-fearing peasant; he prays to that Saint and bears the imprint of that prayer book on his face; you altogether fail to understand, brother, the significance of these, so to speak, emblematical traits; and there's no blasphemy here at all. But if the icon painters did sin, address your demands on them; but to forbid Stepanich to stand under the icon, judge for yourself, that I cannot do—it is not my duty: the temple of God is open to all . . . You'd better keep mum and keep the peace: better think of your own sinful acts." . . . The carpenter spat and strode away from the priest.

The woman teacher also grumbled, "What horror, they have sullied the church." But who pays attention to a teacher? What kind of an authority is she? Another matter if it were a county or a district official or someone else, let's say General Todrabe-Graaben himself, had expressed his judgment on this subject; but the district official was himself a godfather of Ivan Stepanich, and had long ago fallen into his hands; the county official kept his mouth shut while General Todrabe-Graaben had never been seen in our temple. And here, if you please, we must pay attention to one Shkurenkova, a teacher; just consider her looks: a green, verdigris face, always shining, freckled—and she struts about in rose and lilac blousettes.

And her blousettes were of such cheap stuff! The satin was really coarse calico at twelve kopecks per yard; as soon as washed, the blousette would be spotted with stains (the girls just laugh at her); whenever she sees a handsome lad or a summer visitor she picks up her skirts (but her stocking is torn), twiddles the toe of her shoes, and shows pleasure in her eyes.

Who will study the teacher's words? Who, who, indeed, had tripped up the priest? Before whom had the most patient priest humbled himself? Before her, before her, because there was no way of getting under her skin: she's all "he-he" and "ha-ha," as though jesting and joking: but it's no joking matter! She will manage to sting you in the sorest spot: "Why hasn't your wife played the 'Persian March' for so long? I have great imagination and I passionately love music, yes, indeed! You should ask her to play oftener." She would roll her eyes while her lips would dance with laughter: one day, in the presence of the landowner, Utkin, and his six ripe daughters—Katerina, Stepanida, Varvara, Anna, Valentina, Raissa—she stuck a hatpin into the priest. The priest will bear it in silence; another time he will take it so to heart that he will summon the sacristan, send for some vodka—and very soon the guitar would be tinkling in the currant bush garden while the teacher would laugh sardonically.

Only once did the priest lose his temper; as soon as he came home, he sat down to pen a denunciation; he penned and penned it—penned something hair-raising: it turned out she, the nuisance, belonged to some unknown faith and intended, it was alleged, to enter into association with the sect of the Caucasian *Molokans** for the purpose of overthrowing the authorities-in-power; therefore, she was a socialist; and she did not really teach the children, but busied herself all the time with all kinds of filth to which he, the guardian of the Tzelebeyevo temple, could bear witness. He finished off the denunciation so beautifully, tied it up with sense, and singled out Ivan Stepanov as a witness too; it is at once apparent that the priest had imagination, and more than once he had demonstrated the capture of the fortress

---

* A religious sect dating from the 18th century claiming to be "true spiritual Christians."

of Kars. As for Ivan Stepanov, he showed his true colors by
testifying that this same teacher Shkurekova had for the
past two years to the day tried to seduce him, Stepanov,
threatening on the first suitable occasion to commit against
him an amorous violation.

They signed the document and sealed it in an envelope;
just in time, they did not post it and pondered on it: they
might have trouble with the authorities: the authorities
might not believe them. Let us admit, the teacher did practice the Orthodox faith, and that she taught children grammar was evident to all: well, no one could object to
grammar; and with us at that time both the county and the
village constables were very strong supporters of literacy.

But she finds out about the priest's design; and again she
ambushes the priest. The priest was making a round of his
parish; and of course, as everybody knows everyone, put
eggs in his cart, flour, bread, onions (priests lived by collec-
tions from their parishioners); he returned with his cart full
of flour, bread, eggs, and stopped by the school to have a
drink of water from the well; out came the bold maiden and
began to yap and laugh at him: "He-he" and "ha-ha." But
accidentally, she sat herself down on the cart; sat down and
broke all the eggs, broke half a hundred of them: tit for tat
it was, and how could he make her pay?

Since that time they have been apart. Well, what's that to
do with us? when two people quarrel, don't poke your nose
in; if they abuse each other, keep quiet.

Another notable inhabitant of the village was the carpenter: Mitry Kudeyarov. He lived in the hut which
peeped out of the sloping valley; standing on a hillock one
could see his roof over there: moreover, the smoke from his
chimney comes blowing toward us.

The carpenter made furniture and orders came to him
not only from Likhov, but also from Moscow; in person he
was bandy-legged, sickly, pale, and he had a nose like a
woodpecker's. He coughed all the time, but he delivered his

goods to the furniture shops; often enough he had visitors
drop in off the highway; an invisible force drove all sorts of
people along the highway: gypsies, socialists, town workers,
God's folk, they all would have passed by; but no: Kudeyarov happened to be here with us: they turned off the
road to see him. For that reason the path from the highway
to the valley became ever more distinct. Whenever a dark
little figure from the highway happened to hobble toward
him or a yellow dust cloud rose and there in the yellow dust
cloud a cart would rumble, Mitry would climb to the top of
the hillock, shade his eyes with his hand and stand waiting. . . . And what would he always be expecting? So he
waited while an invisible force drove all sorts of people
past: a cart rumbled by, missing the village: one fellow
passed by, another too, bawling a song; yet another would
turn off on to the path: to see Mitry, that is. The carpenter
disliked having to answer questions: "Who and who was
having tea with you?"—"O just so: not a bad fellow." He
frowned and kept his mouth shut.

Not a bad fellow, hospitable enough; if you visited him,
he'd send his woman (Mitry had buried his wife) to the
well: to bring water for the samovar; at once he would
brush the shavings off the bench and begin all sorts of
chatter about his furniture trade: "You make furniture?"—
"We make it, of course; according to *shtyle* and not to
shtyle; when it goes to Moscow, it has to be *shtyle:* there
are solid *shtyles,* profitable ones—because, as you know, it's
carved work: now take *roccoco* or the *Russian shtyle;* and
there is also junk: hip-hop, and it's ready: it's cheap pay
these days for such work, but the orders come in; on such a
shtyle you don't knock off much money: it's false value."
He will say that and his whole face will wink; and what a
face, my respects to it! No face, but a sheep's bone chewed
bare; and into the bargain, no face, but half a face; the face,
let's suppose, resembles a face, but it always looks like half a
face; one side of it winks at you cunningly, the other is

always spying and afraid of something; the two halves converse; one says: "Look what I've done!" the other replies: "Well then, well then: what did you take?" And if you were to stand opposite the nose, there would be no face at all, but just something . . . some sort of blotches.

He would work all day in a red shirt open at the neck and sticky with sweat at the back; when the evening chill invades the far groves with its transparent and sparkling turquoise air, and everything yonder frowns, while gloom gathers and shadows multiply, and the weary sun opposite drips away with its last beams, Mitry will put aside his planes, long planes and drills, let the thin tuft of his yellow beard hang over them, lean thoughtfully on his saw, and then plod peacefully in his worn bark sandals over the common, where the children scattered at his approach, because he had an evil ponderous eye; but he would not harm a lamb; he was not a bad fellow; and everyone already knew where and why the carpenter was dragging himself at that time: to the priest's; to argue over the texts; he was very well read in the Scriptures and had his own views—what they were, no one could understand, though to all appearance he made no secret of them: it was in no wise easy to know what Kudeyarov, the carpenter, meant by the "one essence" and what his opinion was respecting the lawless teacher.

Sometimes he would wipe his perspiring face with his sleeve, turn that half-of-a-face to the priest: "Look what I've done!" and question the priest; thus the priest and the carpenter would hold a disputation on the common at that quiet hour of evening when a thin steamy mist begins to rise over the common. The priest sweated, sweated, while Kudeyarov besieged him with texts, and grew angry when Kudeyarov in pretended innocence would turn the other half of his face against the priest (well, then: what did you take?); having gotten angry, the priest will remember his wife's samovar and close the discussion: "Go on with you, I haven't time to tangle with everybody: there's a lot of you people around here!" The priest would be sorry—he just wanted some tea or had noticed his wife's white neck at the window; he liked to pit his wits against Kudeyarov. The priest would spit, stare at the carpenter, but the carpenter had no face: just . . . some blotches. And the priest would walk away from him; and Kudeyarov would wink at his back, and drag himself across the whole common toward his sloping valley, toward his dewy coolness. And the stars would begin to glow.

What is there to say about Kudeyarov the carpenter? Folk did gossip about him: Kudeyarov, it seemed, barred and bolted his shutters at night (only he and the priest had shutters), and a wondrous light blazed from his cottage through the shutters, and a murmur of voices was heard: some surmised that he and his pock-marked woman were praying in their own special fashion; others hinted at something else: something unclean was going on there. However, they spoke of these things hesitantly and vaguely, and they did not believe it themselves; it was the deaf and dumb man who spread the rumor; he came once into Stepanov's shop, pointing aside to Kudeyarov's cottage and mumbling his *"apa-apa,"* and putting horns to his dishevelled head; admittedly Stepanov did not take this seriously, because he well knew the sort of tidings the deaf and dumb man carried: it was not for nothing that the priest at confession had instructed the deaf and dumb man that he should not eat forbidden food in Lent, to illustrate which he had portrayed a herring's tail with his palm and had made a cabbage out of his hands; the deaf and dumb man understood him, but, as to Kudeyarov, he might well have been mistaken.

As for the woman—that was another thing. He had a wonderful woman, a pock-marked woman: whether he bedded with her or not, no one knew; most likely he did. But the villagers disliked the woman, and she kept to herself. She was a stupid woman: she was always gazing at the stars; whenever the stars began to glow she would come out into the yard and begin singing in a plaintive voice either spiritual verses or an obscene love song. She was often to be seen at the washing boards: she sat on the boards, but did no washing, just gazed at the water, at the stars glowing there. . . .

⁓⁂⁓ The Dove ⁓⁂⁓

In the very blaze of the heat, when the girls skulk at home even though it is a holiday, when their green, red and canary yellow bodices cease to flit back and forth, and when only perhaps a sparrow flutters out of the dust into the bushes, and when only the breeze, the hot breeze, sways in the drowsy pine trees, and the road sends swirls of dust into the fields, then no wagons moved on the highway, no villager walked on his way: the village looked dead—such peace, such absence of people, such drowsiness hung in the glittering sunshine and amid the chatter of the cicadas.

Only where a number of cottages threw themselves in a heap toward the highway, those that were the most wretched and decrepit, did shouts and songs rise from the tavern: the Tzelebeyevo folk who lived near the highway had become spoiled. The folk who were more staid frowned strongly upon this section of the population: the priest frowned, the woman teacher frowned, and Ivan Stepanov (a rich peasant) frowned, as did the bandy-legged carpenter.

The highway ran there—past-past—beyond the village it ran, into the fields—it ran up the smooth slope of the plain and lost itself near the sky, because here the sky came down low over the village (yonder, beyond the frontier and seemingly behind the sky stood the fine town of Likhov). A ragged bush could be seen on that side, but from the village it looked like the figure of a dark wayfarer walking alone toward the village; years passed, and the wayfarer still walked on and on: he could never reach an inhabited place and from afar kept menacing the village.

At that tedious hour, out of the sloping valley where stood the carpenter's cottage, the carpenter reached the top of a hillock and shading his sickly face with his hand, kept peering into the distance along the road: maybe a cloud of dust will rise, maybe a wayfarer is approaching, maybe the Lord is sending a guest; the carpenter waited and waited, the horizon was clear and fluid. There was no one in sight. Again the carpenter returned to his lair; he sat and sat in his favorite corner under the icons; and again he would grow impatient and again he would climb the hillock though it was already time for tea; barefooted Matryona, the pock-marked woman and worker, had already laid the table for him: the white tablecloth with a border of red cocks was already on the table, set with rose-patterned cups, with bread, eggs; and the samovar was steaming already: it was time for tea: but with whom if not with a guest should one drink tea? and the guest was still not there; and again Kudeyarov the carpenter climbed the hillock; it was a long highway; the horizon was clear, there was no one coming; but no, there was some one, some one surely was now approaching the village; that was not a bush, it was a dark little figure; and beside it another little figure, a dark one too; soon it will begin to descend. "Hey, Matryona, be ready for the guests!" . . . And Matryona began to fuss, shuffling from the oven to the table on her strong, white feet: her browless, pock-marked face, with its dark, very dark eyes and barely quivering crimson lips, smiled as though she had long ago expected tidings from afar; she kept glancing at the carpenter who sat in silence without responding to the glances of the stupid wench: he was expecting a guest. And the guest had come.

A strange guest he was: Abram, a beggar, well known in the district; sometimes he would turn up in our local-ity; barefoot he made the rounds of the villages and the country houses; and everywhere he would be given alms: some would give him eggs, others a kopeck (it was the gentry who gave him money), some would just feed him and let him spend the night with them, others might threaten him with their dog on the chain; at times the beggar would entirely disappear: for months there would be no sign of him; then he was to be met far beyond Likhov and he had even been seen beyond Moscow: tall, broad-shouldered, curly-maned, with dark hair streaked with gray falling over his shoulders, with a large nose and narrow, slanting, cunning little eyes, he knew very well what he could take from whom; appearing under a window he would sing a psalm in a chesty bass voice, beating a rhythm to the words with his staff. A strange staff it was: it might have been a stick, a club or a crozier. He was a mighty man in appearance: if you were to meet him in a forest you'd be frightened: what if he hit you with his club? But strangest thing of all was the fact that his club was crowned with a gleaming leaden image of a dove which shone bright as silver. But since everyone knew the beggar, his ways and habits, and that he played with children and on occasion guarded the forest—everyone knew that, even the authorities—so they would not have been frightened of him even in the forest: only strangers would have been alarmed. Abram had only one sin: he often frequented the tavern where he bartered his eggs and bread for snacks and tea; he also frequented the town beerhouse; there he would sit in silence, keeping his ears open: it was said about him that he knew everyone's seamy side, the peasants', the priests', the gentry's, where anyone had gone, what anyone had planned. Abram knew everything; only it was odd why they said this about him: for he was not talkative, spoke little, and when he was asked about anything, he denied all knowledge of it: he said he did not know.

Entering the cottage, Abram crossed himself before the icons, took off his leather satchel and white woolen cap, which had been given him by the gentry, who call it "toadstool": he and Kudeyarov embraced and exchanged three kisses, and then Abram bowed low to Matryona as if she were the lady of the house, while she held out to him her hand with its gnarled, clenched fingers: very simply Abram took off his belt and sat down to tea with Matryona and the carpenter as though he were no beggar but a distinguished guest; and judging by the way they entertained the wayfarer, there was no way of proving that he was a beggar. They drank tea in silence. But when they had finished their tea and turned their cups upside down, while the samovar continued to hiss thinly, Kudeyarov-the-carpenter raised the slim wedge of his beard and stared at the beggar with that side of his face which seemed to say: "I did it, och! and how!" To which the beggar, who understood the carpenter without words, winked at Matryona:

"We know what we know: why hide anything . . . from our own folk!"

Matryona stood a little way off in her red blouse, propping up her pale face with her hand; only her lips quivered and her eyes gleamed mysteriously. She put her finger to her mouth and clearly bent her finger thrice in front of her lips; her lips muttered something; and her eyes again gleamed wonderfully. Then the carpenter, who was sitting in his beauty corner, stared full-face at the beggar and his whole face expressed something like patterns while his hand clearly tapped three times and drew crosses on the tablecloth.

The beggar bowed his head low as if consenting to what he had seen; and he whispered rather than said, "In the likeness of a dove . . ."

All their heads were now bent lower. There was silence. Then the carpenter clearly announced:

"We see that you, friend, are one of us; what have you seen and heard, what are the people babbling about?"

"We'll chatter willingly," the beggar replied with a wink and put his hand inside his shirt; soon he pulled out a dirty sheet of paper folded in fourths, opened it and began to read: "From a humble woman to our Father and Teacher, Mitry. Our brethren and sisters greet you; do not forget to pray for us, Father and Benefactor. We also send to you, Father, our brother Abram, son of Ivan, nicknamed the True Pillar. And we also beg you, Merciful One, to believe this brother in all he says; as you have believed in us, your faithful widows and wives, so believe in him. And Annushka-the-Dovecot also greets you, as well as Elena, Frol, Karp and Ivan-the-Fire. My faithful idol does not know anything as yet; the herbs you sent me I constantly use: what for, that you, Father, know yourself. We pray to the Holy Ghost in our new prayer house, that is, in the bath-house on those days when my faithful husband is absent in the district. A painter among our brethren is painting the likeness of the Dove. Do not forget, Merciful One, to say your honest prayers for us. And to your spiritual spouse," the beggar continued, bowing to Matryona, "my deep bow. Your faithful slave and your dove soul, Fyokla Yeropegina."

"So that's how it is, brother Abram," the carpenter broke his silence, "*himself* then is not in town these days . . ."

"How could he be: he's always on business, making the rounds of his mills," Abram replied. "Our Fyokla Matveyevna is always alone and alone," he went on with a wink, "that is, she is always with the brethren and sisters: she doesn't use enough herbs, there isn't time."

"There'll be time later . . ."

They were discussing Fyokla Matveyevna Yeropegin, the wife of the richest miller in Likhov, who had entered into a certain secret covenant. They said that a faithful brotherhood had already declared itself in the nearby villages, that prayer circles had sprung up here and there, and that no one suspected it as yet; it was a change from the old days when there were only two parishes of the brethren and sisters for the whole district; one parish gathered secretly in Fyokla Matveyevna's house with the help of Annushka and her mother, a centenarian, originally from Voroniye. The rest of the conversation made it clear that Mitry Mironich

Kudeyarov was the secret head of the entire holy enterprise: it was not for nothing that he and his pock-marked
wench Matryona had shut themselves in at night to sing in
secret their wondrous prayers; the Lord must have blessed
them for their holy enterprise of rising up with a new faith,
the dovelike, that is, spiritual faith, and because of that their
covenant was called the Covenant of the Dove. In what the
covenant itself consisted, it was impossible to gather from
their present conversation: one thing was clear, that the
brotherhood put its hope in certain mysteries; Kudeyarov
expected their revelation, but they lacked a man who could
assume the bold accomplishment of these mysteries; without this Kudeyarov and Matryona could not base themselves on the mysteries, of which they alone had knowledge,
so that, until the day came, they had to keep their secret
from the brethren; all that the brotherhood had heard was
that among them were saintly people who remained silent
until the time came when they would engage in battle with
the enemy of the human species on the day that fraternal
strife would spread over Russia; who Kudeyarov was in
reality, that only a few selected members of the brotherhood knew—among them Fyokla Matveyevna Yeropegin.
Abram, the beggar, was the angel of all tidings among the
brethren of the Covenant of the Dove, he carried the
tidings; but, until this day, Abram had never seen the head
of the Covenant and only now for the first time, were his
eyes opened about Mitry.

"Well, have you found the man?" Abram asked in a
whisper, bending toward Kudeyarov.

"Sh . . . sh!" the carpenter exclaimed, turning pale.
"Nowadays even the walls have ears." He looked around
him, rose, went out of the door and, convinced there was no
one near the cottage, came back, shut the door more
tightly, and pointed with his eyes at Matryona. "Ask her.
She is my spiritual bride: she is seeking the man and it seems
she has found someone: but will he bite?" At this the car-

penter laughed spitefully, "She does not want to do it with me: I am too old for her. . . ."

And when the beggar wanted to glance at Matryona, she was already gone: blushing, she had run out: she stood, all flushed, with her face pink and morose on the hillock and chewed a stem while an obstinate thought was imprinted upon her face.

The carpenter and the beggar talked a while longer and then parted; the beggar picked up his staff, girded himself with his satchel, and went his way, kicking up the dust with his bare feet. Soon his staff was tapping under the cottage windows; now here, now there, in the heat his leaden bird-dove glistened and the words of the Divine Psalms resounded in the sultry air.

All was quiet.

Only where the cottages had thrown themselves in a heap toward the highway—the poorer and more decrepit ones—shouts and songs rose from the tavern; the village looked depopulated—such peace, such drowsiness, hung in the glittering sunshine and the crackling of cicadas.

The sun stood already high; then the sun began to decline; it grew sultry; it was an evil day; through the day the dull sun sweated dully, still giving light, but it also seemed stifling and dizzying, attacking one's nostrils with an acrid smell wafting either from the cottages or from the scorched, parched earth. It was an evil day: it was so sultry that one's parched throat choked and shuddered: you gulped water with inexpressible agitation, seeking a sense in everything, while the dim, languorous shroud languorously and dimly heated the surroundings, but the surroundings—the sheep yonder and that fool of a peasant woman—would senselessly occupy your soul and brutalized now, you will seek no meaning, but just roll your eyes and sigh. And those persistent flies? With a sigh you'd swallow a persistent fly: they keep buzzing at your nose, in your ears, at your eyes, these persistent flies! Kill one fly, the air will disgorge hundreds more: in swarms of flies nostalgia itself grows languourously boring. . . .

The sun stood already high, and already it had begun to decline, and the light insolently flew in through the muslin curtains of the priest's little house, so that every grain of dust, every mark on the white plank floor showed clearly, and every stain on the wallpaper dotted with bouquets of roses alternating with bluebells showed clearly too, while the uncleared table with wine spots, bits of cabbage and the dishevelled head of Alexander Nicolaievich, the sacristan, which had drooped on the tablecloth after a good helping of rowanberry liqueur, was covered by a black regiment of flies: they gathered in many-footed swarms around the wine stains and in many-footed swarms again crawled over the face of the drunken sacristan, while the priest (in front of the icon of the Heavenly Queen he had sworn shortly before to stop drinking and was for that reason sober), with a face dripping from the heat and all the glasses of wine he had missed, with a swing of his bony arm was crushing in his fist the black crawling swarms and throwing them in a rage into scalding water. "Twenty-five, twenty-six, twenty-seven . . ." He drowned the flies and in the boiling water the flies floundered, but ever new swarms crawled and flew toward the wine stains, and again the priest caught them, drowned and crushed them: and always new swarms appeared and the whole room seemed to grow thick from so many pricking stings, from so many ringing voices, while yonder, behind the thin partition wall, was a small room with a single window and two wretched armchairs in covers and with the same sort of sofa, in the middle of which protruded a broken spring that might spear an inexperienced guest; the floor of this room was painted over and washed with *kvas** so that one's feet stuck to the floor, for which reason the priest's wife had stretched over it here and

---

* Kvas: a drink made of fermented rye bread flavored with fruit.

there pieces of thin canvas; the room was adorned with: a
card table covered with a knitted tablecloth and a fourth leg
attached only for the sake of appearance, a plaited basket
with the remains of a once luxuriant palm tree now in the
guise of a withered leaf covered with grass lice, a supple-
ment of the *Niva* in the shape of a gypsy with cymbals
hanging on the wall, and a portrait of General Skobeleff*
spotted by flies and pierced with a stick; but what adorned
the room more than anything else was an old piano. Here
was the priest-wife's kingdom; here sometimes she sat knit-
ting alone by the window; here sometimes she became
oblivious of both the priest and their children; here the
remains of some feeling kindled in her, a feeling not entirely
obliterated by disputes with the cook, the slanders, the
wiping of noses and other things having to do with the
scrofulous children; here at times she sat down to an instrument, the piano or the guitar, and played her beloved waltz,
"Times Without Return," without noticing that half the
keys tinkled pitifully or gave forth no sound at all. So it was
now: in a sickly way, as though in the last stages of
consumption, the waltz "Times Without Return" tinkled
forth, the sounds flowed and the sacristan sobbed out in his
drunken stupor, and the priest's fist, full of flies, paused in
the air, fell and opened, when times without return tinkled
pitifully from behind the thin partition wall; the priest
remembered his own "time with return" when as a seminarist he had visited Voroniye, where the little face of his
wife had smiled rosily amid the pink bloom of cherry trees,
a tender maiden then before she became a flabby, grumbling
and unseemly woman; and like a broken string it whined,
the time without return, in the sacristan's soul, too, whenever he raised his head to the puny sounds, trying quite out
of rhythm to join in, intoning: "Bu-u-u-r-r-r-n-n o-o-u-u-t,
bu-u-u-r-r-r-n-n   o-o-u-u-t,   m-m-y-y   fl-a-a-a-m-m-ming

* A Tsarist general (1843–1882), who distinguished himself during
the Russo-Turkish War 1877–78.

spl-i-i-n-n-ter . . . I a-a-m bu-u-u-r-r-r-n-ning o-o-u-u-t
with y-o-o-u-u. . ." And at once the flaming splinter of
the past burnt out in him, and the sacristan's head drooped
again into the swarms of crawling flies.

Daryalsky had become thoughtful too: here, to one side,
he was still sitting at the priest's and smoking, whereas he
should have been long ago in Gugolevo where he had already been missed, where the dinner had grown cold, and
where Katya, from a green bower of acacias, watched the
full dusty road which grinned back at her as it ran on its
way to Tzelebeyevo; and where, leaning on her crutch,
grandma all in lace, in black silk and wearing a white tulle
cap with lilac ribbons quivered in the garden; quivered and
turned among the nasturtiums. Why had time without
return also gripped Daryalsky, why did he also recall his
past life? Lived little, experienced much—enough had been
experienced to last a good dozen lives: Daryalsky remembered his father, an official of the Treasury, a simple and
honest man; he had struggled and struggled, like a fish
against ice, in order to procure his son a proper education;
in the end, he had been sent to an educational establishment
and should have attended it, but no: instead, he visited
libraries and museums and spent his days poring over books
and then, after a month's absence from the school, he had
implored his mother to write for him, secretly from his
father, a letter to the school authorities saying he had been
ill; he remembered how as a child he had declared to his
father that he did not believe in God, to prove which he
had brought out an icon from his small room and had
thrown it into a corner; how his father and mother had
grieved while he, the young non-Christian, had prayed to
the red dawns and to whatever entered his soul with the
dawn; he wrote verse, read Comte and worshipped, he, the
young non-Christian, the red flag, transferring to this material symbol his secret, precious and unknown to anyone,
the secret that the future will come to pass. Time without
return!

His father died; his mother died too. He was still a
student: outstanding among his fellows in their circles, in
disputes with the authorities, a leader, not a follower:
steeped in thick folios, studying Boehme, Eckhart, Sweden-
borg, and at the same time studying Marx, Lassalle and
Comte, seeking the secret of his dawn, but failing to find it
anywhere, anywhere; and then he had turned savage and no
longer influenced anyone; here he was a wayfarer, alone
amid the fields with his strange un-unified thinking, but
always with the dawn, with its crimson flow, with its warm,
avid kisses; the dawn always promised him some sort of
contact, some sort of approach to the mystery; and so there
he was—in the temple; he was already in the holy places, in
Dveyevo, in Optina, and at the same time in pagan antiquity
with Tibullus and Flaccus; and he lacked words to express
his thoughts; and in appearance he had become savage, plain
and crude—but his feelings were warmer, his thoughts
more refined, and there were more of them, more, and from
their plenitude his soul was being sundered; his soul demanded tenderness and love; and then darling Katya had
appeared, bright Katya had fallen in love with him: she
came and loved. But why was Daryalsky sighing now?
"Times Without Return . . ." But this time was no more
than yesterday; only yesterday he had believed that his
secret would be revealed in Katya, in her love and kisses:
she was his path, the indestructive pillar of true life. But
why was even that yesterday a "time without return"? Because the secretive glance of the pock-marked wench had
violently disturbed his soul. The pock-marked woman: her
gaze spoke not of love but of some sort of greed; enough:
neither greed nor love, but especially not love: he did not
need only love; what did he want, if love was the path, the
affirmation of truth? . . . Oh, flies, greedy and spiteful,
don't buzz, don't sting, don't crawl into the mouth! . . .
Oh, plaintive sounds: pitiful sounds, don't tinkle any more!
. . . Away with you, priest: drown yourself in swarms of
flies! . . .

He said goodbye to the priest and left; and the dull sun grew duller still and thundered with light and with thousands of insects from the common; the sun was already declining, and tinkling sounds followed Daryalsky; they broke up the pond into a thousand glitters: glittering splashes like silver doves flashed—in the water or in the sky—when the breeze rippled over the pond and the green air fluttered. Ahead, out of the sloping valley, rose a curl of smoke: there a red blouse flitted by, there a kerchief with white apples flitted by, and both vanished in the sloping valley near the cottage of Mitry Mironich, the carpenter. Daryalsky shuddered.

He walked away from the church, and could not remember how his feet carried him to the naked stone rising above the pond; the rippling waters rocked and soothed him wondrously: he felt drowsy, and already amid the ripples he heard his nurse's cradling voice, "bayou-bayou," and here in broad daylight everything seemed already strange and vague; and with his eyes he sought some passing villager, but no villager was passing here; the breeze was blowing and swaying the bushes; swaying his thoughts— and already he felt drowsy.

Listen—to the babbling streams, the current of the martins: vaguely he could hear the martins calling above the spire which with its gold-fretted cross dominated the village; the martins wove all round it. All day, morning and evening, the black martins bathed in the wave of air above the cross, twittered, darted to and fro, soared and swooped, cut the sky: they cut and scorched the air, scraping and drilling the air with their scorching screams, forever scorching the soul with inexhaustible desire; only at nightfall would they subside; but not altogether: at night too, in the hour of rest and repose, when dogs bark in the distance and cocks crow, a scream will issue from the belfry; the Tzelebeyevo martins were well known throughout the district. But do not heed the martins, friend, do not watch them long: they will tear your heart apart and into your breast they will thrust a red-hot drill. You will want to run, shake the dewy bushes, fall on dewy grass and press it to your breast. Your life will not be worth a copper: you will dry up.

Watch them, how they twitter, cut the air with their wings—they have now glued themselves all over the cross.

Daryalsky stared at the cross, at the belfry: on the other side of the belfry were bushes, a ravine and more bushes: further on, more bushes: as you gazed, the murmuring forest spilled forth its drowsiness, and a stupid bird clucked in the forest; very plaintively clucked.

What does it want?

So Daryalsky had dawdled all day in the village, wandering along the common and peeping into the sloping valley (where stood the carpenter's cottage).

And already the village girls in a choir had passed the pond; they had thrown off their crimson skirts and blouses, and had plunged their white bodies in unison into the pond; how they snorted from there! For a long time they chased each other along the bank—just as they were, without undershirts, plump and white. The village girls in choir had passed away from the pond. The men had also come and throwing off their trousers and shirts had plunged their tanned bodies in unison into the pond; and there was still more shouting and snorting. Just as they had come without singing, so they departed without singing. There was no one now by the pond; only a kingfisher was blackly outlined in the cool air.

Then singing a quiet plaintive song, the pock-marked woman approached the washing planks; she did not throw off her crimson garments: she sat down on the planks, splashing her dangling legs in the water; she combed her reddish tresses over the water. And when Daryalsky passed her, her lips quivered and her eyes mysteriously gleamed— Oh, how they caught fire! He turned around: so did she: oh, how her eyes fixed his! He approached, but the pock-marked woman had already left the pond with her quiet song, her plaintive song. The first little star now glowed, and timidly with its two damp yellow lights the hut peeped out from the sloping valley.

The clean evening breeze spun and swirled over the village, and with summer tearlets joyfully kissed the bushes, the grass, and people's boots, when the daytime sky, neither azure nor gray, hardened into deeper blue just when the West opened its jaws, into which the daytime flame and smoke flowed away; out of there the air cast its red carpet-like patches of sunset and covered with them the door jambs and the logs of the huts, the fretwork angels, the small bushes, studded the cross of the belfry with rubies of vast price, while the tin cockerel weather vane seemed to cut the evening air with a provocative raspberry-colored wing; a clump of crimson carpet-like air struck the priest's hedge of currant bushes, hitting Father Vukol fair and square; the priest was sitting on a birch tree stump in his white cassock and a straw hat; he reddened as he smoked his meerschaum pipe, and looked so very small in the sunset.

The carpet-like air cut the highway with a red canvas, running off to where the smaller and poorer cottages clustered, where songs were being bawled for some reason, and where for some reason the usual accordion tore the air to pieces amid a swirl of dust, and for some reason, as if by magic, a triangle tinkled in response, while at the same time the West shed a dark current and there, into the flow of the dark current—the highway led one away; into the dark blue mist of the blue night somebody was advancing from there upon the village. The dark little figure went on advancing, but it seemed so far off, so far off, that it might never reach our village.

In the Tavern

"Just try and grasp this, you wooden snout, just try and grasp who it is toils for this earth! I'm a peasant! The earth belongs to the peasant, that is, it's his *fully in pharmaceutical possession.* With acres of land they can't give us any freedom; it's just confusing, this freedom. What do we need freedom for?"

"You Berdichev strikers!" a scruffy looking, smallish peasant capriciously intervened.

"Why are you staring at me with your carbuncles, you mug? You will earn your rights only if you fight!" spat out a worker from the Prokhorov mill, a young lad with a fallen nose.

From the side resounded a loud nasty tenor voice:

"There was a wild wind, and it druve me into the tavurn; and my liquor salesman asked, 'Man, what do you want?' And I answered him, 'A drink of water,' and he clenched his five fingers and hit me on the teeth. And, beaten, I collapsed."

"And have you seen, lads, this same forest echo?" a Tzelebeyevo lad with bulging eyes, perspiring from the heat, was asking a couple of gullible persons sipping tea from a saucer.

But stridently a huge accordion drowned it all, an accordion played by a lad in a blue silk shirt and a cap askew, with a pert, coagulated mug; while the drunken voices of the lads lolling around him quietly sang: "Tra-a-a-n-s-v-a-a-l,

Tra-a-a-n-s-v-a-a-l, my l-a-n-d . . . You a-r-r-e bl-l-a-a-z-i-n-g a-a-l-l-l o-n-n-n f-i-i-r-r-e . . ."

The tavern was full of visitors from the neighboring villages; steam rose in a pillar; here and there vodka was being served in teapots; with their hands some were gobbling smelly sausages straight from their saucers.

In a corner a worker with rotted nose and hoarse voice was already defending himself against the scruffy little peasant; at the next table a passing Likhov inhabitant, a seminarist expelled from the seminary, was plucking at his little goatlike beard and intoning in the manner of a sacristan while in another corner lads were talking about "the forest echo."

"Hey, what are you pushing for! Is it fighting you want? for you devil's children we expose ourselves to bullets; he has no understanding: hey, brothers, he'll break my head in!"

"And he went on yelling, 'Isvoschik, Isvoschik! How much will you charge to take me to the little temple?' And he answered: 'There's a coin worth twenty kopecks,' and, after he mounted the cab, the mare took off and galloped away. . . .'"

"They went full steam by the Mare's Puddle and called out 'Devil!' to the 'Echo,' and she back to us, 'Devil!' 'Come out!' and she out of the bushes, you know, all in white, and we took to our heels." But the accordion wheezed and the voices droned, "The bo-o-y o-n-n f-f-o-o-t br-r-o-o-u-u-g-h-t c-a-a-r-t-r-r-i-i-d-g-e-s-s t-o-o t-h-e-e b-a-a-t-t-l-e l-i-n-n-e."

They said the Japanese were trying to stir up the people, that there were spies living near Likhov; they said that the railway workers walked up the permanent way with "red flaks," and that they were headed by General Skobeleff, who had until now been hiding from everybody but had now announced himself to the people; that the witch from the village of "Mare's Puddle" had surrendered her soul to the devil and sought to transfer her occult powers to someone else before she died. But not finding anyone, her occult powers passed into a thin reed; from hand to hand circulated cunningly scribbled notes intended to dissuade the people from rising to work for the landowners; people read them, shook their heads: the contents were tempting; but they only smiled. . . .

To the side, in silence, sat the beggar Abram and the leaden dove dimly glinted on his staff; at times the Likhov inhabitant approached him and after exchanging whispers returned to his place, continuing in a sing-song to bawl out his nonsense: "And bawling in the loudest of voices, 'Isvoschik, Isvoschik! Pull up!' And a mighty voice rang out, 'Hey, stop, you devil's daughter!' And the horse stopped as if grounded. Hey you, freedom!" he tossed at a worker who'd just been bashed and was completely drunk. "So that's the way it is: you have a good script, but do you have your own sicialist god??"

"We'll make a present of heaven to the sparrow . . . and we'll raise . . . the r-r-r-e-d- flag" he muttered, now completely drunk, "to the p-r-r-r-o-li-ta-r-r-r-i-at . . ."

"And not a red coffin?" the Likhov inhabitant suddenly raised his voice so that the accordion stopped, the lads ceased to wonder at the "forest echo," and all the heads turned in the same direction; but how they glittered, the eyes of the Likhov townsman: "Listen, ye Orthodox Christians, the Kingdom of the Beast is coming and we can only destroy this Beast with Spiritual fire; brothers, red death will come between us, and there is only one salvation—the fire of the Spirits, the Dove-Kingdom prepared for us." For a long time the Likhov townsman went on talking and then he disappeared.

The villagers were amazed at these amazing sayings; and some were already departing, others had long gone, while others, having imbibed official vodka straight out of teapots, were lying under the benches, and among them was the worker with the rotted nose.

A clear, pure, quiet, fresh night. In the distance village lads were singing loudly as they went home: "For truth

God will forgive . . . For wrongdoing He will condemn us . . ."

A cart was creaking along; the Likhov townsman was driving Abram the beggar somewhere. "Well, have you found the man?" . . . "We've picked him out." . . . "Who is he?" . . . "An idler from the gentry, only he's still one of us . . ." "Is he biting?" "He'll bite." A clear, pure, quiet, fresh night . . .

CHAPTER TWO

The Town of Likhov

The Highway

The highway ran across woods, bushes, stumps; ran across the smooth slopes of plains, and all of a sudden the attacking wind would rush upon you; ran across the green softly whispering oat field; and running away into the distance the highway crossed streams and gullies: from there a smoky hair shirt stretched and covered the whole sky; and from there rain was sown upon the woods, the stumps, upon the smooth slopes of the plains; and from there a church extended its silver spire out of the mist, although there seemed to be no village within ten miles; the highway skirted the church at a distance, and the village lay concealed between two smooth humps covered with quivering rye. If one were to climb up on a willow tree by the road, which had been preserved only God knows how (in olden days huge willow trees had been planted along the sides of our roads), then one could perceive the village, for it was just an arm's length away if one stood by the willow; but on a gray rainy day when the gray huts like poor orphans hugged the poor gray earth, it was quite impossible to distinguish them through the rain. The hump of earth came to a stop just at the top: the top here cut the plain; the top here tore the village in two and tumbled down here in orchards to the spring before the ravine; the spring was called "The Silver Spring," and in the old days the top had been named by the villagers the "Dead Top"; the top stretched upwards for no less than three quarters of a mile, turning finally to a sandy top, cutting across many other tops and falling into other ravines; the top crawled and crawled, by springtime swallowing up many dozens of acres of plow land; here in the old days the villagers had their fun in the middle of the highway from Tzelebeyevo to Likhov; and the village that lay beneath the top was called Grachikha. It was a poor village, unlike Tzelebeyevo; and the houses here had no iron roofs but roofs of straw; life here had its own character, having nothing in common with Tzelebeyevo; the peasants and peasant women here were different; there were no single proprietors, and the merchants had all gone elsewhere. The village contained only top families: the Fokins and the Alexins; so many of them had been born in Grachikha that those bearing other names had died out, become extinct, so to speak; the Fokins were what are called great hulking fellows: one fool's as good as another—and in practice they were not clean, the Fokins, and they drank besides. The Alexins were not Fokins: they drank less, and if in practice they were not entirely clean, still they were cleaner than the Fokins; but, note, an evil disease had spread among them; but nevertheless the Alexins lived like people should; and they had a priest of their own here, and everything theirs was special, peculiar.

Much could be told about this village, but there would be no point in telling it all because the highway to Likhov bypassed the village; a traveler will pass by the top without noticing anything, the traveler's whiskers will not even twitch: he has no business with the Alexins or their priest. Only the silver spire will project in the mist above the plain between two smooth humps: will project and be no more; will project and vanish in the mist.

Where toward the Dead Top the highway was interrupted by humps of yellow forest and where out of the mist the dark spire was barely visible, Kudeyarov the carpenter was descending the rain-washed road; he walked barefoot, wearing a newly sewn homespun coat; the sticky mud squelched and squished between his toes like a purée of peas

mixed with oatmeal or like a mix of pig slop; the carpenter
had taken off his boots (the boots were new) and hung
them from a stick over his shoulder; his traveling kit also
swung from it. For a long time the carpenter groped his
way through the bushes; walked in between stumps and
through woods; paused to reflect in the fields; he was dragging himself to the town of Likhov; the sleet breathed on
him with its fine dust: the sleet whirled all around him—the
whole space between Likhov and Tzelebeyevo, it seemed,
danced in the tearful wind; the bushes sobbed and danced;
the tiresome stalks danced too; the rye danced; and the
bright, light ripples twisted fussily over the surface of the
cold, still, brown pools. The carpenter dragged himself
across the puddles, the bushes, through the whiskered rye,
and his sickly, miserable face drooped sickly and miserably
over the road, nose down like a woodpecker; his cap hid his
eyes, making his face look blind. Did he see or not see what
was happening all around him? All around him were foul
weather and mud: the rain danced, bubbles burst on the
puddles, but for all that, the carpenter tramped on making a
dough of mud.

The carpenter stared—and there already, on the Dead
Top, was Abram waiting for him; with a reddish satchel
slung over his shoulder and his "toadstool" crushed over his
unkempt hair to ward off the rain, the beggar sat slumped
on a stone, whistling now and then into the wind: he was
waiting for the carpenter. The beggar did not mind the
rain: it was Whitsun—peace was in his heart; so let the rain
be sown yonder, let the neighborhood be sprinkled with
dew, and you, mists, curl and gurgle with rain! Where will
the heart find peace, if it cannot find peace at Whitsun?
Abram spoke solidly, hitting a puddle with his stick:
"Maidens—beautiful, those chambers are all lit up: wait
there for the guest, drink mead and beer. Your wished-for
traveler is near . . ." Water dripped from the dove's beak.
All around the drenched crows were screaming. . . .

Abram the beggar stared—there was the carpenter descending; Mitry raised his nose—the wayfarer was waiting for him beneath the Dead Top: together they were bound for Likhov—theirs was the same way, the same preoccupation, the same business, the same life—and an endless eternal life; they smiled at each other; they met, and so they went on; went up; but the Dead Top was sheer and slippery; if you fell, you'd be covered with mud: no matter—all things were God's: the sky, the earth, the far stars, the clouds, people—and the mud too; the mud was also God's. They went about their business not like other folk, whose ways are known to all, whose acts are unblemished, who go about their business simply and openly; but like black thieves, like wolves, they both picked their way by roundabout paths already for days, weeks, months; so that no one should see how they had joined their paths, they had just now secretly left their human lodgings: the beggar had tramped from Grachikha by way of ravines; and the carpenter had taken a wide circuitous route so that no ill-intentioned neighborly eye should register what road he had taken for his travels.

"Well, friend, you must have got wet sitting there! Have you been waiting long, too long?"

"That's nothing, Mitry Mironich: no doubt you also had to take a roundabout way; no doubt you got up with the cocks?"

"When it's a matter of spiritual affairs, one is ready to do a greater circuit; it's a pleasure even to walk over so many places on earth," Mitry drawled nasally as he climbed out of the gully to where the spaces again unfurled—the spaces that stretched for many dozens of miles: he sniffed the air, staring round him; and the wind seemed to become enraged at this glance; more fiercely the enraged wind whipped the oat fields and the puddles; more madly the nasty sleet whirled about; the clouds dropped and a bush was uprooted: another bush was uprooted, and then a third: now they came upon a thicket of small trees; the road twisted through it; and then the open spaces again: and again the spire spitted through the leaden gloom; spitted and disappeared.

The beggar tramped on, thumping the ground with his staff; it was good to walk thus; to walk on without knowing what was left behind your back; to walk on without knowing what lay ahead: behind your back a heap of huts: in front a heap of huts: behind your back cities, rivers, provinces, a cold sea and Solovki*; ahead the same cities, the same rivers, and the city of Kiev; he had sat there in a hut, between four walls (if he was allowed to spend the night), between benches, peasant women, children, hens, cockroaches and bugs; had sat there and kept to himself, or had begged under the windows; as he had sat there, so he would sit with a peasant's permission and the same sort of peasant woman would start to fidget; and the same sort of children and bedbugs would cling to you. But out here were no children, no bedbugs—instead, a cold free spirit breathed upon you: it breathed where it willed, and no one knew where it came from or where it went; only in the fields could you breathe enough spirit and like a spirit yourself go where you willed; and there would be nothing: you would go over the seas, over the sunflower earth—into the wide world you'd go: an orphan, you'd become spiritual; and that is why to wander—that is, holy idleness, is a spiritual thing: and if every one took to wandering in the fields they would breathe the same air and become one soul: for the one spirit has clothed the earth with its halo. But evidently it is not like that; from merely breathing the open air mysteries were not revealed; the carpenter Kudeyarov evidently knew what mysteries were necessary for the transfiguration of the brethren: a spiritual act was necessary, a great exploit: not until the spirit assumed a human likeness would people be granted joy, and animals and every heavenly bird be granted joy too.

Here Abram looked askance at the carpenter: a sickly looking man with a nose like a woodpecker's, coughing all

---

* A monastery on the White Sea near Archangel. Later a place of exile for political prisoners.

the time, but—he knew the mysteries, had access to all things: men's destinies, the reason why people revolt, and why pains and nausea develop in the belly after giving birth.

And glancing at the carpenter's face, Abram intoned, touching his lips with his fingers thrice: "In the likeness of a khdove . . ." All spiritual intercourse between the brethren began thus. . . .

"In the likeness of a *khdove*," Abram repeated, "we so assume that, for the likeness of a *khdove*, every father will be prepared to abandon his property, abandon his small lot of land, abandon his woman and will take to wandering over *Roosia*, and will breathe plenty of fresh air: spiritual verses or prayers, it may be said, are like spiritual fruit, the breathing of lips that have absorbed the air; and that is the mystery that drives folk from their native land; but here, as we see, they've fenced in our earth, our mother, with spiked collars and wire; sit there, they say, with your rags— there's no freedom for you; your property, they say, is yours, and mine is mine; but can one live a life with just property? My rags, that filth, they mean; and at that rate, there's no such thing as property; your riches will only swell your belly, and then all sorts of things will get at your belly and down you'll go into the tartarian dark: into the earth with your belly; and they'll pile the earth upon you— lie there, rot; isn't that what we suppose? The folk are getting tired of rotting alive: with all these strikes now- adays the folk are putting themselves on a diet of air, so to speak; they'll sit a while, they'll sit—and then they'll go off tramping with flags; and new mysteries will spread, and prayers . . ."

"Well, brother Abram, that's nonsense: you're a Pillar and a True One, but your tongue is false; your heart is gold, but your tongue's a copper penny," the carpenter said; staring at him, winking and twitching his nostrils.

"We, we're just . . . we're just . . . we're what? That you know best: you're the chief . . . We're, so to speak,

neither this nor that, just something else in general; and
everything else," the beggar replied in confusion, panting
into his beard and stamping his bare foot in the mud in a
troubled sort of way. (He was a True Pillar, chanted his
verses well, and had more than enough cunning, but com-
pared with the other brethren he was a simpleton of simple-
tons as far as the destinies and mysteries were concerned:
somehow he could never put two and two together, or
reason out what was what: and, because of that, he mixed
with the "socialists," was involved with the "Stundists" and,
in the summer, went with the *"Beguni,"** and yet, if it ever
was a question of betraying any one of "his own," Abram
could be relied upon not to do so; a Pillar of pillars, he even
held his tongue locked up when necessary.)

"And what day is it now?" Mitry asked him, pulling his
cap still lower, so that only the tip of his nose and his beard
were visible from under the homespun coat as if there was
no man there at all: a homespun coat merely, and on the
homespun coat a cap, and out of the cap—a nose: in this
way the carpenter walked on, stooping more and more
under the driving sleet. "What day is it?" he asked again.

"Whitsun . . ."

"So so, Whitsun . . ."

"And where are we going: do you realize—"

"Don't bother me, we're wandering . . ."

"Just think: to whom are we going?"

"To Ivan-the-Fire, and to Annushka-the-Dovecot . . ."

"So that's it, to the Fire, and whose is the Fire?"

"Whitsun's."

"And the doves, whose are they?"

"God's own."

"So that's it: just realize this: we are entering into our
property, into our possessions, into our church—and there
is a mystery in that. Our spiritual path will be transformed
into a certain convent: like a gust of wind that blows and is

---

* "The Runners"—a religious sect.

gone; and how to change the holiness of spiritual things into
a corporeal essence—that is the mystery. Our essence is
spirit; and property comes only from the Holy Ghost. . . .
Essence is like a chunk of wood: you plane the wood; here
with a jack plane, there with a long plane—here, there, and
you have it finished.

"Just take furniture," the carpenter went on, stuttering,
and his face creased with worry to express something, even
looked depressed and pitiful, even blotchy. "Yes, yes, take
fur-furn . . ." (the carpenter began to stutter when he
tried to reveal in a word the feelings agitating him; we must
suppose that the carpenter's stutter was due to his ailment).

"Take f-fur-furniture!" he finally exploded like a shell,
and from being pale he turned into a beetroot, and per-
spired: "Ah . . . it al-l-l-so," he raised his finger, "is an
important business, brother . . . and don't think about my
delivering furniture; with purpose and p-p-prayer, brother,
with prayer (he had now mastered his thoughts) one planes
and sings those songs, and as for the furniture: where will it
go? Among people: you make it with prayer and it will do
you service: some merchant or gentleman will sit on it and
start pondering upon truth, so prayer helps . . . Take this
furniture again . . ." But he failed to express himself, and
his face dropped: all that was left was the cap, the homespun coat, and the bare feet squelching through the
mud. . . .

"To build, brother, one has to build, to plane—to plane
the House of God: and likewise: here are both furniture
and woman, and all the rest. The resurrection of the dead,
brother, will take first place in the memory, in the spirit:
the dead will come to pass their time with us, friend; that's
the way it is: especially if one places some belonging of
theirs, of the dead—a rag or a portrait—on a table, yes, with
the spirit, their spirit, their spirit, that's the way. Through
that incarnation, it may be said, of our spirit in man: like us
a man will be born; and you talk about the air all the time:
about the air blowing; and then it's gone, the air . . . That's

something . . . As to furniture, leave the furniture . . . The furniture also . . . al-l s-so!" he drawled.

Quietly his face crawled out of the homespun coat, and now it looked quite different: white and luminous: neither pale nor flushed—the carpenter had become all white. The sleet whipped them more and more; and smoky wisps of cloud rushed fussily from horizon to horizon; there was no end or beginning to their armies; a bush sputtered gaily with the bad weather, bending a branch over its hollow; the grasses rustled when there was no rain; there was rain and no rain; there was rain here but none over there: but there were spaces; and in the spaces other spaces hid, lurked, and once again revealed themselves; and as soon as the wayfarers neared any point in the distance it became a space; and Russia was a multitude of such spaces, with tens of thousands of Grachikhas, with millions of Fokins and Alexins, with priests and crows; Likhov rose, only now and then winking with kerosene lamps in the night. The wayfarers were now approaching Likhov, Likhov, but there was no trace of Likhov on the horizon, and it was impossible to say where Likhov was; but Likhov was there. Or, perhaps, there was no Likhov at all, but merely an illusion of it and an empty one at that, like burdock and dandelion: just look: there's a field and somewhere in it is a dry lost broom; but walk further into the mist and look: and you'd say that a wicked man is chasing after you through the field; there's a willow tree; walk past it and look, and it will growl at you.

"And so is a human enemy," the carpenter continued, "just use your brains, friend, an enemy will blow on every sign for a thing, in a word, on corporeal existence; and it's gone, the corporeal life, gone; and the enemy can pretend to be a spirit too; and you (wrack your brains, brother) go on as usual, have to bring a creature to birth; in that way the spirit will assume a human countenance—from a woman such a child will be born; there are spirits and spirits, Abramushka: now one's a spirit, another's an enemy; we understand about the air, what you've been saying about the air; but what about the air that stinks, the air? That also—"

"That we understand, Mitry Mironich, what we are: we have nothing against that—"

"Wait! We've found a man: my wench, Matryona—she's a c-u-n-n=n-i-n-g one, yes! That's what." Here the carpenter choked, "A-a-a-h-h . . . a woman will twist a man round her little finger . . . and the mystery will be consummated: but till then—not a word."

"An idler, you said a while ago, a man of the gentry," Abram ventured carefully and his small eyes seemed to dance mischievously. "You don't mean the fellow that's living in Gugolevo? You couldn't tempt him with a peasant woman: he'll find his own kind and a Baroness's granddaughter into the bargain. . . ."

"All right: let him find his own kind; the Baroness's money is not to be sniffed at: indeed . . . And the little doves will peck at the golden grain. We know he'll marry; but with my wench . . . well, let him . . . let him . . . sleep as he will, and she'll be pregnant by him—that's the cross!"

"But why with him and not with somebody else, even, let's say with you, Mitry Mironich? In what way are you not as good—in your countenance and spirit!" Abram lied because, though Mitry may have turned out worthy in spirit, he was anything but that in countenance. For what sort of a face had the carpenter, it may be asked? And where had such another been seen? No face had he, but a sort of mutton chop chewed to the bone, a mere half face: it may have been a face, but it looked like half a face. . . .

"O-o-o-l-d, I'm old; understand this, friend, in my late years I have arrived at spiritual faith; formerly I badly soiled my flesh—the female essence is harmful for me—it's not for me: to pray, to help: that is a different state—insight would enlighten me about the essence, but that I should do it myself—no; the offspring of the dove," here Kudeyarov sighed bitterly, "will not be my seed, it must be another's, a stranger's. . . . And thus that idler—Daryalsky or whatever he calls himself!" The carpenter hissed with gloomy jealousy as his face darkened. "His flesh is spiritual: when I was mending some furniture last summer at the Graaben's, I noticed him in the garden; and that's the way it was: he looked at everything spiritually, spiritually—on a blade of grass, on his Katinka—he was exhaling spirit; by his eyes I could see he was one of us: and he talks of mysteries all the time, and he is of the gentry; but he can't reason it out, what the mystery is: because he was educated and is too brainy; but mystery nowadays lies with our brother, the peasant; he feels that in his heart, but not in his mind. But he has more than enough spirit . . . I thought that Matryona . . . we couldn't—that's how it is: so I said to my woman, I said, let you and he (for she, the woman, also has the spirit: she has such a spiritual body) . . . At first she was ashamed, but then she thought it over; and much thought went into it at the time: we prayed; and the spirit descended into us at that time (oh how she prayed; and I had a dream vision); well, I said, through you, woman, a great joy, I said, will visit the earth. And from that time I began to give tidings to the brethren: soon, I said, have patience, very soon; and then all sorts of signs manifested themselves; the socialists began to act, people began chattering about freedom; strange clouds began to move in the sky. They remembered Pugachev.* Those, friend, are the flowers: what a fine little berry we shall have . . . yes . . . I'm just full of it!

"And on little Katya's money we shall build a lot of ships, that is, communes—on Katya's and the Yeropegin money: the merchant himself has become rather ill now; I've sent herbs to the wife, but it hasn't helped; his illness grows worse than before: after the merchant's death the

---

* Pugachev, Emelyan (1730–75): A Don Cossack who, claiming to be Peter III, started an elemental revolt against feudalism and serfdom (1773–75). He was executed in the Red Square.

money will seep to us and no one else; that's what we turn
the air, I mean the spirit, into: money, and there's also
furniture . . . Yes, that's the way it is. . . ."

They were silent and only a fine drizzle was falling; only
a light breeze was blowing; and a sparse bush muttered
something, and then nothing.

Already they had passed the hamlet. By the oak grove a
stout, well-to-do proprietor had settled: he had planted an
apple orchard and had girded it with a thick fence of rough
stone at exactly the spot where the village road met the
highway; and the highway stretched on, cutting with its
white stone the fields of oats and other fields—tramped on
with its telegraph poles, flew on with a dark network of
wires; and finally fell in a striped stone scribbled over with
figures, and fell in a heap of roadside flint stones; on the
stones crosses had been carefully marked in tar (they were
collecting the stones): carts groaned, wagons creaked, men
on foot passed and to meet them, caravans of canvas-
covered cases of vodka came dancing; and on every side
hamlets showed more frequently, and villages fell behind:
even a larger village swam out of the mist from behind a
hillock and, close to it, a house with an iron roof standing in
isolation. That was the state liquor shop; in front of it,
attached to a pole, a wooden lantern; the house drowned,
the village drowned—the mist curtained them off. Here,
directly opposite, Likhov stepped out of the gloom, just as
our wayfarers began to think that they would never see
Likhov: then it slowly began to define itself through the
mist in the form of a cathedral and many sad-looking
houses; and already a little to one side the siding rails of the
railway station shone out: from that direction monoto-
nously and dully a train mooed.

⁘⁛⁘ The Dumpling ⁘⁛⁘

"Your wife, brother, is a 'crudity'. . ."

"No, far from it: more than that: one can cope with a 'crudity'; she's not a 'crudity,' but a dumpling!"

Thus, once in drunken company and with a chorus girl on his knees, Yeropegin the miller had characterized his spouse during a spree in the provincial capital. Since he had called Fyokla Matveyevna a "dumpling" in the presence of the marshall of the nobility, the nickname stuck to her: "dumpling" she became and "dumpling" she stayed. In Likhov, soon Fyokla Matveyevna came to be known as "dumpling," not so much among their more intimate friends as among the small shopkeepers, the manager of the farm, the millers and sundry other employees.

Not that she was too obese; but, as it were, all of loose flesh; whether she donned her lilac silk dress after lacing herself up in a corset or the chocolate-colored dress, her belly and breasts just bulged out of her: the chin would swell up and her head would be thrown back; her face could not be called fat: it was rather puffy and pale. An "unhealthy plumpness," as Pavel Ivanich, the doctor, called it: Fyokla Matveyevna had not grown stout, but puffy; and for more than a year now she had been unable to pull off her wedding ring; her fingers had become swollen too. Well, her lips also had gone that way: the lower lip had become separated from the upper one by about a quarter of an inch; and on the very tip of that lip was a wart: that might still have passed, but the fact that prickly hairs had started to grow from that wart, that was more than many could stand, especially the male sex and the tender maidens. One day Fyokla Matveyevna paid a visit to the marshall of the nobility on Easter Sunday; and the small son of the marshall of the nobility (a flaxen-haired boy) took it into his head to ask her: "And why, auntie, have you a little strawberry growing on your face?" His mother at once made the boy stand in a corner, but a sad expression settled on the face of the miller's wife; and her eyes filled with sadness too; her eyes were tranquil and gray: a submissive humility shone in them. It goes without saying that the next day visitors from Likhov began to talk of the "little strawberry" as well as the weather while exchanging Easter kisses with the young ladies. Only it had been a pity, a pity indeed, to hurt her (not the little strawberry, of course, but Fyokla Matveyevna); true, no one had any evil to report of her, and of good she did a great deal: for the benefit of widows and old women; here on Panshina Street there was an asylum for old women. As soon as the hooves of the Yeropegin horses would clatter down Panshina Street, and "Khfedor" would gallop past the windows, while behind him swayed the taffeta flowers, the silk scarf and the fruit on the hat of Yeropegin, an old woman's face would show itself at the window and she would mumble something good. On holidays, as a rule, the old women would flow toward Fyokla Matveyevna—from Panshina Street to Ganshina Street where the Yeropegins had a two-storied wooden mansion with a fruit orchard, stables, storehouse, barn, and even a bathhouse. She was a kindly soul, was Fyokla Matveyevna, and shame upon Luka Silitch for mocking at her— shame indeed! Why, how could she be a "dumpling"? Do "dumplings" have such hearts? One only had to look at her eyes!

But Luka Silitch did not see the eyes of his faithful spouse; he saw everything else; and that is why he had called her a "dumpling," because he wenched on the side, and even, shameful to admit, carried on at home with the servants (it was a good thing that their children, a son at the University and a daughter at school, were being educated elsewhere and even spent the summer with friends. Their children had convictions and that is why they lived elsewhere). From a casual glance at Luka Silitch it would have been impossible to conclude that he was a wencher; tall, dry, with thin compressed lips, with short-cropped gray hair, with a small gray goatee, he walked about in a long black kaftan, leaning on a cane (he suffered from gout), and wore a modest cap; and his eyes, which gleamed severely from under his spectacles, were strictly brown: who could have guessed that these austerely compressed and already moribund lips could joke so much; or that those eyes, so respectably concealed behind spectacles, could wink and sparkle so. It could be said that the modest and well-sculptured image of Luka Silitch expressed the beautiful soul of his spouse, whereas the unshapely appearance of Fyokla Matveyevna represented nothing but the very fetid little soul of her rich husband: in a word, if he were to be turned inside out (soul outward), he himself would have become Fyokla Matveyevna; and, vice versa, Fyokla Matveyevna would have inevitably been transformed into Luka Silitch; they both formed a single image split into halves; but that this image had two heads and four legs, and each half, if we may be allowed to say so, began to live an independent life—this circumstance invalidated the correctness of the suggested comparison.

The two halves had broken apart from each other a long time ago and now looked in altogether different directions: one half watched keenly over the work of more than ten mills, scattered through the district, occupied itself with stud farming and did not let a single attractive skirt slip past; whereas the other half locked itself up: sealed itself off strangely in alarm, fright and obduracy; she no longer raised her eyes to meet her husband's and, sin to say, it might have seemed to everyone as though the "dumpling"

herself knew very well that it was not only official business
that enticed her husband to the town of Ovchinnikov, but
also the chorus girls. Each time her husband returned, the
"dumpling" lowered her eyes, even though her eyes were
clear, sparkling, pure, and there was no reason for her to
lower them; but there were circumstances in the life of
Fyokla Matveyevna that made her lower her eyes before a
husband such as Luka Silitch; it would have been strange to
suppose that such an obese merchant's wife (and a "dumpling" into the bargain and not merely a "dumpling," but a
"dumpling" with a little strawberry on her lip) was given
to amorous pursuits, even though it be with the coachman:
no, there were other reasons that confused Fyokla Matveyevna; for two years already—but just a moment: when
was it Konovalov's pigsty had burnt down? It must have
been at least three years ago since the pigsty had burnt
down. . . . So then: three years had passed since Fyokla
Matveyevna had joined the sect of the Dove and had
become associated with it to such a degree that she had
become its main support and patron; she supplied the sisters
and the brethren with money, she dispatched them on pil-
grimages to holy places and to church readers if the brethren had need of one. More than that: as from this year, ever
since Kakurinsky, the former seminarist, had joined the
Doves with all his household, the merchant's wife had given
quite a large sum for acquiring a machine which could print
appeals to *brother-Russians;* and these appeals egged on the
people to revolt against priests and, at the same time, against
the authorities; the seminarist had installed the machine in
his house and from time to time knocked off something on
it: packets of leaflets were then dispatched somewhere afar
(they were still afraid to circulate the leaflets in our district); and on the leaflets was a cross: in a word, just let go
in all directions—yes. Fyokla Matveyevna understood nothing about all this, but the seminarist had insisted upon this,
and the head of the covenant, Mitry Mironovich Kudeyarov, who lived in Tzelebeyevo, let this go through without

objection, so that it could be concluded that Kakurinsky had printed the leaflets with his agreement. But how came about this transformation of a millionairess from Likhov into a sectarian, a member of a sect, whose content was so indefinite and strange that it was impossible to grasp it as a whole, and what of it was understandable seemed wild and terrifying? But it all came about very simply: about four years earlier they had hired a girl called Annushka to look after the dovecot: she was a young girl (who had seen service with neighboring landowners), pale, very pale, and not pretty: but there was something in her face, because one day Luka Silitch was pleased to visit the dovecot, and— the result was only too obvious: Annushka-the-Dovecot wept bitterly (I forgot to mention that Luka Silitch, before he called on Annushka, had teased her jokingly about the dovecot in the poultry yard; and whomever he himself christened, the nickname would stick to him till death)— well; she wept till the "dumpling" herself came to the poultry yard to comfort her: the "dumpling" did really comfort her; since then they became fast friends, and very soon after Annushka revealed to the "dumpling" in what covenant she was taking part: life was boring, but Annushka-the-Dovecot's wonderful accounts of the carpenter from Tzelebeyevo and of how there was no shame in praying sweetly in the covenant, all this had its effect: on the excuse of mending furniture, the carpenter appeared before the merchant's wife, and once the carpenter had fixed his eyes on anyone, it was all over—that person would not escape his power: in a word, Fyokla Matveyevna, after her interview with the carpenter, was no longer her husband's wife, but the carpenter's fervid prayer-woman; she began to collect certain books: she herself began copying certain prayers; then, at night, she would set to embroidering chasubles, and also acquired ritual vessels and lest we forget: soon afterward the Yeropegins changed the night watchman; in his place came Ivan, a red-bearded lout of a man with red freckles and almost red eyes: "Not a man, but a fire," as Luka Silitch said about him—and that nickname stuck to him, the dunce: Ivan-the-Fire. And it turned out that this "Fire" had been sent there by Kudeyarov the carpenter; thus, little by little, the former servants were dismissed and their places were taken by sectarians from the nearby villages; the Yeropegin house became a *dovecot* (by that time the carpenter had hatched more than two hundred *doves*, though he himself hid his identity from many, while in Tzelebeyevo he did not convert anyone, but kept to himself except that his pock-marked woman was known as a dove). Thus the new faith was brought to Likhov and it spread through Likhov like a sea breeze that knows no obstacles: there were not so many sectarians in Likhov, it is true, but their number increased: several townsmen's families were converted, and so was Kakurinsky. The "doves" told each other in whispers that seemingly two young ladies had also begun to pray in their fashion: but which two young ladies it was—that they did not know; heavens, you will be surprised and you may even report the fact if we confess frankly that an old woman from the asylum took to mumbling integrally the words of the new prayers, abandoned the true faith, and started going to say her prayers in the bathhouse at Fyokla Matveyevna's on the days when the master *himself* drove off to Ovchinnikov on a spree; and the "dumpling" received everyone in secret, giving each a scribbled note from the carpenter, because the whole household, with the exception of Khfedor, was composed of one's own people, of *brothers:* and as for Khfedor, what could he see except a bottle of vodka? He would drive off—for a bottle: and so Khfedor saw nothing; among the household there turned out to be old female doves, bearded doves, clear-eyed, cooing maiden doves; only the atmosphere changed drastically upon Luka Silitch's return: he would stare about him sullenly, and *herself* would look downcast, shrunken, and her lips would hang loosely: she was always afraid that a rumor might reach him, and how she was afraid of that. But *himself* suspected nothing: true, he felt at times that his house had changed altogether: the walls were apparently the same, and yet not the same: the bulging awkward gilded furniture was the same, and yet the furniture was not the same: it was as though the furniture were scowling at him; he would enter a room by chance and that room, like a bathing woman taken by surprise, seemed to be striving to conceal something from his—the master's—gaze, just as Fyokla Matveyevna had for a long time been trying to hide her eyes from her husband's scrutiny: sometimes he had a suspicion—an anxious chilly feeling would come over him and he would glance at the walls—but there was nothing wrong with the walls, which were richly papered and hung with portraits; and yet he would frown and stare at his wife—a "dumpling" she was: he would suspect something and then go off again. And that was all that the "dumpling" wanted; she loved those walls as she loved her whole house, transfigured from day to day by her prayer. But if Luka Silitch had known how to talk with her and had told her that in all the corners in the night there was some buzzing, hissing and whispering going on, Fyokla Matveyevna would not have believed any of it, and would have simply replied: "Must be cockroaches."

It was not this that disturbed her about her husband: his growing thinner and his constant coughing, that's what really disturbed her beyond a joke: she secretly added herbs to his tea, the herbs sent her by the carpenter; but as though mocking the health-giving herb, as though mocking herself, Fyokla Matveyevna, Yeropegin rapidly grew thinner and thinner; and always something drew him away from the house. It was as though he now no longer lived in Likhov; he would go away and come back in good health; after a day or two at home, his face would sink. And Fyokla wondered why, with her herbs, she could not help her husband.

~~~ Likhov ~~~

The dry Likhov dust ate, ate, and ate up the eyes of the passersby; and since the morning of Whitsun Day a gray sieve filled with water descended over the town; through the sieve rain filtered; and soon the streets of Likhov were transformed into a mush in which cabs, carts, wagons and troikas helplessly splashed: if it were still possible to make one's way somehow through the fields, it was quite impossible to do so through the streets of Likhov; as though to spite the townsmen all the filth of the surrounding countryside had been collected there and then scattered all over town; but the astonishing thing was that this filth in the summer had the peculiar quality of drying up within a mere two hours; and whatever there was of it then turned to dust; thus the inhabitants of this God-saved town led a mode of existence between two, so to speak, abysses: an abyss of dust and an abyss of mud; and they could be divided without exception, all of them, into lovers of mud and lovers of dust; to the first category belonged married folk, shopkeepers, townsmen, who produced a heap of hens, rags, children, straw, cans, wooden cases turned upside down, and who threw up, so to speak, their products upon the surface of life in Likhov, for how, I may inquire, could all this heap of stuff find room in a one-storied house with only two or three windows and a fence giving on to Ganshina, Panshina and Kaloshina Streets? The hens scratched among the town dust or in the town straw or

among the weeds and thistles, which so abundantly flourished under the fences and which gave that town, if we may
be permitted to say so, a coquettish air: the children, how
shall we say? . . . The straw very clearly and simply, very
obviously simply, was scattered all over town, for which
reason on dirty, i.e. on rainy days, certain quarters of this
God-saved town reminded one of a cattle pen (the expression *God-saved* is applicable to the town of Likhov as a
rhetorical form for the sake of ornament. Speaking frankly,
Likhov was a town that *could not be saved* ever, so to
speak, by anybody, and by nothing: on the contrary, it was
being decimated by intestinal disorders, fires, drunkenness,
debauchery and boredom). It remains only to tell of three
products of the muddy part of the Likhov population: rags,
jars and wooden cases: well, needless to say, the first
covered the fences, looking pleasing to the eye; the second
could easily be smashed on mounting the steps of any
house, for the inhabitants annoyingly stood in the way;
only the boxes, turned upside down, modestly nestled in the
Likhov gardens; the overturned cases contributed nothing.
Such were the existential products of the most vital section
of the town, the muddy section; I say vital section for a
very good reason; this section of the town population
propagated very willingly, engaged in trade of bread selling
and was more prosperous than the other section, i.e. the
dusty section. Everything pointed eloquently to the fact
that the salvation and the stabilization of the fine town of
Likhov would proceed from here.

As to the other and much less numerous section, the
dusty one, it was composed of civil servants (from the Post
and Telegraph Office, the Metelkinsky Railroad Branch, the
Savings Bank), county clerks, the veterinary, two agricul-
turalists, two midwives, doctors, the agent of the County
Insurance and some others. This section of the population
was quite frankly languishing and nostalgic; in the summer
it flung open wide all the windows of the occupied premises, as a result of which the yellow dust in spirals broke in

and covered all objects of first and essential utility (such as
brushes, combs, toothbrushes, books) with a thick, easily
brushed but even more easily replaced layer of sand; this
section of the population was frankly covered with dust;
thus it could successfully be called dusty; it could also be
called dusty for another reason, namely, to express oneself
metaphorically, because it was puffed with the dust of
tobacco smoke, so that if some wise hand were to remove all
the dust from the premises of this public, the premises
would still be dusty with smoke, and the tables, floors, and
the feather beds would turn out to be littered with crushed
butt ends and ash stains. There is no need to add that the
muddy section of the population was very satisfied with its
situation and contemplated the future with hope; the second
section associated itself with the discontented and innocent
sufferers; and yet the radical feature that separated them
was not this fact, but another—this, to be precise: the
brave, muddy section sent in denunciations against the
dusty one; the dusty section made no denunciations at all; as
a result, its composition in Likhov kept changing; the attitude of the first section to the second was like that of good
to evil and vice versa; there were also some people who
proudly and freely rose above the whole life in Likhov and
stood, as it were, on the other side of either good or evil,
and yet stayed on here both summer and winter, but they
lived neither on Ganshina, Panshina, or Kaloshina Streets,
but on the Dvoryanskaya and Tsarskaya Streets, rising
above the muddy and the dusty sections in two-storied or
even three-storied houses; of their number were a few landowners who had settled in Likhov (and for them in the
Likhov hotel there were always available fruit, French
wines, cheeses and sweetmeats), and also a few millionaires,
who had risen from the Likhov mud and were now accepted in society; Yeropegin was an exception, having risen
into society with the help of a million and the addition of a
second story to his wooden house without changing his
muddy place of residence on Ganshina Street. Just as the

world of the human soul is invisible in space, it is possessed
of a vast impulse, as they say, to imprint itself visibly with
the help of signs of its perishable essence, so the risen and
transfigured society of the town of Likhov had imprinted
itself upon the surface of that town in the form of a
pleasure garden where a band of trumpeters assiduously
roared out marches on the Sabbath, and was reflected likewise in an asphalt sidewalk dotted—honest truth!—with all
five electric street lights: both the sidewalk and the street
lights encircled the huge building of the government vodka
factory, from which wagons loaded with cases of vodka
wended their way toward all the villages of the Likhov
district. The Monopoly, gleaming and transfiguring Likhov,
gathered to itself in the evenings the whole of the Likhov
aristocracy; at the hour when, on tranquil summer evenings,
the dusty section went off to the town gardens, when the
yellow sunset from afar smiled consolingly through the
spreading dusty pear trees, the best families of the muddy
section sent out to the sidewalk of the government vodka
factory their grown-up sons and pale daughters in silk
neckerchiefs, and even in hats, to stroll about under the
"lectric" light and to spit out their sunflower seeds upon the
asphalt; these two Edens worthily reflected the transfiguration into light of a fine little Russian town.

On the day we are describing the trumpeters were trum-
peting their marches in the deserted garden while the
asphalt in front of the government vodka factory was
completely empty; it appealed to no one to get drenched in
the rain either in the garden or on the asphalt, or to have
one's galoshes stick in the oozy mud and sink into it up to
one's knees and there, in the mud, leave one's galoshes. All,
except the pigs and a few unfortunate travelers, who must
have been really passionate Christians, sat at home; some,
because of the holiday, had tumbled into bed since four
in the afternoon, while others, folding their arms over
their bellies, sat by the window twiddling their right
thumbs round their left thumbs; they sat, sighed and stared

at the sky, the rain drumming on the windowpanes, the wet
sky looked swathed in filthy rags, whence a flying crow
might suddenly emerge, or watched how a pig, its snout
buried in the mud, would suddenly pause luxuriously beneath the window with only its tail swirling, and then toss
up its dirty snout and plunge it once more into the mud.
Many sat thus by the windows, drummed their fingers, kept
silent, hiccupped, sighed, drowsed, and yet kept on sitting,
sitting endlessly.

But that day Fyokla Matveyevna did not sit still at all; she
cracked no nuts, she did not scratch her back with the stick
specially intended for that purpose; it was Whitsun and her
faithful spouse had absented himself in the district these last
two days; and, because of that, she had an abyss of things to
attend to: in the first place, she had to see to it that Khfedor
got drunk (and Khfedor was already drunk); in the second,
it was necessary to have everything ready in the bathhouse
for the reception of the guests; so she and Annushka-the-
Dovecot had a busy day of it—in the morning they had
gone to mass, but that was for appearance's sake only; then
they had pulled out a heavy trunk from under the bed; out
of it they had dragged ritual vessels, long white linen shirts
reaching to the floor, a huge piece of azure silk with a
human heart in the form of a dove sewn on with glass beads
(the dove's beak looked like a hawk's beak as a result of this
handicraft); also ritual vessels, two lead candlesticks, a
chalice, a red silk cloak, and a spear—all these were dragged
out of the trunk while Ivan-the-Fire broke up some birch
tree twigs from the Yeropegin garden and carried them into
the bathhouse.

In the master's bedchambers lanterns were lighted; and
only the formal reception rooms were left sulking alone
away from all this fuss; the ballroom sulked with its bulging
gilded green furniture and with its bulging mirror in a
redwood frame and its parquet floor bright as a mirror; the
drawing room sulked, lined with raspberry silk and hung
with soft carpets on which naked youths were depicted

hunting wild boars; and the dining room sulked too; it was empty here and dismal; only rarely a rustling of silk might be heard; and then Fyokla Matveyevna herself would come floating by here in an absurd chocolate dress, bulging out in front with her belly and breasts, and chin, and lower lip; rapidly she would shuffle in her dress over the carpets and creak over the parquet squares, her hands folded over her belly, floating up and floating away in the mirror—swimming on toward her own quarters where, on the contrary, life bubbled like a spring; there, two ancient old women from the asylum flip-flopped with their slippers, quacked, muttered . . . with faces, let us note, of gray color and white, and large-eared mobcaps; and pale Annushka-the-Dovecot, all in white, flew about like a pale-white, bloodless flittermouse; her bare white feet flew about and so did her undone reddish plait; ever since three o'clock that day from Panshina Street to Ganshina Street, over potholes, through the pools of rain, through the mud, the old women and the widows from the asylum had begun to swim there and drowned in the shallow pits: only their gray backs swayed above their heads and only their neckerchiefs swam over the pools, like crows' wings quivering in the breeze. Soon the swarm of old women were boisterously grunting outside the gates of the Yeropegin house, with their umbrellas and sticks threatening the pig that was coming at them from the pool with its penny-round snout; but the gate was opened by a pock-marked peasant, all covered in hair and terrifyingly red freckles; he growled gloomily that they had, so to speak, come too early; after which the gates were shut in their faces and the swarm of old women, pursued by the pig, reluctantly splashed their way back: from Ganshina Street to Panshina Street.

Oh, why did they drive the old women away! Was it not true that, ever since two o'clock, Kakurinsky had been installed in the very study of Luka Silitch: he and two townsmen; all three of them were buried in a heap of leaflets, their voices barked efficiently, and the pages whis-

pered (on the leaflets were black crosses); they gulped tea
and roared with laughter insolently enough; the seminarist's
goatee danced in the air when, holding up a bent finger in
the air, he held forth about the immediate aims of the
covenant, while the two townsmen, a shoemaker and a
coppersmith (whose signboard without any mention of his
trade, but merely announcing "Sukhorukov," was displayed
over the town marketplace, for all knew that Sukhorukov
cast copper pots)—the two townsmen, rolling cigarettes,
agreed with Kakurinsky; the argument turned on the theme
that it was time long ago for the brethren-doves to join the
strikers—it was time to go hand in hand with the socialists
without letting them into the secret and the contrary:
guiding where necessary those same socialists—yes; because
even though the socialists saw the truth, they saw it only
under their noses; and everything else about the socialists
was—rubbish. Thus the Likhov townsmen discussed their
own, so to speak, Likhov political platform, ready as they
were to please both the socialists and the carpenter; that the
carpenter knew everything, though he looked simple, of
that the townsmen had no doubt, just as they were convinced that both of them stood "for liberty."

It was already growing dark. In the small room which
harbored a bed of incredible dimensions, with quilts and
feather pillows also of incredible dimensions, Fyokla Matveyevna had fallen heavily on her knees with book in hand
beneath the ancient image lighted with a holy lamp; the
bulky perspiring merchant's wife whispered the wonderful
words of the new prayers which, like old songs, grip the
heart and speed over the expanse of the Russian land. One
cannot tell where such words were born—for it was no
Fokin, no Alexin, who had composed these words: the very
words of those fragrant prayers sprang from both the
joyful and the chilling breath of the spirit, from the sobbing
of the human heart, from the mutilations of the oppressed
soul—breathe then, breathe those prayers, merchant-wife!

And with all your notions, you will swim away somewhere: and Fyokla Matveyevna breathed those prayers, and the room swam before her; more and more the merchant's wife went out of her mind and muttered, heavily striking the floor with her forehead amid the quilts and feather pillows.

It had already grown quite dark, and the rain beat against the walls, the windowpanes, the fence of the Yeropegin house, and desperately the yellow swarm of chickweed swirled by the fence, and the burdock beat desperately against the wooden steps of the Yeropegin porch; there, in the depths of Ganshina Street, a street lamp ignited as though of itself; and—there—from the windows, pitiful dim lights poured into the mud; a sky, ever more threatening, showed more troubled, gloomy and dark-blue over the fences: it lowered, stole toward the houses and freely poured into the Likhov air, and stuck to the windows, tearing off the shutters.

Then, when the sodden gloom had already poisoned the whole atmosphere, two men stopped under the porch of the Yeropegin house; drenched, muddy, they were grayly outlined in the gloom. It was Mitry and Abram; they stood there a while longer, blew their noses with their fingers, sighed, muttered something and finally mounted the steps.

Through the inner chambers a door bell tinkled sorrowfully, barely audibly; but inside the house everything came to life; Annushka with a candle in her hand rushed through the black formal rooms; in the black formal rooms she slipped over the cold, fleshless surface of the mirror and was drowned in the entrance hall.

The Image of the Dove

Annushka peeped outside through the chained door: she looked—and there was the rain dust swirling madly; but in the glimmering candlelight the silver dove struck her with a blinding light while a human face with damp curls was bending over the bird; a familiar voice languidly penetrated her heart with velvety languor:

"Beautiful maidens
Bright is your chamber!
Soul mates, companions,
Quaff honey and beer!
Wait for the guest, await him:
That guest is not so far—
From a distant land he comes,
Flowing into your chamber."

From the entrance hall doors opened into the ballroom and into the bedchamber of Fyokla Matveyevna; from the ballroom fearfully peeped out the sallow face of *herself* holding a candle in her hand. From the door opposite two old women stared (the townsmen were whispering behind the door); all their faces looked drawn: invisibly the spirit of Luka Silitch struggled among the candle-torn rags of darkness, boding ill. But now Annushka opened the door while the old women stirred more anxiously in the dark gap of the door; the townsmen hissed ever more loudly behind the door, like yellow leaves lured by the gloom, when the wind tears them off and torments them in the sighs of the

air—there, behind the doors, their cordial faces melted in
smiles; they all bowed before the wide-flung door, when the
beggar trod over the threshold majestically knocking on the
floor with his heavy staff; from under his white "toadstool"
his dark curls sprinkled forth; his dark eyes sprinkled forth
from under his swollen temples; the dove-bird sprinkled
forth light on the threshold of that house: grace had descended upon the house. . . .

And when, in the darkness, Abram shook his gnarled rain-
washed hand, rejoicing at the repose and peace awaiting him
after so many cold miles, after so many fruitless spaces—
there, behind Abram, behind the bird-dove, there in the
anarchic dark where it was still impossible to distinguish
anything, there was something already: *it* stamped on the
steps of the porch like the anarchic darkness, like the
anarchic rest; then *it* also showed itself in the entrance hall:
something sickly, pitiful, dragged itself after the beggar;
frowningly *it* entered as though concealing a gift of sweetness in a gloomy image—the carpenter himself built himself
out of the darkness; he stretched out his ailing hand and his
face loomed very close, but they dreamt that there was no
face here, but only wrinkles and blurred traits; but out of
that face, as from the deathless spaces beyond the stars, no
eyes but a warm impact of light entered their sweetly
sighing breasts. . . .

Mitry Mironich was pleased to enter in his new boots (it
was them he was creakingly pulling on and therefore he had
not followed the beggar at once), and he bowed to them in
general; and greedily the old women drew him away from
the others so that he should not lose his concentration, so
that he might concentrate in prayer until the evening—
jealously they led him through the garden orchard, through
the squelching pools of mud: the lantern winked blindly
from the yard, then it winked from behind the apple trees:
for a while the light stood at a distance, in the depths by the
bathhouse; and then the light went out: the carpenter and
the old women were swallowed in the dark. After the

carpenter's arrival, the whole company scattered: it was
time to concentrate: to utter a prayer, first of all, in solitude, to lave one's soul from the everyday worries. And
again through the formal rooms the merchant wife rustled,
the candle glimmered—then everything grew dim, blind,
deaf: the world moved away and the walls dispersed in the
gloom.

And again the bell tinkled; a candle winked in the dark
bedroom; the walls formed, materialized in the light; the
shadow of Luka Silitch quivered pitifully in the corners; in
the entrance hall stood townswomen, townsmen, and
tradeswomen; they stood for a while in the hall and then
they disappeared, guided by someone's hand to someone's
room. And already from Panshina Street once more the old
women swam up toward Ganshina Street; and they banged
and knocked on the gates with their umbrellas. . . .

In a separate wing of the house not far from the gate,
where the servant quarters were, and in the porter's lodge a
samovar was boiling; by the samovar sat the beggar, already washed and steamed; he was winking slyly into the
gloom while sipping the Chinese moisture from a saucer,
and addressed Ivan-the-Fire who was grimly picking his nose
in front of Abram and anxiously snorting.

"Well, brother, soon you will be roaring around the bathhouse with your rattle chasing the devils and fighting the
dragon, when we shall all rise to pray in the bathhouse—it
can be said," the beggar said, adding for no reason the
inexplicable "it can be said."

The rattle was lying on a bench; and over the rattle Ivan-
the-Fire was stooping with his wolfish and forever frightened face; the most unpleasant feature of that face was not
that it was wolfish; but that this wolfish face was tipped
below with a terrifying red tuft of hair and above with a
terrifying red forelock; he was wearing a white shirt with a
red patch under his arm; some unknown face had once and
for all frightened Ivan-the-Fire; most likely it was the
carpenter who had frightened him by pointing once into

the gloom and the raucous laughter of the evil wind in the gloom; from that moment it had been revealed to Ivan-the-Fire that the devil really existed; and Ivan gave up his soul to exterminate this nastiness, whatever form it assumed; like a devouring fire, Ivan savagely walked the wide earth wrestling with Gehenna; and it was not without reason that the carpenter had arranged for him to become the night watchman in this house. In the gloom Ivan-the-Fire saw an evil power; when he spotted something he would wave his rattle, and the rattle would start cracking—the devils were greatly afraid of the rattle; only not so long ago, at the crack of dawn, a dragon had visited him; Ivan fought the dragon, fought him hard—he could not remember what happened: only he almost set fire to his watchman's quarters; thus Ivan-the-Fire just missed turning Yeropegin's house, all the buildings and the stables into a fiery Gehenna.

Of late—had someone suggested it or had he arrived at it himself—the watchman began pondering on who in reality was his strict master, Luka Silitch: was he not a dragon offspring? He grew thoughtful, but kept his silence, and his already sullen face became even more sullen (evidently it is not surprising that one who has beheld the terrors of Gehenna should bear a slight reflection of Gehenna on his own face; such a reflection rested on Ivan).

All things excited in him only fear or anger; and when the brotherhood was praying, when sweet exclamations rose in the bathhouse, and sighs and laughter, full of grace, and the high-pitched roar of the prophesying carpenter—then Ivan boiled over with fervid anger against the enemy of the human race and, as though challenging hell and the dark forces to battle, Ivan's rattle crackled, danced, danced, choked with the gurgling of the wooden trilling, and the rattle leapt out of his hands and tore into the dark, and Ivan's feet crunched among the bushes, and he stamped his feet, choked with whispers, and assaulted the dark; the brotherhood regarded Ivan as a great zealot: some whispered that Ivan had swallowed the flames of Gehenna, had

fallen himself into the fire while protecting his sisters and
brethren; and so they would not allow him into the bathhouse; only he could chase away the buffoons and the devils
who gathered in the night to threaten the prayers and the
vigils.

It was Whitsun now, and Ivan was girding for battle. He
already envisioned the devil and in advance selected his
swear words, spitting on the floor, while Abram the beggar
was sipping his tea without a care, and no power, it seemed,
could tear him away from this everyday task: Abram was
the only one allowed to break his fast by drinking tea
before the midnight ceremony, for Abram was a man of the
open spaces, and his status was wholly different from that
of the other brethren.

So Abram drank his tea, his spirit buoyed up, while Ivan,
his anger mounting, pulled on his short fur-lined coat, and
stepped out into the dark; and in the dark of the fruit
orchard, which separated the bathhouse from the servants'
quarters, a bush would crackle, a branch would bend; something grimly grunted near a tree stump: it was Ivan, the
nightwatchman, wandering about on guard, but not yet
whirling his rattle; the hostile gloom rustled its wings only
from afar: the devils had not yet descended to earth: the
battle still lay ahead—and what a battle!

In the bathhouse everything was still; in the bathhouse it
was cool; the bathhouse had not been heated; but the whole
of it, its inside shutters firmly closed, glittered, shone and
swam in the light; in the center stood a table covered like
the sky, with turquoise satin in the middle of which was
sewn a red velvet heart being torn apart by the dove made of
beads; in the middle of the table stood an empty chalice
covered by a purificatory: on the chalice lay a church
spoon and a spear; fruit, flowers, wafers decorated the table;
and green birch branches adorned the damp walls; by the
table lead candlesticks already twinkled; above the lead
candlesticks glistened aloft a heavy silver dove (whenever
the spirit illuminated the sisters and brethren, the dove tore

itself from the staff and flew about, cooing, fluttering its wings, and played with the broom leaf); in a neighboring smaller room stood a pulpit in isolation, unadorned; on the pulpit rested a book; all garbed in white, with bare feet and with a lighted candle held over the book, now, when there was still no one in the bathhouse, assiduously—no, he was not praying! hysterically the carpenter kept falling to the ground, falling and rising up from the floor, rising up and falling, with arms outstretched, with a flame-white and terrifyingly exulting face. But was that a face? No, that was no face: resembling a pale morning mist which, like lead, presses thickly down on everything around it and then, when the sun comes out, curls up in thin steam before disappearing entirely in the dazzling morning glitter, so his face, now become penetrable like steam, had faded away and then, finally, disappeared; thus over the sickly and sorry features there first passed, and then became outlined, filling and melting with light these decrepit features, another living sun, another living prayer, another as yet unrealized but impending-for-the-world Countenance—the Countenance of the Spirit. And those eyes? There were no eyes: there was something it was impossible to look upon without surrendering, without expressing amazement, without shouting out in terror; the light issuing from those eyes had melted the face and spilled upon the white garment of the solitary man who prayed, who kept falling and rising, dully spreading his arms for the sake of the brotherhood, for Russia, for the fulfillment of the secret joy of Russia, for accomplishing the incarnation of the spirit in the body of man, not as the world, but as he, the carpenter, desired it; and he groaned, cried and implored for that one thing to happen: he wanted nothing more. . . .

It was inexpressible, unbearable in that empty bathhouse in the presence of that vision; but it was not enough for him to pray alone; already in the vicinity of the bathhouse, amid the apple trees, near the house, feet were trampling through the mud—and where the lantern swam in the darkness, and where there was no lantern, feet splashed toward the bath-house: it was the brethren and sisters drawn there for prayer; anxiously the rattle crackled out in the sensitive darkness: in the anxious and sensitive darkness the night-watchman gave warning: the enemy was at hand; and they hastened—hastened to the prayer.

Quietly they entered, now one, now another, the ante-room of the bathhouse: they undressed in the anteroom and changed into white garments. Soon one, then another, took his place in the bathhouse: they stood in prayer around the table, but no one set foot in the neighboring room where the carpenter stood at the pulpit; and, indeed, he is no longer the same: the carpenter's face no longer glowed: his face was white again and looked like a white cloud—there was the long tuft of his beard, and the nose, and all the rest, all the carpenter's, none other's, only it all looked trans-parent—the face; and the eyes were closed: he stood, uttering prayers.

The old women had already pressed into the bathhouse: like corpses they were, the small old women, nasty looking, bent, warty—but all dressed in white: they stood around the walls, mumbling prayers; and Kakurinsky was here already, and Sukhorukov the coppersmith, another towns-man, and the townswomen, and *herself*, and some others. At first it was hard to distinguish who was who: you could not recognize them: so much had the candles lit up their faces, so much had their white garments transformed them: they were praying, the bathhouse was now full; then the brightly-lit bathhouse with the folk in it was locked, as if entirely cut off from the world: here was a new world, and every-thing here was different, one's own, dovelike; in the bright candlelight the dove, raised high aloft, spread over all its wings of bright silver; the azure silk, rich and twisted, was spread underneath it, and seemingly the dove-bird was reflected in that silk.

The carpenter would read, read, then turn, spread his arms over the adorned table, over the silk, the flowers, the fruit and the wafers; and he would spread his hands over the chalice: the chalice was empty; it would be filled on the day when the tsar-dove would be born—the child of light; but while there was no holiness as yet, there was no wine in the empty chalice. The carpenter would spread his arms over the brethren: people bowed and prostrated themselves on the floor; on the day that joy would be vouchsafed them, they would not prostrate themselves, but smiling beatifi-cally they would gaze with clear open eyes into the clear open eyes of one another. And the carpenter would spread both his arms over the birch branches: the birch branches were motionless; they did not whisper or bend; but it would not be thus on the day when the dove would swoop down from his tree, the dove spread on that tree; he will alight with silver feather, gurgle with silver feather and settle on those birch branches. The carpenter was already spreading his weary arms over the white walls: the hour will come when those white walls will turn into white, endless, limitless space; thus, on that day, the walls of that city will unfold; broadly and freely the people will live in the new kingdom, in the silver kingdom, beneath the azure air. In that kingdom, in that silver state, who will illumine the kingdom?—The Spirit. In that sky, above the azure air, who will fly? A gigantic dove-bird with a beak shall fly there; it will peck at the crimson heart of the world, and—the heart—it will spill out purple-purple blood like the sunset. And already toward the ceiling the carpenter quite impotently spread the palms of his hands—and behold: there was no ceiling: it looked covered with icon painting: a blue heaven painted there with gold-leaf stars showing through. It was high, high up; and it was an altogether new heaven, and the carpenter saw it; only the brotherhood did not see it; strictly very strictly the carpenter bade them look only at the sides, and soon they saw neither the ceil-ing, nor the walls—as if there was no bathhouse; holding hands, they were already moving around the carpenter in a circle; quietly, strictly and staidly they moved: they were not dancing—they were not allowed to dance; a great misfortune might befall them from dancing:—they did not dance, but moved in a circle, starting a quiet little song:

"Bright, O bright, is the azure air!
And bright in that air the spirit fair."

They were just chanting . . .

And their faces? Heavenly powers, what faces! No one, never, nowhere, had seen such faces: not faces, but suns; only an hour before their faces had been so ugly, dirty, bestial, but now these faces radiated their bright coolness, as pure as the snow or the sun over everything: and their eyes—their eyes were lowered; the air was no air, but simply rainbow; no prayer, but the shimmering of an airy rainbow.

That was all: they chanted and circled:

"Bright, O bright, is the azure air,
And bright in that air the spirit fair."

And in between them in that golden, azure air the prayer-man was turning with a cup of oil: he would dip two fingers into the oil and make a mark with it on someone's forehead; and that one would raise his eyes to him, or she would glance at him from under brows and he would drench him or her, not with warmth or coolness, but with strength and light; and then already he and she, and this and that already illumined face, would be at the table; now all of them were seated at the table in the seven-colored rainbow, amid the white Eden-like-earth, amid the conifers and the green forest and amid the Favorsky* heavens; a certain radiant man breaks and distributes wafers; and from a goblet (not the chalice) they gulped the red wine of Galilean Cana; and it's as if both time and space did not exist, but there is wine, blood, azure, air, and sweetness; they do not hear the rattle twirling outside or the fiery guardian

---

* A mystical Byzantine light.

defending the door from the dragon—who is not with them does not exist. With them were blessed death and eternal peace. The silver dove, come to life on the tree, gurgled, showed affection and cooed: it flew down from the tree on the table: with its claws it scratched the satin and pecked at the raisins. . . . Ivan, the nightwatchman, exhausted from his battle and his beard all awry, went on making a din with his rattle at the doors of the bathhouse: he was terrified: "Let me in," he shouted. "I can't fight any more." He beat on the door. But he got no response: there, on the other side of the door, dead silence reigned. Did Ivan not know that there was already no one there? If one were to break down the door at that moment and enter the bathhouse, all one would see would be dirty walls and benches, and one might also hear a glowworm: but the people, the candles, the flowers and the church lamps, tell me, where were they all? They must have left the bathhouse by some secret passage in order to promenade in the sky, gather the light of paradise, and talk with an angel.

Ivan sniffled and sniffled by the bathhouse; and then went his way: went to sleep in the servants' quarters. . . .

In the morning all was azure, the sky, the air and the dew: at the first glimmer of dawn the gates of the Yeropegin house creaked; through the gates emerged livid, frowning people, mutely, lifelessly, dispersing to their homes. A little later, reflected in the morning pools, a crimson dawn floated over Likhov and the pig left free to roam grunted and dug in the damp tall weeds, and Khfedor had returned, completely drunk, and knocked at the gates and then submissively, quietly, smoothly lay down in the mud. And when it grew very light, a peasant woman with skirt tucked up high boldly splashed knee-deep through the water; and opposite the Yeropegin house, where hung a sign: "Tailor Tzizig-Isaac," a sleepy Jewish face appeared in the window of a sagging little house.

⁓❧ Life in Likhov ❧⁓

The following day was stifling; a perspiring sun blazed
pompously; and pompous clouds scurried over Likhov; and
the gripping oozy mud was not too bad: it was drying—
with God's help; and the town was not too bad either; it
was drying too; and a desperate Likhov townsman, his cap
askew, ran hurriedly from shop to shop; he was buying
herring and a jar in the market, and for some reason he kept
thrusting a finger into a moldy barrel of sauerkraut and
then bit his dirty thumb at someone; and he would have
been almost crushed to death there by other townsmen and
especially townswomen if he had not managed to shove
others violently himself; carts creaked in the marketplace;
townswomen exchanged abuse with peasant women from
nearby villages; here, according to the popular saying, both
priest and bug stand snug, that is, there were all sorts of folk
in the marketplace: there were people from Likhov, from
Bryuhatovo, and Chmari (the swarthy folk lived in Chmari
and around Chmari, though Chmari was about forty miles
from Likhov—no more); a swarthy man from Chmari was
setting out wheels—one wheel against another—and the
Father Vukol, the priest from Tzelebeyevo, who had come
to Likhov for God knows what reason, was feeling the
wheels with his hands and bargaining with the man from
Chmari; but the man from Chmari would not give in and
Father Vukol, gathering up his cassock, plunged away from
him into the thick of the market, sweating and sighing:

"Och, have mercy, O Lord, there's neither stature nor rank here, no respect at all . . ." The man from Chmari, as if nothing had happened, was now disputing with a man from Bryuhatovo over his wheel, while a man from Kozlikhino almost drove his cart over them.

In the Likhov hotel the county clerks had been drinking hard since early morning: only the day before they had driven in from their district to discuss matters of mutual interest: they arrived and began drinking in the morning: they drank there in that two-storied house which stared with its fiery windows at the marketplace, while over the market, next to the hotel, flared the red sign on which, in fat blue letters, the word "SUKHORUKOV" stood out; and it was all here: more was not to be expected—what more could there be?

That day burnt out with feverish speed; and with feverish speed the night fell upon Likhov; at night Yeropegin, Luka Silitch, returned home; he had his fill of tea in the dining room; and again he felt faint: he looked—it was not his wife, but a "dumpling" of sorts washing up the cups; he'd go into the garden, the trees would be whispering; oh, some evil had crept into the house; in trepidation, Fyokla Matveyevna followed him about: oh, evil glinted under his glasses, in his eyes (in her husband's): she looked—it was not her husband: simply a stranger, gray and dry, ailing besides, subject to gout.

It was dreary for them, stifling for them, and oppressive for them to be together.

A boring, stifling, oppressive night—a June night; in the orchards the rattles clattered; on the horizons glimmers and flashes of light; infrequently, a cart rumbled by, and once, somewhere beyond the sky it sounded as if dumbbells were being rolled: it must have been thunder.

Red, blue, gray, stifling, stormy, windy days completed their turn over Likhov, and in their wake now airy, now blind nights filled with dread fire; and the carpenter lived on in his own way without leaving Likhov; he either made his way stealthily to Yeropegin's wife, bringing her herbs, or argued over texts with Sukhorukov the coppersmith; or he would hold a meeting of townsmen at Kakurinsky's: some sort of papers they read there (yes:—one morning a poster with a black cross was found hanging on a fence urging the people to stop working in the name of the Holy Ghost and to refuse to obey the gentry; the constable took down the poster, read it, and then hid it in his pocket; thus the proclamation never reached the people). Great events were brewing and the brotherhood knew that the spirit of the dove would assume a human countenance, that is, it was being born of woman. . . . Abram had not been seen in Likhov for a long time; he had already left a week ago for the open spaces; but the carpenter lived on in his own way—without going out: finally, he got ready—the time had come: Matryona, having been given her "freedom," must have long ago twisted the lad around her little finger. "By now, no doubt, the lad must be sleeping with her at night!" Kudeyarov thought, grinning into his beard. He was cunning, the carpenter: on purpose he had left her behind in Tzelebeyevo: the workers would do their planing and go home: in the evening Matryona was alone; and under her windows there would be Daryalsky, no doubt. . . .

"They must have got down to business a long time ago: time for me to go home."

Now Likhov lay behind him; if one turned around, there was only dusty gloom where Likhov had been; it was as though there had never been such a place.

"So that's Likhov!" the carpenter exclaimed ironically. He turned off from the highway, skirted the farm of the prosperous owner: from one mound to another; from one ravine to another; further and further. And he was already passing over Dead Top.

The Fokins and the Alexins had plowed up Dead Top: everywhere now there was arable land: the last of the Alexins was plowing the last strip.

The last of the Alexins was already behind him. And there in the blue gloom, out of the dark nocturnal current, from the East, over Tzelebeyevo appeared a dark figure, but it still seemed far away and would not reach the village so soon.

CHAPTER THREE

⚡ He Remembered Gugolevo ⚡

"Yes, yes, yes! (in a moonbeam before him gleamed a
rusty patch of water) . . . It was already night, faster to
Gugolevo . . . (he jumped over a ditch: day, morning,
evening, the water gave off a stench). Uneven the hour
. . . and don't confuse me, you dark thoughts of mine, of
this age my accursed thoughts! (unblinking, a green eye
surveyed him from behind: a glowworm).

I will not go to the village again, nor set foot in God's
temple; nor will I stare into the eyes of odd peasant
women . . . (threatening pine trees bore upon him from
one side: on the other side—from the left—a grove of hazel
trees rustled) . . . I know that only you, Katya, are my
life, and may God be resurrected . . . (damp, unfriendly
ferns wetted his knee) . . . Chase the demon; finish off the
demon (he strode over a ditch, now lost in the shadow, now
appearing all white in the white, luminous, lunar smoke torn
apart by the tree trunks) . . . Katya, my darling!"

Thus whispered Daryalsky, while a stunted bush under
his feet whispered back in reply to his nostalgic, desperate
panting. It was night, and it was steamingly hot as, on the
night of Trinity Day, Daryalsky made his way back from
Tzelebeyevo along a forest path alongside a forest ditch.

"Again you peep into my soul, wicked mystery! Again
you gaze upon me out of the dark past . . . (All around
glowworms, glowworms penetrated the darkness) . . .
Since my childhood, from my cradle, you have pursued me,

you rugged ones . . . (the drowsy forest, the endless forest was creeping up to Tzelebeyevo, encircling it with its two wings; and it stretched further, further) . . .

"From the first instant of my life I had fears; from my earliest infant years my gaze was concentrated on the darkness; since my earliest days that sweet yet ironic song had sounded to me both at dawn and in darkness . . . (somewhere in the forest a glimmer of light seemed to show—but no, no: God knows where that forest ended beyond Gugolevo: it was a state forest). . . .

"And I waited always: and out of the dark people defined themselves; and I waited always for the appearance out of the dark of a terrifying, languorous call, summoning me into the distance. . . ."

A branch cracked, a clearing fell behind: once, they said, the villagers had seen in the moonlight here the deadly face of a shaven convict: the forest has always been the true refuge of convicts.

"I waited, I called: but no one came; I grew up, became a man; still no one came; I called and listened to the rustling of trees; and understood; but when I spoke of that rustling, no one understood me; but as I called someone, so the rustling called me—and someone wept over my life, with an unknown sweet crying; what was that weeping, what was it? Now in the trees, that same weeping; and hark, seemingly distant songs . . . (somewhere in the distance was heard the fading song of the midnight lads, drowning in the night). . . .

"Faster to Gugolevo: forest, always forest: how many times has the she-wolf howled in the forest and in the winter; coming with the frost, here a bear had advanced toward the village, attacked horses, and then retreated into the thickets. . . ."

And like a viper, involuntary fear uncoiled from Daryalsky's breast as a result of all the events of that day, now deepened in the night, as though a viper were stinging his heart, and the heart stopped beating in the breast: the heart.

Like a traveler plunged in the gloom of tree trunks, bushes, forests and forest bogs, blowing the icy sigh of mist to pierce the breast of that traveler and then devour his blood with a burning fever, so that in vain later, staggering, he would seek a path through the forest, a path he had long lost—like such a traveler, Daryalsky had given his bride Katya his life, his light and the noble impulses of his soul, for she had become the way of his life; but already that way was no way: in a day, in an hour, in a brief soul-kissing instant, his life's way had become a way of mists, which now here, now there, raised their cold, high-flying hand: the day, the glance, the instant of the pock-marked wench —and the light, the path, and the nobility of his soul had turned into forest, night, turf and rotting bog.

"Stop! I've lost myself!" Daryalsky whispered; he stopped alone in the middle of the forest; there was neither path, nor ditch; only tree stumps, moss, tree trunks, the twittering of birds, the tolling of the Tzelebeyevo belfry, the far-off, roundish moon falling into the bushes. No one, nothing. Seemingly a ringing sound: then again nothing; like in a dream: dully, dully, in a distant echo the midnight bell fluttered through the thicket. Then Daryalsky realized that he was standing over an accursed spot: at the very spot where the forest rose sheer in bristling pine trees and where the forest ended abruptly in damp shrubbery growing in a mire; over the very spot where last summer his soul had drowned in the boggy window; and on that very spot now stood Daryalsky—stood and listened: "Katya, my darling, I love you . . . Ah, I've remembered!" He stands there and already another face gleams before him; and from behind a bush a face hit him with light: the face of that woman, the pock-marked one, and it was not a woman's face at all: through the bushes stared the large, yellow moon vanishing into the bushes.

"Katya, darling: I love only you, Katya, only you!"

*   *   *

A strange remembrance rose up in his soul, illuminating his life with horrid light: he remembered the night; he was sitting at a table stacked with books; tomorrow was an exam, but his head was filled with childhood memories, and his head was already drooping drowsily over a book (he was running from one stump to another, over bushes, and his boot stepped into a pool of water, on pine needles, into a soft moss-covered ant hill—he was running); he remembered: he had read everything, but nothing was consciously clear; no—no, behind a screen his old mother was snipping with a pair of scissors or scratching a piece of satin with a needle, while a shudder passed over his back and his thoughts disintegrated: his poor, dear mother, she was chiding him as usual for his sleepless nights, for his smoking; at times he would get angry with her for interfering with his work or for scratching the satin with her needle at the wrong time—that's how it was: he remembered—on that night . . . (the trees waved in the wind, a wind-driven bush advanced toward him; bushes and bushes; and the bog was already pouring over him). . . .

That night he remembered the clock ticking, and the tickling rustle of satin: he remembered how he had raised his head over the table and also remembered the phrase he repeated: "In slavonic a wolf is wluf." He saw the open window and a moonlight patch on the floor—and he suddenly remembered . . . (he had reached the road: Katya, save me—it was not far from Gugolevo now: he ran over a meadow, in the midst of rye) . . . Daryalsky recalled the fatal instant of that fatal night when, tearing himself away from his book, he saw the open window—he recalled drawing the curtain over that window: he went up to the window; thrust his head out—and . . . and he remembered nothing at that fatal instant . . . (Here was Gugolevo already: he passed through the stone gateway: there were lions on that gateway; the iron grill was not locked). . . .

When he came to, he saw his mother bending over him: with a trembling hand his mother was proffering him smelling salts, and his mother whispered and sighed over him, "I am with you, my son: I have shut the window, my son: God be with you!" His poor mother: she was resting forever now in a peaceful grave: her needle does not scratch and her scissors do not snip! At that terrifying instant his mother had stood over him; and Daryalsky could not remember why that minute of oblivion had come over him when he went to the window; he remembered that his mother had heard his wild, heart-rending cry; he remembered that after his swoon he was left with the impression that some woman had been standing outside: yes, she had a pock-marked face; and no eyebrows—yes: all this had been in the past: but that pock-marked face had been twisted into such a nasty smile, and such a blemish had twisted that face which had stared so shamelessly at him, and at the same time invited him so unforgettably to share in mutual shamelessness! . . . But why was his secret confined to that face? Did the secret of his soul include a filthy, corrupt sense, even when his soul smiled at the bright beams of dawn? Yes, the dawn both illumined and blotched the face which had appeared to him outside the window . . . (he was already in the alleys of the old park). . . .

But now Daryalsky remembered the face of that ghost because it was the face of the pock-marked woman whom he had encountered in the church . . . (Soul, gaze not into the abyss; here, beyond the iron grill, you—are amid the oak trees of Gugolevo). . . .

He now remembered that the gate was not shut; he went back and locked it; as he pushed in the bolt, it occurred to him to reprimand the watchman and tell him to lock the gates at night, otherwise anyone might enter the grounds; it would be a job finding the trespasser in the bushes; he might even break into the house and rob the Baroness into the bargain.

"I have remembered—so go away, spectre, perish, vanish!"

(His feet crunched on the path stifled with vegetation; and it was already getting light) . . . Sleep in peace, darling Katya: never shall my soul forget you, Katya (the misted lawn appeared, the portico columns of the house shone white) . . . There, there, is your window, curtained in muslin; here I shall pause beneath your windows; I shall protect you from misfortunes, from temptation!"

Daryalsky turned sharply, finding himself in front of the wing drowned in flowers: bell-like flowers, pink and white, swayed at his feet; the key turned, and the stale, spiteful air engulfed him in the cloistered walls of the wing.

"Sleep, Katya, sleep: I shall not surrender you to evil fate."

He's already asleep: he dreamt of a tender maiden's kisses, sighs and silver tears: as if she were a sister, a friend, a bride. . . .

Already a drizzle had started in the courtyard.

~&~ Katya ~&~

The double-lit ballroom glittered in the morning light: the morning light was gray and the light dull; outside in the rain thick stems of *ricinus* could be seen swaying; they shimmered like crystal and silver; muddy rivulets carried the red sand of the paths.

Thus Gugolevo met the sullen day of Whitsun.

In the double-lit ballroom a footman came and went grumbling while laying a table between two white columns with peeling stucco; the columns divided the ballroom, as it were, into two rooms: one half served as a dining room; there was nothing remarkable in it: Viennese chairs stood around the table; Yevseich the footman entered; he laid a clean tablecloth; growling, he arranged the tea service and growling, he opened the door leading to the veranda wreathed in hops, forming a canopy from beneath which could be seen the lawn and a flowerbed, where, on a stone pedestal reposed a headless naked youth raising his yellow elbow overgrown with mold.

In the other half of the ballroom, in the drawing room, stood Katya Gugolevo, the Baroness's granddaugher, bending over the grand piano and absent-mindedly gazing at the old furniture with its patches of faded gold paint and red morocco upholstery.

Here portraits hung; for years a General had pranced here on a dark horse, holding a three-cornered hat in his hand, upon a large dark canvas which had cracked in places;

and for years a bomb was exploding at his feet and for years a no longer vivid flame flashed from it: but amid the powder and the smoke the General smiled for years on end, and the green feathers of his three-cornered hat waved in the wind; stormily the battle was being fought in the vicinity of Leipzig and the brave rider, galloping into battle, smiled on, gazing at the bomb vomiting forth its yellow fire: thus, in a free creative surge, had the unflattering artist depicted Katya's great grandfather, General Gugolev.

There were other portraits here too: a *fräulein* of Catherine's day with a miniscule dog on a cushion and a diamond decoration on her shoulder, a landscape with a love scene and a rainbow hanging low in the sky, over which Cupid had spilled a garland of roses; there were mountains such as were not to be seen in Gugolevo, the ruins of castles, and excellently depicted *fruit*, the creative product of some blue-eyed female person, muslin-wrapped and nostalgic, whose enchanting visage gazed mournfully here from the wall and whose tender diary was preserved in a small cupboard, on which stood cupids, shepherdesses, porcelain Chinamen and a dandy; here likewise was a carved cupboard of unknown origin; from behind the dusty glass peered dully and darkly volumes of Florian, Pope, Diderot and the moldy backs of Ekkarthauzen's *The Key to the Explanation of the Mysteries of Nature.*

Katya stood, leaning over the grand piano, a volume of Racine in her hands; she had been brought up on the French classics.

Just look at her: she was imprinted there over the grand piano in a blue dress, a trifle short and closely clasping her waist, leaning slightly forward and stooping just a little—a little girl she looked, quite a little girl! Her face showed exhaustion; beneath her eyes blue rings were clearly visible; her thoughts had already flown to him: he, he was her master; and to him, to him, she had surrendered her child's heart: her child's heart! There is no crime which cannot be forgiven! But how forgive a crime that wounds a child's heart? You must cherish a child's heart—once a child's heart stops, nothing can make it beat again, nothing. And Katya's childish heart was already barely beating; the worms had already begun to feed on it: those worms—a heavy depression which had imperceptibly crept into her bosom; from the moment—the moment she had fallen in love with him everything had been as of old; as before she fed the pigeons, laughed mischievously at the swallows; her eyes were as innocent and pure as before; Katya was still the same silly girl; in the same way, she moved shyly rather than walked —shyly or was it playfully; but when she sat down at the grand piano, what a wave of thunder poured forth from under her wax-like hands! Thunder, grief, passion had shaken these walls more than once when she sat down at the grand piano since the day of her engagement; but she was still a child. Woe to him who will upset her peace!

The previous day her old grandma had growled against her beloved. She had scolded her beloved, blaming and reproaching Katya for linking her fate with one who was not of noble birth; Katya remembered that she, the young girl, had jumped up like a wild panther, and had tossed a napkin off the table, had reproached her grandmother and scolded her to the amazement of Yevseich: she had managed to flash an angry, hawk-like gaze at the old woman; later, like an orphan, she spent the whole day sitting in the summer house and had wept like an orphan too, no longer smiling at the playful swallows, no longer admiring the little nest, no longer smiling. She went early to bed. But did she sleep?

Now she had blue rings under her eyes; but looking at her, you might remark that the way she was leaning over the grand piano only displayed a lazy grace and a maidenly coquettishness; her waxen hand opened like wax and the volume of Racine slipped noiselessly to the carpet.

Katya had always been like that: if she looked at anything, she did not seem to look; if she seemed to hear, she did not hear; and if she knew anything, she did not seem to know anything at all: composed and quiet always and smiling: quietly smiling she tiptoed through the rooms and curled up with a smile meticulously in an armchair; it seemed she had things to tell and things to think about; but did Katya speak?

It was difficult to decide whether she ever thought: if you approached and talked to her, you would conclude that she had a fine perception of nature, and that she understood and loved every art; but just try and develop your thoughts to her or try and impress her with your gifts or try and display your knowledge and mind: she would not be amazed at your mind—the mind would slip past her, and she would accept your gifts as something due, as something self-evident, as it were, without which it was impossible to live; but she would merely shrug her shoulders, only laugh at your knowledge—and laugh with whom? With Yevseich, the footman!

Was Katya intelligent? Truth to tell, I don't know—and is it necessary to know that? Is she more intelligent than anyone else or is she altogether a fool? Did Katya know many sciences? Not one. Does she have any success in art? Not a little. Why then does she pay no attention to famous and learned men, but rather to Yevseich, a flitting swallow, or her stupid friend, Lelya? Just try and fathom a girl's soul!

Today, oh, there's a storm brewing! Since morning grandma had been frowning, frowning at everything: at Yevseich, still more at Katya, the naughty girl, and even more she frowned at Daryalsky, her fiancé; she would glance with distaste at his not always immaculate boots, she would stare at his angular movements: if he happened to start singing in his hoarse, loud voice, which leapt over all the true notes—oh, oh, oh! what then! How grandma would then glare at Pyotr through her lorgnette!

Pyotr appeared blind; Pyotr seemed to notice nothing. And Katya, the silly girl? Her silly little heart would start pounding and then stop; and then she would flare up and address some new, biting, hurtful, prickling comment to her grandmother. This Pyotr would understand, grasp it all, she thought; but Pyotr, in a merry mood, saw nothing, became boisterous and not quite respectable; Pyotr, in a merry mood, would only quote some esoteric poetic phrase and reply to everything with that poetic phrase. But in view of grandma's attitude to poetic phrases and her sense of decorum, was such carelessness permissible?

Pyotr cogitated much—there was no one smarter than Pyotr: but Pyotr talked on learned subjects with neither Katya, nor her grandmother; only with his friend Schmidt did he discuss those incomprehensible subjects: Aristophanes's beetle, and always about some Villamovitz-Mellendorf; listening to those two, you might think them madmen or stutterers; but they were neither madmen, nor stutterers, but merely philologists and poets: they kept talking about Villamovitz and some Brugmann, whoever he was. The naughty girl knew perfectly well that if the meaning of every exclamation exchanged between Pyotr and his friend about Villamovitz-Mellendorf were to be explained to someone, it would result in a learned book about Villamovitz; for though Katya was quite silly, yet, silly as she was, she knew that Pyotr was smarter than anyone else when he discussed Villamovitz-Mellendorf, and that it was neither for her, nor her grandmother, to understand him; but what this Villamovitz represented, that Katya did not know.

When Pyotr noticed that haughty granny was trying to humiliate him in every way—both him and Villamovitz-Mellendorf, that she stressed her wealth and noble descent or dropped hints as to Pyotr's self-seeking materialistic ambitions, his desire to become rich, and that, if it had not been for him, a priest's son, Katya would by now have become engaged to Prince Chirkizilari, then Pyotr would tap his heel, feel depressed, grow sullen, and sulk for several days on end—petrified and uncommunicative; when anything blew up between him and the old lady, Katya had to bear the brunt of it, both Pyotr's sulkiness and her grandma's vicious hints.

So it was that day: her heart sensed the coming storm; and what a storm! Why did Pyotr fail to understand that grandma's notions about respectability and her whole life were all fixed in a past that was rapidly losing contact with life and that she thought more of a Prince Chirkizilari than of any Villamovitz or Brugmann? Why then had Pyotr thoughtlessly gone off in the morning and been absent all day without a word to anyone? And yet only two days had elapsed since their engagement. What effort, what pretexts that engagement had cost her; but Pyotr did not seem to take that into account.

Pyotr devoted much thought to her, but he evidently thought more about Brugmann. Well, he might have locked himself up with Brugmann, but he had gone off instead to seek company in Tzelebeyevo, and what company! He had gone off to jest with the priest and gossip with the priest's wife; did that signify he had ecclesiastical blood in his veins? No, that Katya could not, would not think; no, these thoughts were bad thoughts, grandma's thoughts: did grandma not realize that Pyotr was a very special person? No, it would not enter her head that Pyotr could be drinking wine there with the priest, though Katya realized, she really did, that Pyotr had got drunk more than once just as he had on that, fatal to her, evening in town.

As she was driving past a tavern in a sleigh in the winter, she happened to see the tavern door open and a drunken band of artists shouting indecencies tumble out of the lighted vestibule; one of them, catching sight of her, gave chase laughing loudly after her sleigh and then fell sprawling in the snow; but what had horrified her more than anything else was the fact that (even though for a second) Pyotr's gaze held her: Pyotr was there and Pyotr was drunk—his collar was unbuttoned and his fur hat was pushed back on his head; he stared without recognizing her:

he was too drunk; at that moment her heart slumped with fear lest he shout at her, Katya, something terribly rude such as men sometimes say to those rouged women with feathers in their hats.

But it was not at her he stared in silence, gazing at her, but somewhere into space, into the blizzard, into the howling storm he stared; and instantly he was drowned in the storm, in the blizzard, but the gaze of those glassy, horrified but terribly quiet and perfectly drunken eyes lingered in her soul. She seemingly forgot about it; but she would never forget that all men—without exception—drank: that even Pyotr, her Pyotr, drank like any other, like the last debauchee. Oh, childish heart, stupid heart: if he drank like any other, then he did all the other things men did, who talked cleverly in the daytime about Villamovitz-Mellendorf, even about Brugmann, but at night sat in restaurants, drinking wine and then, all of them without exception, went off to . . .

Here Katya shook her head and her thick curls fell behind her shoulders; but the frown between her fine brows, her compressed little mouth so inviting to be kissed, her head now held so high, and her light, austerely slight figure, which now seemed taller, expressed some strange, unchildish obstinacy: thus a white-trunked birch tree, suddenly shaken by a gust of wind, will uncontrollably break its silence and spread imploringly its thin nets and weep for a moment—but only for a moment: soon the birch tree would hardly flutter; and no one could tell that a stormy blast had passed through it before leaving no trace: there went its leaves, swirling uncontrollably down the road, but the tree itself? As green as ever, as though it had never lost those leaves claimed by the storm: only those prematurely withered leaves will rustle festively under the feet of a chance passerby; and the chance passerby will not guess that death had been here, the death of a feeling, but nevertheless death; so it is with a young soul; there are many such feelings, and not a few storms; beware of trampling on a leaf by the roadside, never touch a young soul! Never, never, will you learn where, when or why, death comes to a young soul!

Katya shuddered for a minute and then it was as though she had not shuddered; her oval face resting on a swan's neck ringed with curls bent down calmly, her eyelashes closed, and timidly she tiptoed to the tea table past the porcelain shepherds, past the china dandy, past the gaily prancing General, who was not staring at the bomb; and already a smile was lighting her up—but was it an easy smile?—as she glanced aside in the direction of the Baroness's bedroom, whence came the clear sound of splashing water and the smell of toilet vinegar; with apparent gaiety she watched with eyes that had nevertheless turned green the wizened footman, Yevseich, dressed all in gray, mumbling with his toothless mouth as he set out the silver tea service and remembered the cunning and the slyness of the housekeeper whom he had finally managed to outsmart; Yevseich muttered threats against the housekeeper just in case she, the housekeeper, dared venture again into the master's chambers; and outside, looking through the windows, it was wet, outside it was raining; and outside through the windows—God knows what and why!

⁓꙳꙳ Yevseich ꙳꙳⁓

Yevseich! Where find another footman like him: a footman to the tips of his toes!

Try and picture a footman: times are not what they
were; and the footman, it can be said, has been a vanishing
species for a long time; the footman has come to nothing;
and if he still survives somewhere, he is probably very old;
nowadays the footman has become an antique and if you
should have the desire to acquire a real footman then you
must seek an old man; anyone younger, it turns out, is no
longer a footman, but a thief or a rude fellow; and if he is
not a rude fellow, then do you know who he is? he is an
independent man: he will let sprout a mustache or a beard
or, in the American fashion, he will trim his mustache and
pass as a "comrade," or just simply as a "citizen"; and,
remember, my word, such a footman will not last a year: he
will run off to serve in a restaurant or in some lively alcoholic establishment. . . .

That Yevseich was neither a rude fellow nor a thief, that
any one could guarantee without risk; but as to his "citizen-
ship," just ask him. "Yevseich, are you a citizen?"—"He-he-
he!" is his answer. Judge for yourself then what sort of a
citizen he is: well, just look at that citizen, judge his citizen-
ship: he is no citizen, but a subject. He is the Baroness's
subject, and enough of that.

Hm . . . hm . . . Yevseich was old: he had turned
seventy a long time ago, and he is authentic, authentic to

the bone: a footman and nothing else. An authentic footman has gray whiskers; perhaps even here you will wish to
contradict, pointing to the perfect clean-shavenness of a
footman (we shall not quarrel over footmen with mustaches, because a footman with a mustache is no footman);
but the perfect clean-shavenness of a footman is already a
footman's liberty: a shaven footman is a footman second
class: a skullcap becomes a priest just as an epaulette becomes a General, and a belly a merchant. In the same way,
and even more so, whiskers become a footman, and I have
no intention of insisting that the whiskers should be large or
thick, but just so—modest whiskers. Yevseich had such
whiskers.

It also behooves a footman to shave and, God knows, how
often to wear a not altogether spotless cravat, but a white
cravat it must be; and it behooves him still more to wear
white knitted gloves, tolerably marked with yellow streaks;
how shall I tell you, snuff perhaps becomes a footman's
person, just as does a rude attitude toward the housekeeper,
and in the absence of such a person it becomes a footman in
his footman's quarters to strum on strings or play draughts
with the coachman. Yevseich did not shave often; the cravat
he wore was not always clean, his gloves were always
streaked with yellow dust and, even more, with the yellow
stain of snuff; alternately he edged out one housekeeper
after another and was content only when the last housekeeper had lost her last shred of patience and was transferred to the poultry yard; then, in his footman's quarters,
Yevseich would very energetically play a game of draughts
with the dignified-looking coachman, a trickster of tricksters.

Now concerning clothing: footmen have all sorts of
suits—black tails, blue tails; but only gray bespeaks the
footman, distinguishing him both from the rude fellow and
the citizen. Yevseich always wore gray.

In a word, if anyone evoked a footman in his imagination,
Yevseich would have appeared in anyone's imagination with
a tray or a feather mop in his hand.

Yevseich's distinguishing feature was the timidity he displayed toward the Baroness; this was no sign of slavish fear, but rather one of pure adoration; the old lady had only to look at him, look at him haughtily, and the old man would straighten his back, smooth a whisker, mumble with his toothless mouth; as soon as the old lady turned away, he would reach for his snuff: he would sniff it and then shyly sneeze in his sleeve; whenever the young lady talked to him of her joys or sorrows, whatever it might be, Yevseich would die of laughing. "Pfff . . . Pfff," was all that could be heard; he, the footman, looked down on all other people: whether he be a groom or a General, there was no escaping Yevseich's contempt: like a persistent fly Yevseich walked about oozing contempt; he was contemptuous when playing draughts. His contempt would last all day but, when night came, Yevseich could not sleep: he tossed and turned and muttered.

Such was Yevseich: such was the whole life he lived—such he descended into his grave. Rest in peace, last of the footmen!

"Will it be long before grandma comes out?" Katya asked.

"He-he-he!" Yevseich did not straighten his back in front of Katya. Yevseich was no footman now: he had summed up the young lady when still a *child*, and had laughed: according to Yevseich's understanding, Katenka was still a gentry child and, therefore, a respectable footman had no business to heed her childish chatter: childish chatter, as everyone knew, was a bird's trilling, no more than that.

"He-he-he! Young lady . . ."

"Yevseich, you must tell me when grandma is coming out."

"He-he-he!" Yevseich laughed again without paying attention: was there any point in listening to a tomtit, a reed pipe, or a *gentry child*? and so he took out his snuff box, sniffed the sweet snuff and emitted a respectable sneeze into his sleeve. He laughed to himself mischievously all the while—he could not see Katenka without laughing, looking at her jokingly as though he were jesting and teasing her; why that was so, Katenka knew, and she also knew how that game between them had originated; it had all started between them last summer.

Last summer, when she was not yet engaged, Katya had begun playing with the ginger dog Barbos, and Katya had put the whole of herself into it: she had imagined herself to be a cat and had climbed on the handrail of the veranda, puffed out her cheeks, humped her back—and had begun to hiss: she sat there on the handrail with her hair falling over her face: she imitated a cat so well that Barbos kept barking at her; she glanced round and saw Yevseich at the window looking on, snorting and splitting his sides with laughter. . . .

Katya on that occasion had astonished Yevseich very much—indeed, she had shocked him to death: in the whole of his life he had never laughed so much as there by the window; how else: a grown up young lady, a young lady of good birth, a seventeen-year-old young lady, and look how she was writhing there with her back humped and hissing, and all that very seriously, most seriously! But as soon as the young lady had spotted him, Yevseich grew confused, like a preparatory schoolboy caught out of class; out of modesty he hobbled away grunting and began sweeping the carpets with his footman's broom; all the same, to be frank, Yevseich, though he had surprised the young lady, had surprised her in a non-respectable occupation.

A year passed, and he still winked at her mischievously: I, as it were, know you. Though a young lady, you're still a child and no more. Thus, since that day, a sort of special secret developed between them; afterwards, you see, whenever they were left alone, Yevseich and Katya, the old footman let her understand that he, as you can see, was not opposed to playing and having fun with the young lady. From there on, things developed in such a way that Yevseich, the old child, mimed for her a goat and a dog, and he even once ran around like a rabbit or he showed her—and let this not be against him—a shadow pig with his hands; but the Baroness had only to cough from some distant room and Yevseich would straighten his back near a wall, holding his feather mop in his hand; and if anyone passed by, he would have seen no Yevseich, but merely a footman!

Katya was aware of all this, but, on this particular morning, Yevseich's laughter only roused her anxiety: it was no laughing matter when a storm was seething in her soul. She knitted her brows and sadly shook her curls; and as he served the samovar, Yevseich already understood that the child was beyond jokes at this moment, and he compressed his lips with all the dignity a footman could summon; but, suddenly and unexpectedly, he snorted, turned his back on Katya and, like a thief caught thieving, quickly hobbled away.

No, Katya did not smile after him, but neither did her face show any anger; instead, she seemed to collapse on the table in her flowery shawl and with her ash-colored curls; her dark blue eyes were now hidden under her black blue eyelashes, while her pink mouth was compressed anxiously and passionately. The girl in her had died: in that attitude the whole of her seemed to accept the storm, and she appeared like a woman thirsting for caresses.

~~&~~ Tea ~~&~~

It only seemed so: the tapping of a cane resounded through the rooms; somewhere a loose board creaked beneath the heavy tread of the Baroness, and then her heavy snorting sounded behind the wall; a branch by the window shuddered, a loose board shuddered too; Katya also shuddered and, glancing sharply sideways from under her eyelashes, her eyes glared at the door; all this took less than a second.

And then again she was an indifferent, lackadaisical girl, only slightly inquisitive, and so very small. She blinked her eyes, rose up with her shoulders squared and, as was her childhood habit, went to meet the Baroness, wearing a dress too short for her age, with a soft step, a stealthy step, while the squat old lady, dressed all in silks and colored lace, her gray hair streaked with yellow and leaning on a thick cane with a faceted crystal knob, was already puffing stertorously in the doorway.

Proudly, haughtily, austerely, the Baroness's full face swayed there—a face unnaturally white from applications and powder. In her youth the Baroness had been a flaming brunette, and now the dark pouches beneath her eyes looked scorched and burnt, and her smooth skin that emerged from under the powder, her full purple mouth, and her snub nose and the birthmark on her cheek, expressed without comment both stubborness and insolence when she held out to Katish, as she called her, her plump, soft, perfumed hand, a gesture that caused the silk of her morning dress, all hung with fine Lyons lace, to rustle; the smoke of curls tickled Katya's hand; and Katya kissed the soft, plump, perfumed hand: "Good morning, grandma"; with inalterable obstinacy, as though challenging fate, the Baroness's gaze did not fall upon the stooping girl and her lips smiled not at the girl but in some strange way formed a funnel above her, as a result of which the charcoal-marked wrinkles round her lips, and her charcoal-traced mustache above her lips, became more sharply marked while, in the meantime, Yevseich mutely froze to the spot, seeming to grow out of the ground like a gray, mute waxen statue; all in gray, holding a tray straight before him, he stood there, his glance, like himself, colorlessly gray, contemplating a fly that was drowsily freezing still on the wall; this instant seemed to stretch into eternity until the ponderous beat of the clock hoarsely announced it was already midday.

As though challenging fate to battle and casting the glitter of a large emerald ring, the Baroness strode forward ponderously and then quickly sat down at the tea table—as ponderously and quickly as her haughty life had flowed by; and already the strong red morocco armchair creaked and groaned beneath the ponderous old lady and her thick cane tapped obstinately on the faded carpet near her velvet slippers; surprised at nothing, Katya with a calm smile was pouring out coffee while the benign Yevseich assisted the old lady into the chair and then winked at Katya behind her back as he sniffed his snuff-stained gloves.

All this was accomplished in complete silence, and the deep noiselessness of this daily ritual inclined one to meditation, tuning the soul to majestic, endlessly sorrowful sounds.

Is that not the way that you, old and dying Russia, frozen in your pride and greatness, daily and hourly in a thousand chancelleries, council chambers, palaces and country houses, perform these rituals—the rituals of antiquity? But, exalted one, gaze around you and lower your eyes: then you will understand that an abyss is opening beneath your feet: you will look, and fall into the abyss!

"Will you have coffee or tea, Grandma?"

Silence: the old lady's outstretched hand drummed its fingers on the tablecloth and her black, black look was concentrated on her cup as if with her look she had decided to splinter it into a thousand fragments. . . .

"Eh-eh-eh . . . If I may say so . . . m'lady . . . yesterday and the day before you were pleased to have tea . . . eh-eh-eh," Yevseich unexpectedly put in but, suddenly overwhelmed with timidity, died away, nailed to the wall with fear, and his sideways, imploring gaze quickly transferred itself from the Baroness to Katya, then swam about the ceiling and finally came to rest on the toe of his boot; but the Baroness's outstretched hand continued to drum; hardly did she finish one roll than she began another; in grandma's other hand the cane jerked fitfully, tapping fitfully on the carpet.

"Will you have coffee or tea, grandma?"

Silence.

"Well, I'll pour you out some tea."

Silence.

"Eh-eh-eh . . . yes . . . eh-eh-eh-eh—eh-eh-eh! I, your Excellency . . . with your permission . . . h'm, h'm . . . you were pleased . . . n'yes . . . you were pleased . . . eh-eh-eh . . . tea—yes . . . what, your Excellency?"

Silence.

"Now here's some tea for you, grandma—with cream or no cream?"

Silence.

"Without cream?"

Silence.

"Yevseich, will you serve grandma the tea."

Yevseich, trembling like a decal removed from wall paper, became unstuck from the wall, grabbed the cup and stumbling over grandma's lap dog which squealed nastily, spilled some tea on the carpet, scalding his hand, but the Baroness's soft, perfumed, puffy fingers rejected the tea served in such fashion; and Yevseich, failing to guess the Baroness's taste, hastened to put things right:

"Eh-eh-eh . . . Coffee, yes, coffee, Katerina Vassilievna . . . That's it! Their Excellency have always been pleased to . . . eh . . . drink coffee . . ."

But he had hardly uttered this when grandma's chesty, gruff voice boomed:

"Fool! Give me the cup."

The old lady's puffy fingers accepted the cup, and Yevseich, confused and ashamed, retreated into a dark corner, from which his sigh of relief could be heard escaping.

Silence.

"Perhaps that chair is uncomfortable, grandma?"

"Would you like me to bring you a cushion? You will be more comfortable with a cushion!"

"Mimi, Mimi, little white Mimi! Let me give you a piece of sugar; grandma, Mimi's bow is crooked . . . Mimka, Mimka, let me fix your bow . . ."

"Grrr—wow, wow!" came from under the Baroness's skirt and a small creature—no dog, of course—thrust out its nose.

"Ah, you nasty little dog: grandma, she's bitten my finger again!"

"Grrr—wow, wow!" came from under the Baroness's skirt.

"Mimi!"

"Grrrr—wow, wow!"

. . . .

"Don't be angry with me, grandma . . ."

"It hurts me when for no reason at all you say bad things about Pyotr. . . ."

"I shan't do it again, grandma . . ."

. . . .

"We should send the coachman to town, grandma: the

coachman says there's not enough camphor oil left; I think, grandma, you will soon be short of eau-de-cologne as well. . . ."

"It's nasty weather today, grandma, but it was sunny yesterday. . . ."

"Grandma, it's sunny in the summer and less sunny in the winter; but I love both summer and winter, grandma. . . ."

"Lelya also loves both winter and summer, and Prince Chirkizilari, he loves neither summer nor winter, grandma. He lives in Biarritz both summer and winter."

"Will you have some more tea?"

Silence . . . Katya was the only one to talk: silence greeted her every attempt; grandma, though she was forcing herself not to talk, was resolved to avenge Katya's conduct of yesterday. Grandma was always like that; but Katya was not frightened by this, only Yevseich trembled in fear; Katya had now exhausted her whole supply of words: Katya was now talking so little, so little—for silly girls' thoughts do not fit words; remembering that the old lady was most afraid of running out of eau-de-cologne, Katya had used that as a bait although she knew perfectly well there was enough eau-de-cologne in the house; but the old lady had long ago caught on to the tricks of the guilty girl and so the old lady made no reply; finally Katya mentioned the favored name of Chirkizilari in order to extract from grandma at least a grunt to the effect that her Pyotr was no match for the Prince; but the old lady took that in silence too: if Prince Chirkizilari did not dent her silence, what was there left!

"Prince . . . grandma, Prince Chirkizilari!"

Silence: the old lady's plump fingers stretched out tenderly toward her Mimochka, her lap dog, and rested with loving care on the nasty lap dog, while Katya began to feel angry and knit her raging brows; from under her eyelashes a spiteful emerald jealously stung grandma, though Katya pretended she did not mind grandma's maneuver. In truth, she was raging—in a second she would arch her back and spring at grandma—pfu-pfu-pfu: that tiny lap dog, that nasty little lap dog! Mimka! But not a word to her, the granddaughter!

"Eh-eh-eh . . . yes, of course . . . eh-eh . . . the young Prince, yes, Chirkizilari . . . eh-eh, his Excellency . . . I used to know him when he was just this height . . . Chirkizilari . . . yes . . . the young Prince," Yevseich butted in once more but, having been dubbed a *fool*, he now regretfully sulked in a corner.

How could Katya not remember Chirkizilari! She arched her back—pfu-pfu-pfu!! he's balding and burring, drags a leg and has a bad odor in his mouth. Nasty Mimka, idiot Chirkizilari, stupid day—they are all fools! She, Katya would pay them back!

Glancing sideways at her granddaughter, grandma was about to stretch out her plump fingers intending to kiss that little forehead, those little eyes, and that little head of hair when—dong: half-past-twelve.

Thus, in profound silence, was accomplished the daily but majestic ritual of this life that was fast slipping into the past, whereas from the open verandah came the sounds of a new Russia and a throaty song of the lads could be heard as they passed in the distance and the golden screech of a striped accordion accompanying them: "The-e-ey-y-y fol-l-l-l-o-o-w y-o-o-u, the ra-a-an-n-n-k-k-s o-f the n-e-e-w re-e-cru-u-i-t." Then it all died away in the distance.

But those sitting here were ignorant of the new Russia and of the songs of the new Russia, and of those soul-shaking words behind the linden trees; and the lads, and the song, and the words of the song—for surely they sounded, those words, and the lads sang those songs far and wide; but those words and those songs were not destined to reach this quiet retreat, nor were the lads destined to enter this garden. But that is an illusion: both the words and the song are here, and so are the lads: for a long time already that song, full of old sounds, has poisoned the air, making the Baroness's black eyes gape with terror. The Baroness had learnt about it all a long time ago; she had doomed both herself and Russia to death and sacrifice in the fatal struggle; but she pretended to be dumb and deaf as though she knew nothing of those new songs; but Pyotr knew.

And Pyotr entered.

Here he was—in a red silk shirt: his boots creaked courageously and the ash-hued cap of his hair waved in the air; twirling his mustaches and laughing merrily, Daryalsky seized the white lap dog, tossed it up in the air and then, lowering it respectfully, boldly walked up to the Baroness's hand as if he were storming a fortress: "Good morning, *maman*, good morning . . . Good morning, Katya: forgive me, I am late . . ."

An odd thing: after the depressions and the mad flights of a sick soul, have you never felt blessed peace, strange lightness and a boisterous surge of heroic energy? The death of the soul and the terror of dangers threatening you will suddenly appear no more than a childish joke, or rather: something that happened not to you, but was merely related; it will seem to you then that you have heard the song of the chaos which has confused your soul, but where—that you will never reveal: the dream of life will possess you and you will lose your memory: and you will speed lightly on the waves of life, plucking only the flowers of pleasure, the happy gifts of existence: but no, no—your joy will not stay with you: the past, which threatened and which has not ceased to exist, will then confront you in the twinkling of an eye; and you will curse the hour of your lightheartedness—that hour when, watching the winding choir of dancers on the common or the loving glance of a girl, you said to yourself: No, I merely dreamt of misfortunes! no, nothing threatens me now . . . Know then: it will be too late.

"It's late already," the old lady drawled through her nose, haughtily, benevolently swaying over Daryalsky's bowed head and touching with her lips his ash-hued hair while he was kissing her hand.

"Yes, it's late!" Katya exclaimed, flashing her frightened, reproachful emerald eyes at him, while her voice droned on lifelessly.

"He-he-he!" Yevseich responded from his dark corner.

Daryalsky failed to notice the irony, the reproach, and even the fatal benevolence of the seventy-year-old grandmother, and it did not strike him either as strange that the old lady had replaced her daily morning anger at him with an altogether inexplicable benevolence: thus, those condemned to be executed experience in the last minutes of their life the benevolence of those who, in an instant, will lead them to death. Yet it was odd that the old lady, who had grumbled at Daryalsky and had used him to make Katya's life a misery, had already managed strongly and firmly in the depths of her deaf soul to pity her granddaughter's fiancé, of whom she took so unfavorable a view.

Strangely enough Katya realized that there would now be no storm, that an empty caprice or a sudden change of temperature had warmed her grandmother's heart, but she did not rejoice; now that the external anxieties had dispersed, she was overcome with her own particular anxiety; and she kept glancing imploringly at her fiancé: "Perhaps, like all the others, he . . . goes to . . ."

But Daryalsky noticed none of all this: Katya's plaint, like a barely quivering string, hovered in the air; she loved him—of what importance was it to be furious with him for an hour or two!

Did he realize how anxiously her heart had beat when, without seeing her in the morning, he had gone off to Tzelebeyevo: with what joyful expectation she had awaited him when the distant tolling had announced the end of the mass; how yesterday she had gazed down the road, thrusting her face bathed in curls through the green acacias; in the distance she could already make out the red shirts and the golden, blue and green bodices of the Gugolevo girls, and their vivid red kerchiefs burnt in the air while ringing songs began to fill the air.

And he was not there.

Did he realize what strings had sobbed in the golden air—the strings of her soul?

Lunch was already served and still he had not come; when with sharp words she had grappled with grandmother, the sharpness of them had pricked her as with the rose thorn of love; but here he was sitting now, paying no attention to her, oblivious of her flowering; he did not even ask her, *Princess Katya's*, forgiveness; Katya sat, showered with petals of love: the wind whirled the petals, dried them; Katya herself was falling in showers . . .

Did he or did he not possess a single human feeling?

And he? He had become too relaxed; he had an extraordinary feeling of lightness under his heart and, oh, how he laughed at the stupid occurrences of yesterday! The heat, the stifling air, the flies, and the concentrated study of the classics in spite of everything—the engagement and Katenka's kisses—had the effect, of course, of stimulating in his soul such a strange movement that a single glance, a single insolent remark from a stray wench had sufficed to excite him, to disturb stupidly the depths of his soul, and that stupid profundity of soul had swarmed over him; but he would not allow it, his stupid profundity, to develop—he would stifle it, that profundity; and so he laughed loudly, rejoiced noisily, feeling a lightness beneath his heart and a quiver in his heart. . . .

"Certain philologists, *maman*, maintain that the seventh eclogue of Theocritus is the *"regina eclogarum,"* which means the "Queen of Eclogues." Others assert that it is sweeter than honey, the seventh eclogue. To mark this I shall today drink seven cups of tea."

"He-he-he!" came from the corner.

"Regina eclogarum."

And Katya thought: "Yesterday he drank wine—maybe he got drunk and perhaps he's like all of them: before she, Princess Katya, came on the scene, he may have frequented shameless women."

"Once I read in Theocritus, my bride, that they locked someone in a cedar chest, and on that point there is a dispute among philologists; when I marry you, I shall lock you up too, my bride."

"He-he-he!" came from the corner.

"And Theocritus also says that Pan was thrashed with nettles and that afterwards he lay in a ditch and scratched himself; some philologists affirm that he scratched himself because he was lying among the nettles; another philological trend attributes Pan's itchiness to the thrashing. . . . All this is discussed in the seventh eclogue, which is the *regina eclogarum* . . ."

"Oh, do stop it!" Katenka stood up, her eyes filling with tears.

"Very good . . . that . . . that your grandmother was pleased to get up and go away . . . otherwise they would not have been . . . ah, ah . . . at all pleased," Yevseich remarked reproachfully, but Daryalsky no longer saw him, just as he had not perceived the departure of the Baroness, who had retired to her room tapping on the carpet with her oaken cane; he turned and with enthusiasm stared at Katya as she stood nearby while Yevseich fussed round the table, sniffed his sweet snuff and growled: "They beat with leeks . . . Some gent . . . What . . . Can they thrash with leeks? And a gentleman too . . . Must have been nettles . . ."

But now Daryalsky heard the patter of bare feet on the . . . . How she stood there, his own, his bride, who only yesterday had flown away from him only to return to him today—how she stood there wreathed in green intoxication and in dripping drops of rain!

O feast-filled moment!

Two Women

Katya! There is only one Katya in the world; you may travel the whole world over and not meet any other; you may traverse all the stretches and spaces of our broad land, and go even farther: in lands overseas you will be captivated by black-eyed beauties, but they will be no Katya; you may journey West from Gugolevo in a straight, straight line; and you may return to Gugolevo from the East, out of the Asiatic steppes; only then will you behold Katya. This is how she is, look at her now: she is standing there by herself, having lowered her curving, dark blue eyelashes soft as silk; from under her eyelashes gleam the flowers of her distant eyes, vaguely gray or green, at times velvety, at others blue; her gaze is meaningful and with her gaze she tells you things impossible to convey in words—you will think that; but you'll realize that this is an illusion when she raises her eyes to yours; she will say nothing with her eyes; her eyes are just eyes; feel them with your gaze—and your gaze will retreat before the mere beautiful glassiness of her gaze, having failed to penetrate a maiden's soul; you will expatiate upon the glitter of those eyes and you will be wrong: you will understand that in every country estate such as Gugolevo such eyes are to be found; but should she turn and as though by chance glance at you sideways, with eyes half-closed, blushing slightly and smiling: then, contrary to probability, you will believe in the profundity of her gaze so full of meaning; and should she

turn again and speak: speak nonchalantly about trifles;
should she turn just so, her eyes bright, large, elongated like
almonds; and nothing more.

And her rosy, rosepale, unfurled petal, slightly open
mouth—her rosepale, made-for-kisses lips; smile at them
with a smile full of secret meaning—the lips will not quiver
but will just half-open with surprise or close firmly in sorrow; and how enchantingly those lips smile at altogether
hollow words, flowers, expensive dogs and, above all, children; her elongated, pale, somewhat thin face will turn
slightly pink, as an apple petal turns pink when a swallow
squeals at it, snipping the air with black wings; quickly
Katya will turn toward it, her face grown as pink as an
apple petal; and one of her ashen curls will fly up into the
blue air; her oval, lusterless face is all hung with thick,
transparent, ash-colored curls; her curls fall down upon her
breast—and she thrills with laughter at the skill of the black
swallow: she is aware that the Gugolevo swallows have a
reason for darting around her; should Katya fall into a
reverie, a flitting swallow will pluck a silken hair of hers and
carry it away to build a nest for its fledglings; Katya knows
this, and slyly she half-closes her eyes and shakes her head;
but the swallow will come flying by; and the thick, perhaps
even too thick curls will fall back on her shoulders, washing
over her swan-like neck and with their down slightly
tickling Katya's half-open breast; and then again her face
will show white—and just look then; that outstretched neck
and that upraised face all in ash-colored curls agitated by
the breeze, with the rosepale, barely open mouth like a
nimbus, and with the quiet, elongated, unbearably gleaming
eyes—all this, all this, will express the weariness either of a
child or a girl who has experienced a great deal.

But now Daryalsky heard the patter of bare feet on the
verandah and like a singing beam he heard a sweet voice:

"Sweet young lady, can't we give you some lilies of
the valley? We gathered them ourselves for you in the
forest . . ."

He went out on the verandah—and stared: amid the green hops, in the golden and airy hops, as in a dream, in the singing beam stood his yesterday's pock-marked woman, and the pock-marked woman kept glancing at Katya, making up to Katya while the breeze played with her reddish hair—the migrant breeze; the sky began to clear; the gilded rains moved away, and from the rains a seven-hued rainbow sprang up.

"Aha-ha!" Daryalsky smiled ironically into his mustaches, assuming a dignified air. "The mountain did not go to Mohammed, so Mohammed went to the mountain!" and with eyes half-closed he scrutinized the pock-marked woman: the pock-marked woman was not bad-looking—she could comfort: a lusty wench: under her red bodice stirred full-fledged womanly breasts: her sunburnt, sturdy legs were muddy—look how they, her feet, had left traces on the verandah, her nose was blunt, her face pale, covered with large, fiery pock-marks: her face was not pretty, but pleasant and rather sweaty; she held out the bouquet to Katya. "That's what she's like, but where am I, where indeed?" Daryalsky thought. "A fine wench, but a loose one no doubt—that crease about her lips," he tried to convince himself about something, to persuade himself, to stifle and trample down the instant feeling that awoke in him; but he still felt light of heart: "No, I dreamt that."

"Ah, what sweet white lilies of the valley!" Katya exclaimed, pressing the flowers to her slightly flushed face.

"What's your name?" Daryalsky asked the woman bluntly and strictly.

"Matryona—we're from these here parts," she replied and her blue gaze ran over him: at that moment a scorching shriek flew by: someone grazed him with a black wing; a swallow, like a bat, snipped the verandah with its wings, flitting back and forth until it was gone: had flown away.

"That's not a swallow but a martin," Katya said in surprise.

"Ours, from Tzelebeyevo. So will you buy this bouquet, lady? I gathered it for you."

The snub-nosed wench smiled at Katya; and like an innocent angel the silly girl gave her a twenty kopeck piece.

"Lady, be kind, add another five!"

But Pyotr put his arm round Katya's waist: let the whole world see that she, Katya, was his bride-to-be; the wench, continuing to leave traces of her feet, was descending from the verandah when Yevseich, who had appeared in the doorway, mumbled after the woman: "O Lord, O Lord, why do you Herods wander into a gentleman's garden, and why doesn't the gardener keep his eyes peeled? Well, Matryona, look out!"

"Wha-at?" Matryona turned to look either at Yevseich or at Daryalsky, and then her red bodice vanished in the foliage.

Ah, you, golden sunbeam, ah, you, migrant breeze: the flowers bloom, and the gay foliage dances in the beams, and Daryalsky, overjoyed at something, laughs amid the beams; tenderly he draws Katya away from the verandah, and then suddenly in a surge of merriment begins to shout rather than to sing.

But for an instant Katya knitted her brows when, freeing herself from his embrace, with a stately movement of her neck she tossed from her shoulder the ashen smoke of her transparent hair which covered her back, while her bitten lip quivered and smiled, and the broad pink nostrils of her slender nose flared from impatience and controlled anxiety; all this lasted but an instant, and all this Daryalsky saw. As he finished drinking his tea he continued in a fit of joyful heart-beating.

"Theocritus talks strangely about bees: whatever way you translate it, it always comes out 'blunt-nosed bees'; but when are bees ever blunt-nosed?"

When in good spirits, Daryalsky did not like to converse on profound subjects: profound subjects, with whatever feeling he touched upon them, caused him such tormented, complex, nameless and, in their consequences, always fatal experiences, that he piled on these experiences the ponderous heaps of Greek dictionaries; an eternal gravity weighed on his soul and, for that reason, the sunny experience of life in the long-past years of blessed Greece with its wars, games, sparkling thoughts, and always dangerous love, as well as the life of the simple Russian people, always called up to the surface of his soul pictures of a blessed Eden-like life, a clump of shady thickets and honeyed breeze-blown meadows with games and dancing choirs upon them, a notion that his small-minded little girl did not understand at all, the girl who was sitting there sullenly in a corner plucking at the tablecloth and showered in petals.

Ah, these songs, and—ah!—these dances! Are you curtaining or baring still more the abysses of his soul? Very likely, these sulphurous abysses let escape an evil swarm of locusts, so that his heart might be pierced with a locust sting and then be bathed in blood: he struggled with his dark abysses, as Hercules had once wrestled with the hydra, enriching speech with the magic and honey of choice words, a thing people did not understand, as Katya did not, sadly sharpened as she was at this moment into the semblance of a thorn of a rose. Or had his expression become such that she, poor child, could not bear it?

⁘⁘⁚⁙ Who Then is Daryalsky? ⁙⁚⁘⁘

In his speech, laughter, mannerisms, boldness—in everything except the alternating fire or ice of his eyes which
pierced the darkness, my hero reminded one not of a poet,
but of any strutting lad. That is why he created or, more
truly, experienced and still more truly, composed of his life
a strange truth: it was highly unsuitable, highly improbable;
it consisted of this: he dreamt that in the deeper layers of
his native people there pulsed a native and as yet unex-
hausted, ancient way of life—that of ancient Greece.

He envisioned a new light, a light also in the performance
in the ritual life of the Greco-Russian church. In Orthodoxy
and in outmoded concepts, in particular, of the Orthodox
peasant (i.e. in his opinion, a pagan) he saw the new torch
in the World of the future Greek.

But to confess the truth, neither an exchange of winks
with priests, nor his blood-red shirt, silken though it was
and daring, nor his visitation of nighttime city taverns and
beer houses, and the devil knows where else, with Theocritus always peeping out of his soul, added but little adorn-
ment to the appearance of my hero; beginning with the
creaking of his oiled boots, the strong vulgar expressions he
employed, and ending with his suddenly revealed knowledge with an obvious inclination to indulge sometimes in
non-serious and esoteric discussion—all this alienated people
from Daryalsky, just as he himself was alienated from
everything around him; for many, Daryalsky represented a

mixture of odors: those of bad corn, brandy, mucous and
blood . . . with no more nor less than a tender lily, and
these many, in their turn, reminded him of good-for-nothing
rags.

"Ah, you rascal!" was once said to him by a lady drowning in lace, who was ready to do anything with anyone at
any hour of the day or night. Let us begin with words:
Daryalsky's words in other people's ears sounded unneces-
sarily artificial, figurative and, above all, uncleverly distorted, and what especially got their goat was my hero's
chuckling—more than even the distortion of himself into a
simpleton—because the *simpleton* in him managed to exist
side by side with a simplicity unattainable to the mind, a
deafness and a blindness to everything else; Daryalsky reacted violently against every wish to heed any public
opinion formed about himself, just as others reacted violently against his conduct. It appeared then that he distorted
himself for his own, and only for his own sake. For who
else's benefit could Daryalsky have distorted himself?

But in God's sight he did not distort himself: he believed
he was working on himself; in him a savage struggle was
taking place between the hesitancy of weakness and the
foretaste of conduct befitting an as yet unfounded life, a
struggle between the image of the ancient beast and that of
a new human sanity; and he knew that, once engaged upon
the path of this struggle, he could not retreat, that conse-
quently in this struggle for the future shape of life everything was permitted to him and that there was nothing
above him, nothing, no one, never; he had suffered moments
of terror and joy; in the flux of feelings which had outdistanced his contemporaries for perhaps more than one
generation, he showed himself either more helpless than
they or infinitely stronger; their whole outworn heritage
had already become decomposed in him; but the abomina-
tion of this decomposition had not yet been consumed and
transformed into good earth: for that reason, the weak seed
of the future had somehow become withered and frozen:

and it was for that reason that he had become so attached to "the land and the people" and the people's prayers about the land; but he thought of himself as the future of the people: into the dung, the chaos, the formlessness of the people's life, he had thrown down his secret challenge—and wolf-like that challenge went off into the forest thickets of the people: out of the forest, in a howl, something responded to him.

He still waited, he still dawdled; but he could feel already the soft muddy earth sticking to him and oozing after him; he was aware that the people, too, had given birth to new souls, that the fruit had matured, and that it was time to shake the fig tree; there, in the thickets, in the distance and yet in the sight of all, Russia was building, gathering herself together, in order to thunder forth in resounding mountains.

Taking possession of Daryalsky's soul, this struggle called up out of the soul of the earth-depths an army of hidden forces; in order that the evil eye, the eye that hated Russia, should not also strike him down, he began secretly raising, like a holy place, a certain fortification, a fortification of the spirit—the building of his strange fate; but this building stood in the forests, and who could understand the dazzling design of this structure—constructed of his own blood and flesh? We have seen mounds of rubbish and, among them, a carelessly cast away sample of splendid Byzantium; we have seen fragments of Greek statues knocked down shapelessly into the native dust; but the secret enemy slept not; he penetrated into the heart of the people—and from there, out of the poor people's heart, menaced Daryalsky; for that reason, though drawn to the people, Daryalsky fenced himself from it by love, and Katya had become for him that love which blessed him for the battle. An inexplicable foreboding informed him that, if he were to fall in love with a peasant girl, it would prove the end of him; the secret enemy would then get the better of him; and already he was expecting the hostile arrow to strike him out of the dark—

an arrow out of the people; and he defended himself as best he could.

Katya instinctively understood Daryalsky; in her childish, predicting heart she had spontaneously sensed in him something large and altogether unknowable—and with her whole being she leaned on his chest, protecting him from blows: that a blow would fall, this Daryalsky knew; he had a vague premonition that Katya would fall together with him.

There was a wild beauty in the sound of his verse, spellbinding the darkness with an incomprehensible spell amid the rush of storms, battles and enthusiasms. And chaining these storms, battles and enthusiasms, he forcibly broke their daredeviltry of Byzantinism and the perfume of musk: but—Oh, oh: above the smell of musk, like smoke, rose the smell of blood.

For him, this path was also Russia's—Russia's path in which had begun a great transfiguration of the world or the world's end, and Daryalsky . . .

But the devil take him, Daryalsky: let him vanish into thin air: he is already here before us: be not amazed at his acts: there is no final way of understanding them, in any case; well, the devil take him!

Passions approach: let us describe them—not him: somewhere already you hear thunder thudding.

～💥 A Riot 💥～

The old lady in spectacles sat by the window of her
room; she frowned as she bent over her fingers as if attacking them with a needle from which stretched a raspberry-
colored silken thread; she was embroidering a wreath of
green leaves; and now upon that green wreath she was
finishing a cherry; a gust of wind blew outside; dogs barked
in the distance and there was a sound of shouting; the
shouts came from the barn, and the voices drew nearer.

In the dark corridor there was a hurried sound of bare
feet; more and more bare feet could be heard pattering; the
approaching clatter was answered from the kitchen by
thumping and whispering; a heavy door on pulleys kept
opening; here and there bare feet trampled in the corridor;
a woman's face kept peering out of the kitchen; "*v-i-z-v-i-z-
z-z-z*," creaked the opening door and "bang" fell the heavy
block of the pulley; the noise, the squeals, the barking and
the drunken shouts now came from the courtyard; on the
other side of the window a pinkish pig could be seen squeal-
ing and scurrying across the yard from the direction of the
office.

The old lady rose, stuck her needle in the crown of silken
leaves, and the raspberry ball of thread rolled off from her
knees; she pulled off her thimble and calmly sprinkled some
eau-de-cologne on her lace; but nevertheless she listened
intently to the noise.

Yevseich's face appeared apprehensively in the doorway; a barely audible whisper emanated from it.

"Your Excellency. The peasants are rioting there."

"What?"

"Khe-khe . . . the p-p-peasants . . ."

"What is all this nonsense?"

"Can't say . . . The madcaps . . . Mashka, the crooked one, was saying . . . And it's all on account of the manager, Your Excellency . . . He held up the household accounts and seemingly cheated Yefrem and ruined a girl . . . That's what did it, it seems . . ." his voice suddenly broke.

"They're carrying stakes, my lady . . . I'd like to inform you."

The old lady pouted with her full lips and anxiously chewed the empty air.

"Palashka, bring me my mantle!"

Katya and Daryalsky were already at the window; through it they could see the courtyard; the courtyard was green, large, and studded with offices; the offices formed a square; here were the stables, a plank structure with a red iron roof, and on a whitened foundation stood a straw-covered icehouse rotting from the damp, and a hut which served as a bathhouse and was almost drowned in hemp, where birds twittered gaily all day long, and an icehouse, and a half-built chicken coop, and, for some reason, an all-white plastered wall; there were also barns that looked like pondering old men, bulging with grain and propped by stakes, covered over with maple and spread over with sweet brier; here too a proud regiment of raspberry bushes and there hens were scratching; and there was the household office; half of it was occupied by the housekeeper; the other, by the "bloodsucker," Yacob Yevstigneyev who, with the assistance of his plump wife, produced offspring almost twice a year, and his fair-haired children, "the little bloodsuckers," whose freshness, youth and blood belonged, frankly speaking, to the modest little coffins which were not hammered over with glazed brocade and which kept being driven from Gugolevo to the Tzelebeyevo cemetery. It was not for nothing that, for the past five years, Yacob Yevstig-neyev had stuck to the people here like a leech, drinking their blood and passing as a wizard; and though he was a drunkard, he was a circumspect one; and he lorded it over not only his own property, but that of others.

In a leather coat and large hunting boots, he stood on the steps gripping a rusty revolver in his hand, his rasping voice outshouting the roar of the brown peasant mass pressing upon him from all sides, and insolently shaking his whitish beard resembling dishevelled tow above their heads; the homespun peasants surrounded him; the homespun peasants were clambering over the handrails of the steps; the home-spun peasants pressed and pressed on the office; some of them carried stakes; others merely spat in their fists; but they were all shouting.

Suddenly the Baroness appeared on the hop-clad steps; the tresses of her yellow-gray hair unfurled in the wind, in the rain, above the crowd of homespun peasants; and she waved her arm authoritatively; the stares bristled and the peasant mass now flowed away from the office, pouring into the yard and flooding toward the manor house: the peasants swarmed toward her.

"Your Excellency! Allow me to report: dismiss me!" the "bloodsucker" exclaimed, who had outdistanced the yelling crowd and now stood in front of the Baroness, lowering his spiteful eyes. "A man of good birth cannot work with this riff-raff; and they accuse me of supposedly cheating Yefrem . . . But I . . ."

"You're lying, devil take your mother!" a huge lad shouted, advancing upon him with a huge club and, at the same time, brandishing his huge fist before his nose, at which the "bloodsucker's" nose twitched. . . .

"He's a thief, my lady: he ought to be working in the fields, but he plays cards at the priest's."

"He's a thief! Blast his mother, why does he steal from us?"

"He seduces the girls: he's ruined Malashka, he's ruined Agashka, he's ruined my Stepanida!" A sickly looking peasant with running eyes and a good natured expression counted on his fingers.

"And where did you get the master's wheel?"

"Where did you get it?"

"Where, where! So you see, my lady—blast his mother! —he'll drive off on new wheels and get back on worthless ones."

"In a word, he's a chemist: he's sitting on our necks and yours!" They buzzed all round. "You've got a thief there, that's sure!" Noses were raised and hands plucked un-combed beards and huge fists waved in the air as the peasants spat out and stared around them: suddenly the peasants exuded a bad heavy odor.

"Off with your caps, dumbbells! Can't you see—our lady is here!" the "bloodsucker" cut in. And strangely enough, heads were bared submissively, sullenly; red, black and gray-black tufts of hair were exposed to the rain and bald patches gaped; only five young lads who stood to the side shelling sunflower seeds giggled and did not take off their caps.

"Why should we take them off? Soon everything will be ours anyhow!"

"Listen, peasants! Be silent, Yevstigneyev!"

The peasants in front attentively stretched forward their beards; they were ready to discuss the situation; the old man with the tufted beard held his ear forward from behind his shoulders; he listened with his mouth half-open; and his seventy-year-old, rather cunning, slanting eye blinked mis-chievously at the Baroness; and while she was telling them that she would reason it all out according to the will of God, a white louse crawled over the old man's cheek: that was Yefrem who had been to some extent cheated; he was, they said, a rebel, an agitator, and a socialist. Was that so? Attentively examining his face, which bore the imprint of time eternal, one might only read meekness and good will; a peasant hiccupped; another scratched himself; another went the round of his fellows, discussing in a low voice the Baroness's speech and shaking his open fingers under his nose.

Then, suddenly, the speechless silence was broken by the sound of horse-bells; a raven troika then came into view; the driver in a sleeveless velvet jacket raised and lowered his reins, and his lemon yellow sleeves which had been dampened by the rain bobbed up and down in the air; his cap with peacock feathers flashed beneath the willow trees; and the horse-bells tinkled gaily through the park; someone sitting in the troika waved from the distance, first with a red gentry cap and then with a handkerchief.

"Well, we'll finish all this later! I'm standing you, peasants, a quarter of vodka, so go home now!" the Baroness said in haste, staring benevolently from the steps into the distance over the heads of the slovenly peasants. Who were these uninvited guests?

"Thank you kindly, your Excellency! We'll come to some agreement, why not . . . Surely so . . ." came a buzz from all sides. Only gray Yefrem, who had stuffed his nose with snuff, kept angrily scratching the back of his head and grumbling in no very friendly fashion:

"Drink! We'll drink, but only . . . my hay's gone, so much of it . . ."

"And then, after all: he ruined Malashka, he ruined Agashka, and he ruined my Stepanida—and what for? Just so . . ."

That's what the peasants said as they retreated, but a foul little peasant jumped out of the crowd—not in the direction of the village or the town, but right in front of the steps, held out a finger and grinned:

"Now reason it out if we say that it's all right with us and it seems all right with you: because you are ours, and we are yours. But give me a dozen rods for a fence—thin ones."

"All right . . . all right . . . now go . . ."

The troika, like a big black bush, flowering with bells, dashed madly out of the branches, galloped through the courtyard, and stopped dead by the steps.

"Ah, I'm so *vlad*, so *vlad*, to get here at last!" General Chizhikov cried, jumping out of the troika.

⚜ General Chizhikov ⚜

Five and a half years had passed since General Chizhikov
had first appeared in our neighborhood; he made his appearance with a lot of noise, drum beating and gossip; and
triumphant scandal dogged his steps; but in the course of
five years General Chizhikov, if we may say so, overrode
all the scandals—surrounded as he was by money, wine,
women and fame.

General Chizhikov, it was said, had a false passport; but
what no one doubted was: that General Chizhikov was a
General and that of the highest rank; and he was Chizhikov.
That this agreeable personage held the respectable rank of
General, and also wore the red ribbon of a certain order,
was attested to by those who were in the habit of living in
the capital city of Saint Petersburg; they had met Chizhikov in high society and in high official circles, and who
except Generals and sons of Princes frequent such places of
bon-ton where the Messrs. Generals spring to attention
without any undue smartness and where you will find His
Excellency the Minister joking familiarly. There it was that
General Chizhikov had his circles of acquaintances which
he later ceased to frequent: he had grown impossibly radical
and had almost introduced the gospel of red terror into the
provinces; it was said that the secret police were very much
upset by this. Whether this was so or not, General Chizhikov did appear in our neighborhood and made the rounds of
the district: he went from landlord to merchant, from

merchant to priest, from priest to doctor, from doctor to student, from student to constable—and so on and so forth.

That he was the authentic Chizhikov, there's no doubt: it is the job of the police to establish who is genuine and who is not! For no other reason but modesty, under this plebian name was concealed until good time a blue-blooded Count of renowned lineage and family—yes, yes: he was Count Gudi-Gudai-Zatrubinsky. And Gudi-Gudai-Zatrubinsky, it may be said, peeped out of the General—the rascal! He would visit you and not be Chizhikov for more than half an hour; and then the aristocrat in him would press upon you and so much so that you'd grow stifled with aristocracy: he would exhibit his blue blood to you in every way—pull out his handkerchief, and the handkerchief would assail your nostrils with *Coeur de Janet, Houbigant* or even the very Parisian *Fleur qui Meurt!* He would behave with rascally *"sans façon,"* speak in a hotel-like tone, the devil take him, which his very distorted speech illustrated (the General never pronounced an "er" or an "el"); and his noble expansiveness would show itself in his hurdy-gurdying with little ladies; all sorts of *"merci madame,"* would just hang in the air and, let me report this, he would kiss all of a lady's fingertips: no general this, but a sweet soul, a veritable *"crême de vanille"* (don't worry about his being over fifty, or that some of his teeth are missing and that his whiskers— the color of spit—are not of pleasant hue). With a count he'd be a count, with a clerk a clerk: he would get drunk in a tavern and nibble a herring's tail; nor must any conclusions be drawn from the fact that for five spanking years the General idled his time away, preached the red terror, while living on the hospitality of Likhov's rich men. Well, and what follows? Nothing at all! *"Incognito"*—ha, ha! One has to do something; and so the General did commissions for the merchants by way of paying back for the regiment of white-headed bottles he had drunk! You're disgusted at this! Well, you might as well know: mud will not stick to Gudi-Gudai-Zatrubinsky's white aristocratic family tree.

Every sort of thing was attributed to the General: a free and easy attitude to money, unpleasant situations with greedily amorous married ladies, naughty goings on with schoolgirls, an indecent anecdote about the Mordovian servant maid—yet they forgave him, for who is sinless; they all knew that he was a spendthrift and a philanderer; but they were no longer amazed at the General's words! Thrice the General had been ready to put our district to fire and sword, but he still spared us. Even the peasants knew the General! It was not in vain that a rumor had evidently been spread among the common people that the White General, Mihailo Dmitrich, had never died but was still living secretly in our district in the guise of the bandit Churkin. Only the railway workers talked a lot of balderdash to the effect that the secret police were aiding the very courageous activity of the retired General by building up one fantasy after another about him; that he was neither General Skobeleff nor the bandit Churkin, nor even Count Gudi-Gudai-Zatrubinsky, but simply—Matvey Chizhov, an agent of the Third Department.*

---

* The political police under the Tsars.

⚝ Guests ⚝

"There are agrarian disorders everywhere in the neighborhood: is everything all right with you?" General Chizhikov inquired, kissing the Baroness's plump hand and wafting the sweet perfume of tuberose with which he had sprinkled his whiskers shortly before in the troika. "We, Uka Siich and I, Baroness, have called on you on business," the charmer continued, pointing michievously with his red gentry cap at the troika; with dignity, in silence, a tall, dry gaunt man with a small gray beard rose up and stepped out of the troika, raising his modest cap above his gray hair that was cut in brackets. It was Yeropegin, the millionaire; and then the Baroness realized that the troika, the horses, the coachman, and the whole turnout—were not Chizhikov's (the General had no such possessions), but Yeropegin's.

God knows why, but the Baroness stared hard at the merchant and, God knows why, her stare reflected an involuntary question; involuntarily too her face showed a trace of fear and sadness; it was as though she thought spitefully, "How thin he's grown, how thin: he's got nothing left but sinews . . ." Yeropegin glanced shyly at her through his glasses, but his eyes remained absolutely expressionless and reflected only a sedate dignity; but he also conveyed the impression that this sedate dignity was always and everywhere aware of its strength. Yes, yes, yes, the desired moment had now arrived when, in a thrice, the

Baroness's white noble backbone was about to bend before his, Yeropegin's, persistence: "Bend, bend," he thought, "and bow down before me. If I wish, I'll drown you. If I wish, half of the Baronial property will remain with you."

But he showed no sign of these thoughts when he pressed his moribund lips to the old lady's plump hand: white as death, with a face white from powder and applications, her hair white from time, wearing a white fur talma, the Baroness reminded him of a ghost.

Suddenly a sobbing scale of sounds made itself heard: it was Katya at the grand piano in the house; the sounds darted about in a minuet in instants that pursued each other. Time became filled with sound; and it seemed as though there was nothing but sound; and the old lady's spent years seemed resurrected in these chords, golden streams, milky rivers, and a swarm of greedy, spoiled men given to caresses; and among them there was this revelling merchant; but a hussar's spurs had come in between him and her.

And here he stood again before her with his furtive thoughts: "The hour of my revenge is now come: because once you had excited my dreams when I, a young merchant, had fallen for your already aging beauty; and what did you do? You used to come from Paris and London to mock at and torment my youth."

These thoughts flashed through his mind, borne for an instant on the wings of sound; but he bowed to her once more; she was inviting him into the house with a gesture full of majesty.

The legendary General had already danced his way into the hall and, there, had contemptuously thrown—eh-eh— his worn crumpled cape in Yevseich's hands from under which the scent of tuberose-Loubain now filled the air; the General, now in an egg-yellow checkered morning coat, still wearing a glove of even more vivid egg-yellow on his left hand, proudly expanded his chest and stepped into the drawing room, where he at once began to look for a spittoon; this he finally found and spat into it. Thus, this splendid personage's first enterprise in this mansion was recorded.

Daryalsky advanced to meet the General.

"Acting State Councillor Chizhikov," the General introduced himself.

They exchanged a handshake.

"Ah-ah-ah, young man! And who are you, an es-ey,* an es-dek?"** the General inquired. "I suggest you solve the agrarian question—Tfu (he spat into the corner); we, who are suffering the red terror, we understand perfectly that the government should introduce a progressive taxation in order to survive in power, but just try and demonstrate to the agrarians that such a measure . . ." But catching sight of the Baroness entering the drawing room, the wellborn incognito became meek, desisted from his bloody-hued eloquence and, blinking at Daryalsky, purred under his nose: "Taga-ga . . . Taga-ga . . . I have for you some perfect Newfoundland puppies: they were trying my friend's dog in court and," the General exploded like a bomb, "those perfect Newfoundland puppies were born . . . ouai, ouai, yes, they were born in the circuit court . . ." (the General was giving vent to sounds of enthusiasm somewhere in between *ou* and *a*).

"Thank you, General," the old lady gritted her teeth coldly but politely, though her eyes seethed with vague suspicion and fear; politely she pointed to an armchair, which the General occupied forthwith, and then took to sipping a fizzy blackberry drink which, of long summer custom, Yevseich offered the guests even though at that moment it was pouring with rain and there was no heat.

Yeropegin, whom the Baroness had seemingly forgotten and whom she had not invited to sit down, remained stand-

---

* es-ey or S.R.: i.e. Social Revolutionary.
** es-dek or S.D.: i.e. Social Democrat.

ing in an awkward pose shifting his feet, and his dry tenacious fingers began to run nervously up and down the long stretch of his black jacket; finally, without waiting for her invitation, he moved an armchair toward himself and calmly sat down without word.

They were all silent. Somewhere a wave of sobbing sounds burst out: it sounded as if someone had rapidly run upstairs; it was like time had run over somebody's life; and the miller shuddered. Yeropegin's life was filled to the brim—he held the whole district in his fist; if he were to clench his fist hard, all the local gentry would crack up: such were the days of his life. And the nights? The nights soared away—and his icon-like head grayed with the nights . . . wines, fruit, all kinds of women's bodies—everything flew by just as sounds flew. But where were they all flying? He, Yeropegin, for all his brimful life, would also fly into his void, and his chorus girls, like this old lady, would lose their teeth and their faces would become all wrinkled.

So they sat and stared at each other—the old man staring at the old woman; they both seemed like the cremated corpses of their own lives; the old lady had already fallen into the dark; the old man now saw the realization of a dream of many years; but the souls of both were equally far removed from life.

"Time to begin," Yeropegin thought and silently handed the old lady a sealed envelope, exulting as her trembling hand feverishly tore open the package; the old lady, putting on her spectacles, and tapping with her cane, hobbled over to the writing desk. While the papers spilled out of the packets, Luka Silitch, plucking at his beard, coldly examined the china trifles which Katya's careful hands had arranged on a shelf; two Tanagra statuettes evidently attracted his attention; mentally he was calculating their price.

Meanwhile General Chizhikov, who could not keep his seat, had pressed Daryalsky into a corner at the opposite end of the room; puffing his lips, he drummed on the bulky trinket on the watchchain over his belly and continued his burst of speech:

"A strange, a very strange sect has appeared in our region, young man. . . . Doves have appeared, Doves," he said, authoritatively, raising his finger while his high-arched brows looked disdainfully comic. "The sect of Doves: the district police officer told me it was both mystical and revolutionary—Doves! Now what do you have to say about that, dear sir?"

"What sect is that?" Daryalsky asked a minute later, for his thoughts had been elsewhere; he was staring indifferently over the General's shoulder when Yevseich appeared in the doorway with a tray in his hands; but seeing that no one except the General had touched the fizzy blackberry water, Yevseich disappeared.

"Let me show you this, but it's a secret," the General said, pulling out a paper on which a cross had been printed. "Please read this proclamation . . ." and the General began reading:

" 'Brethren, the Word of the Scriptures has been fulfilled, and the day is nigh: the bestiality of Antichrist has put its seal upon God's earth; take up the Cross, Orthodox people, for the Day is nigh: take up your sword against the tribes of Beelzebub; the gentry are the first among them; with flaming fire pass over the Russian land; think and pray: the Holy Ghost is being born: burn the manor houses of the sons of the Beast, for the earth is yours just as the Spirit is yours . . .'

"Shall I read on?" the General asked with a triumphant look, but Daryalsky was silent; he stared at the opposite end of the room where Yeropegin stood over the Baroness like a gray, shriveled corpse; at the writing desk the Baroness quavered, puffed, and her black eyes bulged in horror from their dark baggy sockets, while her fingers leafed through a heap of papers, bills and receipts; or, in a helpless way, she would cover the papers with her body, and her humped,

sideways turned back, as white as the rest of her, moved
restlessly above her bowed lace-foaming head; it looked as if
the old lady were about to press her bosom upon those
sorry remnants of once valuable, percentage-wise papers,
while the arrows of her, as yet sound but darkness-bathed
and somehow childish eyes, described arcs over the cup-
boards, rugs and curtains, but always avoiding Luka Silitch.

On the contrary, the old, grave-faced man, looking as
though he had stepped from an icon, sat quietly, staidly and
humbly before her smoothing his peculiar costume; with his
dry fingers he picked up and with his dry fingers he leafed
through a book; only the cruel glitter of his glasses froze
the old lady—they scorched her with their perfectly de-
liberate indifference; then he put down the book, gently
took hold of his cap, smoothed out the long fold of his
black coat and began to move his lips:

"H'm, yes, Baroness: according to the accounts, then,
you will pay me twenty-five thousand on the first of July,
and the remaining hundred-and-fifty due on the notes I
have acquired—in August. As for your millions, I regret
very much to say, you will have to part with them. . . . As
you can see, the shares of the Metelkinsky branch have
slumped—because of the war;* the shares of the Varaksinsky
mines, after the bank crash, are also not worth a bent kopeck
. . . Strikes and all that . . . I feel deeply on your behalf
and regret all this very much, but . . . Well, what's to be
done? I'll send my business manager to collect the twenty-
five thousand: I delayed doing this but, as you know, I must
have money: moreover, there's the crisis, the economic
crisis in our country. . . ."

He said all this quietly, barely audibly and then sat down
in the armchair quietly, staidly, humbly, modestly; but the
strong red morocco leather armchair creaked and squirmed
under the old lady; only the barely perceptible smile upon
Luka Silitch's puckered, dead, icon-like lips, and the quiver

---

* The Russo-Japanese War (1904–06).

of his beard, betrayed his obvious pleasure at the sight of
the Baroness Todrabe-Graaben who, gripping the arms of
her chair, now stood up; her emerald flashed, the knob of
her falling cane hit the floor with a crack; and out of the
corner an ugly shadow darted upon the wall.

"But you've gone mad, dear sir! I haven't got that amount
of money in cash . . ."

"Well, then, if you haven't got it in cash, that's bad, very
bad for you," Yeropegin continued in the same friendly
tone. "I need the twenty-five thousand at once, and as for
the remainder . . ."

Silence.

"Luka Silitch, spare me!" the old lady burst out.

Silence.

"Well then, on the first, I'll send . . ."

He did not look very majestic; but nevertheless he was
intoxicated with his own corpse-like dignity.

"So then?"

Silence.

He thought: "If she were to fall at my feet, I would
forgive her." But the old lady did not fall at his feet; and
the affectionate Luka Silitch remained merciless.

At the opposite end of the room General Chizhikov continued to trill away like a traditional nightingale:

"Yes, I have always maintained that crude sectarianism
was incompatible with the revolution; in general I stand
for protestantism. And what does the Orthodox Church
teach us? They say we drink the blood and eat the flesh of
God. But how can we eat what we love? And therefore
. . . there's Count Tolstoy . . . Ta-ga-ga . . . Ta-ga-ga,
the Doves, yes, the Doves!" and he spat into the spittoon.

"Here it is, the beginning of disintegration," Daryalsky
thought.

Daryalsky was answering his own question: the raging
chaos of yesterday had just subsided in his soul and a vic-
tory had been gained over the destructive elements and

emotions that had made him deviate from the straight path; the devils had quitted his soul, but now here they were swarming around him again and assuming awkward but entirely real images: in truth, had not that troika and the General himself sprung out of those nasty people who had enveloped the region? The troika had simply materialized out of the mist and someone's revengeful hand had thrown it at the manor house. God knows from where the troika had brought these people? Was it in order that secret disorder of lusts should once more surround him with its swarms?

As though in answer to his thought, there was a sound of steps on the terrace; Pyotr looked at the window; and there in the window now stood a curious creature in a gray felt hat, its small head, which looked as if it had been squashed from above, swaying upon a disproportionately long and gaunt body. "It only required this," Daryalsky had barely time to think when the strange creature, perceiving him, joyfully dashed up the terrace steps while a trail of water dripped from his raincoat upon the steps; the curious creature smiled; it turned out to be a young man with a small, owl-like nose and turned-up trousers; he stumbled over the steps and leapt up precisely on his mosquito feet; his feet came down again and a gray bundle rolled to one side: there was something extremely pitiful and comic about the whole appearance of the new arrival, and General Chizhikov, staring at him through his lorgnette, examined him with amazement; but overcoming all obstacles, of which there were not a few, the awkward young man, blushing pleasantly like a shy girl, enclosed Pyotr in his moist embrace with evident enthusiasm, whereupon the body of the awkward young man formed an obvious question mark and his legs were bent: but imagine the General's astonishment when the awkward creature squeaked in a high pitched tone:

"Highly respected Pyotr Petrovitch . . . I, that is, not I . . . and for the very simple reason that . . . I've come, so to speak, to admire your—above expectation—happy and pleasant situation, called forth by the unbending desire to conclude a legal marriage with an angel-like creature . . ."

Pyotr, freeing himself from the embrace, and suppressing his sadness, tried to change the tactless current of the awkward creature's thoughts:

"Welcome to the house, Semeon, I'm glad to see you . . . Where have you come from and where are you going?"

"Tramping it on foot to Dondiukov, where I have a woman relative . . . and, on the contrary: on the way I thought I'd visit a school fellow, a friend and poet, and, at the same time, congratulate this friend upon the highly triumphant fact of his finding a life's companion" . . . and in such comfortable surroundings! Upon this the young man, thrusting his shoulder forward and twirling his mustaches, suddenly took courage and flew toward the Baroness to make his proper bows. But Daryalsky deflected him again.

The Baroness and Yeropegin, engrossed in each other, apparently paid no attention to the newcomer; but General Chizhikov, sniffing a scandal, was just aflame with interest: abruptly he desired to be introduced and held out two of his fingers to the awkward creature.

"Chukholka, Semeon Andronovich, a student of the Imperial University of Kazan."

"All right, all right," General Chizhikov disdainfully squeezed through his teeth, "it is proper for youth to amuse itself. Are you an ess-dek?" he asked next, looking questioningly at Chukholka.

"Not at all," the awkward creature squealed. "Not at all—neither an ess-er, nor an ess-dek, but a mystical anarchist, and for the very simple reason that . . ."

﹡﹢﹦ A Dream in Daylight ﹡﹢﹦

Daryalsky and Chukholka were standing in the wing; a festive mosquito was beating against the windowpane. Chukholka would glance at Pyotr: Pyotr was a champion standing there and flexing his muscles.

"Well, how is it, brother Semeon?"

"So-so, or rather not at all: and, on the contrary, and yet: I'm reading Du-Prêle, writing a thesis about the acids of the Benzol type."

"Aha!"

"Material needs overcome me, so to speak, while inconstant fate impedes the proper development of my mental shell . . ."

"Well, give up theosophy . . . Do you need money?"

"Yes, that is—no, no," Chukholka replied in a flurry. "I am so to speak here about nothing in particular—just to call on an old school friend and poet in a place of poetic inspiration—I mean!—in a place of his amorous adventures. No, that isn't it at all!" Chukholka exclaimed in confusion as he stumbled against the table. "What I mean is in a herbiverous place and in a circle of observations on the Russian people in the moment, so to speak, of the concentration of its spiritual energies in the battle for right, and for the very simple reason that—"

"Oho!" Daryalsky broke his silence in order to arrest in time this disconnected flow which threatened at any minute to become a veritable ocean of words where the names of world famous inventors were liable to get mixed up with the help of Maimonides, but the conclusion arrived at was mingled with jurisprudence, revolution with chemistry; to complete the disorder, chemistry passed into the kabbalah: Lavoisier, Mendeleyev and Krooks were explained with the help of Maimonides, but the conclusion arrived at was always the same, namely, that the Russian people would win its rights: these rights were interpreted by Chukholka in so modernist a fashion that, from separate parts of his speech, one might easily conclude that one had to do with a decadent such as even Mallarmé had never seen; but, as a matter of fact, Chukholka was a student of chemistry, a chemist who, it is true, dabbled in occultism which had irreparably undermined his weak nerves; and so the student from Kazan had become a conduit for all sorts of astral impurities; and why was it that, though he was a good and honest fellow, far from stupid and hard working, Chukholka allowed all sorts of muck to pass through him and then out of him upon any one he talked to? In his presence every kind of confusion sprang up just like Pharaoh's snakes came to life out of a pinch of powder; his low origins, his squeaky voice, his squashed head and his owl-like nose completed the picture; Chukholka was a nuisance, Chukholka was always thrown out of any place where he had the misfortune to appear: everywhere his arrival started a vibration of disorder.

When Daryalsky led the student into his quarters, he could not help puckering his brows: he had wished to spend that day alone with Katya; did he not have to explain to her finally his disappearance of yesterday? But Daryalsky puckered his brows even more because Chukholka's appearance on his horizon had always proved to be an ill omen—a joke played on him by unseen enemies: Chukholka had once kept Daryalsky standing in a draught and made him catch cold; another time, he had caused Daryalsky to mix up all his dates; a third time, he had turned up on the day of his mother's death; since then Chukholka had vanished; but here he was again. Daryalsky experienced a very peculiar sensation in the stomach, a nauseous and depressing feeling in the pit of his belly after talking with the student from Kazan. "The devil take him," Daryalsky thought, "Chukholka is back again: I'll be spattered again with every kind of muck."

Poor Chukholka was already unpacking his bundle in Daryalsky's room, and Daryalsky was amazed at the order in which everything was packed and tied up; packets of white paper tied with pink ribbon, several new books in new bindings; toothbrushes, combs, brushes—all immaculately clean; there was only one change of linen, two satin shirts and one belt; but to compensate for this, there was a flask of eau-de-cologne, face powder, a razor and even a formidable hairdresser's sharpening stone always of mysterious origin; but what astonished Daryalsky more than anything else was a fresh straw bag from which a large Spanish onion was sticking.

"And what is that you've got?"

"Oh, that's for my mother; living as she does in a village and lacking the superfluities of material life—yes: mother is deprived of comforts, and so I am taking her a present of this Spanish onion and for the very simple reason that . . . Now if that aristocratic old lady were fond of onions, I would onion her—I mean, on the contrary: I would present her with this modest gift."

"Don't be silly . . ."

Daryalsky walked out of his wing: Chukholka positively irritated him; he could not stay a minute longer face to face with this delirium.

The rain had stopped: for a moment the sun shone out again: Gugolevo rose up before him, unfolded, and enclosed him in its flowering embraces—and so it stared at him, Gugolevo: with its clear-streamed lake it stared at him, Gugolevo; and still the singing lake lulled him with its blue silver; and still the running lake reached out toward the shore, reached out with its current toward the shore and could not reach it; and it whispered to the reed grass and there in the lake was Gugolevo; the whole of it seemed to rise up out of the trees, and, then, with a smile stared at the water—and then ran away into the water; and now it was already in the water—there, there.

Just look—transformed, lightly in the depths, the dancing manor house now lightly flowed; and like white snakes, the columns swayed strangely, penetrating the translucence of the waters and beneath them—there: a strangely inverted cupola and strangely there swayed the bright spire spearing the depths and there, on the top of the spire, stood a bird upside down with its feet up; how upside down was now the whole world for him! And he gazed at the bird: it pulled its feet away and sank into the depths.

"Where have you gone from me, my depths?"

And over there, over yonder! O Lord—the whole ringing, splashing watery speed: such now was Daryalsky's soul.

"There, my soul, it is deep: there—it is chill, very chill: and everything there is unknown to me. Can it be it is with me no longer? Can it be that my soul, like that bird that took off from the dancing spires in the depths, has flown away? Can it be that my soul took off from my body and has flown? There, falling into the water, the clouds flow— the underwater is immeasurable—but here is the water's surface; why then has this surface shown me its depths, like my years that flowed on the surface so my years flowed not here but there in mirrored reflection. . . . Listen to the lapping of the streams: gaze into the brightly rippling reflection, more beautiful than life: the streams call, call me yonder, and there, there, the martins weave, circle and cut the underwater air with their wings; and whither now, my soul? It flies to the call; how would it not fly when the abyss calls?

"Aha! Where indeed has my soul gone?" Daryalsky asked himself. A sweet languor and lightness poured through his whole body in tender song and far call of the soul.

And Daryalsky realized that his soul had been lost long ago, that it was not in Gugolevo just as there was no Gugolevo in the depths of the shimmering waters; down there a house, flowers and birds; but if you were to plunge in, you would get stuck in the slime, a black leech would cling to you and suck at your chest. Where then was his soul if it were no longer in his corruptible body? Just like an eagle swooping down on a bird, gripping it tightly in its talons, and circling with it in the sky where there is nothing but currents of air, and in that sky, in the currents of air, a terrible battle takes place and the feathers fly and blood is spattered, so already a long time ago someone had attacked his soul, in currents of air, and the days flew, and the lightnings of his thoughts instilled by someone—someone had attacked his soul in that fatal instant when it, his soul, was taking its flight far from his terrestrial image; for a long time already his terrestrial image had stared around with alarm, glancing at people, in empty corners, at flowers, at bushes—but what could he notice in the bushes except the chirping of the birds? The battle went on: so a mother who had lost her youngling with her arms raised in the air—and already there is no one in the air: neither eagle, nor child; and the eagle is far, far away, and the child is lost to her forever.

So it was with him: Gugolevo stared at him from the water; but tell me, was that Gugolevo? A slight ripple ran over the water but there was nothing there: only white bubbles as though someone had walked over the water on glass beads, on the ancient whispering of the sedge, and maybe somebody else: over there his hand stretches mightily out of the water, an ancient hand.

Daryalsky awoke with a heavy head, trying hard to remember what he had seen in sleep; but he could remember nothing. Gugolevo once more appeared before him, unfolded, and enclosed him in its flowering embrace: with its bright-streaming lake it stared at him now, Gugolevo. And some sweet song rose in his soul. Out of the reeds a rosy childlike face quietly bent over him, and the child smiles, bends over, and raises a pink flower in its hand. Ah, from behind his back a rosebay fell on the surface of the lake. Pyotr turned round.

Katya stood before him: she bent her pale face wreathed in rosebay over him; she was looking sideways at him as though she had discovered him, Pyotr, quite by chance here at the edge of the water; and she did not say a word.

The Everlasting

"Poor Katya, my poor bride! Your Pyotr is not worthy of you; you must realize this and consider what is in store for you."

But Katya did not hear him. Och, how magnificent he looked, what a bronzed chest he had, as though purple were trembling in a cold wind, and how the paws of nettle were beating on his chest; och, what mustaches he had, what a cap of hair, as though hot ash were curling from that head of his, where his eyes, now sparkling with a green fire, were coals burning the soul to cinders!

"Poor Katya, what husband will you now take unto yourself, and will you barter your maiden's life for pleasure or joy? Heavily my hand will fall on your woman's lot . . ."

Och, what a noise of trees, what swishing of Katya's blue skirt, how dishevelled her hair; och, what whistling, what stirring of grass all around; the branches began to sway, the twigs, the tops of the trees and the brightly pink rosebays moved like the youthful upsurge of Katya's soul: a song was being sung and a prophecy was beginning and everywhere there was noise. And there it was, the tender color of her young soul; and around the wind in the distance bagpipes whistled and wooden cymbals shattered, while the century-old oak tree on the mound stretched forth its arms to the forest people.

That was the color of her youthful soul; oh, how she was stretching out toward him, all of her—to entwine him in her arms and to fall asleep on his chest, but the nettles beat against that chest; let the nettles burn her cheeks; why then, let him break her life.

And she placed her gentle head on his burning chest: and her curls mingled with his—the curls, his and hers, combined into one wind-spun smoke—smoke such as is given off by red flame: what a bonfire they had lit in that place. Greedily their greedy lips opened; hands of steel, molding a slender body, stretched out impulsively, a red hot lava of breathing poured into her breast; already her lips met with lips in a long, lingering voluptuous breath; her blue dress, like her blue sky, was against the red sunset of his clothes: and above this sunset of two lives now mingled, the airy ash, the cloud of expostulations, the pink bunches of rose- bay danced all around them.

"Pyotr, enough, be quiet!" Katya, the bride, tried to free herself. "Pyotr, we might be seen . . ."

But Pyotr was lost to the world; he looked into her half- closed eyes, and now he drank those eyes with his volup- tuous lips, and his lips tickled her dark eyelashes; he would throw his head back and with his eyes drink hers—not with his eyes: he'd drink the surge of his soul, now descending to him as a dove: with its wings the dove beat in his empty, empty chest: tak-tuk-tuk.

"Pyotr, enough. How your heart is beating!"

The dove came flying; fluttered its wings, and pressed with one wing against the throat, and Katya's tears, like chilled transparent grains out of the depths of her soul— those the dove will now peck its full: greedy dove; it will peck its full and empty another's soul; and then it will beat its way out from that soul and fly off into the heavens. For the present, then, let the blue elongated eyes melt with those other eyes, and a hand twist hands of steel; to intoxi- cated eyes intoxicated eyes are revealed; souls meet and fly—where?

"Pyotr, stop. Your heart's beating too fast!"

Feeling ashamed, she moved away from him; the sun

looked out and struck her face: there were peacock feathers in her eyes and a network of bright sunlit hares ran over her: but the sun hid itself.

"Listen, Pyotr," the silly girl blushed as she said it, "is it true that men . . . that a man," and she blushed a deep, very deep red, blushed so deeply that she covered her face, "is it true, that men make love to strange women . . . just so: well, when they are not in love!"

"It's true, my beauty; there are such men!"

"And that they kiss them as you kissed me just now?" And as she asked this, Katya thought how prickly were men's cheeks; her face was aflame from the touch of those prickly cheeks.

"Do you love me, Pyotr?"

"How could I not love you, my beauty?"

"Then I'm the first one in your life?"

"Yes!" Pyotr almost said, but stopped in time, while Katya looked up at him timidly, pressing her hands against his chest and half-opening now her raspberry mouth . . . "Yes!" he almost said, but then he remembered his madness of the day before and stopped: he remembered that unique woman he had never met and whom he had not discovered in Katya. He loved Katya, but Katya was not that dawn: nor was it possible to meet that dawn in the shape of a woman.

"Well, tell me?" Katya persisted, her eyes glued to his, and she involuntarily broke the bright pink plume of a flower; but he, he frowned and his shaggy brows hung over his eyes, and the green coals of his eyes darted lightnings on the meadow before her; it was possible to meet her, but the earth would distort her image; of a sudden before him he saw the image of that woman of yesterday: she, perhaps, was his dawn; thus wrapt in a subterranean flame, he stood, his arms crossed, and spoke:

"Listen to me, my gentle Katya! If you will not accept me the way I was born, I shall leave you and go far away, and separated from you I shall fall very low because my passionate blood is all fire; and that blood poisons me. Katya, my bride, whom are you following? If you only knew!"

"I know, I know!" a voice moaned near him. Katya had understood everything: yes, he was like the rest of them; and, like the rest of them, he had had a shameful liaison with a woman before her; oh, how he stood there, as though glowing all red in tender colors, that apostle of hers so disturbing to her peace; and out of him something of a beast peered at her. And all around them a riot of branches: clumps of trees, of beeches, oaks and elms, seethed inter- mittently; and in the distance a ceaseless commotion saying "forgive" to the past. It was as though the red apostles were preaching about what did not exist, but would soon come to pass; while in the neighborhood the trees grew still in expectation of the unsung song that was winging its way toward them: the song of her soul was being sung and the terrible sermon had begun so as to carry the surge of Katya's soul further and further—to villages, huts and the trails of wild beasts; and the beasts responded; perhaps, somewhere out there on an animal trail a wild dog crawled out flattening its ears and staring up at the sky to answer the surge; and, perhaps, that dog had human eyes; and perhaps it, the dog, now stared with its human eyes at some passerby; and the passerby made a sign of the cross and whipped on his frightened nag faster through the mud while a werewolf pursued him through the daylight; and what was so terrible about that if her own Pyotr had turned out to be a werewolf!

Silently Pyotr stood and stared at her with burning coals: but Katya regained her balance: in a twinkling of an eye she had lived through his tempestuous life; with her inner eye she foresaw his fall; and she also foresaw the punishment hanging over him: it seemed to her that his head radiated an invisible, brain-consuming flame; but she did not realize that this hellish flame—was his tomorrow. Katya lived through everything; and forgave everything.

"I accept you as you are . . ."

He dropped on his knees on the damp grass among the nettles and she kissed him sorrowfully on his flaming forehead.

He rose from the ground, girded by the power of her love for future battle.

·ᴥ· The Disorderly Ones ᴥ·

Palashka, the lady's washerwoman, was washing linen in the pond; she was soft, white, buxom and pink-cheeked: little yellow freckles flowered on her cheeks, and her white plump legs were dipped half in water up to her white knees; and her hair was dishevelled. . . .

When the sun glanced at her, its beams hopped about on her like sunlit hares: they also hopped about her bare arms and her bare legs, and over her pink skirt; and through the slender branches she was all covered in sunbeams and flowers—she· was a delight to behold! Thus General Chizhikov began running circles round her till Palashka thought to herself with a smile, "Just look at him, the old dog!"

General Chizhikov could control himself no longer: from behind the branches and the flowers, he attacked her: "Gozy, Gozy, kiss me!" and making antlers of his hands, Count Gudi-Gudai-Zatrubinsky tickled Palashka's breasts and then thrust his hands inside her shirt; they panted and struggled until Palashka tore herself free and, counter-attacking, gave him a swipe on the face with the wet linen: "I'll complain to my lady if you go on annoying me!"

But General Chizhikov, wiping his face with a handkerchief, only blew her a kiss and said: "You're so deliciously soft . . . don't you want a little *baiser?*"

Then the General came across Chukholka, who had become tired of sitting inside the wing; and observing a

Spanish onion sticking out of his pocket, the General immediately forgot the unpleasant incident.

"What's that? An onion, a Spanish onion? What a treat! But maybe it's a bomb? Give me that onion!" And he snatched the onion out of the pocket of the Kazan student.

"Lavoisier, the great chemist, was doing an experiment," Chukholka said, "when the retort exploded and a piece of the eye entered the glass or, rather, the other way around: a piece of glass entered his eye," Chukholka said trying to be witty.

The General took fright, hurriedly put the onion back in Chukholka's pocket and beat a hasty retreat.

"*Suspacious,* very *suspacious,*" he muttered to himself and pulled out his notebook.

Within two hours the guests had departed.

"Young lady, if you should come to Likhov, our house is at your disposal. That will be better than staying in a hotel," Luka Silitch said to Katya when bidding her good-bye and staring lustfully at her tempting face which looked more beautiful than ever.

The coachman waved his lemon-colored sleeves: the bells sounded and the red gentry cap could still be seen bobbing for a time through the trees.

❧ A Scandal ❧

"Time for supper: why, it's already nine o'clock!" Yevseich decided and left his room: the sharp sound of the noisy gong deafened all around; crackling, the old lady appeared and blacker than a storm-cloud she sat down at the table.

She had locked herself in as soon as the guests had departed: but she did not weep; a parching grief choked her and the old lady took out her dissatisfaction on everything around her. Where were they all? What sort of order was this? Ever since this young priestling had settled in there had been all these delays, whisperings in corners, amorous goings on in the bushes.

She was poor now; they would drive her out of the house. How would she be able to pay her debts now? The time of love, youth had passed; everything, everything, was now returning to primordial chaos; the trees outside the window were swaying wildly, and primordial chaos sounded in their pawlike branches: there, outside the window, bad weather was crawling away; a dark, nostalgic, whiteheaded cloud was crawling away toward Likhov; its shining cupolas, spreading their cloaks on high, sank over the forest. The old lady stooped over her lap dog, cooed plaintively: "Mimochka, my little dog, you're mine, you're my only one, my stupid little dog . . ."

Suddenly, an absurd, almost terrifyingly ugly face rose up before the old lady, and a little nose like an owl's swayed above her, it seemed to her a pair of nasty, sugary chinks of eyes winked over her, while a long hand with a Spanish onion in it was thrust right before her nose; at that instant the little white lap dog flew out fiercely from under her skirt and immediately flew back there again, when Chukholka's thin leg apologetically touched the lap dog's white fluffy tail.

"Ah, *pardon, merci*—I'm sorry: I have insulted a respectable, an immortal, so to speak, monad in the age of a dog, that is—no: in the shape of a dog, and for the very simple reason that . . . the reincarnation of earthly substances in their rotary rotation . . ."

"And who are you?" the old lady demanded with boiling indignation, rising from her armchair and gripping her cane.

"I . . . I . . . I . . ." the absurd creature stammered in confusion, "I'm Chukholka."

"What's that?"

"Forgive me, not having been introduced, I represent the image of the best friend and schoolmate of the man of your heart—on the contrary: the man of your daughter's heart . . . I've been strolling here in the salubrious air . . ."

"But where are you from? How did you get here?" the old lady persisted, advancing in a rage.

"I'm . . . from Kazan," Chukholka gasped, retreating and appealingly holding out the onion to her.

"Well then, get out and go back to your Kazan!" she shouted, pointing to the door with a commanding gesture.

But just at the moment Daryalsky and Katya appeared in the doorway; Katya was the first to realize the danger threatening Chukholka; she dashed forward; but Daryalsky, who had grown pale, grabbed her by the arm and threw her back; everything in him boiled with rage at the insult heaped upon a human being; but controlling himself, he crossed his arms and, breathing heavily, silently observed the revolting scene.

And indeed enough was happening to make one mad:

completely bewildered, Chukholka was swaying idly in front of the frenzied Baroness who had finally found an outlet not only for the anxiety that had choked her all day, but also for the storm which Yeropegin's words had raised in her; but the more the old lady pressed him, the more helplessly did Chukholka smile: the whole coordination of his nerve centers had been upset, with the result that the automatic movements of his hands now dominated over the movements of his conscious "ego"; now many egos rushed like a whirlwind through his mind and when he attempted to speak it seemed as if a dozen plaintive imps, all interrupting each other, were shouting their nonsense out of him.

"But listen, nevertheless . . . profiting by your hospitality to make a donation for the table of this onion . . ."

"Get out!" the old lady clucked rather than shouted.

"What? Me?" Chukholka asked, only now realizing the horror of his position and blushing a deep red. "What? Me?" he repeated. "An honorable man? I'll . . . I'll . . . Why, I'll blow you up!" he ended weakly and then burst into tears.

Quick as an arrow shot from a bow, Daryalsky sped forward: he could not bear the sight of Chukholka's tears; it was as though a swarm of little devils which had been sitting in the insulted envelope, as in Pandora's box, now burst out and whirling invisibly entered his chest; and forgetting himself in his rage, he pushed aside the old lady who was attacking the student, gripped her hands, tore her cane away and threw it down.

"Take your words back or I'll . . . I'll . . ." he whispered breathlessly.

Everything was suddenly still: the branches tossed against the windowpanes in the noisy air outside: there the wind raced through the tops of the trees; the spaces grumbled ceaselessly and rumbled; it was as though grain was being poured now in a thick stream, now in a thin stream; grain was being poured here and there: now over there, now here. But it was the wind.

The old lady glanced at Daryalsky with her large and now childish eyes; saliva flowed from her drooping lips . . .

"You pushed me, me?!!"

Mechanically, even quietly, as though performing something inevitable, her raised hand unclenched on Pyotr's cheek: the slap cracked ringingly in the air; five white fingers slowly took fire on Pyotr's white skin: the devils, which had torn apart Chukholka's consciousness and which had penetrated the bodies of these people disarmed by rage, now raised such a whirl that it seemed the very earth between them had yawned and they had all toppled into the gaping void.

In the deep silence the clock sounded hoarsely and donged: half-past-nine.

This chime revived their memory of what had happened: the abyss closed, the devils disappeared, and the people stood facing each other, all equally horrified by what had occurred: Katya screamed; in a flash Daryalsky realized he had been insulted; there existed a mathematics of behavior; and just as twice two equals four so now he must act as the injured party even though he understood that the poor old lady who, now sobbing, had slumped into an armchair in a state of indescribable horror and who held out her impotent hand toward Katya, had only struck him out of helplessness.

"Katenka, my child, my niece, don't leave me now, an old woman . . . Aaa-aa-aa!" she wept like three streams.

In a whirl Daryalsky realized also that now, this very minute, he would regard himself as the injured party and would leave Gugolevo forever and be obliged to spend the night in Tzelebeyevo; and while he was thinking in this way, he was already offended and realized that his presence here was impossible: turning, he quickly stamped out of the door on his heels; a revengeful enemy of his had carried out his execution: destiny sent him back to those places whence only yesterday he had escaped. . . .

"My child, my poor one," the old lady, softened now,

continued to sob. "We're poor creatures . . . We'll be turned out into the streets soon. . . ."

The bright flare of the receding day beat through the window upon those swollen cheeks; and the sun itself, like a glittering phoenix hiding in among the fine network of the tossing branches, spread out its gold tail by way of farewell, blessing the coming of reposeful slumber.

◦◦◦ The Return ◦◦◦

He turned around, he was now bidding farewell to this cherished spot; nevermore would he set foot here again; out there, out of the sunset, Gugolevo showed itself; a short while ago it had been to the right and left of him; it had spread here and there: there the water gleamed, there the huts stood spread out, masses were said, dogs barked and smoke curled from chimneys; and it was all gathered there now in one place; it had all gathered there, sunk in the green foliage of oak trees; no place was more charming!

That is where it was—Gugolevo.

It was singing now in song that came nearer: some Gugolevo folk, it must be, were passing by; the stately ancient manor, all glowing in the sunset, gleaming like a knight in armor, gleaming and glittering on the hillock amid a stormy sea of green leaves; out of these waves it raised up its sunset-pink columns high as the masts of a ship sailing away over the sea: above the columns a silvered cupola was swelling out like a sail: the manor was sailing away from Pyotr toward the horizon over a green sea of crowned oaks; and on the ship Princess Katya was sailing away out of his life.

Out of the irrevocable past the manor house windows in cascades of ruby fire amid the oak tree crowns floating past in the breeze beat straight in Daryalsky's eyes; and the green combs of the forest crashed down on Gugolevo: there a pine tree would start moving; and soon expend its energy, transmitting it to neighboring trees; and another tree would start moving, angrily seething upon Gugolevo; and the seething and singing would go its rounds; the ancient park would surge angrily, the oak tree crowns would toss here and there, rising furiously and furiously marching upon the sunset.

Motionless in the sunset and beautiful that manor-ship on the crowns of the oak trees; deeply immersed in its dream; its red eyes from afar have fixed upon Daryalsky's soul out of the tops of the breeze-blown trees: "Did I not shield your days, unfaithful one; did I not defend you with my breast as a shield; as a shield I stood between you and heaven . . ." That is what the old manor house said to Daryalsky as it receded from him; the golden spire above the manor disappeared among the foliage and the pale transparent sky.

Daryalsky's heart beat fast: turning toward Gugolevo, he cried out, "Forgive me . . ." And started running.

"Mad creature, why are you destroying a man who is so taken with you? Or don't you love me?

"Well, God be with you . . ." It was Chukholka coming to meet him after quickly tying up his bundle and setting off in pursuit; his exclamations could be heard now in the twilight:

"I am greatly grieved that this misfortune should have occurred through my fault; through no evil intention, but for a very simple cause, that . . . a Spanish onion should have stopped the wheel of your fortune . . ."

"Oh, leave me alone!" Daryalsky exclaimed. "Forgive me, Semeon, but just leave me alone . . . Goodbye!"

Chukholka, raising his hat, remained standing in the middle of the road, sighing and wiping off his perspiration with a handkerchief: he had nowhere to go now, nowhere at all; Kondyukov was about twenty-five miles away.

He threw his bundle over his shoulder and set off in the

direction of Kondyukov: that was better than spending the night in the woods. . . .

A drunken band showed themselves among the bushes:

"Wh-y-y-y did y-o-o-u l-u-u-r-r-r-e me, wh-y-y-y did y-o-o-u f-f-o-o-r-r-c-e me to l-o-o-v-v-e y-o-o-u-u-u? It must b-e-e then y-o-o-u-u-u did not kn-n-o-o-o-w . . .

"H-o-o-o-w-w p-a-a-i-i-n-full to be-tr-a-a-y-y-y a l-o-o-v-v-e . . ."

Pyotr's red shirt swiftly crossed their path.

"Hey, gent! What's up with him?"

"Let him be, he's just a hanger-on," one of them spat out.

And the band all together bawled in Daryalsky's wake:

"No other g-i-r-r-l will ever l-o-o-v-v-e me . . . I shall dre-e-a-a-m of one g-i-r-r-l only . . .

"Believe me, d-a-a-r-r-ling mine, I'm in l-o-o-v-v-e with you forever."

The surrounding country tossed up the cloaks of trees in the wind, letting fall the folds of the cloaks from the trees; leaves, branches, dry twigs broke off now into the dark gloom of the East.

"There to the East, into the gloom, without direction," Daryalsky muttered. "Katya, Katya, where shall I go from you now?"

Faintly in the distance the band could still be heard bawling:

"A car-r-r-i-a-a-g-e st-o-o-od by the church: there had been a magn-n-i-i-fi-c-e-n-nt wedding . . .

"All the gu-e-es-s-t-s were finely dre-e-s-s-ed . . . Their faces flo-w-w-e-r-e-d with joy . . ."

"A carriage by the church—not for me," Daryalsky tried to smile, but instead his heart beat achingly.

A heap of straw raised up by the wind from the road swept through the air in high festive hoops, then impotently fell back on the road, started to budge again and ran off somehow sideways.

The distant song could still be heard, but the words could no longer be distinguished. "A-a-a-a . . . a-u-li . . ." a single voice rose higher in the raw air: "the bri-d-e-groo-o-m was m-o-o-st un-ple-a-s-a-a-nt . . . a p-p-i-t-y the mai-d-en was l-o-o-st . . ." were the final words he heard before the song died away in the woods. . . .

It was already getting dark; there was a creak of wheels in the gloom; a voice suddenly shouted "Gee-up!"

"Where from?" Daryalsky absent-mindedly called into the wooded dark.

"Just from around here, from this here same place," a voice replied out of the dark.

"What's going on there?"

"We've got Stepa there . . ."

The wheels creaked again; Daryalsky marched on into the dark blue gloom.

✣ Appeasement ✣

Twilight was falling; and still she stood on the balcony and stared yonder, where only half an hour ago Pyotr's red shirt had been visible as he stood bidding farewell to his beloved past; and long after he had bid farewell to the past, she still stood there staring at the place where he had said farewell; and from that direction, out of the forest, Tzele-beyevo sounded to her in the voice of a plaintive song and in an accordion's moan: "The b-r-r-r-i-d-e was dres-s-s-ed in w-w-h-h-i-t-e: and a bouquet of roses was pinned on her . . . Through her tears she stared sadly at the cruci-fix . . ."

Katya wanted to cry; she remembered her dear one, and her grandma who now felt easier: grandma had just wept her full share on her bosom and had fallen asleep quietly and effortlessly like a child that had been hurt and then asked forgiveness; and Katya had forgiven her everything, forgetting the insult, both on her own behalf and Pyotr's. With their arms peacefully around each other, they sat now, sleepy grandma and gentle Katya; tomorrow both grandma and Katya would write to Pyotr's friend who was living in Tzelebeyevo: the quarrel would be smoothed over.

The pond spread before her; the sunset settled lightly on the damp paths; and the paths showed barely purple; and barely purple was the meadow of high grass; amid the moist gems of dew the white violets were in their last flower; deeply and passionately the little flowers had breathed upon everything around them with their splendid perfume; in the distance rose a hoarse and timid sound, and it seemed to waft something familiar that had been experienced in the happiest days of life: it was a husky woodcock; a white sea of mist poured slowly over the low-lying countryside.

Her Pyotr was now far away; but Katya would return to him; she would live her life, she would; and that life would be as free as she willed it; she and Pyotr would visit foreign lands beyond the sea—lands where malicious gossip would follow them but never catch up: neither malicious gossip, nor grandma's impotent grumbling; the day would come: a happy couple, they would fly out of the old nest to freedom; and that time was not far off. . . .

Katya sat in her room with large windows, listening to the gusts of the rebelling wind: "Somewhere hail must have fallen!"

Knock-knock-knock—someone at the door: who could it be? It was painful now, when night was staring at the windows, for maidens to open their maiden doors; and beyond the door were a corridor, passages, vaults and the attic itself.

Knock-knock-knock—someone at the door.

"Who's there? Is that you, Yevseich?"

"It's me, lady . . ."

"What do you want?"

The door opened: Yevseich's gray head peeped in, shaking with laughter, while Yevseich's shadow darted blackly over the whitewashed stove.

"Well, what is it?"

"He-he-he! that was funny . . ."

Yevseich was laughing, guffawing, snorting; he was satisfied now: the lady of the house was resting, but the old man did not feel like sleeping: he had come to entertain the child.

"He-he-he! Young lady, I've learned to make a new sort of shadow-pig on the stove," he announced. "Look, that's the way: bend your little finger like that and the middle finger like this . . . He-he-he!" Yevseich went on laughing while the dark shadow-pig danced on the wall. And Katya was glad.

"Well, enough, enough, old man: it's time to sleep."

Yevseich went away. Katya watched him depart: it was dark there in the corridors and frightening; and there, by the attic, was a rustling sound above the stair; the old man was still chuckling there, drenched in darkness.

And, och, what a clamor the trees were making!

At night the clouds gathered again; Tzelebeyevo had sunk in sleep; a narrow, ominous band of light still burned in the West.

In the priest's garden nowadays the guitar twanged all day long; then, later in the night, the sacristan's drunken voice cut through the village: "The seminary students stand in the middle of the tavern, calling out: 'Corn brandy, our Holy Mother! Instill in us compassion.' " And the voice died away.

When the black night howls wildly and the sky flashes every minute, falling to earth in stifling clods of cloud, and the marble lightning growls here among us as if it were on the ground without any rain, a horse will not snort peacefully in its stall—but a cock merely crows out at an unaccustomed hour and finds no response—it is stifling and terrifying in Tzelebeyevo. Only a light from an odd cottage will twinkle at you; and if you were to enter into its profuse light the surrounding darkness would grow darker yet; no, do not peep into the window of that villager who does not extinguish the light early that night: he must be strange and fearsome who fears not at that hour the lightning striking at the window.

Without shelter you will be in Tzelebeyevo; beneath the flashes of lightning you will find no night shelter for yourself and you may indeed be struck blind if the red wench Malanya should glance at you from a cloud, and for an instant you will behold the whole horizon red.

And, in the dark, maybe a rickety person will creep up behind you and throttle you with his withered arms, and you will be found next morning hanging from a bush; only blasphemers wander about on nights like these, bent on their thieving missions as they are now doing in the tavern where every sort of scum has gathered, God knows who and God knows where from, drinking vodka and shouting, and glancing at the windows now black, now red from lightning:

"Malanya, darling mine,
With bulging eyes!
You lived in the village
And served the sacristan.
With little experience,
You became a lady's maid,
And then you began to flirt,
And kicked up a dust . . ."

They are singing their heads off there, the lads: on such nights dry bushes crawl about the village and surround the village with their howling pack; the red wench Malanya goes flying through the air, and thunder follows in pursuit of her.

Who was the madman who wandered all night about the village, who put his arms around a bush and who, entering the tavern, drank for more than an hour or two with all that scum? A drunk—who afterwards sprawled in a ditch? Whose red shirt lay in the early morning by the steps of Kudeyarov's cottage? Whose shrill whistle had cut the night and who, in answer to that whistle, had opened the window and had stared for a long while into the dark?

CHAPTER FOUR

Temptation

Life As It Is Lived

"Let us," Matryona Semeonovna's man, the carpenter, would say, "let us," he would sometimes say, "tread the locality of the earth: let's take a walk . . ." So he would sometimes say on a holiday and rise creakingly from his favorite corner, turning upside down the cup with the design of roses on it, on which he would inevitably place a chewed morsel of broken sugar loaf already dotted with flies: he'd say that, and Matryona Semeonovna would pin on a shawl: off they'd go. . . . Thus they would stroll together on our street, spitting melon seeds.

It would be he, the carpenter, who'd throw on his home-spun coat over one shoulder on top of his red shirt: he it was, groaning, pulled on his creaking boots which had been drying on the stove: and with great dignity even he would assume an air of importance and start walking; Matryona would follow him wearing half-boots and a canary-colored bodice with an ornament (the gift of a rich relative). So they would stroll, man and wife! They'd crack open their melon seeds: worthy, most worthy people; as if they were not peasants, but rather middle class; should anyone pass them, immediately a cap was removed and a bow so quick as to make the hair leap:

"Good day, Mitry Mironich . . . A happy holiday to you, Matryona Semeonovna!" If the sacristan should pass, immediately: "To the carpenter Kudeyarov!" he'd bow.

All around were white huts, red huts, green huts, with

window frames oil-painted white, ornamented with fret-work and with a third attic window under the roof dazzling your eyes with the reflection of the sun; and all around wholesome sweet scents: at his feet the small lake rippled blue and cool, luring him with fresh air, while yellow streams of liquid mud flowed noisily into it down the slope, while a kingfisher with a fish in its claws paused in flight just above the surface of the lake, thrashing in one place with a sharp, snow-white wing! Or, from the blue sky itself, a tree seemed to suspend a red, withering leaf, from which emanated the sweet autumn twittering of a tomtit: thus, every autumn after the lapse of all the three holy Savior holidays,* this pair took their walk year after year: the carpenter and the carpentress; the pair would walk as far as the edge of the forest and then turn back: soaring high into the azure there stood the jagged combs of ten-derly roselit hue amid every sort of shimmering, and the birch trees already reddish in hue quivered excitedly in their rust and brocade, like a priest garmented to celebrate the first capital Feast Day; and a red squirrel's muzzle would be thrust out of a hazel grove; and amid this scene, if one glanced at him in profile, Mitry Mironich's face stood out like a countenance in a Suzdal icon.

Just look, look closely at the carpenter, at his face: nothing there, and yet there was something there, a certain dignity; but how explain it? An ignorant fellow, an object of the most trifling quality; yet it was manifest that though Matryona was plain, she was a queen; the effect she pro-duced was icon-like; and though they led a scruffy, peasant-like life, the carpenter was a little afraid of the carpentress, scraped and faltered a little in her presence—not because she had taken him strongly in hand, but rather because the carpenter had need of this woman for some reason; and she

---

* Three popular church holidays in August: first, Honey; second, Apple; third, Linen (August 1, 6, 16, Old Style).

it appeared had noticed his need of her: well, it goes without saying, the fact was obvious . . .

But if you were to hint, let us say, that this was the case,
it would have turned out a different story, my dear fellow:
something not quite like that: the carpentress had bound
her life to Kudeyarov's to the very last breath, and you
could never unbind them: where the carpenter ended and
where Matryona began no one among us could tell; they
washed their hands of it—yes: on days when they sent their
working carpenters home, they'd eat some onions and a
dish of bread steeped in *kvas*, and a few more things, lick
their spoons, wash the plates, and then stand side by side
and bow together before the icons; and then they would
bow to each other, uttering special phrases; Matryona
would say to him: "My Sovereign," and he to her: "My
Spiritual Bride!" just as if she were a *Countess* or a *Goose
Queen*, the way he said it: the elegance of it! Or they'd sit
down to table at sunset; a yellow sunbeam full of whirling
dust grains filtered through the window; the carpenter,
spectacles on nose, would sit by the window reading a book.

The carpenter would read for a while, put his book aside,
then place his hand on Matryona Semeonovna's breast and
from that hand, invisibly and visibly, prickling, tingling
currents would pour into her breast and from his fingers
threads shimmered paradise-warm and caressing through
her breast and mounted to her throat; and, after this, her
eyes grew even more enormous; she could not live without
the apposition of those hands.

So it was: the touch of hands rather than the union of
flesh bound them together; the carpenter poured his
strength into her and afterwards nourished himself on that
transference of energy as though on capital deposited in a
"bank"; and because of this, around Matryona the carpentress (though she was plain) there spread so much
sweet and pleasant excitement that it gripped the heart; and
because of that, when you entered the carpenter's cottage
and saw there every sort of rubbish: benches, plates, rags,

even that rubbish will hold your attention, and that's a fact; even the big stewing pot will transfix your soul and perhaps you will begin to imagine that the obscure icon-countenance was staring at you in no simple fashion from its golden halo and that, in no simple fashion, was a finger raised at you from behind the icon lamps; and neither did the samovar boil so simply, and you began to wonder why a bright "hare" of light ran capering over the red cockerels on the tablecloth on a holiday when your hosts were serving tea; nothing of the kind seemed to happen in other people's houses and, indeed, these particular hosts seemed so very different from the general run, and so were their surroundings.

And what were their surroundings? Everything seemed normal: as soon as you entered the yard, your feet would shuffle over straw with here and there liquid manure splashing under your feet, a horse snorted, and in a garbage dump in a corner a bristling hog was rooting while, as in every properly run farmyard, a familiar rustling and twittering came from the hayloft; and as you stepped into the hut, you most likely would bang your forehead against the doorjamb and only then, after such an entry, would you find yourself in a workroom full of worktables and benches; and here you would see two barefoot journeymen (the "shaggy" fellow and the "noseless" one) amid a pile of wooden blocks, boards, chisels, fret saws, saws and gouges; on the blocks you would see drills, files, planes, long planes of huge size, an unfolding yardstick, and a meter-stick among the shavings, the sawdust, the splinters and, here and there, a jar with lacquer, paint brushes, and a small bucket of dissolved carpenter's glue and near the blue light a paint rag; against the wall you would see window frames side by side, unplaited straw seats without legs and further you would see plaited straw seats without legs or with only two legs—legs of many different styles and brass rollers; the "shaggy" journeyman would not even glance at you, but the jovial "noseless" fellow would begin talking to you in a hoarse voice; and you would notice at once that he smells strongly of vodka; and in a corner, dominating the scene, you would behold the icon of Our Savior blessing the harvest. And stepping over the threshold of the carpenter's shop, you would send the sparks flying again as you hit the doorjamb with your forehead: then you would see a tidy, cleanswept room covered with wallpaper of a miserable color; you would be surprised to see curtains on the windows, Viennese chairs even, and other such comforts; here also you would find benches and an icon hung with many lamps; here too would be a Russian stove and a wooden frame bed with a patchwork quilt; and if you happen to visit here at night you would hear the disturbing rustle of cockroaches which threaten you with their whiskers from all the crannies, as well as from behind the chromolithographs hanging on the wall and depicting, respectively, the brocade-clad image of Our Lady "Light of Paradise" and also the austere image of Gregory "The Word of God," standing with a cross, in a mitre, behind a mosaic rim, in an omophorium, and an azure halo, his white beard glittering like snow; and among these chromolithographs, you would notice a photograph showing a group of seductive girls—the gift of a rich female relative, who had long kept a house of pleasure for the benefit of young men in the town of Ovchinnikov.

You would see all that. But where have you not seen similar things?

Yet all these things which you have seen so many times would astonish you afresh, and for a long time you would ponder on the carpenter's way of living; and you would sigh.

⁓⁓⁂ Ivan Stepanov and Stepan Ivanov ⁂⁓⁓

Well, what about it?

Oh, nothing: no more than usual. Daryalsky had been in Gugolevo—that's what: just look, good people: he's now in our village. A fine village ours: there's room here to spread oneself, to go on a spree and to drink up all you have: money, boots, and even your soul: if you don't drink, then don't: a free man has his choice; but if you do drink then drink properly; well, many did drink properly: first they drank away their money, then their clothes; they drank away their harness, their cottage, their wife; and finally they drank away their very soul; and once you drink away your soul, then go and lose yourself in all the four quarters of the world: without a soul, man is like a glass jar by the roadside; hit it with a stone—Crack! and nothing's left.

Well, and what about Daryalsky?

Oh, nothing: he got up drowsily in the hayloft; he was giddy from the stifling smell of hay and because a fly had flown into his mouth, and because a litter of pigs was loudly gobbling garbage below; his head was swimming and splitting from drink; the hayloft whirled like a wheel under his feet; and his swollen tongue moved drily in a mouth that felt bitten by acid. "I'd like a lemon," he moaned, and then fell asleep again.

"Where am I?" he thought, wakening again, but he must have uttered his thoughts aloud, and already the sun must have stood high because at that moment, from the hay above him, there peered down at him a swarthy face, that of Stepka, the shopkeeper's son. The swarthy face peered down at him, exuding the fumes of liquor:

"D'ye not remember, sir, we did a bit of drinking a while ago? I was telling you then to have no doubt about my supporting the popular cause and also about the verse writing I do, and other things about *women*."

"Well, and what about it?"

"About Matryona . . . I took you to that cottage of theirs. And you whistled at the window; and that wench put her head out and laughed . . . You were so drunk she got frightened . . . And then I brought you here to the hayloft . . . Don't you remember? Only not a word to my father: he's a scoundrel."

Daryalsky remembered nothing of all this: he remembered only the insult and promptly clapped his hand to his cheek; his Katya rose before him, plaintive and reproachful, but the dull pain in his head hindered any further remembrance; and why remember? Did not destiny itself bring him to Tzelebeyevo? So let come what may!

They went into the street; a passing cart creaked by slowly; in Tzelebeyevo the puddles were drying even more slowly in the sunlight; most slowly of all, an old Tzelebeyevo man who sat on a tree stump was mending his worn breechcloth; slowly too, an old rag furled and unfurled itself as it hung from the broken window of a sagging hut, the hole-filled roof of which revealed the beams and supports, and the owner of which had disappeared a year ago.

Daryalsky stared dully at Tzelebeyevo; his cheek was marked with a livid bruise, his shirt stained with God knows what, and his hair dishevelled. "I'd like a lemon!" he said.

"Well, sir, let's go to my father's shop," Stepan suggested, pulling him by the sleeve. "Looking like that, you'd be ashamed to go back; so come and sit down in our place."

But Daryalsky had no notion of returning to Gugolevo; he had already decided to go and stay with his friend

Schmidt, who every summer rented a cottage in Tzelebeyevo; only in his present drunken state he was reluctant
to face his friend; there was also, in truth, another circumstance, why . . . well, but let that pass!

"Stepa, my dear, d'you think I could get to know that
woman? Ah?"

"You mean that Matryona? Eh!" Stepan shook his head
sorrowfully.

"Tell me what you know about her."

"What I know? I know nothing, and people say nothing.
Did you mean you want to have some fun with her?" he
inquired, shaking his head severely. "She's no wench, she's a
fine woman. Vodka, that she drinks all right; sometimes it
does happen (she went out with me), especially when the
carpenter is away: she does go out—but only in a manner of
speaking, for appearance's sake; but not in the way you
think. No, no, she doesn't yield!"

"A-a-a-kh!" Stepan grunted after a long silence. "If you
wish, I'll take you to see her (the carpenter's away now).
. . . Want me to?"

Stepan Ivanov was a man of boisterous character. His
father, Ivan Stepanov, was on the contrary a strict man;
east and west of Tzelebeyevo he burnt, uprooted, and
soiled our locality: quite simply, he made money: Stepan
Ivanov spent that money on women and that sort of thing;
Ivan Stepanov from the left of the choir of the church
helped the sacristan to sing in the mass; but Stepan Ivanov
hiccupped loudly in church and was rude to the priest. The
icon painters, when they decorated the church, had represented Ivan Stepanov as an image in an omophorium; but
they had cleverly converted Stepan Ivanov to *"socialism"*:
Ivan Stepanov became a free-thinker. Some evenings Ivan
Stepanov would start clicking and clicking on his stained
abacus! In the evenings Stepan Ivanov, if he was not wench-
ing, would be drinking or composing verses. Ivan Stepanov
left the village only when he went to Likhov. Stepan Ivanov
had even been to Moscow: he returned from Moscow on

foot, minus cap, boots and watch, and with only a ragged book purchased in the flea market; the book turned out to be the poetic works of mister "Heini";* and Stepan Ivanov developed a fondness for "Heini."

"What a brain: he cuts his verse in Russian as well as in German!" he used to say as he entertained the sacristan with his own compositions; the sacristan took a special liking to Stepan Ivanov's verses "Petya's Sorrows." The verses began thus:

> "Autumn. The heart aches—
> And goes on aching:
> Reveals not itself,
> But oppresses me,
> I am always very poor,
> And always very sad!
> O to hide in any abyss,
> In the earth or under the sand."

Stepan Ivanov had another ballad, "Nenila"; he wrote well, turned out to be a poet; had his father not pulled his hair and pulled it unmercifully in his youth? It was true, Stepan Ivanov had indeed lost more than one tuft of his hair; but inside his head Stepan Ivanov did not change, foolishness took root in him and thrived; so his father threw up his hands in despair, kept his own counsel (the son bit back); only he concealed the profits.

Entering the shop, they bumped into Yevstigneyev Yakov the bloodsucker; he touched his cap perfunctorily and began to untether his horse; then he got into the droshky—yes, that's the sort he was. It was stuffy in the shop; at the counter, Ivan Stepanov in spectacles was clacking away on his abacus; snuggling against the counter, the sacristan and the constable were sipping tea from saucers and tricking each other in a game of soiled cards; on Daryalsky's entry, the sacristan bowed then snorted, while

---

* Heine, Heinrich (1797–1856). German poet of Jewish origin; wrote in German as well as in French.

the constable, without looking at anyone, said through his nose: "N-yes! Where were we? So you trumped my jack with hearts?"

"Hearts are trumps!" The sacristan snorted again for no apparent reason; but Daryalsky at once understood that just before they had been discussing the unfortunate slap on the face he had received; and that Yevstigneyev Yakov had already bruited it abroad: now that "slap" would go the rounds of the village; as bad luck had it, he had a bruise to show; he blushed red, very red: then he and Stepa sat down by the window, and Stepa, taking long gulps out of a bottle, dinned into his ear:

"Ah, it's boring and it's sad,
Alas, nowhere joy I find!
Wherever my glance roves,
All I see is spilt tears."

Daryalsky resolved to bear with everything as long as he could get Stepa to take him to her, the pock-marked woman: his head was splitting and it gnawed in the pit of his stomach; he kept thinking, "I'd like some lemon now."

"Hey, diamonds are trumps now!" a voice said from the side, and there was more snorting and whispers amid such exclamations as: "Serves him right . . . Don't rouse the people!" And Stepa went on firing away:

"I rolled on the floor,
Writhed on the sofa,
Wriggled on the stove,
Crawled on the bed . . ."

"Do trumps exist in themselves?" the sacristan asked profoundly with a sigh, stifling a yawn; Ivan Stepanov continued clicking on his abacus; a hornet buzzed at the window.

"In a wood 'mid the trees a hunter rests,
But his thoughts are roving far . . ."

Stepa burst out, emptying the bottle.

Three peasants entered: a corpulent peasant, a red-haired peasant, and a peasant with a hoarse voice (however, all three of them had hoarse voices); when the corpulent peasant uttered a sound that suggested "kha," the red-haired peasant, "tfu," and the one afflicted with hoarseness, "khrpliu," then the corpulent peasant grunted "nails"; the red-haired one grunted: "tobacco"; and the third peasant grunted, "some sugar!" "Nails, sugar, tobacco . . ." Ivan Stepanov clicked off on his abacus.

Picking up his nails, the corpulent peasant scratched himself: "The carpenter's in town," he said. "He's got mounds of business, he has!" the red-haired peasant scratched himself too as he picked up the tobacco; and the third, scratching himself, grunted: "Sectarians, that's what!" and grabbed his sack of granulated sugar.

"K-kha! Tfu! Khrpliu!" and the peasants left.

Daryalsky glanced at the window: a path had been trampled through the hemp. Drawing Stepa from the shop, he implored him: "Stepa, let's go to her now . . ." In his head, God knows what was going on: from the thumping, it swayed from side to side.

"We can't do it," Stepa assured him, now completely drunk. "What are you about? And what am I doing? Let's have a drink."

Well? Oh, nothing; they drank till evening; and what of Katya and Theocritus and Daryalsky's psychic depths? He could not think of Katya or Theocritus while his head was splitting, and in his head at least twenty willow-rattles rattled full blast.

When he finally emerged from the tavern, he sat down in the hemp field; the priest's wife happened to pass by:

"Why aren't you in Gugolevo, Pyotr Petrovich?" she asked, looking at him quizzically. "Do come and see us: my priest's in Likhov now . . . Ai, ai, ai, what's that on your cheek, a bruise? It will heal by the wedding day!" And off she went.

He did not remember the moon mounting in the sky; but

was it the moon? In his drunkenness he thought it was a slice of lemon.

The little angels, the fretwork of the window frames, and the roofs of the houses were already glittering silver; the puddles shimmered and shone, and a thick dew had spread over the hemp field; in the distance a woman in red walked to the pond, filled her buckets, and was already returning when a woman in blue passed her; she filled her buckets too, and was returning when a maiden in yellow with a yoke and skirts tucked up came to meet her; but in the darkness it was now impossible to recognize her; it was as though she had sunk in the pond; and only the bushes along the banks kept on swaying for a long time; and then from that direction came the sound of laughter and ringing kisses.

About What Was Being Said
and Who Rode on a Bicycle

The expulsion of my hero from Gugolevo was long gossiped about in Tzelebeyevo, though he himself seemed to have been swallowed up by the earth; but to tell the truth, his boggy boots left many a trace winding and weaving round the village; it was also true that Ignat had transported his belongings on a donkey from Gugolevo to Schmidt's cottage; Pyotr, however, did not show his nose in Mister Schmidt's place, but accommodated himself, instead, independently in the village of *Mare's Meadow*, where he had struck up some unsavory acquaintanceships and where every sort of riff-raff visited him. But in the village of Tzelebeyevo my hero no longer shone with good repute.

Day succeeded day, and every day new rumors were rife in the village; on an azure day in June a pillar of smoke was seen rising above a distant fir tree grove: it was a fire; that very day, in the vicinity of Dondiukov, they scoured the countryside; they arrested a student; they turned everything upside down in his lodgings, but all they found was a head of Spanish onion, a rarity in our district; they ate the onion and put the student on bread and water; also on that memorable day, Yevseich, pulling a cap over his eyes, set forth with a letter from the manor house toward our village; here he kept searching for someone, but departed empty-handed; he whispered a lot with Mister Schmidt: well, he was watched too: one villager, another, a third, besieged the shop; because, as you might expect, our shop

served as a "*clup*": who, even on a brief visit to Tzelebeyevo, ever failed to run over to the shop? In the shop,
where Stepa had just hidden a batch of fresh manifestoes
among the stock, Yevseich had sat for a while, chewed some
sausage and then taking off his cap, had croaked out that
back home the young lady was desperate and weeping;
within an hour everyone was repeating that in Gugolevo, it
seemed, the young lady was desperate and weeping; the
priest's wife at once decided that she had not been in Gugolevo for a very long time and that she must set out there
this instant: "Don't go, my dear," the priest reasoned
with her.

That's what happened on that azure day in June.

Then a cloudy day followed, thundery and patchy; on
that day Yevseich's cap again flitted between the huts; on
that day Stepa set off running to *Mare's Meadow* to sniff at
strange people, and they painted for him in bright colors
that "aliberation" came from the Holy Ghost, and that
there were certain people who, in secret, were expecting
the coming of that very Ghost on earth; through the same
person Stepa learned that the whole of the district was
making surmises about what had happened in Gugolevo,
and it was being said that the young lady had almost taken
the final step, but that, as yet, good people had counselled
her to desist.

The next day turned out to be like a whitehot oven: on
this day the priest's wife, all in rose, in a hat and earrings,
rushed off in rustling skirts to Gugolevo, but she was not, it
seems, received there; to annoy her the teacher had also
gone there later on the same day and she, it seems, had been
received; breathlessly on her return she related how she had
been treated to all sorts of sweetmeats, and how Katerina
Vassilievna had wept on her bosom as a result of entrusting
her fate to a monster of the human species; all that day the
priest spat in sorrow at the teacher and scratched himself:
only a denunciation could have kept her down—manifestly:
the teacher was a liar and a harmful subject.

Yet another day turned out to be like a whitehot oven:
on this particular day Tzelebeyevo gave one great gasp, so
much so that when the sky had already become starless,
groups of people still stood chattering: about the theft of
"prilliants" from the Baroness Graaben, but no official
action was being taken because it was a patent fact: that
Daryalsky was the thief; others swore that all the events had
a secret significance, namely: General Chizhikov had been
pleased to indulge in a joke; on this day, too, Yevseich
dragged himself about the village shaking his head and kept
seeking someone: but he found nothing for his pains.

By this time the green common had grown yellow with
chickweed; the cloves had shot up purple on the common,
the camomile had turned white and from the oat fields the
pinks had awakened to stare at the highway. . . .

That was all that was memorable about those days, yes.
But why have I said no word about the most important
event of all? Excuse me: it's my defective memory! It's
about the bicycle of course (the priest had a bicycle); not
this priest, but the one who—but you can already guess
whom we intend, and the bicycle, let me testify, was an
excellent one: a fine lad, the priest, to possess such a
machine: a bicycle toy—new, accurate, with good brakes,
excellent tires, and very successful handlebars! Hatless, the
priest leapt from under his awning, wearing only his cassock, and jumped on the bicycle: that's the man he was: a
pillar of dust on the highway: a small priest, like a mushroom! His spectacles slid to the tip of his nose (they were
gold spectacles), his black hair in disorder, his cross swinging to one side, his black beard covering the handlebars, and
his back arched . . . Well, well . . . Folk gaped at the
priest as he scorched past them along the road on the
bicycle gripping the handlebars, his cassock billowing like a
sail and displaying, to the amusement of passersby, the
pedalling motion of his boots with reddish leather uppers
and striped bottoms; but he merely blew the dust into their
gaping mouths as the milestones and villages simply flew

past him: the very highway budged and sprinted under his
bicycle as if it were a big white ribbon being rapidly un-
rolled at one end of the horizon and rolled up at the other.
In this way, the priest rode rapidly into Tzelebeyevo with
much din, disgrace, and pepper; and off he jumped at Father
Vukol's house and burst in to see him.

There is no need to stress that the priest in question was
Father Nicholas the scholar from Grachikha who, for some
reason, had woven his nest in Grachikha and sat in it for the
last two years without moving; he sat there and gave no
breath or sign of life. The inhabitants of Grachikha gave no
sign of life either, since they lived off the main highway;
and since they were small, unfamed and swarthy, God had
rewarded them with a small, swarthy priest: Father Nicholas was a flaming brunet. In the past there had been no news
or sign of him; but latterly a black rumor had spread about
him and a black spirit had emanated from his sermons;
whatever the case, one fine day he got up and streaked over
to us on his bicycle. It was a most awkward time for a priest
to visit a priest: Father Vukol was sitting at home in his
underwear catching flies, while the priest's wife, since her
maid had the day off, was tramping about barefoot in the
drawing room with her stained and spotted skirt tucked up
very high, making a loud noise with a slop pail and splashing
a dirty mop about. But Father Nicholas confronted her in
his creaking boots, orating without stop and scattering
cigarette ash, while his kindly eyes filled with tears and his
voice trembled despite the fact that the priest's wife, caught
unawares, had bolted from him in order to change her
dress; and the more calculating Father Vukol watched carefully lest the priest from Grachikha trip over a roll of
canvas and thus upset the basket containing the consump-
tive palm tree or the redwood card table on three legs, on
the knitted tablecloth on which reposed the missing fourth
leg; at the sight of Father Nicholas the priest's little children
began to howl. Father Vukol answered the agitation of the
priest from Grachikha with silence: Father Vukol was

calculating; looking at the swarthy priest, he thought: "Don't go to peasant meetings and don't mix with riff-raff— live as others do and then you will not have to lament being soon unfrocked or becoming a political prisoner."

Already the samovar, the lenten sugar and the honey had been served, and the flies, having already gorged themselves on honey, were now stuck to the rim of the plate, their legs wobbling and reminding one of sparkling golden stones, but Father Nicholas was still crying out loud and alarming himself without heeding any advice, and so he finally departed without easing his soul.

⚜ The Hollow Oak ⚜

Stepa kept our hero Daryalsky informed of all that was going on; and our hero Daryalsky was amazed at all the talk and the rumors, and the visit paid by the priest from Grachikha. If that hero's star had fallen in Gugolevo and Tzelebeyevo, yet it nevertheless unheroically lighted up his days in Mare's Meadow: people called on him and talked about "Liberation"; his tongue was already sore from such talk, but the local free-thinkers kept pushing and pressing upon him: the district doctor dropped in to see him as he was driving by: the old veteran of the days of Nicholas I with a wooden leg and four St. George's crosses hobbled over to see him: he was the "arorator of the forest meetings": there, in a forest glade, he stamped his wooden leg on a tree stump and incited his audience to rebel: the old soldier took snuff in the company of our hero (Daryalsky) and showed him his four St. George's crosses; and finally the student who lived in Likhov expressed the intention to come and shake his honest hand.

What more could be desired!

One day Stepa ran in and informed him that he was no longer a "socialist," but a bird of note, that he had made friends with the small family of the "doves," and that now he was a "dove" himself: rumors about the "doves" now crossed all of Daryalsky's paths and he greedily absorbed those rumors; but judge his surprise when Stepa whispered in his ear that the "doves" were very well informed about

him and that they were now inviting him to be present at
sunset at the old hollow oak tree and that after dark, on that
spot, a certain good man would meet him.

"Matryona must have had a hand in this, I can assure
you!" Stepa said with a wink; but as soon as some strangers
entered the hut, he tossed his head and bawled out a song
that was quite unfamiliar to their ears:

"Ay, you elephant, elephant, elephant,
Mister Trunk,
Tusk Tuskovitch,
Trumpet Trumpovitch,
Trembole-eel-ski . . ."

At the appointed hour Daryalsky was already waiting by
the old oak: his heart stood still; he fancied that his days and
nights had become confused; but there was no turning back
now; and he was already finding it delicious to live in a
feverish dream; it was better not to think of Katya: that
past had died; in the forest glade he stood thinking hard;
then he had a sudden impulse to tear off a branch of fir, to
tie its ends together and to crown his head with it; and that
is what he did; and crowned with this green prickly wreath,
a piece of which stuck out like a horn above his forehead
while another hung down over his back like a green feather,
he climbed into the hollow oak; he did not remember
whether he waited there a long while or not; and he did not
know what he was waiting for.

He looked—and there she was, Matryona Semeonovna,
coming out of the forest with an empty linden bark basket
and flowers; he realized then that she must have arranged
the meeting through Stepa; he pulled himself together and
leapt out of the hollow oak into the path in front of her; he
even startled her a little with his charcoal-smeared face
(shepherds must have lighted bonfires in the hollow).

"Oh, you frightened me!"

She was pock-marked and ungainly; with a large belly; he
could not understand what it was that drew him, attracted

him to her all the time; and she did not even blush, but just kept staring down at her feet; under her feet was a stump turned yellow with rotted leaves; and beneath the leaves were ants crawling.

"Are you picking mushrooms?" Daryalsky asked. "Did you call me?"

"Me? What do you mean?" she replied. "Why should I want to meet you?"

"Well then, you've been gathering flowers. Do you love flowers?" Daryalsky pursued.

"Ordinarily, I love them."

"Give me one of your flowers!"

"Here, take them, make your choice . . ."

And she looked him over, and how! From her eyes out of that pock-marked face blue seas began to move; the abyss yawned in her eyes and he was already swept away into a cold whirlpool of passion.

"May I walk along with you, Matryona Semeonovna?"

"Come along if you'd like to, it's common ground here."

She smiled to herself, her eyes shone and she was cross-eyed: while one eye was fixed on you, the other looked sideways; and so she strode quickly toward the village, kicking up her heels; and the much worn path was all of fine dust; she kicked up a lot of dust under his nose; and he kept thinking that she was cross-eyed and he liked the idea.

"I've long been looking for a chance to speak to you."

"Well, you've found it now . . ."

"I wanted to go up to you when I saw you yesterday."

"Why did you run away then?"

She laughed as though wishing to provoke him to laughter too; she wriggled her bosom and lowered her eyes, and for an instant her lips folded in a way that excited him greatly; and he thought that fold of her lips a very good sign; but she didn't seem to care; she kept trotting fast and there already was the village; and there coming out of the village and cutting across was Stepa with an accordion who pretended not to notice them and who was bawling at the top of his voice:

"Ay, you elephant, elephant, elephant,
Mister Trunk,
Trumpet Trumpovitch,
Trembovee-eel-ski . . ."

"And now go back to your oak," Matryona said, suddenly turning, "Or the neighbors may see us together and report it to your French girl, to Katerina Vassilievna, your painted little angel," she concluded, laughing insolently.

"So that's the kind you are!" Daryalsky exclaimed.

But Matryona only snorted, snorted into her apron at him from a distance; then by the village palisade she turned again to him:

"You can call on me if you like me."

And she climbed over the palisade . . .

The five-hundred-year-old, three-headed oak tree, composed only of a hollow, spread out its three crowns into the burning-out evening; for an hour already our hero had been sitting and pondering inside that oak; many thoughts had passed through his head; he was not even thinking about Matryona Semeonovna, she had become the sweet murmur of a song; his thoughts were light and elusive—about his destiny and the oak tree. . . .

It was still unknown what the oak tree could tell, of what past things its leaves were whispering now; perhaps of Ivan the Terrible's famous *druzhina**; perhaps some solitary *oprichnik*** had rested here on his way from Moscow into the wilds, had sat here beneath the oak tree in his gold-woven fur cap with tassels of brocade which kept brushing

---

* Bodyguard organized by the Tsar to fight feudal nobles in the 1570's.
** A member of that bodyguard.

against his shoulder, an *oprichnik* in red morocco leather
boots pressing against his mace while his white charger,
untethered, grazed peacefully by the oak tree, a charger
with a raspberry saddle-cloth under the saddle whence
stuck out a broom and a grinning dog's head gaping at the
road; and perhaps that *oprichnik* had gazed for a long time
at a velvet cloud floating by and had then leapt on his
charger—yes, everything is possible; and perhaps in that
hollow oak a runaway convict had sought refuge before
ending his days in a stone cell in Solovki; and a hundred
years more will pass and then a tribe of free people will visit
these roots projecting out of the ground; and that tribe of
free people will hear the moans of the convict, the sorrows
of the *oprichnik*, who had galloped off on his charger into
immeasurable time; and that tribe will sigh about the past.

Everything is possible, and in his thoughts he returned to
Matryona Semeonovna, and he suddenly realized he was no
longer in the hollow oak, but almost in Tzelebeyevo itself.
How had his feet of their own accord brought him there? It
was already dusk, and the villagers were still coming to the
pond with buckets: a peasant woman in red would come up,
turn toward the bushes, set down her buckets; just look
again: there she would be all in white; she'd be sitting at the
water's edge in only her shift; then her shift would fly up
over her head and there she'd be in the water; a woman in
blue would walk up to the pond, turn toward the bushes, set
down her buckets, and just look through the reeds; a long-
legged woman would be moving toward her, looking like a
man in the twilight; and way off a girl in yellow could be
seen carrying a yoke; and in the pond, of course, there
would be a lot of laughter and splashing going on; ducks
quacking and the hoof beats of village horses galloping off
into the night dust, barking, and the clear sounds of words
carried over the dew. And the gentle stars were already
shining and palely the quivering waters cradled them. . . .

Night flew down upon the forest; but in the bulging
hollow of the oak a red-hot handful of heat crackled, shim-

mering with the first powder of ash, while a blue bud of fire
leapt above it; there was a crevice in the hollow; and its red
glow stared out into the thickly wooded darkness; and out
of that glow a voice was raised and Abram's curly head,
thrust from outside into the crevice, was nodding to
Daryalsky, who was concealed in the hollow: Abram the
beggar was hugging a staff to his hairy chest; and from that
staff the wing of a leaden dove hung heavily massively over
the fire; the pale stars from on high peeped into the opening
of the hollow oak; and Abram was gazing up at them; only
the whites of his eyes lit up by the fire looked into Daryalsky's soul.

So that's who he was, the "good man" for whom Pyotr
had been waiting for more than an hour or two; he was a
beggar, that man—and now here he was staring squarely at
Pyotr; and from his beggarly chest a soul-disturbing speech
burst out; in a singsong voice he drawled and drawled these
tempting words:

"If only you knew how sweet are our chanted proverbs;
and the services—sweeter than those songs; with kisses,
with beautiful sermons; and the breasts of sugar our women
have; and whiter than snow the ritual dress we wear; and
we are always talking with each other about the adamantine
gates and the land of freedom.

"And they call us the '*khdoves*'; and we fly over the
whole region, friend; and in our midst there dwells a big
man; himself a great big, dark-blue *khdove;* and that's why
throughout Russia holy rebellion has spread, why under the
blue little skies free cossacks are up in arms.

"And that's why those cossacks are free, above all; like
darling birds they'll spread the Holy Ghost throughout
Russia; and as they'll spread grumbling over the land, so the
'*khdoves*' will fly out in their wake.

"So . . ."

"Enough!" Daryalsky said. "I'm yours."

"Behind that free, so to speak, cossackry, the very church
of the Holy Ghost is being built," Abram went on. "And if

you join us, brother, Matryona Semeonovna shall be yours; and for that reason, without us, brother, an evil end will befall you."

"Enough: I'm with you."

Pyotr sat in a corner of the hollow oak, his face on his knees, and it was as if he were dreaming a dream; and his wreath of fir, pushed to one side, like a stag's green horns, projected a horned shadow in the oak's hollow—a shadow running away high. The bursts of red light threw up high from the top of the hollow the falling dusk, and the shadow did a mad dance, like some winged denizen of hell trying to stifle a man girded all around by the fire.

"Abram, why did you trust me?"

"By your eyes!" Abram replied.

Ever more darkly the night settled on the forest; more than one seer no doubt lamented now: "May my eyes burst—what use are they?" And the blind assuredly mocked the seers.

⁓⁓⁂⁑ Events ⁂⁑⁓⁓

By day, and in the beams of sunset, and among flowers, Daryalsky wandered around our village, drawing attention to himself by the green branch of the fir wreath and by the crimson color of the shirt he wore; and Abram the beggar was always at his heels: and caught up with our hero.

By day, and in the beams of sunset, and among flowers, Matryona with nothing to do also wandered around our village; and Daryalsky, sunburned and unshaved, would come out to meet her from among the bushes: he would stand there in front of her shifting his feet and plucking at his mustaches glancing shyly at her at first: he spoke little, but for some reason kept following her and watching her all the time; she only had to come from behind the palisade, or stroll along the road, or go into the oak grove after mushrooms, there would be a crackle of dry branches behind or a branch would shake in the air even though there was no wind; Matryona was not in the least afraid; if she willed it, the gentleman would get out of her way quickly enough; but she already had a liking for the gentleman; a certain community of spirit was being born between them even though they exchanged few words; on one particular occasion she was almost frightened; she had gone into the forest and a branch behind had begun to sway of its own accord; well, she wanted to surprise him: she pretended to be looking for mushrooms and furtively approached the branch; she bent down, raising her skirts, thrust the bushes aside and at that instant someone ran away from her; it seemed she recognized the Peeping Tom—who was not her young gentleman at all: that Peeping Tom had a spade beard, wore high-top boots and a brass watch and a chain; and then Stepka also stepped out of the bushes and went up to her:

"Matryona Semeonovna! I assure you I'll strangle that parent of mine, I'll not allow you to be offended since, for your sake, I have become a "dove"; and even if you have turned me down, I shall bear all that, and I shan't be long with you here anyway, for I'm no competition for that gentleman of yours and God be my witness, I like that gentleman: we are of one mind now. . . . But that my accursed parent should be against you and following you— why, I'll pluck the old devil's beard out, I'll drive an aspen stake into his heart!"

That made Matryona Semeonovna think long and seriously, to know there were three men on her trail, and it was not so much about her fears that she thought; rather she felt sad at being watched so closely; and she was alarmed lest Ivan Stepanovich might spot the chief thing: her prayers and willful spiritual behavior; and why wouldn't he be able to sniff out all that was hidden under the quiet roof of Kudeyarov the carpenter? At the slightest provocation, he would send in a report and the authorities would crack down on their heads.

In the village rumors were already circulating about the slap on the face, the revolt in one restless village, the cossacks and the purple pillars of distant fires: a neighbor had again set fire to a neighbor's house; arson was again running wild in the region; it was expected to appear any day with us too. "The red gent must have had a hand in this!" the staid folk muttered; no wonder the red gent had started wandering about like a wolf; the deaf and dumb villager had seen him lurking in the bushes where the lilac-yellow eyes of cow-wheat peeped at the road, and the priest's wife had observed him in a field of rye; when she had been about to pick a cornflower she had spotted his

crimson shirt there; and he had been seen in the Tzelebeyevo tavern when the riff-raff gathered there: not those
whose reason kept the village meetings going, but those
who had become separated from work, who went about
bawling and whistling under girls' windows, who spread
nasty scribbles and kept watching the man in the highway;
by night all sorts went walking about in the village; perhaps
they were the visitants of another Likhov who had long ago
abandoned the village, who had long ago rotted in the
Tzelebeyevo cemetery, and who had now arisen from their
graves in order to set fire to villages and blaspheme; that
was the sort of riff-raff that gathered at night in the tavern;
and with them, that riff-raff, now the gentleman drank, who
had been chased from the estate and who now wore a
horned wreath of fir on his head.

He had also been observed by the summer resident, who
had rented a cottage in Tzelebeyevo—that resident who did
not believe in God even though he was Orthodox—by
Schmidt himself; he still sought out Daryalsky: to give him
letters perhaps; but whenever the red gent Daryalsky
caught sight of him, he'd run away and hide himself in a
hollow; and off he'd go without greeting his friend.

Two village lads decided to beat him up, and I don't
know how that affair would have ended if thunder had not
struck our village; a man from Likhov who was passing
through related that the Grachikha priest, with a crowd of
peasants armed with sticks and stakes, raised his honest
Christian cross in his sacrilegious hand against the restraining authorities, and went on strike with the whole of
Grachikha, and now in Grachikha there was such a
roundup going on, caused by the cossacks who had been
brought there, that God alone knew how it would all end;
then this was followed by the news that the old veteran of
the armies of Nicholas, having pinned on his four St.
George's crosses, hobbled along in person to join the
swarthy priest; but that turned out to be sheer nonsense;
for, by that time, the cossacks had caught the swarthy

priest, torn off his cross, and, having bound his hands
behind his back, had taken him straight off to Likhov
(there's the bicycle for you!); and since Grachikha was
populated only by two clans, the Fokins and the Alexins, so
all the Fokins and all the Alexins were picked up and put
into the town jail.

Stepka, the shopkeeper's son, sneered at all this talk: evidently he knew what was a secret to others, and it was not
in vain that good folk had entrusted Stepka not only with
the task of collecting a militia, but also with that of driving
a wedge between that militia and the socialist strikers; the
aim was to instill into the militia the rules of a new faith and
form a free means of support for the brotherhood of doves;
Stepka knew all this and kept quiet: Stepka cast more than
one look at the dusty road: his feet drew him toward that
dusty road, and he would have marched off further and
further: there, where the sky hugged the earth, where the
end of the world was, and the ancient refuge of dead men;
and if anyone should stare long at the highway, then that
dark figure that stands there and beckons will lure him with
a wave of a hand from afar, but if he walks closer, the
figure will turn into a bush; and for more than a year or
two the figure stood there, now coming closer, now receding, and soundlessly it threatened the village and soundlessly
it beckoned. . . .

A lump of granite falls into the dread depths of a crevice;
if those depths happen to be water, the lump of granite falls
still deeper, but in the sticky mud at the very bottom
there's no more falling: here the limit has been reached; but
the human soul has no such limit, because the fall can be
eternal and it astonishes one just as the trail of stars flying
over the abyss of the world: you are already swallowed in
the black throat of the world, which is without heights or
depths, and where everything that exists is in a state of
suspension at the center; and in the world of being you may
account for that falling or flight—it is all the same. . . .
Thus, for Daryalsky, his fall became his flight: without

looking back, he was running in the direction where Matryona's sarafan flitted; but why was he so shy of her? And she, laughing at his childish shyness, pursued him, followed him from the village, as though catching up with him and yet not pursuing him, laughing in his steps and ahead there, a dark little figure lost in the fields summoned them all to attempt the wide, unknown, terrifying spaces.

So the days flew—azure, misty, dusty days; and in the village teeth were also being ground about Daryalsky's involvement with the carpenter's wife, and about the fact that the carpenter Kudeyarov was still away in Likhov because he was developing *anormous* affairs, or because he'd come together with the dark folk of passage—the sectarians.

No wonder people gossiped about Daryalsky, but they no longer avoided him: the phenomenon was explained—in the sight of everyone he'd begun to go about with Matryona; the coppersmith related how a while ago a pleasant company was drinking at his house: the red gentleman with the fir branches on his head and with Matryona on his knees (she looked as if she'd gone crazy, the fool); Stepka, the shopkeeper's son, had played for them on the accordion; and Abram the beggar, to get a tip from them, had been dancing on the floor in his bare feet, in his torn trousers and had kept waving a leaden dove.

Well, well! . . .

Matryona

When you take a fancy to a dark-eyed, painted beauty,
with lips as sweet as ripe raspberry, with a light face un-
creased by kisses, like the petal of an apple bloom in May,
and she becomes your love, do not affirm then that this love
is yours: you may not tire breathing the fragrance of her
rounded breasts, of her slender figure, softly melting like
wax in fire; you may not tire gazing at her little white foot
with rosy nails; you may kiss again and again all the fingers
of her hands in the beginning—all this may be: and how she
will cover your face with her small hand till you see
through the transparent skin in the light, the red glow of
her flowing blood; and may this also be true that you will
ask of your raspberry love nothing more than the dimples
of laughter, the sweet lips, the smoke falling down from a
head of hair and the shimmering blood of her fingers:
tender will your love be, for both you and her, and you will
ask nothing more of your love; but a day will come, a cruel
hour will strike, that fatal moment will come, when that
little face crumpled by kisses will grow tarnished and the
breasts will quiver no more at the touch: that will all come
to pass; and you will find yourself alone with your shadow
amid the sun-scorched wastes and the exhausted sources
where flowers do not bloom, but merely a dry lizard's skin
shimmers in the sun; you will also see, perhaps, the hole, all
woven over with cobweb, of a black shaggy-legged taran-

tula. . . . And your thirsting voice will then rise from the
sands, appealing avidly to your native land.

If your love be different, if ever the black itch of
smallpox had passed over her browless face, if her hair be
reddish, her breasts drooping, her bare feet dirty, her belly
protruding in any way, and she is nevertheless . . . your
love, then, whatever you sought and whatever you found in
her is the holy land of the soul: and you have looked into
her eyes, into that land and you'll no longer see your
former love; your soul then will converse with you, and a
guardian angel, winged, will descend upon you. You must
never forsake such a love: she will satiate your soul and you
cannot betray her; in those hours when the longing comes,
and when you see her as she is, that pock-marked face and
the reddish looks will excite in you not tenderness, but
greed; your caresses will be brief and rude; she will be
instantly satisfied and then she, your love, will look at you
reproachfully and you will begin to cry as if you were not a
man, but a woman: then only will your love be dovelike
toward you and your heart will beat in the velvety dark of
feelings. With the first, you are tender, though a powerful
man; but with the second? Enough, you are not a man, but
a child: a capricious child, all your life you will be drawn to
the second one, and no one ever will understand you here,
nor will you yourself understand that this is no love between you, but an unsolved mass of the mystery crushing
you.

No, it was no rosy mouth that adorned Matryona Semeonovna's face, nor the dark arcs of her eyebrows that gave
that face its peculiar expression; what did give that face a
peculiar expression were the prominent lips—red, moistly
protruding, and as though passionately smiling once and for
all, upon a blue-white, pock-marked face, by some fire-
reduced-to-ash; and yet tufts of her brick-colored hair
insolently stormed forth from under the red kerchief
adorned with the white apples of the carpentress (car-

pentress they called her locally, although she was only a work woman): all those features of hers expressed anything but beauty or a maiden's well-preserved chastity; the movement of her breasts, her thick legs with their white calves and the dirty soles of her feet, her big belly, and her sloping and rapacious forehead—all frankly bore the imprint of lust; but her eyes . . .

Looking into her eyes, you will ask: "What plaintive bagpipes are weeping there, what songs is the vast sea sending us, and what sweet perfume is covering the earth?" Her eyes were so blue they plunged one into the depths, into the darkness, and produced a sweet headache: one could not see the whites of her eyes: two vast watery sapphires slowly rolled there with the languish of the eyes in the depths—as though the blue-ocean-sea had begun moving out of her pock-marked face, and there was no limit to it, the blue-ocean-sea with its rolling waves: her eyes spread like waters all over her face, washed by dark circles under her eyes—such indeed were her eyes.

Gazing into them, you will forget all else: drowning till the Second Coming, you will flounder in those blue seas, praying to God that the Archangel's resounding trumpet might free you soon from that marine prison, if you still had any memory left of God, and if you still did not believe that the devil had stolen the trumpet of judgment from heaven.

And the strangest fancies will come to you: her blood will seem to you the blue-ocean-sea; and her white face will seem blue-white because it is transparent-blue; and in her veins you will see not the blue sea, but the blue sky, and in place of the heart a red lantern, like the red sun; and her lips will appear purple: with those purple lips of hers she will tear you away from your bride; and her ironical smile will seem like an endearing smile, endearing and . . . mournful; and she becomes for you a sister, not forgotten as yet in the life of dreams—she will become for you that native land which we sadly contemplate in the autumn on days when the orange-colored leaves swirl in the farewell blue of cold October; and the carpentress's red hair will be like a leaf swirled by the wind into the sky, like the gleams and the quivers of autumn; but then you will notice that these all-illuminating eyes are squinting eyes: one of them stares past you, the other at you; and you will remember how insidious, deceitful, is the autumn.

But should the carpentress roll up her eyes, then the whites of Matryona's eyes will stare at you; you will understand then that she is as alien to you as a witch, monstrously ugly; and if she lower her eyes a fraction and stare at the mud, the straw and the shavings, and hold her gnarled hands over her belly—a shadow will run over her face, the folds near her nose will sink deeper into her pockmarks—and she had a great many pockmarks—and her face will crumple and perspire, and her belly will bulge again, while such folds will quiver at the corners of her mouth, in a way that is quite obscene: to you she will seem just . . . a wanton wench.

Matryona was in her yard driving a cow into the shed; soon her pail creaked, and she was under the cow; and very soon a warm jet of sultry milk began splashing on the tin bottom of the pail.

A sound of steps, of voices, in the darkness:—"Matryona, ah, Matryona?"—"Wha-a-t?"—"Embrace me, darling!"—"Go on with you, I'm not in the habit of kissing . . ."—"Are you alone?"—"Let me be!"—"Let's go into the house!"—"Oh, what do you mean?"—"Well?"—"The master will be back soon, I'm sure. . . ."

The sounds of sighs and stifled exclamations: hurried steps across the yard and noise; the hens cackled; with flapping wings the crested pigeon flew up to the hayloft and from there, on someone's head, drily fell a pigeon dropping.

They were already in the parlor: a green icon lamp illuminated the bright countenance of the Savior blessing the harvest; their hair was full of shavings, sawdust and wood splinters; at that moment all the objects in the room, whatever they were, fixed themselves silently on Pyotr; in the green light, there was Matryona Semeonovna's perspiring face with sunken eyes and teeth glittering out of a grinning mouth: in the green light before him was the white face of the witch sitting there like a green corpse; now she herself was upon him, pawing him and pressing her plump breasts against him—a grinning beast; somewhere in the immeasurable space of a green sea floated away from him now that ancient house in which Princess Katya was standing and waving farewell.

What was happening to him, O Lord, O my God?

And he burst out sobbing in front of that she-beast, like a big forsaken child, and his head fell on her knees; a change came over her; she was no longer a she-beast; those large eyes, now full of tears, swam away into his soul; and a face, no longer crumpled by a surge of passion, but somehow full of grace, was now bending over him.

"Oh, sick heart! Oh, little brother: here, take this cross of mine. . . ."

She unbuttoned the collar of his shirt and, taking from her warm body a tin cross, hung it around his neck.

"Oh, sick heart! Oh, little brother: take your sister, all of her, as she is. . . ."

Night was already squatting among the bushes when Daryalsky walked away from the carpenter's hut, while a dog barked at him, and the darkness was already swallowing him when, turning, he perceived someone's hand holding up from the threshold a twinkling torch which soundlessly threw into his darkness a dull-red flood of light and also lit up Matryona's face beneath a kerchief with white apple-dots, a face illuminated in the dark with a voluptuous smile and eyes dazzled by the glitter; she seemed so small there in the distance; and, though Daryalsky had already melted into the dark, she stood there still, holding out the torch in pursuit of his vanished trace; for a long while yet the purple eye of the torch winked in that spot; but finally that seeing spot went blind; and soon, from that spot, for all Tzele-beyevo to hear, a cock crowed lustily; and a barely audible song answered as though from . . . However, God alone knows where it came from.

~❧ The Encounter ❧~

They were still standing there embracing, and an ineffable closeness kept them together, when the sound of steps near the threshold at the entrance barely gave them time to jump apart before the master himself, Mitry Mironich Kudeyarov, the carpenter, who had just returned from Likhov, crossed the threshold and confronted them.

"O-o-o-o!" he began to stammer as he entered.

Matryona Semeonovna's bare feet beat a retreat to one side; there she covered her incredibly dense burning face with a dirty apron and kept glancing expectantly at the two of them; her face seemed even to reflect a curious mischief and a certain shyness; for what had she to fear? She had performed her acts of endearment with her husband's approval and, what is more, even at his behest; yet a shudder of fear passed through her, and her teeth chattered. Was it because she had not executed the carpenter's secret command in the manner he expected: in her soul, his command had become a sweet and impetuous urge; within a second everything within her went cold when half of the carpenter's dead, lean face fixed itself dully upon the icon and his dead, lean hand, like a fish bone, was raised to make the sign of the cross; her heart sensed that she had committed a sin before her husband; with trembling hands Matryona Semeonovna began to arrange her face which had become all dishevelled from the kisses, embraces and caresses and, unnoticed in the dark, she did up her unbuttoned blouse.

But the carpenter had apparently noticed nothing; he glanced affectionately at Daryalsky, though it would be truer to say that it was his pointed nose that glanced at Daryalsky; his beard alone hung down reproachfully toward the floor.

"O-o-o-o . . . I'm . . . I'm (he had already stopped stammering) . . . I'm very pleased at seeing a man of your intellectual stature in our lair . . . yes, very . . ."

And he held out his broad calloused hand to Daryalsky.

But the carpenter saw everything and it, as it were, frightened him too: to see it all so plain and to have it follow this course. "No, I can't, I can't," he thought to himself, sighing, but what it was he couldn't stand, that he obviously had not yet thought out very clearly; but he felt stifled by the odor of black bread in the closed hut.

Daryalsky, frowning severely and his head lowered, stared with wildly glittering eyes at the carpenter from under his brows, ready to answer or repel him; not a trace of his previous excitement could be observed: in a flash our hero had taken in the situation and was prepared to meet with dignity whatever might arise between them; but the carpenter's affectionate manner and even more, his calloused hand had robbed Pyotr of his strength.

"I'm here . . . I'd like you to know . . . I've really come with an order," he said. "I need a chair, a wooden chair, with a carving of a cockerel," he went on, blurting out the first words that came into his head.

"That you can have . . . yes," the carpenter replied, shaking his hair. "Yes, that you can have," he repeated, and there was a trace of condescension in that shaking of his hair, even perhaps of approval, and mainly of an almost imperceptible mockery: for if the carpenter had really acted as he felt, he would have grabbed the shameless hussy by the hair and banged her head on the floor and then, pulling up her skirts, would have kicked her black and blue; and there she was, the shameless hussy, watching him from a corner; and her eyes were saying: "Was it not you, not

you yourself, Mitry Mironich, who gave me the instructions and put your strength into my breast?"

To give instructions, that indeed the carpenter had done;
that is exact; but the acts that followed were not according
to the rules: without prayers, purpose or rank: and if the
acts took place without ritual, without God, then they were
merely the result of mutual lust; he himself was ailing; he
had grown lean from fasting and coughing: it was not the
moment for him to occupy himself with the nature of
women: he had occupied himself with all those things in his
good time: Matryona had to give birth—that was certain:
he knew what would result from this and what consequences would follow that: the consequence would be the
birth of the spirit, the respiritualization of the earth and the
freeing of Christian folk; but things were not turning out as
they should: Matryona had to couple with the gent; but
things were not right if, in his heart, he had pangs of
jealousy . . . "They were at it, they were, without me!"
he thought, spitting contemptuously and scratching himself,
without looking at Daryalsky.

"So it's a chair you're after . . . We can do that for you.
A wooden chair with a carving; we can do all that," he said
aloud. "With a dove or a cockerel on the back of it, that
also we can do. There's no difficulty in that: there are all
sorts of styles. . . ."

At the word "dove," Daryalsky shuddered as though
someone had broached the secret of his soul; and he
snatched up his cap.

"I stayed here, so to speak, for a while without you . . .
It's time for me to go now."

"What's that? You'll offend us if you go: I can see you're
one of us," Kudeyarov replied with a wink. "I've just come
in and you're off; that won't do!"

And Kudeyarov plainly sketched a cross three times on
the table for Pyotr to see; and in Pyotr's head everything
turned topsy-turvy; he was now no longer able to tear

himself away from the carpenter; and he almost exclaimed, "In the shape of a Dove!"

The carpenter went on fussing around him:

"Here's how: you must do us the favor of breaking bread and salt with us . . . Heat up the samovar, Matryona Semeonova . . . What's got into your head, stupid, not to have asked the guest into our best quarters?"

Then the carpenter suddenly stamped his feet and hissed:

"Look at you, keeping the guest here in the dark and getting him all untidy with shavings and sawdust: go at once and put on the light!"

Matryona stamped past them, glancing apprehensively over her shoulder into the carpenter's eyes: she could not understand the way he was behaving now; did he not, Mitry Mironich himself, tell her how to approach the gentleman, the dear gentleman; and now it looked as if the carpenter was angry with her.

"You fool!" he hissed under his breath as she passed, thinking to himself: "You coupled with him, but for what? You sniffed together, but couldn't you wait till I came back!"

Then, coughing and with twice as much affability, he rushed to Pyotr.

"You must forgive that stupid woman," he fussed. "Look at those shavings on your clothes, and the sawdust on your mustaches and the sawdust in your hair! Won't you come into the sitting room now!"

Daryalsky again felt agitated; but within a minute the agitation had worn off.

The three of them were now at table; small talk was exchanged between them; they sat, drinking tea among the pictures and chromolithographs. Daryalsky was speaking excitedly about the people's rights and about faith.

The carpenter was thinking hard: maybe all sorts of things did happen without ritual, prayer and brotherly presence, well, it can't be helped this time; still that wasn't

in order: "Tfu! How could they go about it without me?"
And the carpenter felt hurt again; though he kept himself
away from her, yet he could not resist at times the pleasure
of stroking her: and now no doubt the gentleman had
stroked her too. But the carpenter pulled himself together.

"H'm, yes, that's right," he said. "They're oppressing the
people; near Likhov, in the gorge, there was a meeting and
with orators. . . ."

"If we weren't peasants, but free—that is, citizens, I
mean, we'd show them!"

"Yes, that's a manifest fact: dignity is lacking to the
powerless. . . ."

Hardly had Pyotr passed out of the gates, when Mitry
Mironich turned at once to Matryona:

"Well, hussy, tell me at once: have you established rela-
tions with him or not?"

"Oh, yes, I have!" Matryona howled rather than spoke, as
she fussed around the bed and wrapped herself in a quilt;
she glanced at the carpenter sideways with an angry stare.

"You have, have you!" the carpenter groaned.

In the end, there was peace. Matryona had already tucked
herself under the quilt, while the carpenter, with his belt
off, still stood motionless with one of his calloused hands
pressing down on the table, while with the other, which
bonily protruded from a red sweaty sleeve, he plucked at
his scraggy beard, at the opened collar of his shirt and the
large cross around his neck and then, raising it above his
head, let it drop with all its five fingers into his matted
yellow head of hair: so the carpenter stood, his mouth half-
open, his half-closed eyes turned in upon himself, his forehead still painfully furrowed: his face had become covered
with small quivering wrinkles, and it seemed as if one
dominant thought, profound and painful, glimmered beneath the changing expressions of that icon-like face; a bead
of sweat trickled down his forehead, trembled on his eyelid,
twinkled on his cheek and vanished in his mustaches.

Finally that still face was turned toward Matryona, and then it grew contorted:

"Aaaa! Wanton!" the carpenter exclaimed.

And then again he did not see her; he stood there, his nose pecking toward the floor, shaking his head and muttering:

"Aaaa! Wanton!"

Then slowly he let himself down on the bench; slowly he let fall his hands on the table; and a quick-legged cockroach ran over the table toward him, stopped under his very nose and twitched its whiskers.

❧ Night ❧

Bushes, tree stumps, ravines; and again bushes; through all the tangle of branches, shadows and sunset hues winds a meandering trail; Pyotr was rapidly moving out there—into the depths of the East—into the bushes, the tree stumps, the ravines, among the green eyes of the glowworms.

Yevseich was catching up with him.

"Sir, dear sir, Pyotr Petrovich—ke-he, k-ke-he—what is going to happen to us? Have pity—just take a look at the young lady; she's desperate, she's weeping!"

The only answer he heard was the cracking of dry branches and the gurgling sound of feet running through a bog to Tzelebeyevo.

"Keche, keche, keche," Yevseich coughed. He couldn't catch up with Pyotr Petrovich; how's an old man with sore feet to chase after a young one!

Yevseich turned in the direction of Gugolevo; the last daylight was gone; troubled night fell on him with the chaos of ash.

In the Gugolevo park all was dead: the old grandma, all surrounded by pillows, was drowning in furs beneath the window; from outside the open window the dusk fell upon her; a sheaf of golden light from the lamp inside the window rushed to meet him; a slight breeze blew the half-lit paws of wild vine into the window.

But where was Katya?

There, there Tzelebeyevo was ahead: and Katya was

terrified; pale Katya crept alone; and Katya had grown thinner; like a gray slender stalk wrapped in a white cobweb, in ash-pale dress and with ember-like hair, veiled in a pale shawl, she palely melted in the ash-blue turbidness, drowned in a nocturnal sea; her thin face barely rose above the surface of that sea; she was going there in secret from her grandma, from the Gugolevo servants, even from Yevseich: to meet her steps in the pale glitter of the heat lightning there, coming toward her from behind a bush—Yevseich; Katya hid from him in the bushes; it meant the old man, the old man . . . had also begun to go there in secret.

The old man was now far behind her back; in the pale glitter of the heat lightning the footman's gray back flashed once more when she turned:

"Yevseich, Yevseich!" the frightened girl called into the dark, but Yevseich did not hear; Katya looked in his wake . . . and wept.

Her eyes were like pieces of nocturnal blue, the nocturnal blue which scrutinized Katya from behind the black lace of leaves gathered around; Katya stopped . . . and wept.

Grandmother's ruin, the slap, the stupid loss of the diamonds, the terrifying disappearance of Pyotr, gossip about *this* disappearance and *that* loss, and finally this vile, anonymous badly scribbled letter, altogether illiterate, in which some simple-minded person arrogantly reported to her that, as it were, her Pyotr was involved in a romance with a newly come wench. Katya gazed at the little stars and wept, and her small shoulders shivered from the shudders of the nocturnal leaf; everybody has heard such shudders: that special shudder which does not exist by day.

Schmidt will tell her everything: he will find Pyotr for her.

Already the huts were there; they have settled squarely into the black stains of bushes, have scattered—and from there they blinked angrily at her with their eyes full of cruelty and fire; as if a swarm of enemies now hid in the bushes in fiery patches, the doorposts of houses a mesh of shadows and from there will rise the black fingers of a starling coop—all this now stared at the forest, all this had picked out Katya on the fringe of the forest and was now revealed to her; but at first only a confusion of lights emerged from the dark forest; and while the silly girl was approaching the village, the heavy white belfry swooshed past her to the right, squeaking with a momently awakened martin.

Her light slippers were drenched in the high grass, the grasses spilled water on her dress, and a shiver travelled down her spine; look, Katya had lost her way, wandered up to the smooth slope; out of the bushes a small hut sprang up, with smoke falling out of a chimney and glimmering with light; a blood-red patch of light was falling out of the window on the grass; and on top of it fell the black cross of the window; and it all projected upon the bushes where Katya now stood; she felt a little afraid and at the same time happy with an uneasy happiness to see in that reddish glow the slightly quivering diamond of dew upon the leaves and the slender stems; and then, all of a sudden, she felt simply terrified: she saw a blood-red face, that of a man in a peaked cap under the window; his beard and red nose were fixed upon the window; his eyes too were fixed upon it; and for whom was that red-lit, shaken fist intended? Stealthily Katya crept away—away—from that place. But how was she to find Schmidt's cottage?

Only at a safe distance did she realize that the man standing beneath the window was the Tzelebeyevo shopkeeper, Ivan Stepanov: why then had her childish heart taken fright?

But if she had approached him, he would have pointed to the window, and in the window she would have recognized Pyotr, dirty and unkempt, in the company of the snub-nosed, pock-marked peasant wench and, likewise, the carpenter's sickly, cunning face winking at Pyotr over a saucer of tea raised to his yellow mustaches; all that she would have seen; but it was better for her not to have seen it.

For a long time yet the Tzelebeyevo shopkeeper watched there under the window, whispering wild threats: "You wait, I'll make you sing, you old pimp!" Eventually his face was shrouded in shadow and for a time only, his hairy fist showed blood-red in the light, but it too was lost in the shadow; a few branches crackled underfoot and then all was silence.

Daryalsky was already leaving the hut, already in the dark he began to lose the light from the hut and turning around, he saw a hand back there holding a kerosene torch which soundlessly threw a flood of dull red light into his darkness and, in the center of that flood stood Matryona, and her face shone sweetly into his darkness and shone too with her light-dazzled eyes. How small she looked there in the distance!

Daryalsky wandered about the village and the dogs howled; the dogs followed, snapping at his heels and then loudly leaping away. Aimlessly Daryalsky wandered toward the priest's garden and by chance he passed an open window. The voice of the priest's wife reached his ears:

"I tell you . . . he has a little black mustache. There's a bridegroom for you: he's come back on leave—he's of gentle birth."

Daryalsky could not resist glancing in at the window— and what did he see inside? Katya, who looked very small and green as she sat hidden in a corner, was forcing herself to smile: the priest's wife was pressing down upon her with her belly, bosom and her gossip; and the sadly silent Schmidt pretended to listen to Father Vukol's chatter; beneath a lamp Father Vukol in a white under-cassock was rolling cigarettes; Schmidt was watching Katya carefully and a barely perceptible anxiety for her passed over his face.

Daryalsky dashed away.

In the hazy dark, quiet voices came nearer; over the dew in the hazy dark quiet words could be heard:

"No, that's not slander; it's a fact."

"But he's no thief."

"He's not a thief. But here we have a coincidence of some deliberately planted circumstances; the enemies have concealed themselves and are controlling his acts. The hour will come when they will pay for it—for everything, everything; for him and those they have already destroyed."

"Pyotr, my Pyotr, with that peasant woman.!"

"Pyotr thinks he has left you forever; but this is not a case of betrayal or flight, but a terrible compelling hypnosis: he has stepped out of the circle of aid—and the enemies, for the time being, are triumphant over him just as an enemy might triumph over and scoff at our country; thousands of innocent victims and the guilty ones are still in hiding; and none of us, poor mortals, can tell who is really responsible for all these stupid occurrences. Reconcile yourself, Katerina Vassilievna, do not despair: all the dark forces have now fallen upon Pyotr; but Pyotr can still get the better of them: he must first overcome himself, he must give up the attempt to create life personally; he must re-evaluate his attitude to the world; and then the spectres which, for him, have assumed blood and flesh, will disappear; believe me, only great and strong souls are exposed to such temptation; only giants collapse as did Pyotr; he did not accept the helping hand held out to him; he wished to attain everything himself; his story is stupid and formless; it's as though it were narrated by an enemy who was mocking every bright aspect of our country. . . . In the meantime, you must pray, you must pray for Pyotr!"

That was what Schmidt told Katya as he accompanied her back to Gugolevo; suddenly there was a crackling of dry branches in front of him; an electric torch threw a sheaf of white light and Katya perceived: in that circle of white light Pyotr's head was straining forward like the head of a wild wolf; his troubled eyes wandered drunkenly; just an instant and then it was dark again.

Strong hands kept Katya riveted to the spot as she was about to dash after Pyotr:

"Don't move!" Schmidt exclaimed. "If you follow him now, you will never return!"

For more than an hour or two already the blue, moist mist had drenched the fields with its fragrance, flowing easily into the green parts and the opal glow in the sunset places, where the black comb of the wood was set in as yet clear remnants of recent splendors; the moist misty haze was in the East, with the exception of only one place, which was luridly swollen by the as yet unrisen moon; though it was black all around, it was also transparently clear; the bushes were clearly cut into black patches, hemmed by the lace and the whisper of leaves; a black piece of this whispering, as though of a loose leaf, crawled here and there; there it went rolling into the lace of the bushes: that was a bat; overhead the spreading sea of cupped blue was flowing with the summer tears of near-and-far glittering tiny stars; and both Daryalsky and Katya, from different spots of the sadly whispering wood, gazed at those stars. They gazed at those stars and wept for their memories.

PART TWO

PART TWO

CHAPTER FIVE

On the Little Island

Strange thing: the more Pyotr's friend demonstrated his cleverness, the more subtle, cunning, capricious and complex seemed the zigzags of his speculation; the easier Pyotr breathed in his presence and the simpler he appeared to himself. The young man's superfluous sophistries merely enlightened Pyotr as to his own intelligence and simplicity, for he was weary by now of conflict and deeply heartfelt emotions. Here he was at Schmidt's, sitting at a table, sunburnt and unshaven, reading through a pile of letters addressed to him; a blissful smile hovered over his face; and yet the smile seemed carved of stone. Sitting there, he was at the frontier of two very contradictory worlds: that of his cherished past and that of a new reality as voluptuous as a legend. A lofty, deep, clear-azure sky strung with woolly clouds peeped into Schmidt's window together with a vista of Tzelebeyevo; in the distance the priest could be seen sitting on a stump and fiercely holding his ground against Ivan Stepanov. Ivan Stepanov was saying to him:

"I'm by way of thinking it's about time to have that carpenter arrested. He's one of those sectarians and troublemakers, that's what he is! And as for that wench, why, pfoui!—she's just a shameless wanton. It's very likely that these same people are the 'doves.' I've been keeping my eyes peeled on them for a long while."

"Well, Stepanov, I've been thinking you're doing it for

fear of God: that's true," the priest answered. "Mitry Mironich is interested in texts, you see . . ."

"And as for that Gugolevo gent, if I may say so," Ivan Stepanov continued, "they've tied him up, cast a spell on him. Why, otherwise, has he taken a job with the carpenter?"

"Oh, that's just a bit of gentry fun!" the priest exclaimed.

Father Vukol dropped his head and then, puffing at his pipe, spat with gusto on the sun-scorched grass. The pure, tender sky, palestrung with curling lambs' wool and the lofty azure, beat down upon his eyes.

Soon Stepanov started walking back to his shop; and a man whom he passed on the way held out his hand and insolently barked out: "Aah . . . Aah . . . your hand, Ivan Stepanov!"

"Go your way," Stepanov growled, walking on. "I don't shake hands with strangers; for all I know, your hand may be infectious!"

And he went on.

Daryalsky heard none of this as he stared out of the window; all he saw was the sky, the lambs' wool, the painted peasant huts, and the priest's figure standing sharply etched against the meadow; and as he stared Daryalsky exchanged every now and then a few brief, random remarks with Schmidt.

Schmidt sat engrossed in his papers. In front of him was a large sheet and on it a circle had been drawn with a compass and within it were four triangles and a cross in the center; lines divided the angles and cut the circumference of the circle into twelve parts, which were marked off by Roman numerals, where *Ten* stood above and *One* on the right hand side; this strange figure was further surrounded by another circle divided into 36 sections; each section had within it the symbols of the planets arranged in such a way that a sign of the zodiac stood above three symbols; the twelve large cages held crowns and crosses and the symbols of planets from which, through the center of the circle and intersecting the star, thin arrows projected here and there; on the figure were also inscriptions in red ink which read: *"The Scapegoat," "The Reaper," "The Three Goblets," "The Dazzling Light"*; in the margin of the page were strange inscriptions, such as *"X-10: Sphinx (X) (99 scepters); Venus at 9 Leo; Jupiter at 10 Virgo (The Ruler of the Sword); 7 Mercury, The Seventh Mystery,"* and so on, and so forth.

Schmidt was saying to him:

"You were born in the year of Mercury, on the day of Mercury, in the hour of the Moon, beneath that section of the starry heavens which bears the name of 'The Dragon's Tail.' The Sun, Venus, Mercury, are afflicted for you by unfavorable aspects; the Sun is cursed by a conjunction with Mars; Mercury is in opposition to Saturn; and Saturn is in that section of the soul of the starry sky where the heart is broken, where Cancer vanquishes the Eagle. Saturn also presages misfortune in love, lingering as it does in the fifth house in your horoscope; and it is also in Pisces. Saturn threatens you with destruction. Think better of it—it is not too late yet to turn aside from your terrifying course. . . ."

But Daryalsky did not reply. He stared at the bookshelves. There were strange books here on those shelves: the *Kabbalah* in an expensive binding, the *Merkabah*, the volumes of the *Zohar* (an open page of the *Zohar* always glowed golden in the sunshine on Schmidt's table); the golden page spoke of the wisdom of Simeon bar Yohai and struck the eyes of the astonished beholder; here were manuscript notations from the works of Julius Firmicus, astrological commentaries on Ptolemy's *Tetrabiblon;* here too were the *Stromataeis* of Clement of Alexandria, Hammer's Latin treatises, among which was the *Baphometis Revelata,* where a connection was established between the Arab branch of the Ophites and the Templars, where the Ophite abominations intertwined with the marvelous legend about Titurel; there were manuscript notes taken from *The Shepherd of the Nations,* from the eternally mysterious *Sifra di-Tseniutha,* from the book which has almost been ascribed to Abraham himself—the *Sefer*, to which Rabbi Ben Hannana swore he was indebted for his miracles; on the table were sheets of paper with signs on them drawn by a trembling hand—pentagrams, swastikas, circles with the magic *Tau* inside them; here was the tablet with the sacred hieroglyphics; an elder's hand had traced a garland of roses above which was a man's head and, below, that of a lion; on each side were the heads of a bull and an eagle; within the garland were two crossed triangles in the shape of a six-pointed star with the following numbers in the angles—*1, 2, 3, 4, 5, 6*, and with their sum of *21* in the center. In Schmidt's hand, beneath the emblem, was written: *"The Garland of the Magi—T=400."* There were other figures too: that of the Sun dazzling two infants, with the inscription, *"Quilolath—the sacred truth: 100."* There was the image of a Water Spout above two bound men, beneath which Schmidt had written: *"This is number sixty, the number of the mystery, of fate, of predestination, that is, the fifteenth hermetic glyph* Hiron." Also here were the altogether incomprehensible words, *"Atoim, Dinaim, Ur, Zain."* On a chair to one side lay a mystical diagram with the ten Sephiroth beams drawn in a certain order: *"Kether —the first Sefiroth: the Divine halo, the first gleam, the first shimmer, the first pouring out of flight, the first motion, the canal going back before Creation, Canalis Suprumundanus,"* and the eighth Sefiroth, *Yod*, bearing the inscription *"ancient serpent."* Strange scrawls marked the white wooden surface of the table, scrawls such as *"the straight line of a square is the source and instrument of every sensible thing"* or *"every material substance is calculated by the number four."*

Schmidt's bald head rose from among this pile of books, signs, and diagrams; and his elder's voice continued to enlighten Daryalsky:

"Jupiter in Scorpio would have foretold your ascendancy, nobility, and priestly dedication, but Saturn has overthrown all this; when Saturn enters the constellation of Aquarius, misfortune threatens you; and just now Saturn is in Aquarius. I am warning you for the last time: watch out! Mars too is in Virgo; you could avoid the consequences of all this if in your horoscope Jupiter were to be situated in your birth sign; but Jupiter is situated in the place of your destiny. . . ."

Pyotr was shaken. He recalled those past years when Schmidt had ruled over his destiny, revealing to him the dazzling path of secret knowledge. He had been on the point of traveling abroad with him to join *them*, that mysterious *brotherhood*, which had influenced his destiny from afar. But now Daryalsky stared out of the window and all he saw through the window was Russia: gray, white, red huts, peasant shirts silhouetted against the common, and voices raised in song. There was the carpenter in a red shirt ambling across the common to call on the priest; and there, above, was the tender affectionate sky. Daryalsky turned his back on his past: he turned his back on the window, on the dying Russia that was beckoning him through the window, on the supreme new master of his fate, the carpenter; and he said to Schmidt:

"I don't believe in fate: in me the creative life will conquer everything."

"Astrology does not teach the power of fate," Schmidt replied. "On the contrary, it maintains that thought and the word have created the world and omnipotence, and the seven spirits—beneficent geniuses—who have manifested themselves in the seven spheres; their revelation *is* destiny; man ascends through the circles; in the lunar circle he becomes conscious of immortality; in the circle of Venus he assumes innocence; in the solar orb he bears light; from Mars he learns humility; from Jupiter, reason; on Saturn he contemplates the truth of things."

"You're treating me to *The Shepherd of the Nations*,

which bears the stamp of late Alexandrianism," Daryalsky
replied. "We philologists set value on authentic sources, but
there is no authentic element of the Magi in this."

"You have forgotten that I am quoting from oral tradition rather than the external records," Schmidt replied.
"Some of the ancient documents, which are still ignored by
your formal science, I have seen with my own eyes—
there, with *them*. . . ."

But Daryalsky got up: a flood of sunshine poured in on
him through the window.

"Do you have anything more to say?"

"No, nothing!"

"Goodbye then. I am off—not to *your* people, but to
mine. I am going off forever. Don't think evil of me."

He went out; the sun dazzled him.

Schmidt continued sitting for a long while among his
calculations; a tear of regret was drying on his old cheek:
"He's done for!" he thought. And had any Tzelebeyevo
villager unexpectedly entered, he would no doubt have been
astonished to find Schmidt weeping bitterly.

Schmidt was the only summer visitor to reside in the
district; he always arrived in our remote locality in March;
and he departed when the first blizzards began roaring
stormily over the village; he was toothless, bald and gray; in
the summer heat he wandered about the nieghborhood in a
yellow silk jacket, leaning on a cane and holding his straw
hat in his hand; he was always surrounded by a bevy of
village boys and girls; frequently he visited the priest; and
he used to bring with him a Persian powder which was
effective against bedbugs; but though he was Orthodox, he
did not believe in God; and that was all that was known
about him in Tzelebeyevo.

·⚡· A Scandal ⚡·

What happened in Ivan Stepanov's shop? Why was there a splintering crash of breaking jars? What made the shop-keeper dash out of the hut with sticky cherry jam dripping from his head on to his face? All this remained a mystery. He dashed out and made straight for the trough and began to wash himself; he washed and washed himself, and when he was washed clean, then a bloody scar became visible across his nose as if someone had swiped him across the nose with a knife. Only when he was washed clean did the shop-keeper collect himself and only then did he remember that he should avoid showing himself outside his yard in such a state.

But they did not think of paying attention to him; for, as a matter of fact, while he had been energetically washing off the cherry jam from his hair and face, the Tzelebeyevo folk were preoccupied with something altogether different, another event as extraordinary: a cloud of dust had suddenly swirled along the Likhov highway—and there, from the cloud of dust came a frightening soul-rending roar. The cloud of dust bore down on our village with incredible speed; ahead of it rushed a red monster: it was as if a red devil had jumped out of the horizon and rushed at the village. The old folk, men and women, had barely time to dash out of their huts before the red devil was already standing immobile in the center of a green meadow, puffing and gasping, but no longer roaring, and tickling people's noses with a stench of kerosene. That was a machine—the same about which it was said that apparently it could drive people without the help of horses; out of the machine leapt a man all wrapped in gray canvas, with great big black glasses over his eyes; he tinkered with the wheels, took off his spectacles, and nodded affably to the folk standing around; his plump, crumpled face, somewhat yellowish in hue, and slanting eyes that peeped from behind wrinkles of fat, winked at the Tzelebeyevo villagers, but they timidly retreated from that high-cheek-boned face; even the priest stared at him from behind his currant bush garden, restraining, as he did so, his son from dashing toward the machine; in the meantime, the gentleman with the Jewish-Mongolian face, donning his spectacles again, seated himself once more in the red devil; the devil roared and then took off with a hissing start. That's the way it was.

It was this circumstance that distracted the attention of the Tzelebeyevo villagers from Ivan Stepanov the shopkeeper and his efforts to wash himself clean in the trough from the cherry jam juice which was dripping abundantly from his head to which, revoltingly, was sticking a pile of jam and fragments of the broken jar; it might be thought that someone's vicious hand had been smashing him on his venerable head with jam jars; but how the Tzelebeyevo folk would have laughed had they been told that the vicious hand belonged to no one but Ivan Stepanov's own son; the two had been quarreling for an hour already and had used up all their stock of swear words, after which the lad, losing all sense of honor and reason, had expectorated, spat in his parent's face, and then attacked his elderly parent with a knife; and, to round off the indecency, smashed a weighty jar of jam on his head. Not without trepidation Ivan Stepanov now reentered the shop; the floor was a mess of jam and splintered glass; a disgraceful sight for anyone to see. Ivan Stepanov locked up the shop, propped his beard in his hand and thought hard; it would have been difficult to decide whether the assaulted parent was angry at his son or just frightened. What he thought was, "I wish Stepka would get out of here, the sooner the better; and then nobody will know about it . . ."

The instigator of this scandal was not only getting out, he was quite ready to depart: he was sitting at a greasy table in his cubbyhole; on the chair beside him lay just one small bundle. He was now about to forsake this locality for more distant, deep-forested, freer places: he had long planned his flight from our neighborhood; that is why he had often importuned the "doves" to send him on some mission which would have allowed him to depart from this place forever. He had become disgusted with our locality; he was also disgusted because Matryona had preferred the gentleman to him, Stepka; but what disgusted him even more was the realization that his father had been spying on Matryona. Stepka could no longer bear the sight of his father, and yet he could not help watching him spying, and in the process he had caught him in a criminal act; the previous night, when Stepka was loafing in the vicinity of Kudeyarov's hut, he very clearly spotted his father, wearing just a shirt and no cap, fumbling round the cottage, piling up brushwood, pouring something over it (kerosene probably) from a bottle, and striking a match; a minute more and flames would have wrapped the carpenter's hut; but Stepka, needless to say, gave a shout, and his father took to his heels.

Just now they had settled accounts. Stepka might have thrashed him harder; he had itched to do so long ago; but the devil take him; Stepka had already informed the "doves" as to the shopkeeper's intentions; they had already set a certain man to watch him; who'll get whom, as the old woman said ambiguously.

Unhindered, Stepka was now quitting those regions where his riotous life had flowed; and he thought hard, carried away by his thoughts (it was not surprising that he turned out to be a poet): it occurred to the lad, as an act of forgiveness before quitting the parental home where, whatever may have happened since, his deceased mother had been good to him—it occurred to him to write the opening part of a short novel he had been planning. Thus, Stepka pulled out his greasy notebook and with his rusty pen began to scratch down the following opening paragraph: *"All was quiet: the whole village was asleep; only somewhere a cow mooed, a dog barked, the shutters creaked on their rusty hinges, and the wind howled under the roofs. And, as it turned out, it was not quiet at all but, on the contrary, even very noisy—if you object, then please do so . . ."*

When the stars began to glow brightly, Stepka's black silhouette began to advance along the glimmering road, growing ever smaller, ever smaller, and finally blended with the dark, distant figure which threatened the village from time immemorial. Stepka never again returned to Tzelebeyevo: he hid his days in the deep forests; maybe there, in the North, a dark shaggy-haired hermit only now and then appearing on the road was the former Stepka, if Stepka had not already been laid low by a vicious cossack bullet, or if, bound in a sack, he had not already been hoisted skyward upon the gallows.

In Ovchinnikov

"A wit! A terrible wit!"

"So?"

"An incredible, monstrous wit!"

"Well, and so?"

"In one aristocratic family he flies up to the grand fiano and, d'you know what . . . 'Do you flay?' the lady of the house inquired.—'I flay.'—'Ah, flay then, flease!' and just imagine what he answered."

"??? . . ."

" 'Lady, I only flay with my—eyes!' "

"He-he-he!"

"Ha-ha-ha-ha!"

"Kwho?"

"A m-a-a-a-n! Biegogogovensky!" General Chizhikov cried out, a chorus girl on his knees.

"So, where is he now, General?"

"Drank too much—burned out with drink; I myself saw a blue flame in his mouth!"

"Well?"

"Soaked in alcohol like a wick: a match would set him alight."

"He-he-he!"

"Ha-ha-ha-ha!"

"Kwho?"

"A m-a-a-a-n! Biegogogovensky!" General Chizhikov cried out, a chorus girl on his knees.

"Where did you get all the money, General?"

"Eh?"

"Well?"

"A man from the pawn shop swore that you were pleased to pawn a marvelous diamond—he-he-he!"

"Not a stolen one, I hope?"

"He-he!"

"I hope so!" the General laughed ironically.

"No, gentlemen: that's not it—that's it there: go on, talk . . . however it may be! I'll tell you about it: a friend of mine, he keeps liquors, liqueurs and wines, all in alphabetical order, from *A* to *Z* inclusive . . . what's that about his 'burnt-out alcoholic': is nothing to him! Now this friend of mine: you'd visit him and he would immediately offer you a concoction based on the word 'abracadabra' or the word 'Leviathan'; 'abracadabra'—'A' is for the anisette he'd pour in; 'B' is for barbery; 'R' for—Riesling; and so on; you'd drink it and you'd be 'ripe'!"

Thus the dull-eyed county officer from Chmari recounted, gesticulating.

The cabinet, woven in rose-colored silk, glowed with fires; a footman kept bursting in through the doors; in and out flew chorus girls; the provincial rich and the nobility sprawled carelessly, one on the sofa, one on the divan, one on the table, while a handsome graying man without a jacket, standing with his back to the piano, suddenly flopped down on the keys and sighed:

"The best years, the best years! Moscow—the Noble Assembly: ah? Where is it?"

"Ah? Where is it?" sounded from the corner.

"Mazurka! Tra-rara-ta-trarara! In the first pair, Count Berci-de-Vgrevien with Zashelkovska, in the second pair . . ."

"In the second pair, Colonel Sesley with Lily," a voice from the corner interrupted.

"Yes. In the second pair, Colonel Sesley with Lily. The Best Years! And now: half-a-quarter a day!"

"How's that? I've moved up to a quarter long ago!" came from the corner. . . .

"Maybe you still have a spare diamond?" a stout man who had accidentally come into this aristocratic gathering inquired, bending over the General. "I could arrange a sale for it."

"My soul, make me a present of it!" a chorus girl exclaimed, approaching Chizhikov.

"What do you mean? Never! It's an extremely rare case when one is forced to part with family valuables. What will you have me do—a temporary need!" the General replied in confusion.

From the side came:

"Theatre! Operetta! You recall *La Mascotte**? Chernov, Zorina, and the unforgettable 'How I love a gosling . . .'"

"But I love little lambs," a voice from the corner joined in.

"How they cackle: gau-gau-gau . . ."

"How they bleat: B-a-a! B-a-a!" came from the corner.

"Gau-gau-gau—b-a-a-a!"

"B-a-a-a!"

"B-a-a-a!" a chorus of aristocrats joined in recalling their youth, never-to-be-forgotten Moscow, the unforgettable *La Mascotte* . . .

Luka Silitch was perspiring heavily as he sat in a corner; this day his eyes did not shine; no painted chorus girl was sitting on his knees today; distinctly over the champagne his back stooped; distinctly the pouches under his eyes hung down; his gray beard trembled distinctly under his lips, and distinctly his gray checkered knee shook visibly: he felt feverish—not for the first time; a sweet faintness and dizzi-

---

* A French light opera, 1880, by Edmond Audran.

ness carried him back home, back to Annushka-the-Dovecot; where were the chorus girls? There was Annushka—
Annushka indeed! Near the full moon when, secretly from
his wife, at his, Luka Silitch's insistence, she visited him at
night—to sleep together; those nights they drank sweet
wines—and in every way amused themselves; after those
nights, more than ever, weakness conquered him; like any
boy in his old age or worse: like the last beast he barged
into his wife's barefoot housekeeper. . . . What of the
chorus girls! Annushka—was Annushka! His knee shaky,
his beard, his spider fingers, his goblet; golden drops, cold
drops of champagne splashed on the table. He thinks—to go
to Annushka! Everything here now disgusts Luka Silitch:
aristocracy disgusts; lo, there, drunken faces; they had
gathered at this Provincial assembly to save Russia from the
Revolution; what else! Luka Silitch was likewise revolted
by the tradespeople; by the champagne; and more than anything else he was revolted by the little General, by Chizhikov; only nasty things from the General; for a certain
percentage he'd brought him promissory notes of the Baroness Graaben; Graaben was in his hands, he no longer
needed the General now; he was a great drunkard, a gour-
mand, and on top of that, a thief, an investigator and a
scandal-monger.

But the little General was whispering in the corner:
"Well, I may even show you the diamonds. . . ."
"Yes, dreams are all full of significance . . ."
"Ye-e-e-s—dreams are prophecies."
"Fu-u-u-l-l . . ." the drunken gents roared and their eyes
wanted to leap out of their orbits; one of them turned in
song to another; the other made a gesture toward the first;
and another one, thrusting out his neck, pecked at the
ceiling with his nose; yet another had long hidden himself
away with a chorus girl.
"Yes, dreams are all full of meaning. . . ."
"Yes, dreams are all prophecies. . . ."
"Fu-u-u-l-l," roared the drunken gents.

Luka Silitch imperceptibly glanced at his watch so as not to miss the train departing from Likhov at an unreasonable time—at four o'clock in the morning; he got up, paid his bill, stared around at the nobility, remembered the incendiarism on the estates; and quit.

"Dir-dir-di," the four-wheeler leapt with him over the Ovchinnikov cobbles; it was getting light; Luka Silitch was thinking that Annushka had white feet and that after tomorrow's night he would feel sick: faintness and perspiration, perspiration and weakness—time to die!

"I couldn't survive more than a year of such a life—*kaput*," he thought and plaintively whispered:

"Annushka! . . ."

"Dir-dir-di," the four-wheeler leapt over the Ovchinnikov cobbles. The Metelkinsky railway branch was already there: there it was, shining with its siding rails.

·····⚬ A Traveling Companion ⚬·····

Inside the station the heat was oppressive and stifling; it was already light but the lamps were still twinkling annoyingly; a beefy officer, whose punitive detachment had been quartered for over a month in the villages around Likhov, was devouring a veal cutlet with great gusto, making eyes at the same time at a lady in a bright green hat and a purple coat who was aimlessly strolling back and forth, and whose face disclosed nothing beyond white powder and cream, lips delineated in purple hue and rouge on her cheeks.

Here too, on a bench heaped with cartons, bundles, sacks, bird cages, and umbrellas fastened together with string, a lady was fussing about half drowsily, her jaw bandaged, her hat askew; and she had in her charge a bevy of five children, one of which had fallen asleep holding a homemade pie in its hand. A traveler of indeterminate profession strode up and down, waiting for the train to Likhov; the newspapers were no longer on sale; the last cutlet had been ordered at the station buffet, and the final glass of beer had been consumed; everyone was tired out, curled up on the benches; only the harsh yellow lamps continued to fire their stifling beams.

On the platform outside it was very different: there it was already morning, fresh and full of movement; there were many intersecting railway tracks; on the tracks stood lilac-trimmed yellow carriages; and on the rails a locomotive was maneuvering and whistling; the mechanic, in a uniform cap, had thrust his head out and was washing his hands with water blown from his mouth; there was a twinkling of many signals; and the guard was running about there and swearing; he had a lantern in his hand and from his lacquered belt hung a furled flag; a circular building gaped with many open jaws at the platform; a locomotive peeped out of each pair of gaping jaws; but then the semaphore leapt sixty degrees and a freight train came rolling over the spare track.

Luka Silitch, yawning lazily, stared lazily around him, trying to identify the various inscriptions on the freight cars flashing past him: among them he could distinguish *Vladikavkaz, Zabaikal, Rybinsk-Vologodsk, Yugo-Zapad.* Involuntarily he read the numbers of the inspected cars: *1910, 1908, 1915.* . . . The cars flashed past, some with their sad burden of oxen chewing the cud and then a white refrigeration car also flashed past; and open cars also flew by, some empty, some filled with sand, others loaded with timber; an open car flew past on only two wheels; a *Ter Akopova* oil car also flew past, followed by another open car; and then came the last car; the train had sped by; the conductor was flying away, and beneath him near the railway track a red lantern was flying away.

Again many railway tracks; a locomotive was dragging itself over them; emitting a shrill whistle as it poured out white curls of smoke into a white morning: it was a mad, gay, shrill whistle!

A clean-shaven gentleman with grizzled hair, in a tightly buttoned brown overcoat, was slowly pacing the platform; and he kept passing Luka Silitch. The gentleman wore a cap with earmuffs; his long nose and aristocratic upper lip protruded well in front; all else had retreated far back; the gentleman was erect of carriage though advanced in years; he had tucked his hands in his front pockets; and he kept on pacing up and down in front of the merchant; now he would come up at him from the right, now he would catch up with him from the left or he would let him walk ahead; he was followed by a lackey carrying a plaid.

Luka Silitch became interested in the gentleman. The gentleman would walk ahead and Luka Silitch would stalk him: he would come up at him from the right, catch up with him from the left, let him walk ahead; it looked accidental, but he thought to himself: "Where have I seen this gentleman before? He must be an important personage; about sixty years of age, I'd say; from the back he looks a young man; he has squared shoulders and is walking about there with a lackey."

The gentleman would walk up to the very edge of the platform, and Luka Silitch would drag himself after him out of sheer boredom and empty curiosity; and if Luka Silitch ventured to the edge of the platform and then turned around, he would find the old gentleman standing behind him and the lackey with the plaid would be right behind the gentleman.

In this way, they dogged each others' footsteps for more than an hour while waiting for the train to Likhov; and now the train was approaching and the semaphore had been raised. The people from the waiting room were crowding the platform: the lady with the bandaged cheek, the five children, the bundles and cartons; and the portly officer now without the lady, and a traveler of indeterminate occupation, a crowd of peasants with saws and sacks, a gendarme and the station master himself in a red cap who bowed respectfully to Luka Silitch. Then Luka Silitch watched with amazement as the clean-shaven old gentleman approached the station master and pointed with his nose at Luka Silitch as though inquiring who that person was. Luka Silitch compressed his lips and gave his face a haughty expression. "Where have I seen that old gentleman before?" he asked himself. "He must have been younger when I saw him last. . . ."

But the Likhov train had arrived, and Luka Silitch settled

himself down in a first class compartment; it was a three-hour journey to Likhov and the Likhov miller felt faint, weak, and nauseous.

He had just made up his mind to lie down when the compartment door opened and the old gentleman came in and sat down opposite him; a lackey brought in his plaid and went away; and there they sat, opposite each other, exchanging glances. Luka Silitch did so stealthily, while the old gentleman stared at him straight in the face. Shame! to stare at him so brazenly!

Luka Silitch got up and walked into the second class (where there were some empty carriages); five minutes had not passed before the gentleman appeared in the second class too, and sat down opposite Luka Silitch, who just could not restrain himself any longer.

"Are you, sir, if I may ask, going as far as Likhov?" he asked.

"Yes, Mr. Yeropegin," the old gentleman replied in a thin drawl, something between laughter and crying.

"Whom have I the honor of addressing?"

"I am traveling from Petersburg to the country on my mother's business—yes!"

"What age is his mother, I wonder?" Luka Silitch thought.

"And my name is Todrabe-Graaben . . ."

Confusion seized Luka Silitch: he saw spots before his eyes and shivered. He had forgotten all about the Baron, but now he would be obliged, obliged, indeed, to discuss business with the Baron. The business was not aboveboard and the Baron was, moreover, a Senator in the "legal department."

The Baron kept his silence: he smiled in silence; he said not a word about the business; Luka Silitch began to feel nauseous; he could not bear the Baron's eyes fixed on him; he had a sinking feeling in the pit of his stomach; he got up and went back into the third class.

In the third class the atmosphere was thick and stuffy;

there were no "vacant places"; a worker was sitting next to the lady with cartons; the seat opposite was heaped with bundles.

"Every citizen with a ticket has the right to a seat," Luka Silitch drily announced; at the same time, he felt revolted—revolted with the lady, revolted with her five youngsters, revolted with the worker; but it was better for him to be here than over there alone with his enemy, the Senator.

Luka Silitch continued to sit. Through the carriage window he could see the yellow, blind, drooping willow trees, sheaves here and there, and the reddish ripening groats; in the distance the dust-blue horizon kept parallel with the train, taking a sharp turn now and then, while the same sort of willows ran up to meet them under the window. It was as if the spaces were whirling in a circle; everything running in the distance was now carried back beneath the window-panes.

The talkative worker with the humble face (evidently a loafer), unable to bear the silence, turned to Luka Silitch:

"I'm traveling now without any supplies; so I'm bringing some sugar and tea, and bagels. We got together to ask them to make a distribution of seeds; but he wouldn't agree: so I'm traveling."

The merchant was fuming and sweating: he interrupted the worker.

"You shouldn't have gone: they acted rightly toward you—according to the law!"

"How do you mean?"

"You needed it, but the manager risked being punished!"

The worker listened attentively.

"One hundred and twenty men went to ask for it again; they were refused again—he didn't give any."

"I explained it to you. Do you understand?"

"I understand."

Silence . . .

Through the carriage window they could see the telegraph wire running up and down, the windowpane was all dusty; the telegraph wire ran up and down; a midge sitting on the windowpane looked like a bird flying over the fields. "The devil take the General's wife!" Yeropegin thought. He thought he had detected something sinister in the Baron. Did the Baron know of his dealings with his mamma? How couldn't he know—he must know: if he weren't careful, the Baron could corner him here in the third class; and why was he, Yeropegin, afraid of that?

But the worker was not to be repressed.

"I'm carrying tea, sugar, and bagels," he started off again. "This year we have nothing to sow . . ."

"What do you mean we have nothing?" Luka Silitch asked, pointedly voicing his surprise as he plunged into the discussion so as to stop thinking about the Baron, the General, and Annushka.

"There is no grain, that's it, for sowing the fields . . ."

"Why do the others have it and not you?"

"Why don't I have any? But the others haven't got it either; we wrote a petition, seventy-five of us wrote it; but they turned it down."

"Because that's the ruling all over the state . . ."

"I wasn't implying anything in particular: I merely remarked that life has become harder for us."

"Well, that's not a very clever remark."

"But I . . ."

"You should listen to what you're being told: don't interrupt . . . With us, in the whole of the state, it might be said, people are busy with agriculture and the raising of wheat, and our state is not lagging behind any other state. And we are living, thank God. . . ."

"Yes, thank God, thank God: this year again we have nothing to sow . . ."

"That's a stupid statement again; only a hooligan would say that . . . If you want to be a hooligan, you can talk like that (Luka Silitch had made it a rule to enlighten ignorant folk). As I have already told you, you should speak only when I have finished; but if you wish to interrupt me, you must give me warning, do you understand?"

"Have you finished now?"

"Yes, I have finished. You can speak now."

But that conversation was fated to come to a sudden end. The door opened and the conductor courteously bent over Luka Silitch.

"There's a gentleman in the first class who begs you to call on him to have a chat."

There was nothing to be done. His bones creaking, Yeropegin got up and made his way to the first class: he had no wish to decline such a conversation. Some of the passengers joked as he left.

"He's a real commander, that . . ."

"He must be a cadet!"

"A regular dog, that's what!"

"A gentleman!"

Yeropegin was now already installed in the first class compartment facing the Senator.

"I've been wanting to see you, Yeropegin," the Senator said. "We'll have a chat now on the way. . . ."

And so they had a chat.

For the two hours that remained to them before reaching Likhov there was nothing but talk—talk of shares in the Varaksinsky mines and in the Metelkinsky railway branch. Yeropegin got in one word to the Baron's ten; when Yeropegin tried to be evasive, the Baron was ten times more so; and thus he attacked Yeropegin with legal paragraphs and clauses . . . attacked him so persistently that Luka Silitch, for all his business acumen, was forced to retreat before the Baron; and the Baron kept after him, threatening him with legal action; and he did it all so quietly, courteously, and properly that he simply wore down the merchant who felt all tied up in knots from weakness, nausea, dreams of Annushka's kisses, and fear of the Senator's legal threats.

At last they arrived at Likhov.

"I advise you to give up your claims of your own volition," the Senator concluded. "If the matter comes to court, I shall have you jailed. They'll put a ring in your nose and drag you off to hard labor." (The Baron always expressed himself in images: he was a great eccentric.)

Thus, abruptly, the Baron ended his speech with a heavy sigh, as he carefully blew a gram of dust from his traveling bag.

Now they both fell silent: their elderly silhouettes, those of the gentleman and the merchant, swayed in the azure space of the window: the silhouettes of a merchant and a squire; one sickly and green, with eyes glittering in the sun and a grayish beard; the other, rosy, clean-shaven, and long-nosed, smelling of eau-de-cologne—the silhouettes of two old men: one had on his finger a gold ring with a large ruby; the other wore no ruby, but had on black gloves; one had a plaid and a cushion strapped together; the other had a plaid without straps and a small traveling bag; the former's face, which was plain and icon-like, showed lips all parched with debauch; the other's sexless face was sadly pink, while his full lips played ironically; the former was tall, angular, dry and when he changed his jacket for his merchant's garb, wore a coat with artificial shoulders; the latter's shoulders were rounded, his back straight like a young man's; the former was wearing a cap, the latter had donned a black silk cap with earmuffs and also wore an expensive black blouse; the former was gray; the latter was still graying though he was the same age as the former; the former was a miller and a peasant; the latter—a Baron and a Senator.

"And do you have children?" the Baron asked.

"Yes I have."

"What do they do?"

"My son's at the University."

"Poor fellow, in that case it's the end of him," the Baron sighed in genuine horror.

"How do you mean?"

"Oh, very simply: mental work requires selection and a sound heredity. . . ."

This Yeropegin failed completely to understand. He only understood one thing: the Baron, though an eccentric, was also a sharp dealer, and it was better not to get entangled with him.

The Baron began to sway from side to side: from the hunchbacked plain the Likhov spire already came in sight; a windmill passed, so did a line of wagons; the train stopped; a couple of Likhov porters played the gentleman, besieged by imploring passengers; here an economic elder with a flaxen beard down to his waist was darting up and down, peeping in a frightened way into the windows and searching out the gentry; an energetic lackey ran into the Baron's compartment and the Baron handed him his plaid and traveling bag: "Do me a favor and lighten my burden, friend!"

"Goodbye," the Baron said to Yeropegin, curtly holding out his hand, but without removing his glove; and then he disappeared in the thick of the crowded Likhov platform.

Sultry Weather

It was scorching. Luka Silitch almost burned his hand when he touched an iron part of the four-wheeler; he could not get the Baron out of his head, just as he could not forget barefooted Annushka. Was she up and waiting for him this early? But no doubt she was asleep. As for Fyokla Matveyevna, she got out of bed around eleven. Strange, but the walls of the house seemed infected with some disease; he had hardly set foot in the house before a malignant odor overcame him and made him feel faint: Fyokla would never look him in the eyes now; and the servants glanced sideways at him as though they were concealing something. He had difficulty in breathing; and there was also the Baron with his threat of legal action.

They were already approaching Ganshina Street, at the bottom of which his wooden mansion could be seen, while all around him out of the sky stifling clouds were falling to earth, although it was hardly eight o'clock in the morning. There had to be a thunderstorm, indeed.

For a long time Luka Silitch kept ringing his doorbell: there was no answer; were they all still asleep? From a window of the house opposite, occupied by a tailor, a certain "Tzizik-Izic," a Jewish woman all in wrinkles and rags stared sympathetically and waved her hand at him:

"Ring, ring . . . you won't get any answer," she shouted. "Your servants had a party there last night: at five o'clock this morning Sukhorukov came out, and so did

Kakurinsky, and so did the women from the old people's home."

"What's this?" Luka Silitch asked himself. It wasn't enough for fate to wear him down with faintness, nausea, and lustful thoughts for barefooted Annushka; it wasn't enough to have had that Petersburg Senator persecute him to the point of exhaustion for three hours in the railway carriage; but now, if you please, on returning home he was obliged to put things in order (Luka Silitch always made a strong point of order). Despairing of any response to his ringing, Luka Silitch descended the steps and started banging with all his might on the gates: then he made out muttered words and hoarse breathing behind the gates; the hinges creaked and Ivan-the-Fire thrust forth his drowsy, swollen face; catching sight of his master, he looked confused and lowered his eyes.

"What's this I hear about your having visitors here at night in my absence?" Luka Silitch demanded, rushing up to him, but Ivan-the-Fire remained as dumb as a tree stump.

"Well?" Yeropegin continued, trying to force an answer. But Ivan-the-Fire merely replied with a show of anger:

"What guests? We've seen no guests!"

"Don't wave your hands, don't get into that habit. Drop your arms."

"I didn't mean . . . I've never seen no guests. I'll swear on the cross, I didn't."

"All right. But what did that Jewish woman mean?" Luka Silitch turned to the tailor's window, but the Jewish woman had disappeared.

"A Jewish woman's a Jewish woman," Ivan-the-Fire put in. "A Jewish woman will say anything; you just believe a Jewish woman . . . a Jewish woman . . ."

"Don't argue with your hands, drop your hands, sew them to your trousers. Pick up my things," Luka Silitch shouted, beside himself. "We'll go into all that later . . . It looks like a thunderstorm. . . ."

"Yes," the Fire replied, scratching his ear and staring up at the sky, "it's piled up. . . ."

The master, his boots creaking drily and impressively, strode into his study; there was a heavy atmosphere in the empty study; he dropped into an armchair; soon his abacus began clicking, there was a clang of keys, a rustling of papers in his fingers, of receipts, bills, and promissory notes; he was anxiously examining the papers that had to do with the Graaben affair, and he began to comprehend that perhaps the Baron had been right: these papers were sufficient to frighten, but not fleece the old woman; for an hour or two or more the master suffered from his thoughts, from weakness, nausea, and a sort of parching sadness. There was Ivan the porter, too; more than once it had seemed to the master that Ivan the porter had been keeping watch on him grimly with some deceit in view—he must get rid of him, get rid of him quickly. . . .

His attention was suddenly diverted; he noticed a cigarette butt in his ashtray; the merchant picked it up, examined the butt from every angle, and decided that none of his guests could have smoked such a cigarette. This meant that, in his absence, some stranger had been sitting in his study; but who could it possibly have been?

He looked around him. An armchair cover had been moved and on the carpet under the chair was a dry patch of mud; Fyokla Matveyevna had no business in his study and, in any case, she would not bring mud in. "There must have been visitors here without me," Yeropegin thought. "Fyokla must know about this, but she is hiding it from me: that explains why she hasn't looked me in the eyes for a long time now; maybe she's begun to have a lover. Pfu!" Luka Silitch felt so sick at the thought that he spat out at the idea of even imagining the "dumpling" in the role of a lover.

"No, that's not it!" he decided. Then he remembered what the Jewish woman had told him: Sukhorukov the coppersmith and the women from the old people's home had been there at night, she had said. "The devil! What do they want here at night!" And Luka Silitch remembered the buzzing and the whispering that went on in the house, the way the walls had frowned on him for over a year, and sweat broke out on his forehead. "I'll get to the bottom of this," he muttered. "Just you wait, Fyokla Matveyevna, just you wait; I'll teach you to have secrets from me in my own house. I'll teach you to have parties here without my knowledge . . ."

He rang the bell:

"Call Fyodor."

Fyodor appeared, still tipsy from the previous night.

"Who was here last night?" Yeropegin asked.

"Dunno: seems no one . . ."

"You've been at the alcohol again."

Fyodor scratched his head:

"I had a little. I was offered some."

"Since you admit it, I must tell you that you're an unfortunate man to use alcohol. It's a great evil, and it's a lost man who uses alcohol."

"Quite true, I admit it—a human parasite . . ."

"Well, that's a stupid thing to say. A human *parasite?* Do you know what *pa-ra-site* means? Can you make anything of it? Well, off with you!"

So! they were getting Fyodor drunk. Fyodor was not one of them; all right, we'll get to the bottom of it. Luka Silitch sat there with gleaming eyes and compressed lips; he felt nauseous, his temples throbbed, and a faintness greater than he had ever experienced stole over him. Fyodor, the Baron, deceitful acts . . . A dry sort of sadness was gnawing at him. But in the house people were already getting up: there were footsteps, a clatter of plates, the shuffling of Fyokla Matveyevna's slippers; everyone knew that their master in person had returned from Ovchinnikov.

Not on the appointed day had Luka Silitch been pleased to return from Ovchinnikov: no one had expected him at so early an hour. And the things that had been going on here!

THE SILVER DOVE

263

In his absence the "doves" had prayed the whole night
long—not in the bathhouse, but in the dining room; before
the prayers began the "doves" held an important consulta-
tion; they had discussed the advisability of temporarily
desisting from their political propaganda and proclamations;
the police were already on the track of the "doves"; leaflets
with black crosses on them had been distributed in Likhov;
if they were not careful, they would be caught; all sorts of
restrictions had recently come into force in Likhov, especially after the Grachikha disorders and the revolt of priest
Nicholas; a whole squadron of cossacks had been quartered
in the district; the townspeople of Likhov remembered how
the Fokins and the Alexins had been taken off with their
hands tied, in carts down Panshina Street in the direction of
the jail.

A seminarist, who had been expelled from his seminary,
attempted for a long time to defend the Likhov political
platform, but Sukhorukov the coppersmith stood his
ground; and, on this account, an unpleasant conversation
had developed between them on the subject of intelligence.

"I'm no fool, if I may say so, and in political affairs I'm
smarter than many a one . . ."

"I am no fool either: we'll see who's smarter . . ."

"How oddly you talk! Rudely, one may say, and insult-
ingly. I've never met a man smarter than myself. There may
be some, they can be found, they're very rare. I have not
yet met any . . . I can't continue this conversation with
you any longer, I don't want to. You can speak, if you like,
but I won't listen," Sukhorukov concluded, sulking. But
they were eventually reconciled. Nevertheless, the coppersmith won his point, and the "doves" for the time being
stopped their political activities.

In the midst of the lamentations of the old asylum
woman, the "dumpling" read the carpenter Kudeyarov's
epistle announcing that a "dove" child, a human one, was
being generated from two spiritual human substances; the
"doves" told each other that around Tzelebeyevo a whole

movement was under way and that the "doves" there were entertained with hospitality and affection.

On the morning before the meeting Fyokla Matveyevna received the epistle by hand from the beggar Abram, and she at once resolved to visit Tzelebeyevo on the following day to have a look at those places, her excuse being that she wished to inspect the mill. At that time, in her husband's absence, Fyokla Matveyevna used to pray day and night and, as a result, she lost weight and her flesh hung loosely; but also, as a result, her eyes had become all the more radiant and pure: she might have resembled a pug dog, but she had angelic eyes.

The master had come back earlier than expected; she had planned to depart before his return and then to invent some excuse; but now she was puzzled how to explain her projected trip. Fyodor was already polishing the harness: it was too late to put it off.

These were the thoughts weighing on her mind when she met her spouse: they shook hands drily; the master stared at her—at the nasty, deceitful, little "dumpling."

"All right, all right! Drop your eyes!" he thought. "I know why you won't look me straight in the face: there are secret goings on here."

The "dumpling" stared at her master. The Lord Save Us! he looked like Deathless Kaschey* in person; lean, pale, perspiring, with shaking hands and dark bags under the eyes.

Her heart almost stopped beating when the "dumpling" informed her husband that she'd like to breathe the *aramatic* country air for a day or two, visit the priest's wife in Tzelebeyevo, and to inspect the mill—needing the master's attention.

At first Yeropegin thought, "Now, my darling, I'll put the pressure on you." But he thought better of it: in the

* A character out of Russian folklore.

first place, in her absence, he could really investigate who it was visited the house at night; and, secondly, without her, he could enjoy himself all the more with Annushka.

"Well, go then," he said.

"I'll take Annushka-the-Dovecot with me . . ."

"You can't take Annushka!" Luka Silitch hissed. "The house will fall into disorder without her. Annushka here, Annushka there . . . Annushka hasn't time for every-thing. . . ."

The troika arrived; with tied up cushions, tubs, and quilts, the "dumpling," all wrapped up, took her seat; the carriage rattled off.

As soon as the house was emptied, Luka Silitch began to explore that empty house—to sniff in every corner, to turn everything over, to examine the shelves; finally he reached Fyokla Matveyevna's room and lo! and behold: under the pillow he found the keys of the trunk and a wrapped up piece of embroidery with a number of crosses on it and, in their midst, a silver dove with a halo around its head: "H'm, h'm, h'm!" Luka Silitch muttered with a gesture of surprise; he grabbed the embroidery and carried it away to his study: he locked it up there and returned again: he picked up the keys and crawled under the bed; under the bed stood a forged metal trunk; he pulled out the trunk and opened it: "H'm, h'm, h'm, proclamations! I must let the district office know . . ." So thought Luka Silitch as he bent over the trunk. He began to remove various objects from it: ritual vessels, long shirts, a large piece of azure silk with a human heart embroidered on it in red velvet and a white beaded dove tearing at the heart (on that embroidery the dove's beak was that of a hawk); he then pulled out two leaden candlesticks, a goblet, a red silk purificatory, a church spoon and a lance; Luka Silitch pulled all these things from the trunk and fumbled among them, pale of face, sickly-looking, yet strong-fingered; wearing his long black coat among these pieces of silk and these shirts he looked like a spider in his web.

"Aaaah! Aaaah!" was all he could utter as he left the room somewhat apprehensively; and in the dark corridor he was obliged to lean against the wall, so faint did he feel; the perspiration poured off him, his breath came in gasps, but what it was all about he could not very well explain: there was something criminal about it, that is all he felt.

Annushka-the-Dovecot was shuffling along the corridor; her plaited hair was rising and falling behind her supple back; without noticing Yeropegin who was crouching in a corner, she was smiling to herself. He grabbed her by the skirt. "Oh, you frightened me!" she exclaimed, laughing, and pushing him away with her bare foot. Evidently she thought he was merely indulging in a little license. But far from it! Luka Silitch dragged her off to the "dumpling's" room and shoved her face into the "objects"; and in the ensuing tussle they stumbled among goblets, silks, and shirts. "What's this? Eh! What's that?" the master of the house kept demanding with a note of apprehension in his voice as he pushed her close to the chalices.

"That's . . . That's . . ." she began, turning pale, and then stopped.

"Out with it!"

"I won't . . ." she gasped, turning paler still.

Bash! he struck her on the face.

"Out with it!"

"I won't!"

Bash-bash-bash! the blows rained upon her.

Then, suddenly, with a squirming movement, she rapidly tore herself away, dashed aside, and then burst out laughing, laughing insolently. The way she laughed when the old man made advances to her at night.

"Why are you hitting me?" she asked. "You don't know yourself why! Can't you see it's your wife's secret here; and if I was to tell you about it, it should all be done in good order. Now this evening," she said, winking, "I'll tell you everything; I'll do you a service. We'll lay out all these objects in their proper order; we'll drink wine from the chalices, and we'll have mutual pleasure; I'll try very hard, you'll see!" Thereupon she bent toward him and laughingly whispered something that made the old man's face light up.

Ting-a-ling-a-ling! the bell had already sounded more than once; it was time to go and open the door. They locked the room; a visitor had come at an awkward moment on some business about wheat; unwillingly Luka Silitch closeted himself with him.

Meanwhile, in the orchard, Annushka-the-Dovecot was holding a whispered conversation with Sukhorukov the coppersmith.

"So, Anna Kuzminishna, you mustn't leave a trace: not a trace, I tell you; otherwise, if there is even a trace left, it will be the end of us all. . . ."

"Oh!"

"Groan as much as you like, but we have to put an end to him."

"Oh! I can't!"

"You must trust my judicious sense: I've never met a more able man than myself . . ."

Silence.

"Whatever you may feel, you must give him that powder.

"I can't give him that powder . . ."

"You must, I tell you. I assure you I've never met a smarter man than myself. . . ."

Silence.

"So it's decided, isn't it?"

"Taste this sweet wine, my handsome one, my loved one."

The sound of a kiss: again and again . . .

"Annushka, my Annushka, my white-breasted Annushka!"

The sound of a kiss: again.

"Here, my joy, taste this sweet wine; and take something to eat . . . take more . . . more. . . ."

The sound of a kiss: again and again . . .

The old man, wearing only a nightshirt, displayed his parched, hairy legs; and the white-breasted Annushka was seated on his knees; on the table lay an azure piece of satin, wafers, a goblet; two candles burned on either side; the door was locked, the blinds were drawn. From afar Ivanov's rattle could be heard rattling madly.

"Help yourself, my beautiful, to more sweet wine. O Lord!"

"What's the matter?"

"Something pricked at my heart; it's nothing; eat . . ."

"So it turns out that this 'dumpling' of mine prays at nighttime in her nightshirt. Ha-ha-ha!"

"Hi-hi-hi!" Annushka laughed in response, hiding her deathly pale face on his hairy chest.

"And they call them the doves?"

"Doves, my darling . . ."

"Ha-ha-ha!"

"Hi-hi-hi!" in his hairy chest the sound was more like a squeal than a laugh . . .

"Why are you trembling so?"

"There's a pricking at my heart . . ."

She raised the goblet and carried it to his already stupidly drooping lips.

The rattle was rattling madly into the darkness under the windows.

🐍 Necessary—Unnecessary 🐍

The sun, great and golden, with its great golden beams was bathing the parched, slightly sunburnt meadow, and the grasses were baking in the beams of the great sun; here a flower swayed upon a dry, slender stem; there a white-trunked grove of birch trees was inviting you and, amid the white trunks were moss, stumps, and fallen leaves; and amid the heaps of fallen leaves, here and there, a mushroom cap would peep at you; an old birch mushroom will just beg to be picked and stowed away in your linden basket; a sweet, autumnal twittering of a tomtit—do you hear them? It was still July; but all of nature was already staring at you, smiling at you, whispering in a murmur of birch trees, "Just wait till August . . ." August came swimming in the noise and rustling of time: do you hear the noise of time? August was already sending the squirrel to the hazel grove; and the month of August was already rushing through the high heavens in triangles of storks; hear then, hear, my dear, the farewell cry of fleeting summer!

Among the purple flowers, the little birch tree stumps, stood Fyokla Matveyevna in quiet adoration: submissively she had folded her hands over her belly; the sun played on her chocolate-colored dress, on her veil, on her hat of enormous proportions ornamented with cherries. Like the goddess Pomona, Fyokla Matveyevna paraded deeply moved amid the pleasant gifts of summer; and the spirit filled her heart: aromas tickled her nostrils; she melted and grew faint from sweet, sweet sneezing, and Vukol, the priest, striding after her in his cotton cassock intoned each time she sneezed:

"Praise be to you, Fyokla Matveyevna!"

To which Fyokla Matveyevna modestly responded:

"Thank you, Father Vukol: a fine man you are."

But she had other things on her mind: here, here, were aromatic places, favored places, sacred and spiritual places; here, here, the joy of all Russia was being born: the Holy Ghost. Keenly the merchant's wife glanced from behind bushes, stumps, ditches, for some kind of a blessing.

She was now in the holy, health-giving places—in Tzelebeyevo places; beneath her feet a stream gurgled and splashed; and when Fyokla Matveyevna stepped on the log thrown across the stream, the stream protested and gurgled all the more; the waters splashed and growled, wetting Fyokla Matveyevna's feet.

"Be careful, mother, the log's unsteady here: it's not the time to slip . . ." the priest fussed behind her. In his impatience, he gathered up his cassock and jumped over the stream and, shaking his reddish beard and laughing, held out his hand to the merchant's wife. Fyokla Matveyevna laughed too.

And there, there, beyond the stream: there, into the distance, ran the birch tree copse; white yards of cut logs, glowing in sunlit brocade; and in that golden brocade a white dove spun, beating its wings and cooing: it settled on the logs and then ran across them: and over the dry bark its claws sounded: tsa-tsa-tsa!

"What blessed places we have here, mother Fyokla Matveyevna!" the priest exclaimed, smiling and wiping his perspiring face with a red handkerchief.

How could they not be blessed: Fyokla Matveyevna remembered how she had driven yesterday to Tzelebeyevo and prayed all the way; she recalled how her heart had pounded and how, when they had neared the holy place, each stump by the roadway had assumed the semblance and image of a devil; all the way the wind had whistled about Fyokla Matveyevna and showered her with dry dust, and out of the dust the stumps, the bushes, the branches had peered at her like devilish faces, wickedly grimacing at her in the sun, trying to drive her back to Likhov; and only then did Fyokla Matveyevna comprehend how many devils there were always threatening human nature; invisible to the eye, they swirled about us; only prayer, fasting, and the aspiration to saintliness, to chasten the flesh, can endow with spiritual vision the corporeal sight itself; and by means of this spiritual vision each material object became the image and semblance of other invisible objects; all this Fyokla Matveyevna had comprehended yesterday as she came near Tzelebeyevo from Likhov: the entire road as far as Tzelebeyevo had been planted with terrifying devils; it was as though an ambush of hostile powers had been thrown around the sacred precincts: from one small stump to another, from one devil to another. On the road, as many devils entered Fyokla Matveyevna's soul as there were devils in the semblance and image of stumps rising up on each side of the road beneath the sun; but she had prayed incessantly—and then Fyokla Matveyevna found herself in Tzelebeyevo.

Here everything went differently: already, as she sat by the samovar with the priest's wife, Fyokla Matveyevna observed some strange occurrences: the bushes, the huts, the tin cockerel on the roof of the hut all stared her straight in the eyes as though saying with pensive sweetness:

"Look at me: I have a secret. The village, the pond, the roof peeping out of the smooth slope—have all preserved the secret of these places. Even the priest appears to be an inhabitant of a different, better world."

That evening they stood on the Tzelebeyevo common: a choir of maidens was dancing on the common; their feet were stamping out every sort of rhythm, and around them waves of grass were scudding and the evening breeze lulled them, while a shaggy curtain of dust rose up on the road and the large, yellow moon ascended above Tzelebeyevo; it gazed down into Fyokla Matveyevna's soul and bade her, "Gaze, be silent, and keep the secret. . . ."

That night in sleep, a vision was vouchsafed to Fyokla Matveyevna: the carpenter appeared and stood by her head; spreading his pale hand over her, he enjoined her not to speak of him or see him; in silence, with his eyes only, the carpenter conversed with her: "I am now bound by a great secret, and it is forbidden now to see or hear me, or to think about me in these places. . . ."

In the morning, having awoken from the vision, Fyokla Matveyevna reversed her intention: she was not prepared to visit Kudeyarov in his dwelling; for that dwelling was now the holy of holies; it was not accessible to strange eyes. . . .

Thus thought Fyokla Matveyevna as she contemplated the holy places in the company of Father Vukol. And what places they were! Yonder a blue lake would gleam with loud streams running down to it as though from mica, there a tree would hang down its withered leaves, and from among the leaves would come sweet autumn twittering of a tomtit; a golden beam fell on her breast and that golden beam on her breast emanated a hot, powerful current and a command as though from some invisible power: "As from this day, all that will come to pass shall be good: and so it should be."

"And so it should be," the priest confirmed; but saying this, he confirmed something else; the priest stood before a pool of water, showing Fyokla Matveyevna how to cross it; but Fyokla Matveyevna, flowering in an angelic smile, flashed her eyes sweetly and tenderly at the priest: "So it should be," she said and stepped into the mud.

As for the priest, he thought to himself, "Why am I fussing about with this stupid head? She does nothing but smile. And what is she smiling about?"

And with its large beams the large golden sun was bathing the parched grass; and the month of August rushed through

the high heavens in a triangle of storks. Hear now the familiar cry of departing summer. . . .

They had barely settled down over a samovar in the
priest's currant bush garden, and barely had the priest's
wife, bowing low, served before the "dumpling" the Lenten
sugar and the golden honey, above which the striped wasps
circled, while at the same time, the brass shine of the
burnished samovar distorted the merchant wife's face, when
a messenger galloped up and tethered his horse to the
priest's fence; he quickly ran up to the table and handed
over a message; the message informed Fyokla Matveyevna
that her husband, Luka Silitch, had fallen ill overnight and
that he was now bereft of his tongue, hands and legs.

Strange thing: while Fyokla Matveyevna was reading the
note, in her soul echoed the powerful command: "As from
this day, all that will come to pass, shall be good: so it
should be . . ."

Fyokla Matveyevna almost said aloud: "And so it should
be . . ." Her heart bade her weep and be horrified, but
Fyokla Matveyevna, accepting the tidings as a dream that
had long passed away from her, continued to rejoice.

Already the horses were rushing her back to Likhov; all
those stumps and bushes, which had recently menaced her,
now swayed gently in the evening breeze and sang a new
song of ineffable joy; in the fine whistling of the branches
sounded: "And so it should be . . . When the horses
mounted the Dead Top, the whole countryside unfurled
from the Dead Top; and such was the silence all around that
it seemed the grief of the world had departed forever from
the earth and the earth was exulting in its triumphant
glitter.

In the Yeropegin house all was empty and terrifying:
through the dark chambers sin was fluttering; it seemed as if
from all the corners Luka Silitch's spirit was straining and
complaining. Luka Silitch was fluttering through the empty
halls as through an empty, stupid, and aimless world, and

there was no escape for him out of his own house, because he had himself built his house; and this house had become his world; and there was no escape for him. . . .

There, there, in the bedroom, lay something pallid, pitiful, and speechless. But this was not Luka Silitch. What was it then? You might of course find some dry skin and a grayish beard: all this carefully wrapped in sheets; and bending over *all this* an old crone from the old people's home, quietly mumbled over *all this*. But *all this* was not Luka Silitch: in vain *it* stared at the world with meaningless eyes, in vain *it* tried to move its tongue, in vain *it* tried to remember—*it* did not remember. Luka Silitch had already become separated from *all this*. Invisible, he pressed against the windows, but the windows were firmly shuttered, and Luka Silitch, though fleshless, deathless, could not penetrate through the wood, his corporeal soul fluttering futilely against the walls and rustling over the wallpaper as cockroaches do; voicelessly, Luka Silitch screamed that they had poisoned him, that then they had carefully wrapped him up in sheets: that in *all that* there was now throbbing poison, not blood. In vain he implored the General, who had dropped in by chance, to expose this criminal activity, but the General did not hear him; the doctor and he were both stooping over the gray beard.

"A terrible thing to happen, doctor!"

"It was to be expected: a stroke—one can't burn the candle at both ends without consequences."

"It isn't true, it isn't true!" Luka Silitch assailed them. "It's sheer murder: they poisoned me—avenge me, avenge . . ."

But his voice was soundless, his soul invisible. The doctor and the General bent over the gray beard; but the gray beard was not Luka Silitch.

But where was it? Luka Silitch no longer saw his gray beard protruding from under the sheet; to left and right of him he could only see the edges of the pillows; the doctor was bending over him and feeling his head. Where was

Luka Silitch? Was it all merely a dream? Had he not flown through the rooms? Or, perhaps, he had just regained his body? What had really happened to him?

The disk of light came nearer; candle in hand and pale as death, there stood the "Dovecot." Luka Silitch came out of his delirium: now he remembered everything, but he could express nothing; he knew that he had been poisoned, that a terrifying mystery was being enacted in his house; appealingly he stared at the doctor; he felt the tears pouring from his eyes.

"Does he understand?"

"But he cannot say anything."

"Never . . ."

"He can't move?"

"Never . . ."

They were exchanging whispers about all these things with the doctor; but Luka Silitch's hearing grew sharper; he heard both what was being said about him and what Sukhorukov and Ivan-the-Fire had said to each other in whispers in the kitchen, as well as the noise that a cockroach was making as it ran over the wall of a far room.

He hears everything, but he says nothing: they had poisoned him.

Now Fyokla Matveyevna, in a chocolate dress, was standing over him, smelling of the sweet aroma of the fields, but her eyes were hidden behind a veil; she had not yet taken off her hat. Was she weeping or smiling there beneath that veil? Luka Silitch tried to open his lips and move toward her: "They have poisoned me, poisoned me . . ." But she did not hear him; she smiled: nothing was clear through the veil. . . .

Fyokla Matveyevna stared at her husband and saw that he was no longer her husband, not himself, but merely something wrapped in sheets; she wanted to weep for her husband and grieve; but she felt no grief, *merely something:* a blue lake gleamed suddenly in the sun, and toward it from the mica flowed babbling streams; there a tree let hang its withered leaves, and among those leaves there was a sweet autumn twittering of tomtits. There was no grief in Fyokla Matveyena's soul, but memories and the sweet autumn twittering of tomtits, and she heard an authoritative command within her, "As from this day, all that happens shall be good: and so it should be . . ."

"Not that way, not that way," Luka Silitch tried to say. "You should weep for me, not laugh."

But Fyokla Matveyevna did not laugh. Tears poured from her eyes, and yet . . . in her soul a beam, a golden beam, rose on high, and, within that beam, a white dove fluttered, beating its wings and cooing.

"Not that way!"

"That is the only way!"

In the Yeropegin house all was dense, empty, and terrifying, and shuffling sounds began to make themselves heard in dark corners. Luka Silitch was again fluttering through the rooms.

ꞏꞏꞏ꙾⤸ Pavel Pavlovich ⤵꙾ꞏꞏꞏ

Above the high ravine into which the pine trees tumbled
Katya sat, gazing in front of her at the angry chill evening
light over the forest expanse; a gray plaid covered Katya's
shoulders; her youthful shoulders shivered now and then
from the raw air; the day before, on this spot, the poor girl
had almost thrown herself into the pond; the day before, on
this spot, the wretched girl had forgiven Pyotr; the day
before, on this spot, she had stretched out her slender arms
to him—beyond, over the expanse of forest, into the angry,
chill evening light.

But the thought of her grandmother had stopped her.

Katya mastered her impulse. She returned as usual to play
a game of patience; and they played *durachki**, the grandma
and the young girl. They smiled at each other; and then
toward evening uncle Pavel Pavlovich arrived after having
been delayed for a day at Likhov.

Her uncle had grown grayer, but otherwise he was much
the same as he had been when she last saw him a couple of
years ago; clean-shaven, neat, smelling of eau-de-cologne, he
had kissed with a sort of detached affection the old lady's
fingers and, afterwards, at tea-time, while sipping cream, he
had told them in his querulous voice of Petersburg and of
his travels abroad; and Yevseich, who looked as if he were

---

* "Fools," a game of cards.

stuck to the wall, greedily absorbed these traveler's tales;
Strigachev, Pavel Pavlovich's butler, who was dressed no
worse than the Baron himself, came and went carelessly
among the gentry and, whenever Pavel Pavlovich became
confused in his narrative, he corrected him without the
slightest compunction.

"If you will allow me, Pavel Pavlovich, it was not like
that: we arrived in Nice not on Thursday, but on Friday
morning; you were pleased to take a bath on arrival, and
then we . . ."

"That's quite correct, my friend," Pavel Pavlovich
agreed, continuing his account.

In this manner the three of them sat on the terrace: in her
sad way, Katya was pleased at her uncle's arrival; and the
uncle, blowing his nose loudly, was saying to the old
Baroness:

"*Maman*, what a pother about nothing: I thought you
were threatened with ruin which would have been in the
order of things. But this is no more than a little affair of
cheating, a confidence trick; no one at any time has the
right to deprive you of your estate. As to the shares in the
Varaksinsky Mines, we shall discuss this with Yeropegin. I
don't think he is as dangerous as he would like it to appear."

(For some reason, Pavel Pavlovich concealed his encoun-
ter with Yeropegin on the train).

Pavel Pavlovich sat down above the high ravine, into
which the pine trees tumbled; Katya sat beside him on a
bench; and in front of them, over the expanse of forest, the
angry chill evening light; there, in the distance, an aspen
tree was the first to turn red; the summer had been hot: the
red, golden age of autumn was nigh.

Uncle and niece sat there, each thinking his own
thoughts. Katya was thinking that, as soon as her grandmother died, she, poor child, would enter a nunnery; while
the long-nosed Senator uncle smiled sorrowfully that Katya
was so young, suppressing in his soul an involuntary sigh:

"You're such a child, little Katya. You don't know life: time will heal everything."

"But why did he abandon me, uncle?"

"I can't tell you that, dear girl. You are so young, and I sincerely wish you happiness. The fact that he is no longer with you raises him in my estimation."

"?"

"It proves that he was seeking your hand because he was genuinely attracted to you, and not for the sake of money . . . He's a poet, isn't he?"

"Yes, a poet."

"That is, a vulgar aesthete . . ."

At that Katya blushed profusely! What an arch her brows made! What a glance she darted at him! But her uncle's beardless face looked sad and humble.

"My child, I did not wish to offend you," he said. "I must declare that all men fall into two categories—parasites and slaves; the parasites in their turn are divided into magicians or magi, murderers or vulgarians; the magi are those who invented God and by means of their invention procure money; the murderers are the warrior caste in this world; the vulgarians are divided into plain vulgarians, that is, solid, learned vulgarians, such as professors, lawyers, doctors, the men of the liberal professions and vulgar aestheticians: to this last category belong the poets, the writers, the artists and the prostitutes . . . I have finished, my friend," the Senator uncle concluded with a sigh as he sniffed a flower.

It was already getting dark: they were sitting on the edge of a ravine; low, chill, black clouds were sweeping past them.

In the distance, along the garden path, among the branches and the shadows, and bats flying up into the shadow, the Baroness was walking listlessly, leaning on her cane: her dull leaden eyes and her hanging mouth all spoke of an old woman's ruin, of her ruin, and the fact that her days were numbered, that the gloom of eternal night, having stuck to her eyes, was already peering into her soul, calling her.

All three of them now walked back toward the house: the uncle supported the grandmother; Katya walked a little ahead of them aimlessly chewing a slender reed.

The mother whispered to her elderly son:

"That ruffian robbed me into the bargain; I missed my diamonds the day he left the house."

"Don't say that, mamma: he's an eccentric and eccentrics, as we well know, do not indulge in thieving."

"But the diamonds . . ."

"Who else was at the house that day?"

"I don't think there was anybody else . . . But wait, yes, Yeropegin was there that day . . ."

"Alone?"

"No, he was with General Chizhikov!"

"Well, there you are, mamma, and you're making up stories. It was General Chizhikov who stole the diamonds."

That is what Pavel Pavlovich softly told his trembling mother as he blew his nose into the condensing gloom. . . .

Baron Pavel Pavlovich Todrabe-Graaben was a big eccentric; but all the Barons Todrabe-Graaben had the trait of eccentricity and walked about with prominent red noses which, by the age of sixty, became covered with a network of purple veins—the consequence of their measured use of the rarest and finest wines still to be found in their ancestral wine cellars. In the case of all of them, their upper lip protruded far forward under their nose; in all of them their chin was conspicuously absent, and this made the lower part of their face appear monstrously small by contrast with their bulging eyes which never stared at women's faces, with their enormous noses and receding foreheads of vast proportions. There would, perhaps, be something about them that was gloomily raven-like were it not for their pale-chestnut, unusually washed out, silken hair. All the Barons Todrabe-Graaben sobbed pitifully rather than talked if one elected to ignore the meaning of their words, but the substance of their high sobbing note was always jocularly ironic.

The Baronesses sobbed too; and the Baronesses also wore foreheads and noses as did the male line; but the Baronesses had chins; for that reason many of the Baronesses were stupid: like so many empty quivering jars, they walked about in lace and, as adolescents, they had already left Russia for Nice and Monte Carlo.

Pavel Pavlovich's father, who also bore the name of Pavel Pavlovich, was, like all the Graabens, a big eccentric; he developed such a bee in his bonnet about cleanliness that he instituted an odd custom in his house; he would use a towel or a handkerchief only once; whenever he had a cold and felt the need of a handkerchief, he clapped his hands thrice; the door of his study would open and in ran two little serf-cossack boys, each of them holding in the tips of their two fingers the end of an absolutely clean handkerchief; Pavel Pavlovich would then pick up the handkerchief by the middle and blow his nose loudly (all the Graabens blew their noses loudly); the cossack boys would immediately rush out of the room with the used handkerchief; and if a handkerchief were needed every other minute, the cossack boys would keep running in every minute: an endless succession of handkerchiefs was brought in and taken away.

Pavel Pavlovich was also a musician; he played Beethoven symphonies on a violoncello and made his son sit down to accompany him: at the least mistake, the symphony had to start again from the beginning even though ten pages of it had already been played; and so it went on *ad infinitum*. Because of this, Pavel Pavlovich, the father, could never play a single passage to the end; as a result, his son from early on developed a hatred for music. Everyone in the house fled from Father Pavel Pavlovich's music, but he would always settle down to play on the threshold between two of the most frequented rooms; on one occasion he locked in an acquaintance of his and played for him a good many hours without pause until the acquaintance swooned away. Shortly after this episode Pavel Pavlovich, the father, died.

Pavel Pavlovich's uncle, Alexander Pavlovich, was an even greater eccentric; as a young man, he ate up three quarters of his estate and drank up the entire ancestral wine cellar; at about the age of forty he moved to his country estate where, for five years, he rode all over the district, pouring forth witticisms on every side; then, for the next five years, he isolated himself on his estate, visiting only the harvest fields and expending his wit upon his estate manager. At this point he developed a certain peculiarity: he went about both winter and summer in a sable overcoat and a fur hat; for the next five years Alexander Pavlovich confined himself within the precincts of the park: here he planted fruit trees and trapped birds; then, with every year, he cut down on his walks in the park, so that by the age of sixty, he found himself driven to the terrace where he fed the pigeons bread crumbs; then Alexander Pavlovich incarcerated himself in only three rooms of the mansion; and, finally, in his last three years, he remained secluded in his bedroom where, at his orders, they used to bring a servant girl, Sashka by name, whom Alexander Pavlovich stroked with extraordinary tenderness on the shoulders and that was all. God be my witness, that was all! As for Sashka, she gave birth every year to a child fathered by odd young men here and there. The most astonishing thing was that Alexander Pavlovich was firmly convinced that these children were his own; indeed, in his will he left the richest domain to Sashka's children.

Another uncle of Pavel Pavlovich's, Varavva Pavlovich, was an even greater eccentric; like all the Graabens, he was distinguished by his wit, honesty, and a special passion for cleanliness; it was this latter trait that found expression in such an unlikely idiosyncrasy (in one only) that it might be indecorous to refer to it and, indeed, you will hardly believe it; living as he did in the country, Varavva Pavlovich went visiting in a carriage drawn by six horses; this carriage was always preceded by another carriage drawn by four horses; two cossack boys stood at the back, while a postilion waving a whip rode the front horse. But what did Varavva Pavlovich carry with him in that front carriage? Yes . . . it's rather embarrassing to admit it: he carried, in case of need . . . a certain "utensil," the nature of which is indecorous to define more exactly; on arriving at some manor house, the leading carriage stopped first; the two cossack boys jumped down to open the door and the "utensil," well covered, was solemnly borne into a room specially reserved for it; and only then, after this had been accomplished, did Varavva Pavlovich in person draw up before the manor house; and only then did the hosts appear to welcome him on the threshold and lead the old gentleman to his appointed chambers.

This striving for cleanliness had also mutilated the life of Pavel Pavlovich's aunt, Agnia Pavlovna. In her old age she washed everything that fell into her hands, and she held towels in contempt: she dried her hands by waving them in the air, with the result that her hands were always chapped. Finally, one morning she washed an enormously large fur coat of silver fox—washed it with her own hands—and, as a result, a small pimple appeared on her finger; the pimple turned out to be the Siberian plague, and of this the Baroness Agnia Pavlovna very soon died.

It was in this family of eccentrics that Pavel Pavlovich Todrabe-Graaben, Baron, grew up together with his sister Natalia, who was distinguished from the rest of the female line by her beauty and intelligence. At that time, when their mother was leaving her husband to run away with a hussar, Pavel Pavlovich became very attached to his sister; this attachment later assumed an even tenderer form; in those days Pavel Pavlovich had entered upon a legal career, was a slender young man, and wore a three-cornered hat. His sister had married a man of the gentry, Gugolev by name; the news of her marriage had so shocked Pavel Pavlovich that he too decided to marry as soon as he had completed his course, and this he did. In his choice of a wife he was guided by two principles: in the first place, his wife must always be silent; in the second, her hair must be as fine as flax; and so Pavel Pavlovich married his wife's silence and her fine hair.

By virtue of his intelligence, eloquence, and ability to disentangle the subtlest legal matters with all due honesty, the Baron very rapidly advanced in the service; moreover, at that period he was a moderate liberal; as soon as he had quite imperceptibly earned the right to wear the white trousers of a senator, he immediately abandoned all professional activity; a radical change came over him. Pavel Pavlovich had become a fierce disciple of Proudon. In the Petersburg salons people began to fear him for his witticisms, which spared no one; in the Senate a benign attitude was adopted toward his escapades, but he was made to understand that there was nothing more for him to do there. In no way perturbed, he transplanted himself to his grandfather's estate; but he still used to visit Petersburg for three months at a time so as to keep in touch with his friends.

In the country, the eccentric traits of the Graabens quickly and vividly manifested themselves in him: he made depredations on the wine cellar and squandered money; the library grew at a monstrous rate; since Pavel Pavlovich remained a serious man at heart, he found time for every sort of collection. To begin with, he filled the house with old china; on the tables, sideboards, and shelves there appeared all kinds of statuettes without noses, heads or arms, cups without handles, angular lamps, and rubbish of that sort; then Pavel Pavlovich traveled all over Europe in search of a certain, quite unnecessary engraving. After this expedition, he ordered some half-a-dozen bicycles; he himself took to riding a bicycle and made his wife, butler, maid, and his quite small son, do the same; within half a year he had given the bicycles away and concentrated on educating his children at home; he imported a French woman, a German woman, an English woman, and a Negro woman. Treatises on education were studied; finally Pavel Pavlovich adopted the system of Jean-Jacques Rousseau: all books were taken away from his son; the English woman, the French woman, the German woman and the Negro woman were sent packing; and the fair-haired boy began to swing from trees like a monkey. Then Pavel Pavlovich relaxed and gave all his time to books; in his library one could find everything other bibliophiles lacked, but the most essential books were missing; he had the rare books bound in moiré leather bindings of tender blue, pale-rose and straw-colored hues. Only his closest friends were admitted to the library; but woe to the friend who inadvertently left even the slightest mark on a book; a damaged book could no longer be kept in the library; and with cleverly veiled contempt he presented the book to the person who had damaged it. His closest friends went in fear and trembling of receiving a present of a book from Pavel Pavlovich: such a present signified only one thing, that they had fallen forever in his esteem.

In the country Pavel Pavlovich got up as soon as the cocks began crowing; for three hours, while everyone else in the house was still sleeping, Strigachev the butler washed, massaged and doused him with water according to a set rule, after which Pavel Pavlovich retired to his study and scribbled—but what he wrote had always remained secret to everyone. In all likelihood he was developing some improbable treatise in which he set down for the benefit of humanity some original revelations in the spheres of anthropology, philosophy, history, and the social sciences. Some people would have it that what he was writing was mere nonsense, but Pavel Pavlovich was not discouraged, and on occasions he corresponded with scientists; true, his correspondence touched upon the fine points of bibliography rather than of science, but he did conduct a correspondence.

Before breakfast, Pavel Pavlovich ran through the gazettes and made clippings; afterwards, just before lunch, he would run through the park, looking fresh and sprightly, to the swimming pool with a towel over his shoulder and a tea rose in his hand.

Pavel Pavlovich's attitude to the servants was benign; it was not his principle to lecture them. Pavel Pavlovich allowed everyone his freedom of action, but this freedom was worse than serfdom; without watching anyone, he saw everything; and since his concept of tidiness was intolerable to anyone else, any observed departure from this concept resulted in his sudden flights for an indefinite period from the house, to the horror of the servants; the whole house would be shaken and put on tiptoe when, from afar, his querulous and gloomily benign voice was heard. Thus, as he was walking through the house on one occasion, he noticed several cigarette butts stuck in a vase of flowers; this produced such an effect on him that he was unable to do more than sadly cast a look full of reproach at the servants and then quickly retire to his study; two hours later Strigachev carried out his master's suitcases and trunks, and two weeks later his inconsolable wife received the tidings that Pavel Pavlovich, alive and in good health, was sailing on the steamship "Victoria" to the island of Madeira.

In Petersburg, friends always seemed eager to see the Baron; but in his absence, they all expressed indignation at him, calling him an "eccentric" and, moreover, a "harmful man and an anarchist." On his arrival the doors of the salons were all opened to welcome him, the "eccentric"; and Pavel Pavlovich, seated on a plush ottoman, with a glass of cream in his hand (the Baron avoided tea), expatiated much and at length on the destiny of Russia, the Mongol invasion, the harm caused by Christianity, its influence on the spread of alcoholic beverages, and on the political order in the future. He talked mournfully and slowly, shutting his eyes; he talked with disarming conviction, but he said such strange things that a circle of people would gather around him; and afterwards, this circle of people would make ironical comments about Pavel Pavlovich's opinions. No one contra-

dicted Pavel Pavlovich while he talked; and indeed, it was
difficult to contradict him; the Baron's logical premises
seemed highly contestable, but he defended and developed
them with an iron logic, brilliance and almost inspiration.
He had a number of favorite themes, but he varied these
themes in many different ways; every conversation in
which Pavel Pavlovich was involved seemed to lose its
autonomous sense and became a mere canvas on which
Pavel Pavlovich embroidered his themes.

In this way, Pavel Pavlovich mercilessly continued to
sharpen his wit in the salons of Petersburg; at other times he
made the round of the bookshops and bought many a book.
There were also occasions when Pavel Pavlovich recalled
his legal experience (and he was indeed a remarkable jurist
—cool headed, balanced, and persistent); in the course of
things he would disentangle some dirty business; and having
unmasked the swindlers, he would return to the country.

Having learned that some swindlers and sharpers were
threatening his mother, Pavel Pavlovich set out for Gugolevo. After making a few preliminary inquiries, procuring
some essential documents, and writing for some additional
information, he set off hastily to break up the dastardly
plot. His conversation with Yeropegin had reassured the
Baron: he understood that the merchant would discontinue
his threats.

However, Pavel Pavlovich's haste to depart from Gugolevo was not due only to his anxiety about his mother's
condition; he was even more perturbed by his thought of
his niece Katya, who reminded him of his love for his sister
who had died before her time; Katya was very much on
Pavel Pavlovich's mind; he had for her a very special, tender
feeling, a feeling that was too tender, perhaps, for a relative;
but like a decent man, he restrained himself from building
anything upon this feeling; and yet the knowledge that his
niece was now engaged to a young man, and an eccentric
into the bargain, disturbed him; that her fiancé was a boor
affected Pavel Pavlovich only emotionally and not at all in

principle: in principle, Pavel Pavlovich was a democrat; the fact that this boor was a poet and an eccentric helped to reconcile him to the idea of their marriage (as is well known, eccentrics entertain a certain respect and mutual understanding for each other). Now, having learned of the boor's flight from the Gugolevo estate, of his infatuation for some sectarian peasant woman, and of the Baroness's suspicions which reflected on Katya's fiancé, Pavel Pavlovich Todrabe-Graaben, Baron, for reasons known only to himself, unexpectedly concluded that this "boor" was a decent fellow and a proper match for Katya.

For the past year Katya had indeed preoccupied the Baron's thoughts! He had suddenly initiated with her a sadly languorous correspondence; he wrote her gloomy letters signed "Uncle"; from a distance he attempted to guide her reading; he wrote to her on azure-colored paper which he kept in a sachet, and sealed his letters with an ancient image of two trees and an engraved quatrain, which read as follows:

> "A stream here separates two trees,
> And yet their branches mingled grow;
> Thus fate divides one heart from t'other,
> But as one heart they think and live . . ."

Over the last few years Pavel Pavlovich had grown leaner and grayer; his nose grew sharper like his judgments, which had become intolerably sharp; like the blade of a sharp dagger he gloomily displayed his flashing wit; but he spent his wit mostly on himself; young people were very attracted to him; but he drove them away; as for old folk, they fled from him of their own volition. On the threshold of two centuries, his superfluous wit illumined Pavel Pavlovich's lonely path for the remainder of the journey which he was destined to make in this world.

It is understandable that the aging old gentleman should have grasped at his friendship with Katya; it is understandable that, abandoning his affairs in Petersburg, he should have turned up in our locality; and now in the dark, to the sound of the mumbling old crone, Pavel Pavlovich fixed his gloomy eyes on Katya: a plan was forming in his mind to bring back her fiancé to Katya; how he was to accomplish this plan was still an enigma to the old gentleman; but he was very positive about the success of his enterprise.

Such was Pavel Pavlovich.

CHAPTER SIX

Luxuriant Fire

⟫⟪ Men ⟫⟪

Mitry Mironich dismissed his hoarse, noseless worker; his second worker, the shaggy one, was a "dove." For the past two weeks, the noseless one's place had been taken by our hero.

For Daryalsky, at the carpenter's, an abundant yet rather terrifying life had begun; a bright light glowed in his breast; his passion for Matryona was bursting from his breast like a torrent of fires; like a torrent of fires, Matryona's glance also rushed to meet him; like a torrent of fires the carpenter pored over them; and the carpenter's fiery prayer safe-guarded both of them with the light of the blessed and the brightness of the illuminated; it was as though a white-hot stove with its open jaws was scorching them unbearably, raising them high and bearing them on—but where was that prayer bearing them? Yet, in the torrent of days the shores of a daily laboring life were also visible: in the morning the three of them met, avoiding each other's eyes, avoiding all memory of their ash-turning flame; with grim faces, which could only be moved by nocturnal prayers or the silence of nocturnal caresses, they shook hands; and they carpentered in the level noonday flame; and it was as though there were, between the three of them, all three of them dumb, a con-spiracy; and it even looked as though the carpenter had blessed Pyotr's love for Matryona, and as though through that blessing the amorous flames were smelted into the flame of the Spirit. But among themselves they never referred to this at all: it was a strange, awesome life; and the trees were growing yellow, pink and withered; a rustling emanated from the dry, pink, lilac foliage, leaves fell in a shower, a squirrel's red muzzle peeped out and a bird trailed its paradisiacal note; and in the meantime rumors flew about the spiritual union of these people: Vukol, the priest, was now to be seen at times in the vicinity of the carpenter's window. At someone's malicious instigation, Vukol the priest now began to visit the hut; he would call at the slightest pretext, trying to ferret something out: he would leave looking disconcerted; and Pyotr and Matryona continued their courting and loving in the fields and the woods, gazing into the flames of vanishing sunsets and weeping for the flame; in the blue skies wavering stars swayed, falling into the earthly vales, falling and burning themselves out; days passed, and they passed from day into night; and out of the nights they passed into days.

And so it went on.

In the daytime, Pyotr, in a red shirt, the back of which was damp with perspiration, planed the boards to the merry screech of big saws and little saws under a shower of sawdust, as tiresome as falling snow, under the wearisome buzzing of flies in the carpenter's hut.

In the mild sunlight bursting in through the windows, a pillar of sawdust was spinning and the clear grain of sawdust, like light-dust, poured from under the saw; in that clear light, in that clear dust, the austere icon-like image of the worthy master was bent over a board; he spoke little when at work:

"Pass me the meter stick, sir . . ."

"Here's the meter stick."

"And now we have to level off these armchair arms . . . like this . . ."

And he would fall silent.

Mitry Mironich worked hard: now he would apply a chisel to the wood and hit it with a hammer that flashed above his head in the glittering sunlight, now with his bony hand he would seize a saw and saw off a piece of wood, sweating and breathing hard as he did so—but whatever the carpenter did had solidity and sense: the carpenter satisfied all kinds of customers; and that is the way he worked; and there was always work; and the customers paid not at all badly. And all around them was the dazzling heat or a pale glitter, and over it all the Savior's image blessing the harvest; beneath the icon a little lamp, full of oil, spurted, glimmered and twinkled. The worthy labor of these men might well excite a quiet feeling of sympathy; there was no fuss about that labor: gazing at it, one might say: "Bless, O Lord, the labor of these men!"

By evening six new chairs, not yet put together, would be standing by the wall: men weighed down by thought will grimly sit down on these chairs, but the prayer put into the wood through labor will invisibly pour forth in smooth flame into those who, plunged in thought, sit on the completed chairs: all kinds of people will buy these chairs: they will be taken to Moscow, Saratov, Penza, Samara, and to all sorts of other renowned Russian towns; they will be brought there and people will set them out and sit down on them; and for a long time those people will think, sitting on the chairs, on the ways of life and on what exists; and things will become separated from their accidental names; and he who sits in the chair will say: why is a chair called a "chair," and not a "spoon," and why am I "Ivan" and not "Marya"?

Labor then, workers, on new objects: and bless, O Lord, the labor of these men!

At other times, amid the hammering and the buzzing of flies, these austere men, all damp with perspiration, started to sing their austere songs; the "shaggy one" would be the first to start; leaning grimly on his hammer against a board, he would begin:

"In my very tender years
I was fading like sweet light,
The Lord have mercy on us!"

It was as though a certain dream which had been but had not yet become manifest, had now returned, beating against the windows with a marvelous light, illuminating these men's joy which had lain hidden behind their moroseness—of these men, who, by the sweat of their brow, were planing a new life for themselves; something indescribable was taking place; the rainbowed curtain of light was torn from the light of the curtain: in the light everything was torn off, baring the indescribable, when the carpenter nasally sang:

"Since my early infant years
I have been visited by God.
The Lord have mercy on us!"

And from the main room came Matryona's affable voice, rising and falling, as she sat there peeling potatoes:

"Forsaking all our dear ones,
We shut ourselves within holy walls.
The Lord have mercy on us!"

And they all joined in:

"The Lord have mercy on us!"

There, in the main room, God knows what was happening: neither the shaggy-haired worker, nor Pyotr, dared look in that direction: there, there, O Lord, you might see Matryona's red skirt: there, there, through the half-open door, their eyes might pick out her bare foot under the table; and the luminous beam of life intersected that foot; the light had cut their hearts; in their breasts beat the severed parts of their hearts: they carpentered and sang:

"In the endlessness of times
There is joy for us in heaven.
The Lord have mercy on us!"

The air in the chamber warmed with light, and there was an odor of perspiration in the air: the austere song rose and broke off; after breaking off, it rose. It was as though a world of its own, a new world, had come into being here in a space of only a few square feet, a world divided off from the other world by wooden walls. During the chanting

Daryalsky began to have the illusion that the Holy Ghost was descending within these few square feet; the Holy Ghost poured out as if from nowhere; there were creaking noises in the corners: there a piece of wood placed on the table leapt up, moved by the Holy Ghost, and rolled down among the shavings. But neither he, nor the shaggy-haired one, nor the carpenter interrupted their work; it was as though nothing existed. Then a patch of light resting on the carpenter's chest detached itself on two luminous wings from the carpenter and, growing rosier, flew along the walls toward Daryalsky's chest: a block of wood with its purple light illuminated the wood for him; but that was only the sun's reflection; it moved rapidly: the sun rolled away; it was already evening.

Outside the house, somewhere very near, a Tzelebeyevo lad was yelling out in a dull happy way a fashionable song, which someone had introduced among the villages into the countryside:

"Ah, you elephant, elephant, elephant—
Mister Trunk:
Tromb Trombovich
Trembovelski."

It was evening: with his work-hardened hands Daryalsky was gathering up the shavings glowing yellow-rose from the sunset; shaggy-head, puffing, was picking up the nails and putting them into his mouth; then he took them one by one from his mouth and hammered them rapidly into a board; Matryona passed, shuffling over the shavings; her brows were sternly knitted: foolish woman—why should she hide herself—it was already evening and the stars were swarming; the cool air was already covering the distant thickets with its draughty, grained turquoise hues, and all around everything was beginning to frown—the dusk was descending and the shadows multiplied—and on the opposite side the weary sun was expending its ultimate fire. Mitry put aside his plane-irons, planes and drills, hung over them for a moment with the thin tuft of his beard, thoughtfully leaned on his saw, and then quietly plodded out of the hut in his worn bast-shoes; soon he was crossing the common, and the children scampered away from him; the evening frowned: very soon all those who walk about with dull eyes in the daytime will have bright, languishing eyes like those azure icon lamps full of oil; and their speech among themselves will be sweet as honey.

The bright light, born of the morning, already glitters dazzlingly in the evening from the eyes of these men who, through labor, as through fasting, transfigure themselves.

⁓⁓ The Catch ⁓⁓

In the damp air mother-of-pearl ripples were running. For over an hour in the damp green air Daryalsky sat hunched in a red patch; he had thrown his fishing line a long way into the water where moist bits of mother-of-pearl danced on the water, breaking against the banks in bubbly, plaintively lapping water; and the line could be clearly seen stretching down from the rod and the float swayed, and a sad-looking duck swam past, pulling the ripples after it; bits of mother-of-pearl danced and over them danced the dragonflies; a mosquito, which had survived God knows how since the spring, buzzed into his ear; in black earth in a paper at his feet wriggled red worms; the setting sun made the village which was to one side of him look amethyst, all shining with roofs, windowpanes and timbers; in front was a wildly glittering piece of sky; and it also looked amethyst.

Alexander Nicolaievich, the sacristan, sitting somewhere to the side, suddenly stretched himself; his float had begun to bob and up flew his fishing rod; and a fluttering little fish, flashing bright signs with its scaly body, found itself in the sacristan's hard fingers which tore its mouth, and plumb: the little fish had fallen into the bucket.

"What a catch, ah!"

"Indeed!" Pyotr responded out of the air.

"Praise to you too!" the sacristan cried shrilly.

"They're not biting for some reason."

Silence: in the silence dusk was descending.

"I've been looking at you there, Pyotr Petrovich, and excuse my frankness: I can't make out what's got into your head: you're a gentleman, that's for sure; and God did not cheat you in appearance, and of learning you have quite a store, and yet, the Lord have mercy on us, what sorcery is this: with all you have behind you, here you are working as a laborer and for whom?! For Mitry the carpenter!"

Daryalsky's legs were sore, his back aching, his hands were numb from work, but in his soul there was sweetness and joy, an unutterable bliss; he smiled at the sacristan's words; he was gazing into the distance, beyond the village: a rhythm was beating through his head and the words fell into measure:

"A bright clear sapphire
Into cool moisture falls . . ."

All this repetition of vowels: what about a rhyme for sapphire? But he couldn't find a rhyme—what the devil! And his float had begun to jump: a largish fish must have bitten.

"And why shouldn't I carpenter, Alexander Nicolaievich? I'm out of my mind already from books and learning; so I'm carpentering."

"It's for exercise then, as I see it," the sacristan relaxed. "That's it. It all depends on whose head a book falls; some heads simply go bald from books. Take me for example: as soon as I open a book, all sorts of wheels and whorls start spinning in my brain."

"A bad joke, learning!"

"He-he: a log will stay a log!"

"*Vzz-vzz-vzz*"—a swallow swerved past.

Silence: the sunset was fading.

"The last swallow!"

"They haven't got long to fly here, they'll perish—where should they go?"

"To Africa, Alexander Nicolaievich. To Africa, to the Cape of Good Hope."

"You don't mean Africa?" The sacristan was very surprised.

"Yes, they'll go there."

"They're real fliers."

"Real fliers," Pyotr agreed.

They both watched the swallow, the white-breasted swallow, circling and flying, calling and twittering, here and there, there and here: "*ivivi*"; there it went brushing the pond with its breast, there it soared right under the cross on the steeple and went on dancing over it—a sapphire sign in the sunset in its airy enthusiasm, that dancer-swallow: "*ivivi-ivivi . . .*"

"Look at it dancing!"

"Like King David before the Ark of the Covenant."

And Pyotr thought: "Dearest, dearest, sacred swallow . . . And it's twittering about Katya. '*Ivivi! Ivivi!*'" The swallow swept off toward Gugolevo: "*Ivivi . . .*" died away above the trees; it was quiet now: rippling circles spread in the water, the thought-aching soul, the plaintive sound of a bucket being hoisted from a well: all was quietude, smoothness, drowsiness, duskiness. The sacristan disappeared in the dusk; there was just no sign of him; a soul-disturbing thought.

Where had Pyotr gone? What was the matter with him? Never, nowhere, nothing of the sort had happened to him. Nowhere, never, is anything of the sort dreamt of in Russia; yet here, among these plain, unsophisticated folk, all this is dreamt; the Russian fields know secrets just as the Russian forests knew secrets; in those fields, in those forests live bearded peasants and a multitude of peasant women; they have few words; they make up for that by superfluous silence; come and live with them and they will share with you this abundance; come and live with them and you will learn to be silent; you will drink in the dawns as if they were precious wines; you will nourish yourself on the odors of pine sap; Russian souls are dawns; the strong resined Russian words: if you are a Russian, you will have a beauti-

ful secret in your soul, and your spirited word will be like
sticky resin tar; it has no shape, but it will stick, and the
breath from the word will be abundant and pleasant; and if
you utter that plain word, it may seem there was nothing
much in that plain word; those words are unknown to those
who live in the cities, crushed down by stones: those who,
when they come to the country, merely see dirt, gloom and
a heap of straw and, looking at them out of the straw, the
grimly scowling face of a dirty peasant; but that this is no
ordinary peasant, but a secretly evangelizing carpenter
Kudeyarov, is something they will never understand or
realize; they see before them merely dirt, gloom and a heap
of straw, and out of the straw a peasant woman's stupid
chatter; but that this is beautiful Matryona with lips of
sugar and the honeyed sweetness of kisses—all this is hidden
from them.

Poor wretches! Pyotr thought: already the whole dream
of the West had passed before him and had passed away; he
thought: a great multitude of words, sounds, signs the West
had thrown away to the world's amazement; but those
words, those sounds, those signs—like werewolves, when
dying out, yet lure men after them. But where? The silent
Russian word, issuing from you, remains with you: and that
word is a prayer; like golden wine splashed from a goblet
into the air, where its drops burn like precious stones in the
sun and then fall in drops underfoot into the mud and leave
you unquenched, even though you had called upon
strangers to admire the shower of golden drops—such are
the words we are taught by the West; they splash their
words out into books, into every sort of wisdom and
science; and because of that there are attributive words and
an attributive order of life: that is what the West is. But the
word is not the soul: it grieves for the ineffable, it is nostalgic for the unspoken. It is not like that in Russia: the people
of the fields, the people of the forests, do not dress in words
and do not delight the eyes with their form of life; their
word is coarse; the way of their life is drunken and quarrel-

some: untidiness, hunger, dumbness, darkness. And you should know: the spiritual wine is there on the table in front of each of them; and each one of them will drink that wine of unspoken words and ineffable feelings for himself. He will talk, stammering apparently, and always of such simple things; when he falls silent, what a monstrous silence! His lips will swear at you with the worst words, while his eyes drown in the bright dawn; the lips swear, but the eyes bless; he'll start talking as though he were planing your board; and when he sings, then . . . in a word, the fame of those Russian songs has spread far and wide through the world. And who sings those songs, who has composed them? That same bumpkin has composed them, who, on occasion, will turn his coarsest swear words upon you.

To live in the fields, to die in the fields, repeating to oneself the one spirit-marked word no one knows except he who receives that word; and they receive it in silence. Here among themselves they drink the wine of life, the wine of new joy, Pyotr thought: here the very sunset is not squeezed out into a book: here the sunset is a mystery; many are the books in the West; many the unuttered words in Russia. Russia is that against which a book is shattered, knowledge crumbles, and life itself is burnt; the day the West is grafted on to Russia, a universal fire will spread over it; everything that can burn will be consumed, because only out of the ashes of death can issue forth the paradisia-cal soul—that of the Fire-Bird.

Daryalsky remembered his past: Moscow and the affected assemblies of fashion-conscious ladies and ladies' men—poets; he remembered their ties, studs, scarfs, pins, all imported and French, and the whole fashionable gloss of the latest ideas; one such young lady shrugged her shoulders whenever the conversation turned on Russia; afterwards, she had made a pilgrimage on foot to the monastery of Saarov; a social-democrat had laughed at the superstition current among the people; but how did he himself end?

One day he left the party and turned up among the North-eastern *Khlysti*.* One decadent had papered his room in black and done many other strange things; then he suddenly disappeared for many years; later he emerged as a wanderer through the fields of Russia. Many, many men are consumed by the dream of the open spaces; O, Russian field, Russian field! You reek of resin, herbs and lovage: in your expanses there is room to breathe one's last and die.

How many sons have you nourished, Russian plain; and your thoughts like your flowers have grown chilled in the heads of your restless sons: your sons run away from you, Russia, and try to forget your expanses in foreign lands; and when they return later, who can recognize them! They have acquired foreign words, they have acquired foreign eyes; they twist their mustaches in another way, in a Western way; and their eyes shine in a different way from all other Russians; but in their souls, they are still yours, O field: you burn their dreams, you shiver in their thoughts with the flowers of paradise, O dear native meadow-like path. Hardly a year will pass and they will take to wandering over the fields, through the forests, along wild beast trails, to find their death there in grass-grown ditches.

The number of those who will escape into the fields will grow and grow!

And the number of little watchtowers in the deep Siberian forests will increase! Does any one of us know how he will end? Perhaps in his declining days he will refuse to sit quiescently in his city armchair poring over wisdom-packed volumes and smoking fragrant tobacco, but will end up by swaying from the crossbar of two posts in the open air; perhaps he will end his days in a country ditch or in some hermit's cell in the Vologodsk forests? Who knows? Who can tell? Young men, you know nothing about yourselves! Listen, wives, listen, the glad tidings are free: in the wide open, free fields glad tidings are heard from time immemo-

---

* A mystical and secret sect, the Flagellants, dating from 1645.

rial; and who has once heard those tidings will find no peace in the city; he will only languish in the city; half-alive, he will run away abroad; but even there he will never find peace. His soul will be torn by weeping, his mind will dry up, his tongue will stick to his palate: he will have to take the waters for his nostalgia-sickness, and he will spend time in a madhouse and in prison; he will end by making his way back to you, O Russian plain!

"That's what will happen to me!" Daryalsky shuddered: he gazed up and saw the cubed blue falling over his head; fields, forests, huts—they were all cubed, nocturnal: the yellow moon will rise and so will the shadows.

"It's as though I have found new spaces, it's as though new times were mine," Daryalsky remembered the lines of his once favorite poet; he too was exhausted; he'd die if he did not leave the city; in his soul likewise the dream of country had strongly taken root. Involuntarily, the favorite poet's lines reminded him of other lines, which were both precious and terrifying:

"In the endlessness of times
There's joy for us in heaven,
The Lord have mercy on us!

"Forsaking all our dear ones,
Hiding in the empty fields,
The Lord have mercy on us! . . ."

And lo! from the vicinity of the pond came the familiar response:

"I was visited by the Lord
Ever since my infant days . . .
The Lord have mercy on us!"

That was the shaggy-haired one on his way home after finishing his day's carpentering.

"I'm no longer a philologist, a gentleman, or a poet; I am a dove; not Katya's fiancé, but Matryona's lover," Daryalsky said to himself ironically, and this sweet reality frightened him; he felt anxiously tortured; to deaden this anxiety, he sang:

"It's as though new spaces I have found,
Found myself in endless times."

"Why am I confusing the lines?" he thought; and he felt alarmed.

"What are you singing, young man?" a querulous voice inquired behind his back.

Daryalsky shuddered and turned around.

A sad looking, clean-shaven old man with a very prominent nose stood before him sniffing at a flower; he wore gloves; he had a plaid over one arm and a cane in the other hand.

"Oh, I'm just singing songs. And who are you?"

"I'm from the neighborhood," the old man sighed gloomily.

"Where have I seen him recently?" Pyotr thought; and he detected in those features a strange resemblance to something dear and familiar, but now already remote. But a resemblance to what, to whom? He examined the old man carefully—he was as neat as a pin; and Daryalsky thought, "He must be a Westerner!* That's it!" And the old man in the form and image of the West carefully unfolded his plaid, laid it down on the grass and sat down on it with Daryalsky; the moon was already out and bathing them in its gentle light, and Daryalsky was thinking that it was time for him to meet Matryona at their trysting place, but the clean-shaven old gentleman had put a spell on him; the old gentleman's voice was as plaintive as that of a bird in the bog; that cry in the autumn reminds one of the dear past, and we stand spell-bound for a long time at the rotten, boggy windows listening in fear to the voice of the familiar, sobbing bird.

---

* A Russian influenced by West European thought, traditions and manner of dressing and behavior, as distinct from a Slavophile, who stressed Slav origins.

"Everything's gone, everything's gone," the water lisps while we smile in disbelief. "Nothing's gone," we object; but we never say what has gone and why . . . but "*chu*"— there it is again, that cry of the sobbing bird. . . .

"Young man: you're an eccentric?"

"???"

"You're an eccentric because you're a Russian: all Russians are odd."

"Where have I heard that before?" Pyotr asked ("*chu*"— there was that cry again).

"You heard that in your own self," Pyotr said to himself, amazed; it seemed as if he had merely thought, not said, those words.

"Just a minute, wait. Where have I seen you? You remind me of . . ."

"That's mere fantasy. We all remind each other of ourselves, and we all meet."

"What do you mean?"

"I don't mean anything in particular . . ." the quiet gentleman plaintively continued, stroking his knee.

"How nervous you are. You're very odd, my dear sir; you'd better look out or you may have to pay for your nervousness."

"And how do you know?"

"You're a young man; and young men nowadays leave no issue; that's sad, but it's a fact; Russians are dying out; the Europeans are dying out too; only Mongols and Negroes are breeding."

"Russia has a great future," Pyotr protested, staring at the clean-shaven gentleman: the gentleman looked all right—he was a quiet, demure gentleman; he was probably a Westerner. "Where have I seen him before?" Pyotr thought, while aloud he said: "Russia hides an ineffable mystery."

But Pavel Pavlovich (for it was he), having broached his favorite theme, now coolly began to embroider upon it at Pyotr's words.

"Russia is a Mongol country," he said. "We all have

Mongolian blood in us, and it will not resist the invasion. We are fated to prostrate ourselves before the idol."

"Russia . . ." Pyotr protested.

"Russia—is an unfortunate country," the old man interrupted. "You speak of the ineffable. That means you have something on your soul which you are unable to express. Young man, you're not only an eccentric, but you are moreover a pagan eccentric. You're an unfortunate, dumb young man, just as all young people today are dumb; they all talk of the silence of the womb, because they're incapable of expressing themselves clearly. When one speaks of the ineffable, that's a dangerous symptom; it merely proves that humanity is retrogressing to a bestial state; a pity, but now everyone is bestial, not the Russians alone!" Pavel Pavlovich, the Baron, sighed sadly and blew his nose loudly.

"*Chu!*" Again that far-off, familiar bird cry from the bog: "Everything is gone, everything is gone!" As though struggling, Daryalsky exclaimed:

"No, no, it isn't true, it isn't true!"

"Unfortunately it is true. Now you, young man, are apparently an intellectual; but to look at you, you're just a peasant. That is because authentic culture is too hard for you to grasp; because you play the eccentric; you force yourself to see dreams; better wake up. . . ."

Once more Daryalsky listened to the ancient words. Was not everything that happened to him a miraculous dream, a living dream? He stared in astonishment at the clean-shaven old man, but the clean-shaven old man, having stood up, was folding his plaid and politely holding out his gloved hand to him:

"Good-bye now. I have a long way to go still. . . ."

Soon he was far removed from Pyotr—so was the West. "Where have I seen him?" Daryalsky continued to puzzle. A chill, autumnal breeze touched a small tree: a yellow leaf fell into the shadow; the stream at his feet babbled:

"I shall tell you everything, everything, everything. . . ."

"I know that myself!" Daryalsky smiled ironically; and

he suddenly caught himself: "What, what, what—what do I know?"

But it was time: Matryona must have been waiting for him a long time.

"For a second I didn't sleep—I woke for a second," Pyotr thought. "But now I'm already plunging into dream."

The nearer he approached the old oak, the more it began to seem to him that he was falling asleep again; and then it seemed to him that there was nothing left of what had been: the clean-shaven old man, his strange speech, all that was a dream which had moved long ago to the West; he was swallowed up again in a terrifying reality: that of Russia.

A stream of autumn water babbled at his feet: "I shall tell you everything, everything, everything, everything—everything—everything . . ."

"I know that myself," Daryalsky smiled ironically.

Making It

"Sit here, Matryona. You're a fine lass: sit here, Matryona. Must be sad for you to be with an old man like me—d'you think . . ."

The carpenter's eyes glittered wildly: his lame legs bore him to the window, his hands gripped Matryona and pulled her after him to the window:

"Sit here, Matryona . . ."

"Oh, what's this!" Her eyes glittered wildly; her unresisting legs carried her to the window; having caught her by the arms, the carpenter stroked her, whispered, and pulled her after him.

"Come here, come!" he sat her down beside him. "A fine lass you are of mine, big-eyed and large: though you're a little disfigured by a birthmark; but that lover of yours won't mind . . . He's waiting for you, I'm sure, that lover. . . ."

"Pff . . . Pff . . ." Matryona snorted shamefacedly.

"He's waiting?"

"Waiting . . ."

"All right. Let him wait awhile: all the sweeter for him afterwards."

"Oh, I can't stand this!" Matryona hid her face from her aged consort, but the aged consort had already sat her down on the bench. "A fine lass, a fine lass," he thought.

"Oh, oh, oh!" Matryona sighed.

"Give me your hand, won't you, Matryona. You won't? Well, don't then, I was only just . . . that's all. But listen

to my words. I'm not against all that. Only there's this: you
both are being sweet too often: every day, every day, something happens between you. And all without prayers, without sighs—that's what I mean. And what for? Don't you
know the mystery of this event? When you are with child?
Remember what a spiritual burden you'll bear for the joy
of all of us."

"But Mitry Mironich, it's not just what happens when
we're together," she said, confused. "We sigh for the spirit;
we adore the fields, the flowers, all the sweet smelling things,
we sing songs . . ."

"Let me put my hand on your breast, dearest," the carpenter said softly, his eyes shining wildly from the flame
that had been lit in him. "It's a soft breast you have,
Matryona!"

"Oh, leave me alone, don't touch me!"

But a magic power had already stuck her dumb; a current
from the carpenter's hands split her bosom; the current
from those perspiring hands, those grasping fingers flowed
around her in fine streams, poured into her; she stopped
resisting, all willpower left her blue-pale face, which began
to take on color slowly as the current poured into her and
made her blush like an autumn apple.

"Are you warm, are you warm, are you warm?"

"I am warm: still warmer—hotter . . . Oh my breast is
burning: I'm all on fire . . ."

"Pray then, pray: sigh, not for yourself, but for the
child; every evening that you walk, be it in the fields, or in
the forest, by the oak or in the hayloft when you are
making love together—who but carpenter Kudeyarov prays
till the tears come for the spiritual impregnation of the
soul? Yes, carpenter Kudeyarov. And take this into account: I am not pushing you into a shameful union of the
flesh—to that I am prone myself—but for the sake of the
advent of a Holy Ghost. A fine wife, that I have . . . and I
myself am not against the flesh . . . Pray then, pray, sigh
. . . Let me, my love, put my hand on your breast again."

The carpenter's hand scorched her with its flaming brilliant crackling strength: crushed by his will, she did not resist; her kerchief had slipped from her head, her hands covered her face, as Matryona Semeonovna wept and spilled her tears tenderly; and she felt both well and terrified, like being in a steam bath: she felt drowsy.

And the carpenter? His face seemed to have fallen away from him like the skin of a molting cockroach; his dread, dread, slightly squandered face, with spectacles balanced on the tip of his nose, glanced anew from under that transparent, empty skin: savage and dread the carpenter's face; and savage and dread it was in the hut; the air was strangely tense between objects, like the weave of a spiritual force; and the weave glowed and crackled: there were sparks in the room, dry crackling sounds, and little fires ran about as though a spider were spinning a bright web. Muttering spells and words, the carpenter threw up his arms; and then again pressed his hands to his chest; up, down—up, down— his arms flew, as if the flaxen hair of his ailing chest were stuck to his grasping fingers: sweet-smelling, god-given hair; and he plucked the sweet-smelling, god-given hair from his chest. The carpenter's finger fell, fell, fell, on Matryona Semeonovna's breast, shoulder, belly—and fast-fast, his hands enmeshed her in a web; drowsily she moaned, drowsily she drowned in the barely perceptible abyss of light torn from the carpenter's chest and wrapped around her, and over all this the carpenter's eyes, like devious holes, poured buckets of light over her. Thus they sat by the window; the evening light humbly stretched its last beams through the window and then, more fiercely, spread in a purple jamb over the table, and it was difficult to distinguish which was the sunlight and which the carpenter's light—the carpenter's web of prayers, woven in sunlight and darkness into a single carpet of air; the carpenter's soul, strangely, invisibly, flowed out in filaments of cobweb, in light and flame; around his hands, around his head now was a purple-golden halo: drowsily Matryona saw all this; stupidly, drowsily, she fell on her knees before him; she was kissing his hands and—ah!—she was praying. But Mitry Mironich

was no consort now, but a great prophet who had exterior-
ized his flame; and Matryona knew that when he wished,
Mitry Mironich could set the straw ablaze with this flame:
he would put his hands together, make of his fingers a
wedge, and to this spearhead of his fingers would flow a
terrible force which, gathering there, would shine forth
with whitehot flame. She had once seen how, one dark night
through the window, lightning had flashed forth and thunder had boomed from the carpenter's charged fingers.

As in a dream all this now passed through Matryona's
head; she was all enmeshed in a luminous, warm web; and
green coals poured buckets of light over her while his
crooked fingers spun a golden thread; the carpenter now
moved aside and from him a bright band stretched, ending
on Matryona, as well as in her, as a large ball of light; the
carpenter moved there: drowsily Matryona followed him;
the carpenter moved here: drowsily Matryona hurried after
him.

Now already with his gaunt arm the carpenter cut the air
between them, dividing in two the mesh of light: the band
of light was torn in two; swaying and quivering in the
darkness, its fine blades flowed upon Matryona; a fragment
of the mesh, swirling—the part that remained with the
carpenter—floated into the carpenter, and the third part was
dissipated in the air, and she now rested alone in the light
given her—Matryona Semeonovna slept and saw nothing:
the dazzling, the intolerably shining carpenter paced up and
down, throwing up his arms: up, down, up, down, up,
down: he enmeshed the objects about him with a lightbear-
ing weft pouring out of him, muttering the while: he would
place his hand on the table and then walk away again from
the table; and from the table a thread would stretch after
him; and he would stretch that thread further toward the
window, toward the lamp, and toward his favorite corner;
the spider wove his web around the whole room; everywhere now there was a thousand-fold glimmering, glitter
and twinkling of the finest, brightest threads, and the
crackling of threads: a golden, terrifying complex of

threads; all those threads spun out of the carpenter came together again either on his chest or his head, while he, sitting in the corner, rapidly gathered them up in his hands like a spider with its paws quickly spinning a web; and so it seemed—as if he might hang suspended on his own web on the airy wave of the night; and rapidly, rapidly, he mumbled his indistinct sorcerer's speeches; hoarsely, gabbling, a torrent of praiseworthy words flowed from his throat; well then, listen: dazzled by the glitter, what sort of speeches was the carpenter whispering? You'd be horrified not by the ineffable sense of these instants; you'd be horrified by the frenzy of their meaninglessness:

"*Staridon, Karion, Kokiré, stado, stridado:* I shall pray to the Lord God and the Holy Pure One. Young hero lad, you have a glad golden horn . . . *Staridon, Karion, Kokiré— stado: stridado.*"

Thus, in a state of terrifying bliss a wild incantation poured forth: that luminous body, rapidly groped by fingers, which not so long ago considered itself to be the carpenter, was no longer the carpenter: it was a legion of suppressed furies; now a flood of ineffable joys; just watch; flying out of the carpenter, the sheaves of light gleam golden, grown pale, flare brighter, turn blue, spinning red flames from his mouth, hissing as they strike the floor, and flutter out of the half-open window; if one were to stand by the smooth slope concealed in the high grass, watching the hut closely from afar, then it certainly would look as if a samovar pipe was thrust out of the window, spitting into the dark in sheaves of red sparks.

The carpenter's eyes were not turned inward; only the whites of his eyes could be seen in the sockets: the spider's web, all invisible, which had become visible only for an instant, no longer glowed and hung listlessly, as though nonexistent; but it still hung there; anyone entering the cottage would trip over it, would become entangled in it and, on leaving the cottage, would pull it after him; and if such a person had a wife, his wife would become entangled too; between them and the carpenter's hut would stretch these malicious threads; and it would seem as if the objects stared ambiguously at him, at his wife; he might leave the village, but the threads would follow him and pull him back; the chance visitor would then keep visiting the carpenter, bringing his wife and children too, until the whole of his family would be enmeshed in nets.

Now the Doves will be praying throughout the region, and they will sing their liturgies about the white dove; now from early morning, from the carpenter's cottage bittersweet things will spread in flight to all those places where the Doves' huts stand; not in vain did the sun set so sweetly just now. If you have been delayed in the open fields and night is already catching up with you, if your eyes have not been dulled with grammar—remember this: in the darkness you will see a golden, noiselessly alighting thread; and don't think those are stars falling through the sky: it is a fraction of the carpenter's soul, sweetly stinging you with a luminous arrow, flying through the darkness toward the praying dove. But what of the carpenter?

With drooping eyelids, with his beard drooping into his hands, he now stoops over the bench, his face frowning and taut, while his soul rests far from himself; he had spun much light, had hung up many of the sweetest, finest nets: he had surrendered his sighs through space to his brother Doves; and now, his soul wandering in the spaces, he caught up with Pyotr on the road to Laschavino; he caught up with him on the road by the oak tree; and, finding him there, the carpenter spurted his word-flames at him: a word would fly out, flop on the floor, turn into a luminous cockerel with beating wings: "*ki-ki-ri-ki*"—and in sheaves of bloody sparks it fluttered out of the window.

"To the Lord God I'll pray, and bow to the brave lad: the brave lad, the brave lad—in the clear field of Laschavino; in Laschavino an oak tree stands; in that oak a hollow: in that hollow make your choice of girl friends, all sorts of girl friends:—rotting, foresty, nettly, drunken: in the oak there is a golden shingle, a golden branch, in that branch a willow, a yawl, and a third juniper—sisters, half-sisters, uncles, half-uncles . . . Uuugh . . ."

A flood of light gushed from his mouth and—flutter: a red cockerel ran along the road in pursuit of Daryalsky.

Daryalsky was walking toward the oak to meet Matryona, already forgetting his conversation at the pond; a rivulet at his feet whispered, "I'll tell you everything-everything-everything, everything-everything-everything . . ."

How odd! Under the moon a big red cockerel ran across his path; he crossed himself; he went on skirting the wood. In the distance was Laschavino: there was the oak and Matryona.

He reached the oak—the hollow was empty: Matryona was not yet there.

The carpenter, curled up on a bench, still continued his mad muttering:

"Fire, fire, fire, all-seeing,
Fire, fire, fire, flying . . ."

"*Dir-dir-dy*"—a cart creaked under the very windows of the carpenter's hut; Andron the peasant, sitting in his cart, was hoarsely shouting at the carpenter's window:

"Mitry Mironich, eh, Mitry Mironich!"

The carpenter's frowning face was thrust out of the window:

"Wha-at do you want?"

"I'm driving to town. Do you want a lift?"

"Thank you for the thought, Andron. Drive on and God be with you."

Creak-creak-creak: the cart moved away.

"Aaaah!" Matryona yawned, wakening on the bench. "Who's knocking there?"

"Andron in his cart!" the carpenter grimly cut her short and began to light the lamp.

Matryona then remembered that her lover was waiting

for her; she got up, yawned sweetly, and glanced mischievously at the carpenter.

"I'll go and take a walk, Mitry Mironich . . ."

"Well, go off with you and walk," the carpenter replied, coughing quietly.

"Creak-creak-creak"—somewhere in the distance Andron sat still in the cart; he felt cheerful; he was driving to town where he would meet all kinds of folk.

And Andron filled the night with his deep bass voice.

⚓ Trinity Day ⚓

Then off she ran: ran along the road to Laschavino; and och, what a night, what strength in it: she'd halloo—the very moon would roll down from the sky at that hallooing of hers; thus, a mare, neighing suddenly, would gallop with a shepherd in pursuit; from afar the wicked eyes of villages, many eyes; from afar, a bird out of the bog would raise its voice, and then sink into a long silence; och, she ran, Matryona's heels twinkling: the moon rolled on, as though a wheel rumbled in her breast: forcefully thumping out of her, throwing her, throwing her over the tree stumps; her kerchief askew, her hair awry: when her fingernails touched her hair, sparks flew. "Where was her darling now? Was he still waiting, waiting so long? O to embrace her gentleman lover, to kiss him!"

"My bright one, my bright-eyed one, he'll wait.

"Wait, my joy, wait, don't go away . . .

"My bright one, my bright-eyed lover—wait for me."

Thus she whispered: ran; jumping over one tree stump, over another. Sh-u-u-u—the rooks, disturbed by her running, took off from the branches; the twigs crackled under her feet, the moon dazzled her eyes.

Behind her, from bush to bush, someone was hurrying after her; if she'd turn, she would see a dark figure skulking behind her; but Matryona did not turn.

On and on, one stump after another, a ditch, a ravine; the carpenter, breathing hard, came jumping after Matryona: he can't keep up with her—he's lagging behind, but he hasn't the strength to turn back. The carpenter couldn't bear to stay at home without a woman; he resented Matryona's carrying on with the lad; he'd like to love and caress her himself.

He knew it himself very well: there was a necessity in that infatuation of Matryona's; he himself had spiritually made her love blaze; and here he was now dragging himself after her to observe their tryst, and he was lagging behind; he could not keep up with the young. Was it jealousy or mere curiosity that pulled him toward those spots where they spent their amorous nights? He stumbled on, spitting and blowing hard into his beard, raising his bony arms toward those wooden places: in full force he blew the clouds upon them, but he was afraid of coming too near to spy on them; at times the lad was more bitter to him than wormwood—he would rather not look at him; at other times, he was dear to him, dear as a beautiful maiden: "He is giving birth to the spirit within her, that's what. If only they would embrace in my presence, if only they'd caress under my eyes; but, like wolves, they run away from me into the forest. I'd rather they did it in my presence, here in the hut; I'd watch over them; I'd make the samovar for them; and if anything didn't go right between them, I'd instruct them—that's what."

He was running, panting: branches beat against his chest, bushes beat against his chest, the grasses and the wormwood beat against his chest; under his long-nosed face angry dogs stuck to his beard; dragging his feet, the carpenter coughed and stumbled in pursuit of Matryona and, lagging behind, muttered threats:

"Hurry, hurry . . . he-he-he: shameless ones!"

"I used to go fast myself when I was younger . . ."

"O Lord, have mercy on us, Your folk, and blessed be Your property . . ."

"He's waiting, no doubt, waiting: you just wait, it wasn't just for that sort of thing I involved you . . ."

"Turn and turn their love into prayer."

"I'll teach you, I'll—you abductor, you adulterer!"

"I'll show them! *Staridon, karion, kokiré—stado, stri-dado . . .*"

Dry fragments of curses, prayers, incantations and cries flew croakingly out of his throat: he coughed them up; and all this variegated herd spat out by the carpenter now set off in pursuit of Matryona, while the carpenter himself, cough-ing, sat down on a hillock and brandished some dry branches in the direction of Laschavino: he might have been threatening or blessing them.

Matryona neither heard, nor saw anything.

"My bright one, my clear-eyed one, wait for me, wait . . ."

"Clasp your sister to your breast!"

"My bright one, my clear-eyed one—don't go away, wait for me."

Night. All around emptiness and unease; wild shouts in the distance; Daryalsky waited and waited for Matryona in the hollow oak; no Matryona as yet; the translucent moon rolled through the sky; from afar a swamp bird raised its voice and then sank into a long silence: the minutes flowed by, like eternal ages; as though it were not the night fulfill-ing itself in the skies, but human life itself, as long as the ages, brief as an instant.

Shouts in the distance, and still no Matryona; Daryalsky stood waiting outside and then went back into the hollow oak: there he kindled a fire, and the raspberry coals glowed with heat; the red grin of the crack in the oak expanded into the thick-trunked dark. A sound of hooves, someone pulled up a horse by the oak: the ringing sound of a bridle dropped. What's happening out there? Daryalsky thrust out his head: nothing, no one; it must be that escaped *oprichnik* who had galloped up here out of the abyss of time; over five hundred years ago he had rested, perhaps, under this oak, had pulled up his horse by the oak, looked around him, and then rushed off again, that homeless *oprichnik*, into that deaf darkness, until he came to revisit that familiar spot again some two hundred years later.

"Darling, my love, why are you not coming?"

A moan close to his ear. An owl perhaps? Or maybe rather the moaning of that lost soul of the fugitive convict who had rested here over two hundred years ago and who had ended his days in Solovki? Daryalsky looked outside: again no one there.

"Darling, my love, why are you not coming?"

"Here I am, here I am."

"My treasure, why so long? What kept you?"

"Ah, I'm bitter, bitter: the old man was kissing me: crumpling my breasts . . ."

"Stop that. Don't talk to me about the old man: it upsets me whenever he comes between us."

"The old man recited prayers: he is awaiting the white *khdove.*"

And Matryona began to sing:

"Bright, Oh bright the azure air
And bright in the air the spirit dear!"

"*Cocorico-coco,*" came the crowing by the oak, and out of the darkness a throaty cockerel peeped into the hollow.

"Darling, darling, I'm frightened. Where did this one come from?"

"Yes, it's strange."

"Darling, I'm frightened!"

"Stop it, Matryona, stop it; and yet it's strange: speak of the devil and he appears, as it were; but we're not afraid; do you think the old man is casting night spells upon us?"

"Don't you touch the old one: he's awaiting the white *khdove.*"

"Whether he is waiting for a white dove or a black raven, that I don't know: all I know is that you and I, and some others, are caught in his net."

"Don't touch the old man: he is awaiting the white *khdove.*"

"And I tell you: he is waiting for a black raven."

"Don't touch the old man: he hears everything."

They became thoughtful, both of them, watching the crackling of the raspberry coals.

Pyotr stared at Matryona and wept: such fragrant eyes she had, like bluebells; she had spellbound him, the female dove; but was it the sweets of paradise or the abyss of hell?

"Brother dear: let me unbutton your collar and kiss your white breast: your white breast. And what have we here: a birthmark, like a little mouse, on his chest: little mouse, little mouse, go away, leave the young man's white body.

"And what have we there? My little copper cross on his chest!"

"Ah, my dove, leave me! I can't look at you, my dove, without weeping."

"Why, O why are you weeping, my darling child?"

"O Lord, My Lord! What is all this!"

She seized hold of him; she rocked him like a baby; she pressed his head against her breast. They drifted away into the dark crack; and she said, turning somewhere:

"Look at us now, old man. Come here, old man, and see if we are loving without prayers or spiritual joy."

Was it dream or no dream? A body woven of gold detached itself from Matryona and covered Pyotr: their flesh vanished, burnt out: only a gold woven cloud of smoke filled the hollow oak. Was it dream or no dream?

It lasted only a brief instant; but during that instant there was nothing: no world, no space, no time. And then again their bodies defined themselves; it was as though from above, from the opening to the sky, out of the dark heaven, bright purple threads had been poured, sparkling threads, like bright Christmas gold or silver thread to make children happy.

And out of those bright gold and silver threads a human image formed itself again; dark-woven, floating, dumb, they glowed there, settling down in their places.

Miraculous: Matryona gazed at her darling friend; Pyotr's body still looked transparent, and she could see the purple blood in him flowing, and a paw-like fire dancing here and there, thumping—*tok-tok-tok, tok-tok-tok*—on the left side where his heart was.

Miraculous: Pyotr gazed at his Matryona: Matryona's body was transparent too: he could see her black blood flowing, and a blue snake writhing there, on her left side, where her heart was.

Between them were the bright threads which formed their bodies; between them was one bright patch: for an instant the patch quivered between them as though alive: what—it was an airy dove fluttering there, beating with its wings against their bared breasts: they embraced; the luminous dove, pressed between their breasts, fluttered more wildly than ever: *tu-tu-tu-tu-u-u* . . .

"Darling, how your heart beats: where were we just now?"

"Darling, is that your heart beating?"

The dove was pecking at their hearts.

"O darling, there's a jabbing pain in my heart."

But Matryona no longer heard anything: she could not tear her red lips away from red lips . . . Then she tore free: her kerchief fell off—the little dove fluttered away over their heads. . . .

"Look at us now, old man. Come here, old man: are we loving without prayers, without soul, without sweetness?"

"I am here: I see everything, everything you do," came a voice overhead accompanied with hoarse laughter.

Pyotr and Matryona looked up in alarm toward that place in the hollow where a portion of the sky and the stars could be seen; but there was no sky there: someone had blocked the opening.

"It's the carpenter . . ."

They both lowered their eyes: for an instant it seemed to them as if someone were climbing down from the oak tree and then running away. Pyotr once more looked up impetuously: now the dark blue sky and an edge of the yellow moon peeped at them again. Pyotr quickly ran out of the hollow oak: for an instant, in the moonlight, there loomed before him a peasant—a bearded, shaggy figure in oiled

boots, with a watch chain, but without a cap: the figure
loomed up and then jumped into the bushes: Pyotr recognized Ivan Stepanov, the shopkeeper: picking up a stone, he
hurled it fiercely after him.

The stars were already fading, a pale stretch of dawn was
showing in the East: there was a rustling of dry branches
along the ravine, and it was difficult to make out what was
happening, whether it was a bear creeping away from the
village, or some drowsy "doves" on their way home from
their prayers, or folk stealing away at dawn from meetings
in the forest huts. All that could be heard was someone
nasally singing a song there where the branches of a hazel
tree rustled in the breeze:

> "Fabulous sea—sacred Baikal,
> My fabulous sail—caftan all in holes.
> Hey, Barguzin, make the wheel turn.
> Already the storm's on the way . . ."

Most likely a convict was creeping through the bushes.

⁓⁑ⅇ On the Eve of a Holiday ⅇ⁑⁓

Thus Pyotr and Matryona shortened their pre-autumn summer nights: night fell behind day, night led the day away. Days passed. After them clouded mornings met the nights: the sun blazed; a bright cobweb stretched through the air; a fragrant light penetrated everything; the pale faces of grimly working men gave no sign of agitation; the shavings fell; a white stream of sawdust fell upon the bare feet of the carpentering folk. The huts of Tzelebeyevo begged admittance through narrow windows; beneath the windows a pig was digging; a red cockerel strutted importantly upon the straw or, with neck outstretched and feathers bristling, chased a hen over the parched meadow. Far off, in Laschavino, smoke curled over the trees: the azure sky there looked a troubled gray and there, on the outskirts of the forest, shepherds were kindling a fire; a herd of horned cattle was grazing in the meadow; in the hollow oak a silly shepherd sat, mending his whip and puffing at a pipe; a small fire danced before him.

On the morning after the night we have described Yevseich came into Ivan Stepanov's shop, bought kerosene, various brands of tea and other such things, mopped his brow with his red foulard handkerchief, and let his tongue wag about the affairs of the estate:

"Their Baron-son in person turned up on a visit on Throne Day to see how things were . . . about five days ago, yes . . . an important bird, a Senator-General, and the amount of fuss he caused: of water alone in the morning he would use up five or six buckets: and nobody was good enough to clean his trousers except his own valet; a handy lad by the name of Strigachev . . . and he talked to us about French women. 'French women,' he would say . . ."

But Ivan Stepanov frowned angrily at all this, drily clicked on his abacus, glanced up now and then from beneath his spectacles, and finally muttered:

"Rumor says you're being ruined . . . let me tell you . . . Five-and-a-half rubles," he exclaimed, cutting short his surmises.

"And who dared to say so, may I ask?" Yevseich asked furiously, puckering up his face and putting on his cap.

But the shopkeeper merely shrugged his shoulders and went on clicking on the abacus; after a silence, he casually threw out:

"Nobody told me nothing: what business is it of mine? But the rumors are going around. They're in debt, according to the bills . . ."

Yevseich no longer lingered in the shop: formerly, it was otherwise; formerly every respect was shown him; a present of mushrooms or a little tobacco, or simply a few verbal compliments, but nowadays it had become impossible to chat. As he was leaving the shop, the old man noticed that Ivan Stepanov was limping; he could not resist saying ironically:

"Did you damage your leg?"

"I hurt it a little," the shopkeeper replied with a show of perfect indifference while, in reality, he turned pale with rage.

"He got beat up!" Yevseich thought as he left, carrying a bottle of kerosene in one hand and the packages in the other. It was the sabbath; at the carpenter's they finished work earlier that day; by four o'clock the saws, large and small, and the other tools, had been put away; a red tablecloth embroidered with cockerels had been laid; the carpenter was now having tea at an unusual hour with the house folk: with Daryalsky and the shaggy one; Matryona had donned her ornamented bodice; the carpenter had

pulled on his boots and the shaggy one had changed his
shirt; Pyotr also dressed up. Since four o'clock the carpenter had begun to look whiter (on work days he looked
green and ailing); looking at his freshly washed face and his
oiled hair, one might assume that he would pore over his
sacred book well into the evening: till midnight of that day
they whispered that the guest would arrive, but who the
guest was Pyotr had no way of knowing yet.

"A notable guest," the shaggy one kept slyly winking at
Pyotr.

Strangely enough his former fears melted away like wind-
blown smoke in Pyotr's soul; even Matryona's loveliness
had paled in his soul: No, Matryona remained Matryona,
but he began to have an inkling of something not obvious to
the eyes; Matryona turned out to be not independent but,
so to speak, part of the carpenter: the enticement she
offered did not belong to her alone, and it was not in the
least curiosity; it was not the feminine essence that attracted
him to her, but the soul: but her soul, all of it, had turned
out to be patterned on the carpenter's: it was apparent that
the carpenter inflated her with his soul and she, inflated by
the spirit, astonished Pyotr with her languishing eyes, her
sarcasm, and her greedily twitching nostrils.

A monstrous thing: There was something in his soul
Pyotr had not sensed, not felt for a long time: true, Pyotr's
soul had become numb, gave its master no voice: everything inside him seemed empty and vacant: but moments
came when this, as it were, vacated space within him
seemed to brim over, splashing and pulsating with fullness
of life and ineffable strength, warmth and the joys of paradise: "What is it within me that passes through with such
sweet fire?" Pyotr asked anxiously: what was it that went
on in his breast, that quivered in his breast and cried; as
though an electric motor had been started up to work in his
breast: what was that lump of sorrow that choked his
throat; and when it choked his throat, the village was no
village, the peasants no peasants, and the familiar space
seemed quite unfamiliar and altogether new: as though in

that new space everything was arranged in bright splendor and only externally filled with huts, peasants, straw, and, when one turned away, out of each object creatures of another world, bright angels, nodded to one, and the bright, long-awaited bride said: "Wait—I shall come!" And one did not believe in the straw, in the mud, and in all the visible deformity; it no longer existed.

"Is it your birthday today, Pyotr Petrovich, you're so dressed up?" the schoolmistress shouted ironically as she rode past in a cart.

"I've done my day's work," Pyotr answered exultingly, "and that's that!"

"Looks as if someone's forcing you," she retorted, and off she went.

Indeed, he was a birthday boy: from early morning, as soon as he went on the binge after the night before, his heart had beat faster, was all a-din, and he didn't know what to do with all that joy: whether to seize hold of a paring chisel, scribble some doggerel—the devil take it—or go fishing on the pond. He settled down to fish, and guffawed; he hooked the worm, cast his bait far: the damp air runs upon the light-catching nets of the waters: a gold snake runs, another after it, a third: in between them blue wrinkles, the waters run breaking against the shore, merrily splashing; swimming by, to one side, a duck quacked; the float began to bob, the bait drew taut and a flapping fish fell into Daryalsky's fingers, where its mouth got torn and— plump: it fell into the bucket.

"What a catch!"

"Yes!" Out of the air responded Alexander Nicolaievich, the sacristan.

"Will you be serving at mass this evening, Alexander Nicolaievich?"

"Yes, I'll be doing that. I have just prepared a golden halo with blue bouquets for the priest."

"I love, I love the mass . . ." Pyotr enthused for some unknown reason.

"You can love it, but we just perspire, we perspire."

"I-vi-vi"—a martin flew past. *"I-vi-vi.. . ."*

As Daryalsky gazed, an autumn thread of cobweb stretched into the azure of the sky; the bright thread ran away toward the carpenter's hut; with rainbow glitter, from there, from the valley the window shot its rays; and it looked not like glitters, but a cobweb: everything around was cobwebbed; in the sweet azure day the cobweb settled on the grasses, stretching taut in the air; and smoke rose from a hut and settled on the grass; and it, too, seemed to be a cobweb.

Daryalsky looked—there was a cobweb between his hands sticking to his chest: he wished to disentangle himself from it, but it would not yield: his eyes saw it, but his fingers could not grasp it, for it seemed to have grown into his chest in a tangle of glitters; he unbuttoned his shirt collar and looked down: red, blue, golden, green threads stretched into his white chest, and rolled back from there— you couldn't tear them off, it would be easier to pluck them out of his chest together with his quivering heart like the stem of a little onion; he gazed on the twigs, in between the twigs was a tangle of glitters; on the blue pond too—a tangle of glitters: and if he half-closed his eyes, the same glitters: the same glitters in his soul: plainly not the world, but some sort of radiance.

Pyotr was in the grip of religious fear: was this the world's transfiguration? Or was it that sweet poisonous premonition—the end of the world? But for Pyotr only one thing stood out clearly: Tzelebeyevo had now become a new earth; it was no longer just air, but a sweet honeyed herb; breathing it, you became intoxicated; but what would it be when it was time to sober up? Or from now on no sobering up; you will drink till you see the green serpent, but what afterwards—death?

"What am I thinking?" Pyotr tried to formulate, but he understood that it was not he doing the thinking, the *"thinking"* was being done in him: it was as if someone had extracted his soul, and where was it now, his soul? Where was everything that had been? He gazed, the threads stretched on, criss-crossed each other, in the bright air the threads became enmeshed: and Pyotr thought: those were no threads, but souls: they flowed through space in a weave of cobwebs—souls of doves divided by space . . . they stretched, the souls, toward each other and enmeshed themselves in azure. Daryalsky made a movement with his rod.

"How goes it? Have you caught a small roach?"

That was Alexander Nicolaievich, the sacristan, calling to him, having thrust his curly head into the autumn azure day.

"Alexander Nicolaievich, it's a fine day!"

"He-he-he: a pleasant sunny day!"

"And we'll have an even better, more favorable day!"

"He-he-he: it's steamy and a little damp!"

"What do you mean? We don't know yet how it will turn out."

"What'll turn out? A revolt, d'you think?"

"Far from it: days of paradise . . ."

"He-he-he! There'll be great drunkenness! It's a long time since the priest has danced 'The Persian March.' Tomorrow, I'm sure, his guitar will start tinkling. . . ."

"Well, let it tinkle!"

"Our Father will do a scene, the 'March over the Balkans.' "

"Let him, let him!" Pyotr cried with holy enthusiasm, shaking his finger; and as he stared, he saw a fine thread flying from his pointing finger and getting entangled in the sacristan's beard.

"*And I—I too—am giving forth light,*" Daryalsky said joyfully, but the sacristan observed nothing.

"My dear, let our priest be merry and dance: the spirit will move him and the priest will pick up the guitar."

"He-he-he! It's from the wine, Pyotr Petrovich, from the wine, and not from the spirit."

But Pyotr was not listening to him: he was in a state of blissful enthusiasm.

"But I tell you, Alexander Nicolaievich, the priest will dance for the glory of God."

"Christ be with you, Pyotr Petrovich, what's that for the glory of God: in that way any raving tavern drunkard is a town crier: that happens with the *Khlysti*, none other; they confuse their shameful merrymaking with spiritual enlightenment. . . ."

And the sacristan chanted:

"Oh, I'm an orator
Of the green, green serpent . . ."

But Pyotr did not listen; in a state of holy bliss he picked up his fishing rod.

"Where are you going?"

"To the priest's!"

Alexander Nicolaievich, the sacristan, could grasp nothing: "He must be drunk!" he thought and as he fingered his rod, he sang into his nose:

"My wineshop wife, my soul—
I just can't live without you."

Pyotr crossed the common, staggering from enthusiasm if not from the poisonous exhalation of the locality; great was the divide in his soul now; it seemed to him that he now understood everything and was able to say, tell and demonstrate everything; but another voice kept whispering to him: "There is nothing of that sort and never has been," and he caught himself realizing that this other voice was really himself—the authentic self; but no sooner did he catch himself realizing that he was out of his mind than it began to appear to him that the voice that had caught him was the voice of the devil tempting him. . . . This is what he was thinking as he crossed the common; suddenly behind him, from behind his back, a strand of bright cobweb floated before him; he turned around and saw some twenty paces away a peasant from the village of Kozhuhanetz, one of the doves; around that peasant danced a network of threads, issuing from his head, splashing with beams of light: "One soul gives tidings to another!" Daryalsky thought joyfully and bowed to the dove; they exchanged a subtle, mutually understood smile and went their ways.

"May I perish," Daryalsky thought, "if I betray the cause of the Doves . . ."

"O-ho!" his other voice teased him. Did he realize that by those words he had attracted death to himself; no, he did not realize that; if he had realized it, he would have howled in horror, seized his cap and run away over land and sea from the village. . . .

He had hardly taken a hundred paces from the pond toward the highway when he saw an elegant carriage dashing along through the dust of the road; evidently a young lady in person was driving a horse of fine breed; she wore white gloves, her pale pink dress fluttered in waves in the warm air, and on those pale pink waves there were what appeared to be white clouds—muslin and lace; the white muslin curled in the air, unfurling from a straw hat; and tender curls danced from under the hat.

Pyotr looked and his heart gave a jump: his heart beat fast, he did not know why; he stood in the middle of the road and shouted gleefully:

"Stop, young lady, stop!"

The small carriage pulled up: an oval face lost in ash-blonde hair peeped out from behind the horse: it was a childlike face, serious, with blue rings under the eyes, with velvet black eyelashes masking a pair of brilliant eyes; the young lady's apprehensive eyes stared wildly at Pyotr, her rose-pale little mouth quivered, her hand tremblingly clutched a whip; the young lady stared at Pyotr . . .

But . . . it was Katya.

To Pyotr at that moment it seemed as if nothing had happened between them and everything was as before: the quarrel, the betrayal, the engagement—could all that change what they had in common between them? there had been no quarrel and, even if there had been, who would want to remember it now, in these new spaces? A warm cheerfulness pervaded Pyotr.

"A fine day, Katya!"

Silence: the horse snorted and pawed the ground.

"Beloved child, a long time since we saw each other . . ."

At the words "beloved child," the rose-pale mouth quivered, the eyes seemed to hesitate for a moment whether to flash back or not in response; but instead, Katya contemptuously compressed her lips; from under her lashes a look of blue horror; the whip cracked and the thoroughbred almost knocked Daryalsky off his feet.

Daryalsky swung around and shouted after her:

"I hope grandma is well! Give her my respects too . . ."

There was only a cloud of dust on the road as if Katya had never been there. Drunk with air, Pyotr did not understand the monstrous nature of what had come to pass.

"That's Katya for you," he thought, striding swiftly on to the priest's.

At the priest's were gathered the village constable, Ivan Stepanov, the shopkeeper, and a young Utkin lady.

"Good day, Father Vukol: tea and paradise for me."

But the priest shook hands with him drily.

"Sunshine and light make the heart glad! Good day to you, Stepanida Ermolayevna . . ."

"Pfff, pfff, pff," the young Utkin lady puffed, turning her face and glancing at him not without mischief.

The shopkeeper at first sight seemed uncomfortable: the shopkeeper by the window was already hobbling toward a bench.

"Why has he gone lame in his left foot?" Daryalsky asked himself.

The occurrence of the previous night did not enter his head.

Drily the constable held out two fingers to Pyotr: the interrupted conversation was resumed; as if deliberately, they paid no attention to Pyotr; a feeling of hostility toward him became evident. But Pyotr was like a blind man: in all humility he proffered the brief gift of his benevolence to these people.

They were discussing Yeropegin: "Who could expect it? A big ace like him and then suddenly paralysis!"

"It can happen to anyone: to a beggar or a moneybags," the constable put in.

"Poor Fyokla Matveyevna," the young Utkin lady sighed.

"Why poor? She's glad, no doubt. To whom but to her will those millions flow!"

"You can say what you will, but when it's a question of death, disease or the law, everyone's in the same boat: a merchant, a nobleman, a General or a chemist."

"It's a pity, though, about Yeropegin . . ." the Father said, glancing round him with a sort of guilty grimace, while to himself he thought: "If I go on drinking, I'll get a seizure like that too."

"Don't worry: all's well that ends well!" Daryalsky exclaimed, enthusiastically jumping out of his seat, but at this everyone else looked embarrassed, dropped their eyes, and turned their backs on him.

"Don't worry," Daryalsky continued. "We must understand only one thing, that everything is nothing: just look there—at the glitter, the cobweb, the sunshine; and on your table, Father Vukol, stands golden honey; and outside, there, the aspen trees are already turning red . . . Ha-ha-ha: all is well, and the Honey Savior holiday has already passed. It's time for the Third Savior holiday—aha! And you talk of death: there's no death—ha-ha! What death can there be?"

They all turned away: a fly flew noiselessly in through the window with a dirty piece of down sticking to its back, and it settled itself near the young Utkin lady's muslin blouse.

"Ah!" the young lady cried out: the fly noiselessly described a deathly circle and returned to its previous place.

"A strange fly!"

"It's been feeding on a corpse . . ."

"It's epidemic . . ."

"And the fly . . . the fly is also fine!" Daryalsky continued. "What's the matter with you: I'm calm; the Third Savior is already approaching, so why should we grieve?

God willing, we shall survive until the Beheading—that will be a radiant day . . . And you're worried about a fly!"

"Now please tell us, Mister Daryalsky, is it true what they say, that you have written a book about young goddesses?"

"He-he-he!" the young Utkin lady snorted, for some reason lowering her eyes.

"That's the way things are," the priest said with a wink at Daryalsky, "you talk as it were of the Revelation, and under it all you publish books with a fig leaf, but, pfu, pfu, and there was Father Bukharev, he kept reading the Revelation, but in his old age he went off and got married. You shouldn't joke with the Revelation."

"It's nothing," Daryalsky went on. "Everything's nothing: everything is possible; let us rejoice; why not play the guitar, Father, find joy in the sweet strings, make the heart go round. Praise the Lord God on the *gusli* and the organ . . . Mother, bring the guitar, and we'll dance!"

Hereupon something indescribable took place: snorting, the young Utkin lady ran out of the room, stumbling over the threshold; the constable's face grew fierce and savage, while his lips shook with laughter; and the awkward and at that moment blushing priest's wife threw herself at Daryalsky, choking with rage like a sow defending her litter from a wolf.

"Strange, very strange words to hear from you: no sense or order in them at all. What if the Father does ask me to play on the guitar? You may see dust in other people's eyes, but just look at your own—there's a whole log in them: the whole district can see that; thank God, we're not that sort of folk: we don't filch diamonds and don't peep at barefooted women from the bushes."

"But, Mother, I never thought . . . I'd no intention of saying anything bad against Father Vukol."

"Pf-fff-fff!" a snorting issued from the next room, from which a slobbering priest's child now thrust his head and stared with popping, bulging eyes.

"Kh-ho!" the constable gasped, red as a lobster, and his

face assumed an even more savage expression as he contained his laughter.

"I must ask you not to visit us again."

"They don't see, they don't think, they're blind!" so thought Pyotr as he left the priest's palisade; and out of the window, in his wake, the priest's wife continued to abuse him:

"Maybe you are that same thief, who . . ." But he did not hear: his eyes were raised to the sun: in a sunbeam a bright strand of cobweb stretched, stretched; in it a fly was caught—*"Buzz-buzz!"*

In the distance on a hillock, Schmidt, surrounded by children, was returning from the forest with a basketful of mushrooms; Pyotr waved to him, but Schmidt did not notice him, did not want to see him.

"What have I done to them? They're all sulking, they don't understand, don't want to see!" He thought about the carpenter's hut where right now, in a space of thirty-five square feet, the coming of the Holy Ghost was taking place.

"That so!" a voice mocked him.

"That so!" Pyotr mocked that voice.

"Fine day, young man!" as though in reply a voice sounded behind his back.

Pyotr turned: facing him was a clean-shaven gentleman, laughing; his hands were gloved; over one arm a plaid; behind him—the West; in the West—the sun.

"You're strolling: whispering to yourself!"

"No, I'm only counting the days on my fingers."

"I've already stopped counting the days: you shouldn't count them either."

"It's fine, warm, lots of light!"

"Think so? What light? Where did you see light? Now the Italian sky gives light and warms; but that is in the West . . ."

"He doesn't see the light," Pyotr thought, "and what about the hands!" He looked at his hands, his hands gave off no light: they were cold and white.

"Or did I imagine all that perhaps?" he unexpectedly asked aloud.

"Yes, yes," Todrabe-Graaben, Baron, whispered to him, "you imagined it: those are only images, images."

There was a strange authority in those words; and the Baron continued to whisper to him.

"Awake, come back," the Baron pointed in the direction of Gugolevo.

"Where?" Pyotr cried, startled.

"How where? To the West: the West is over there. You are a Westerner; so why are you wearing a Russian shirt? You must come back. . . ."

For an instant his life flashed before him, and Katya too: he felt full of enthusiasm for her. Good God, what had he done? Crushed her young life? Katya was calling him— listen: somewhere a white dove was cooing: somewhere a swallow streaked through the air; "*i-vi-vi*," the plaintive cry rose. There, in the green thicket, was time's unchanging noise: the rush of wind and its battle with the trees; and that made for the incessant noise in the trees. The Baron Pavel Pavlovich's shadow was spread on the meadow; out of the wood a section of the Gugolevo spire glittered; there, over there, an old mansion was waiting for Pyotr: Oh, go there, to the West.

"Avaunt, Satan! I am going to the East."

~~&~~ Twilight Falling ~~&~~

At the priest's house endless chattering and whispering was going on.

"Yes'm, strange things are going on in the district: this one has made up his mind, that one has run off to the socialists, and another has been gored by a mad bull . . . that's the way things seem. Diamonds are ace," the village constable said, surrendering his cards.

But the priest did not reply: he had stuffed himself sullenly into a corner, propping his chin with his fists and pursued his quiet thoughts: "It's evidently my destiny that everyone can catch me out drinking, what's to be said?" The priest sulked, rubbing his eyes with his fists.

"There was a wolf cub running about the district not so long ago: someone managed to look into his eyes: his eyes were humble, human-like; and as I see it, he wasn't a wolf at all; the peasant lowered his cudgel; the wolf cub ran off into the bushes and stared from there with glittering eyes!"

Still the priest did not respond; all the more he huddled in his corner, huddled pitifully, and two teardrops rolled down his cheeks: "What sort of a life is this? A wolf's life: you are always dependent on someone, and they all turn out to be smarter than you!" The red-gold sun was beating down on his red-gold hair and making it downy.

"Most likely you saw a squadron of cossacks riding in the distance; they all had rifles and shaggy fur caps, and they were riding to the East; the folk stood about talking: means there have been peasant uprisings everywhere; and everybody is fed up with these uprisings . . . Your card, young lady, I'm taking it."

"Here!"

The priest filled his pipe: it would soon be time for the mass; he'd sweat it out and then what? A little cordial perhaps!

"A woman went picking mushrooms; she heard a peasant yelling in a thicket—a bass voice he had: it made her feel queer; she hid in the bushes and watched: and there along the path comes a woman striding, holding up her skirts and you could see her peasant boots underneath: and there she was yelling, loud as could be: 'Christ has arisen!' Who could it be but a werewolf?"

"A werewolf, that's certain!" The constable laughed at what the priest's wife had said. "I know that werewolf: it's Mikhailo, the watchman.

"O Lord, O Lord!" The priest's wife sighed. "What's going on if a peasant turns into a woman?"

"He was hunting for an escaped convict," the constable said with a wink. "There's a convict crawling about in the bushes around here, but I'll ask you to keep this secret for the time being."

"But it's time for vespers; after the service I'll—well, I shan't break my fast tomorrow!" the priest said, smoothing his red hair and fitting on his gray cassock; he walked out on the common to signal the church watchman with a straw hat. The moist dewy grass of the common had already turned yellow like a sunbeam; and both were now turning slightly red; the priest screwed up his eyes in the sunlight, the sunset was rosily freckled; the priest preened himself.

From afar came the words of a song:

"Transvaal, Transvaal, my lovely land . . .
You're all enwrapped in flame,
Under a spreading tree
A worthy Boer is sitting."

The priest signalled with his hand and already the watch-man was on his way to the belfry: Ivan Stepanov's shop was already closing: soon he would plod on his way to the church.

"On foot a little boy did bring
A bullet to the trenches . . ."

came the words from somewhere far.

Then, once again, the Tzelebeyevo belfry cried out into the red abyss of the sunset; the shudder of that ringing spread far and wide; far and wide from Tzelebeyevo that ringing re-echoed: the peasants took off their caps.

The priest looked up at the cross, threaded with red sparks, and crossed himself too; and off went the priest to conduct his evening vigil.

In the distance voices continued to bawl:

"Pr-r-r-a-a-a-y then, you w-o-m-e-n,
Pr-a-a-a-y for your s-o-o-ns."

Of a sudden a breeze made itself felt in space, and every-thing was thrown in motion: thousands of trees nodded from afar and moved; the gnarled, triple-crowned oak tree started and shook its foliage threateningly at the village, its coarse green garment moved; its green brocaded masses rustled; when the church bells stopped ringing, the family of red aspens made their fill of noise against the village; and then retired into silence waiting for new torrents of air, and only the golden, lisping leaves swung in the air, and a tin cockerel on a gaudy hut continued to creak; and detaching itself from the sagging roof of a poorer cottage a strand of straw flew up and then fell to earth. The air was now full of chicken down.

Making It

The shutters of Kudeyarov's hut were fastened tight, the gates to the yard were also firmly locked; the only sound that could be heard coming from under the rotted board at the entrance of the stable was the grunting of the pig and the dull snorting of the mare. Not a soul seemed to be breathing here at this hour; but that was not true: hotly and avidly four souls breathed here, calked up from the outside; avidly and hotly the dove's lips kept silence; and the silence overflowed into the space of an area of thirty-five square feet; and the rooms were brimmed with bliss like a full goblet: the descent of the Holy Ghost took place here in the space of thirty-five square feet; a heavenly cupola, fallen to earth, was held up by four human body-pillars; and those four pillars were the white-breasted spirit-woman Matryona Semeonovna, the crooked-legged carpenter, Pyotr, and the shaggy-head. All those threads which, day and night, the carpenter spun out of himself—all those threads, formerly unseen—glittered now with a thousand splendors; it was as though the yellow wood of the walls had been covered with golden paper and, brighter than the sun, the room glowed in the dim light of four smoking candles. Brighter than the sun reflected on three of the faces did the face of Mitry Mironovich, the carpenter, become illumined.

All of them were already sitting here at the table; they had not donned their white shirts; they did not have to look white for anyone, there was no one they had to dress up for; just in their things night had clothed them, so they stayed at the table; in her ornamented bodice Matryona Semeonovna sat solidly on a Viennese chair; on a plate before her lay a French loaf—for breaking; nearly opposite her sat Pyotr, glancing at her from time to time. Miraculously he now understood that a wonderful mystery flowed from the carpenter into Matryona, and that Matryona had nothing to do with it, she herself was just a wild animal; he glanced sideways at her and her speckled, later covered face that looked crumpled and yet was very, very white, and also terrifyingly blue, and the azure-like circles under her eyes, her soiled red hair of dusty shade, and her blood-swollen lips wildly excited him; he remembered both the tenderness and the fury of her embrace; he thought: "A beast or a witch?" But the witch sat motionless in her ornamented bodice hanging formlessly on her as on a coat hanger; she had folded her gnarled hands over her stomach, her eyes were fixed on the French loaf which she was supposed to break and distribute; but just as sweetly licking her lips, the witch stared at him, so in her eyes large blue waves began to move, and a droning ocean-sea looked out of her eyes; then it seemed to him that until the Second Coming, he would flounder, drowning in these blue seas, that he would be drawn to those lips till the Archangel's trumpet pealed, if, indeed, there was to be a Second Coming, if, indeed, the devil did not steal that trumpet announcing the Last Judgment. But he was already beginning to understand that this was—horror; the noose, and the pit: not Russia, but some dark abyss of the East was pressing upon Russia from these bodies wasted by sectarian exultation. "How terrible!" he thought, and remembered the clean-shaven gentleman, his impressively enunciated words that had fallen on the ear like the cry of a startled nocturnal bird announcing to a traveler that he had gone astray in the night, calling upon him to turn back, to return to the land of his origins: "Return home!"

For an instant the image of Gugolevo floated before him,

and he thought: "Everything is so clean there and uncorrupted; there is no secret call there, so luringly sweet from afar, so unclean at close quarters."

The carpenter sat sternly in front of him with a sunwhite face and a candle in his hands; on the occasion of the festival he wore a pair of high boots greased with tar, a watch and chain, and a jacket with a matching pair of pants; a green flood of light gushed from his head like a shimmering halo; but what was most terrifyingly arresting about him was the broad crimson satin ribbon that hung down rustling and furling in folds from his neck, like a priest's stole, while his sorry little goatee quivered over it.

"How strange!" Pyotr thought. "He's all alight—illumined with sweet joy; but why is his face so sinister and terrifying?" Pyotr stared closer and saw: a long-nosed man sitting in front of him, all glowing.

They all sat there in silence, crossing themselves, sighing and awaiting the desired guest: the desired guest did not knock at the door: knock-knock-knock; it was their hearts beating; the four wax candles licked their faces with four red flames; in a tin jug on the table wine that had just been poured was still foaming; that day was one of silent prayer; sighs and hoarse moans burst from the carpenter's mouth; at times they sounded like threats; at other times they resembled the dull roar of an oncoming flood; sometimes a cockroach would scramble across the table and stop dead before the French loaf, twitching its whiskers; and then it would rapidly run to the edge of the table: Daryalsky was thinking that all the wealth and wisdom of this age had failed to tempt him, and that a young maiden's pure love had not stopped him from flight; but an animal of a woman and a long-nosed man had led him into the abyss; but the long-nosed man was staring sternly at Pyotr. Pyotr shuddered.

It seemed to him he was already in the abyss; and the four walls were a hell in which he was being tortured; but why in that abyss did his soul catch fire and his fingers glow? Was it the abyss or the heavenly heights? If it were the heights, then why was the carpenter long nosed? The long-nosed man stared sternly at Pyotr. Pyotr shuddered.

Pyotr stared back: the halo of light, crackling, expanded over the carpenter's head, and the carpenter no longer seemed to be the carpenter but a sort of manifestation of light; the sharp beams of light beat, pricked, cut and burnt Pyotr's body as though penetrating his thoughts; it seemed to him there was something menacing about the carpenter: no—it was just a momentary premonition.

A jug of foaming wine made the rounds of them all; on the carpenter's yellow mustaches the wine dried like black blood: the French loaf was broken at last; they greedily swallowed the white chaff dipped in wine; and the walls already began to melt, doubts had begun to melt, the yellow wax of the candles was melting: the wax was dripping on the crimson satin ribbon: everything was melting, a feeling of gaiety and lightness was all pervasive.

Their eyes flashed as they looked at each other; drunk with happiness, they laughed and spat out; the shaggy-head roared out in his bass voice; they all clapped their hands. Matryona began to dance: she danced and the carpenter encouraged her: "Hey-ho, up and go: tarabom-bom-bom . . . The Lord have mercy upon us!" With their tramping, stamping and shouting they solaced each other, laughing; their teeth glittered; their eyes glittered. Matryona pulled up her skirts and did the will-o-the-wisp; their eyes were bedazzled by those bodies illuminated by prayer; a knife glittered on the table, left there for some purpose; suddenly the knife blade squeaked out: "A white body—a brave lad's body." Shaggy-head began kicking out his legs in front of Matryona. And then everything began to move: it was as though these four walls, separating this space from the rest of the world, had shifted from their place: all the signs showed that this was now a ship flying up into the blue sky; just step outside the porch of the house now, brother—outside there's only emptiness below, far off, deep underfoot, in the dark of night, the lights of Tzelebeyevo twinkled like

far stars, or the moonlit reflections of puddles on the
ground; separated by the sweetest airs from the life inside,
all four of them flew into the void.

Everything moved: the walls crackled; the hut-ship was
leaning over to the right, the table poured upon Pyotr; the
jug, emptied of wine, rolled to the floor, and the carpenter
himself stood over Pyotr . . . The walls crackled—everything moved: the hut-ship swayed over to the left and the
table rolled off Pyotr: down went the carpenter, up bobbed
Pyotr: was it infernal punishment in the abyss or blessed
paradisiacal joy—who knows, who can tell?

Matryona was stamping about, her skirt lifted high; but
her face was blue, her eyes hidden; only the whites of her
eyes could be seen, spilling their blueishness beneath her
eyes; her white teeth had bitten her lip; she was stamping out
a rhythm with her feet in short boots; shaggy-head rolled
into a corner, breathing hard. Pyotr danced, and so awkwardly! Then Matryona suddenly began to throw off her
clothes, but then thought better of it: half-dressed, hiccup-
ping, she looked at the carpenter, stamping her feet. The
carpenter himself plunged into the dance: he pulled off the
ribbon from his head, his hands to the sides: he did it seriously. Matryona clapped her hands, and kept time in a soft
voice: it was an amusing song, lighthearted and pleasant.

"An old man—
Tartara roaring tartararik . . ."

And the shaggy-head from the corner took up:

"Tartarara-tartarara!
Tarara-tararik . . .
Bang goes the priest,
Falls he low
With his brow
Into a coffin!
Tartarara-tartarara—
Tartara-tararik!"

They do it well, smartly: they dance, all four of them,
but it seems they are five . . .

Who is the fifth?

Yes, brother, here all is possible," the carpenter giggled;
the air was invisibly gracious both below and above; behind
this airy fortress they could not see the world, nor could
the world see them.

Matryona jumped up and ran out laughing from the room
and for no reason at all Pyotr ran out after her; they ran
toward that blessed spot where the yard used to be spread
over with dung, but now it was no longer the yard, nor was
there dung underfoot, but soft, cool velvet; they opened the
gates and beyond the gates, as might be expected, nothing
was to be seen: neither Tzelebeyevo, nor any other place:
cool black velvet whistled about their ears: the hut was
standing in the air.

All their sins remained there below; here—all was possible,
no sin, for all was grace: they returned to the room.

The carpenter was already on his feet, raising his bright
arm over them; as if it were he—as if it were not he, as if he
were speaking, as if he were not: the words seemed to form
themselves in the air. "What you see, children, at this time,
in this time I love in that eternity, for I am sent to you here
in this world from where I live in eternity to accomplish
that which is needed. Be merry and sing and dance, for all
of us are saved through grace . . ." That is what Pyotr
seemed to hear, but they were not the carpenter's words;
they were just words that formed themselves in the air.

But here are the carpenter's words: quietly he came up,
with his sickly hand stroked now Pyotr, now Matryona: "A
lusty wench—no? That's it. Well, Matryona, *ambrace* your
gentleman. Well, children, what about it?" He smiled with
the side of his face that winked; "Didn't I do it well?"

A hot flame already bound Pyotr and Matryona, a pillar
of smoke between their breasts; they went off to bed. And
from there they returned to the carpenter. But look—

everything had changed; as soon as they entered the room, they saw: the shaggy-head kneeling before the carpenter, knocking on the floor with his forehead while the carpenter sprawled on a bench all bright and luminous; he was moaning sweetly, his belt off and his chest bared—transparent as a clear December day, it stirred, and from his chest, as from an egg, peeked out a small, white-beaked bird's head; behold—from the ripped, bloody chest a small dove fluttered forth as though knitted of mist and began to fly about.

"*Co-co-co*," Pyotr called to the small dove; and he made crumbs of the French loaf for it, and the dove threw itself on his chest; with its small claws it tore at his shirt, and with its beak pierced his chest; and it was as though white, chill December was ripping at him and spilling his blood; Pyotr looked: what he saw was not a dove's head, but a hawk's.

"Ah!" Pyotr fell on the floor; and the bloody hole in his pecked chest poured out a fountain of blood.

Then the small dove threw itself upon Matryona; and soon there were four torn bodies lying voicelessly on the floor, on the table, on the bench—four bodies with bloodless, pale yet luminous faces; and the small dove with the hawk's head kept fluttering round them, caressing and cooing; then it alighted on the table and ran along it; its claws went "*tza-tza-tza*" as it pecked at the crumbs.

But everything melts away like a fugitive dream, like a fleeting vision, and already there is no *child*, no red flaming sphere: above—an azure sky; in the distance—rosy dawn; in the West—nocturnal shade and smoke; and in that smoke the sinister, dying, now-dulled circle of the moon, which had been purple not long ago. Below, at the bottom of the slope, the village stood quiet; the white belfry was still wrapped in darkness, but the cross already showed clear gold: that was Tzelebeyevo: there the throaty cockerels crowed lustily, smoke poured out from some of the huts and the cows lowed. Very soon the dust will rise there and a horned herd will lazily start out for yellow-brown fields.

A cart was rattling along the road from Likhov: it was the peasant Andron returning from a spree: in his cart he carried some sacks, a bottle of crown liquor, and a batch of crisp biscuits. Andron felt in fine spirits.

The horse suddenly halted: a body was sprawled on the roadway.

"Tpru! Why, isn't that the Gugolevo gent?" Andron asked as he bent over the body.

"Sir, wake up, sir!"

"Ah, where are you, bright dovelike child?" Pyotr muttered drowsily.

"He's got a child on his mind," Andron said sympathetically. "Why, he must be drunk . . . He must have swallowed a barrelful. . . ."

"Sir!"

"And is it my breast the dove clawed?"

"Get up, sir."

In a stupor, Pyotr got up and began to dance:

"An old, old man—
Tar-taratovy tararik . . ."

Andron picked him up around the middle and put him in his cart: "Ah you, I ought to whack you with a rolling pin. . . ."

"Matryona, witch: go away, long-nosed one," Pyotr continued to mutter; but Andron paid no attention to him; Andron smacked his lips: "*dir-dir-dy*," the cart rattled and bumped, and there at last was Tzelebeyevo.

Pyotr now came to: he jumped up in the cart, looked around: in front was a ditch; and from it the wormwood was whistling into the turquoise morning.

"Where am I?" Pyotr asked.

"You've been drinking a little, sir: you'd still be lying on the road if it wasn't for me."

"How did I get here?"

"That's simple. There are worse places you can end up when drunk."

Pyotr remembered everything: "Was it a dream or no dream?" he thought and began to shiver.

"Horror and a ditch, and a noose for you, man," his lips involuntarily whispered: he thanked Andron, jumped out of the cart; staggering drunkenly, he made his way to the carpenter's hut.

All was quiet: near Kudeyarov's hut a boar which had been set loose was grunting; the door to the yard was not shut: "I must have come out through the yard," Pyotr thought, but he could not remember that: all he could remember was the dancing, Matryona with her skirt raised, and the bird of prey, God knows where from, throwing itself on his chest. . . . He also remembered some sort of a bright vision; and he remembered . . . nothing more.

He entered the hut: there was the sound of heavy breathing, snoring, and the thick smell of charcoal fumes: on the table a tin jug lay on its side: on the table, on the floor, spilt-wine stains.

A clock was ticking evenly.

Threats

After a long disappearance the beggar Abram, who'd gone somewhere, finally reappeared in the morning under the windows of the huts; in his deep bass voice he sang psalms, drumming a tune with his staff: dry soundless lightnings flashed from his little leaden dove; his white wool "toadstool" was thrust here and there toward a window, for an egg, a crust of bread, a penny; from a window a hand stretched out either with an egg, a crust of bread, or a penny *for the sake of appeasement;* but the hoarse beggarly bass voice was not at all appeased: it became drier, dreader; the beggar's voice threatened unknown misfortunes just as a dry August day threatened misfortune; on a dry August day Abram drummed with his staff, and thrust his "toadstool" toward a window, while soundless lightning flashed from his leaden dove.

There were only three beggars in the Tzelebeyevo district: Prokl, Demyan and Abram; the fourth, nicknamed the "Abyss," rarely showed up in our district; Prokl was a drunkard with a good-natured smile; Demyan stole hens; the fourth beggar, nicknamed the "Abyss," was a paralytic.

One way or another, the beggars were accepted and supplied; the beggars were their own kind: and Abram, making his round of the huts, demanded his share; and hands stretched out with crusts, pennies, eggs, and the beggar's sacks swelled up.

Now Abram turned up by the shop door, pounding with

his staff, and started singing not a psalm, but an ancient song:

"Brethren, understand,
All you friends of mine,
Be attentive, listen
With your ears.

Brethren, now display
Your mercies.
Do not tempt yourselves,
All my sin's in vain."

But this pleasant song, hiding a gentle threat, created a commotion; out jumped the shopkeeper, Ivan Stepanov, from the shop with spectacles on his nose, limping with his damaged foot, and "A fig to you," he said under Abram's nose.

"I'll give it to you, you sluggard, carrion, sectarian dog, just wait, wait till they get you!"

The constable was already coming out of the shop, snickering to himself.

Abram bowed and quietly made his way to Gugolevo.

Over the Gugolevo window limply hung the red leaves of the withering vines; Katya stood by the open window, her hands placed on her grandma's shoulders; grandma was winding wool; Pavel Pavlovich, the Baron, standing over the old lady with respectful condescension, was holding the woolen threads on his fingers.

Suddenly, under the window, a song resounded:

"In the East the brightest paradise,
The land of joy eternal
Unnoticed in depravity,
To the virgins shall be given.
Better than the Tsar's the chambers there.
The orchards and the gardens,
The women's chambers, golden halls,
And in the gardens wondrous fruit."

Under the window stood the beggar Abram drumming with his staff and holding out his "toadstool" toward the window; the leaden lightning flashed drily from the soundless dove; already a silver coin rolled down to the "toadstool," but he still continued:

"Smoothly there the rivers flow
Purer than tears those waters flow—
And there eternally she dwells,
The daughter that I love so well . . .
In the soul all passions will die down,
For there is only joy and peace . . ."

"A-aa-a!" Katya burst out sobbing; she fell into an armchair, covering her face with her slender fingers. . . .

"Get out of here, you scoundrel!" grandma shouted, banging with her heavy cane; but Abram had already vanished; confusion ensued.

In deep silence, Abram, smoking a cigar, sat beneath the icons in his favorite corner; the bandy-legged carpenter was pacing before him from corner to corner, picking at one of his fingers; furious rage shone from his frenzied eyes: they complained to each other:

"The shopkeeper ought to be flayed and sprinkled with salt; nasty beast; he keeps spying!"

"He'll get it in the neck!"

"Is everything ready?"

"Everything: the dry straw, the tow and the kerosene: he's started enough fires—his turn now to be scattered in ashes!"

"Anyone picked yet to light him up?"

"No one's picked . . . there's no need . . . I'll light him up with my glance."

Silence.

"And that lad: I don't like that lad; he may get frightened of making it."

"And have you made it?"

"We've made it."

"Is there something wrong with you?"

"Things are so-so: not much—the lad's afraid of making it. There isn't much strength in him; we did it; and though a corporeal child was formed from our prayers, it wasn't a strong child—it vanished like steam, did not hold for more than an hour; and it's all the result of the lad's weakness. And such strength I put into him! Matryona too . . . And the lad's afraid . . ."

"Did you tell him?" Here Abram whispered something to the carpenter.

"I didn't at all: he'd get frightened—run away."

"I'd catch him then."

"But if he'd get away?"

"It's a lost cause then: he can't get away now."

"And yet if?"

"Ah-ah-ah . . . I-I-I," the carpenter began to stammer, "why then . . ." and his compelling eyes pointed to the knife.

"Ha-ha! Then he won't get away?"

"There's nowhere he can go from me! If he goes I'll cut his throat."

Silence.

On that day, as it happened, a guitar began to tinkle in the priest's currant bush garden: the strings could be heard all over the village; wine glasses were emptied, the priest's wife shed tears, the guitar tinkled so boisterously, so smoothly. Vukol the priest was building a fortress of chairs and then, arming himself with a fire-iron, captured the fortress with the help of the sacristan: it so happened that the priest's son was inside the fortress: the priest took the priestling prisoner; but here the angered priest's wife intervened; and her guitar began banging on the priest's back; bang-bang-bang; the guitar broke in bits; in the bushes there was guffawing; to save himself from his wife the priest rushed to the well; seizing the ropes, setting his feet on the

boards, he slid down to the very bottom of the well; he sat
there with water up to his knees looking up at the azure
aperture of sky; he saw that his wife up there was beside
herself: tearfully, the "wretch" was asking the priest to
climb back; but the priest sat on there with the water up to
his knees and to all her entreaties—"I won't, I won't; I'm
cool down here." They wished to go down for him; but,
finally, recovering his good spirits, the priest agreed to have
the good folk fetch him out of the well; they lowered a rope
with a bucket attached and pulled the priest up; with legs
propped against the bucket, all frozen himself, water pouring from his cassock as from a wet hen. The lads laughed
derisively, so did the woman teacher from a distance.

It turned out a stormy day: beyond the trees the thunder
was already tarara-ing with the trees; and dully the trees
whispered back; where the dusty road ran away to Likhov,
that dark figure which had distantly watched the village for
years desperately waved its arms at the village, and the dry
torrents of dust rose and bore down on the village and
licked the feet of passersby, threw themselves at the sky and
whirled there in yellow clouds; and the dread sun itself,
looking red through the dust, presaged a long drought for
the inhabitants of our village, who were already wilting
under the heat.

CHAPTER SEVEN

The Fourth Man

⁓⁌⧺⧼ Evening Speeches ⧺⧼⁓

With a garland of five-fingered beams the red, vicious sun
assaulted Tzelebeyevo over the crests of the yellow forest;
the sky above glowed tenderly azure; and that azure looked
like cool panes of glass; on the rim of the horizon stood a
thicket of clouds that resembled massive golden icebergs;
there, the setting sun flared; and all this glittering glow
concentrated itself in the small window of the carpenter's
hut.

Pyotr and Matryona were at the window.

"Do you know, the carpenter's planning to destroy me."

"Shhh . . . Here he is himself."

So said Matryona, leaning out of the window. Pyotr
stuck his head out too. In between the bushes and the tree
stumps, which were covered with red patches of sunset as
though with patches of carpet, the carpenter, spitting out
sunflower seeds, was slowly making his way toward them.
He wore a pair of new boots; his blood-red shirt stood out
scarlet amid the bushes, and over a shoulder he carried a
heavy homespun coat. The carpenter was followed by a
visitor: a bloodless townsman with dull eyes and thick lips,
surrounded with wiry, colorless hair; he looked moribund,
but had a certain dignity of carriage.

"Who is that, Matryona?" Pyotr inquired.

"God knows! I don't know!" she replied.

The visitor was already standing on the threshold of the
hut. "He's the fourth man," Pyotr thought in fear (thus he

answered a secret question); and he already felt his strength
ebb and his resolution wane in his attempt to resist the flood
of all these last days. "The fourth man!" he thought, feeling
a weakness steal over him: it was as though strong, transparent ice were melting beneath a July sun. . . .

"Put on the samovar, Matryona: greet our dear guest," the
carpenter exclaimed.

The guest entered, crossing himself with dignity before
the icons, and then, pointing a finger at Daryalsky, was
pleased to say:

"And that must be that same one of whom you spoke,
Mitry Mironich. The object, that is?"

"Himself," the carpenter replied, fussing around the dear
guest, glancing at Daryalsky, and making signs to him not
to interrupt.

The sun had already sunk behind the yellow tree tops of
the forest; the five-fingered garland was already regally
ascending into the tender azure of the sky; the evening was
now all purple, porphyry-like.

"So . . ." the guest squeezed through his teeth as he
played with his brass watch chain; and then he sat down
without being invited in the sunset-red corner of the hut.

"Good evening!" Pyotr said at last, offering his hand to
the moribund-looking man.

"Good evening, good evening," the townsman replied,
condescendingly holding out two fingers. "I know about
you . . ." he went on. "You are engaged in matters of the
spirit. . . ."

"Just a little," the carpenter put in, while the wrinkles
collected on his face moved, and the half of it that was
turned to Pyotr promised no good.

"You must continue, brother, with your spiritual affairs.
That is a good thing to be doing, occupying yourself with
spiritual matters; I, too, am involved with that . . . I do my
little share. . . ."

"And who are you?" Daryalsky asked, unable to restrain
himself.

"Why, I am the coppersmith—Sukhorukov. You have heard of me of course: everyone has heard of Sukhorukov. I'm known in Chmari, Kozliki, and Petushki."

Pyotr remembered the signboard he had seen in the public square of Likhov, on which the name of "SUKHORU-KOV" had been painted in bold letters.

In the meantime, Matryona had served the samovar, some biscuits, and sugar, and the carpenter sat down to tea with his guest who, biting off a lump of chipped sugar, blew with his thick lips upon the boiling liquid. But Pyotr thought one thing very strange: they did not light the kerosene lights; and so they sat in the thick, red twilight of the village dusk.

"Sidor Semeonich has been doing some important business for us, lad, that's what," the carpenter said, winking at Pyotr; and he added, "He's a regular dove."

And the regular dove added:

"All the Sukhorukovs are like that: the whole race of the Sukhorukovs have been of a kind, it may be said . . . And how are things with you?"

"With us things are like this: in a small way, in a light way, we are also *making* it."

"Well, and is he also *making* it?"

"He is also making it. . . ."

"With the woman?"

"With my woman . . ."

"And is the woman making it?"

"She's making it . . ."

"Well, lad," the carpenter turned to Pyotr with a sort of special sweetness in his voice, "don't mind us talking like this, and so on. Now Sidor here, Sidor Semeonich," the carpenter seemed to go all soft as he said this, "he, too, you know, he, too, is making it: he's a real, regular dove."

The *real dove*, sitting at the table, was blowing importantly with his thick lips at the boiling liquid. One circumstance seemed odd: they did not light the lamps.

But Pyotr felt no fear of the moribund-looking craftsman; he saw that there were three of them seated at the table: he himself, Mitry, and the shaggy-haired one. Sukhorukov was the fourth among them; but Pyotr felt no fear at all; true, he experienced a sort of disgust, a revulsion almost, for the coppersmith; it was soon clear to him that this craftsman was capable of every sort of nastiness the human race could imagine; that was clear to Pyotr from the way the carpenter honored his guest. Pyotr guessed that they must share some shameful secret in common; but the coppersmith continued quite dispassionately and with staggering importance to breathe on his hot tea, as though the carpenter, Pyotr, and Matryona were just objects that had fallen in his, the coppersmith's, hands, and had fallen into them so surely that they would never again escape from the coppersmith's grip.

Pyotr felt sick; he went outside. The five-fingered purple garland was still remotely aloft. Pyotr remembered how imperceptibly the days had gone by, how autumn was already there with its shrill tomtits and its yellow-clad, far-carrying trees.

Matryona was sitting close to a cow in front of the hut, and was pulling away at the cow's teats while the milk splashed into a copper pail.

Thoughtfully Pyotr stood over Matryona.

"Do you know, the carpenter is scheming to destroy me?"

"Go to the devil! What else can you think of!"

"And he'll destroy you too."

"And what for?"

"He's a menace to all good people."

"That's just impossible: there's no such danger at all."

"Then why does he glower at me so and spy on me?"

"It's just his master's eye; he keeps watch."

"Haven't you noticed, Matryona, we are the carpenter's captives here: both you and I; neither of us can take a step without him; at the least provocation, he trails after us into the woods; or he's hanging out of his plank bed to spy on us . . ."

"It's sinful what you're saying, Pyotr Petrovich!"

The milk continued splashing into the pail as she pulled at the cow's teats; somewhere in the distance the purple streams of clouds burned clearly; in the East the darkness of ash was already turning a blue-black; and from there, out of that blue-black gloom, shy stars began to glow and the chill, autumn breeze was already rustling in the bushes.

Pyotr remembered, God knows why, his now remote past; he remembered Schmidt and the books Schmidt used to give him to read; he remembered, God knows why, Paracelsus's treatise *Archidoxis magica,* and Paracelsus's words about the way an experienced hypnotist can use human sexual energy for his own ends; he remembered also the physicist Kircher* and his book *De arte magnetica;* and he remembered the words of the great Fludd.** Oh, Pyotr would have said, Oh, he would have said to Matryona as regards the carpenter and everything related to them; but Matryona would not understand that; Daryalsky shuddered and stared at Matryona: the crooked-kneed wench was evidently turning something over in her mind as she sat there under the cow, and she let slip the slender teat from her hands; her brick-red curls had thrust their way from under her kerchief: she squatted there, picking at her teeth with a manure-smelling finger: a veritable witch she looked; but her eyes—that was the trouble! And the chill red beams of sunset were now bathing her; and the slenderest puffs of evening clouds now curled up into the deep azure of the sky.

"And all these prayers?" Daryalsky asked. "How do we

---

* Kircher, Athanasius (1601–1680). German scholar and mathematician, author of *Ars Magnesia* (1631).

** Fludd, Robert (1574–1637). English physician and mystical philosopher. A disciple of Paracelsus.

know, Matryona, what spirit is descending into us? It's all at his, the carpenter's suggestion; and he needs you, Matryona, just as he needs me. Without us his energy would kill him. There is a word, and I'd say it, but only you wouldn't understand it . . ."

"What is the word?"

"I'd say it, but you wouldn't understand it."

"A miraculous word, I'm sure you've invented. Just leave Mitry Mironich alone, for Christ's sake. I don't like your talk, so there."

Matryona picked up the milk pail and went into the hut; as she entered she found the carpenter and the coppersmith huddled in a black corner, whispering; they had not yet lighted the light; it was dark in the hut; the cockroaches were rustling behind the chromolithograph; and the light rustling of human voices accompanied the light rustling of many cockroach legs: *shu-shu-shu* . . .

They did not notice Matryona enter: they were immersed in their whispers; frightened, Matryona called out:

"Mitry Mironich, ah, Mitry Mironich!"

They took no notice: they were immersed in their whispers—whispering into each other's ears: "*shu-shu-shu-shu-shu-shu.*"

"Mitry Mironich!"

"What?" the carpenter finally responded in a thin voice from a corner, startled by her voice. It sounded like a rooster crowing rather than Mitry Mironich.

"What are you up to there?"

"What?" the coppersmith creaked like a rusty cart wheel.

"What are you whispering about there?"

"Oh just so! We're creating prayers. Go your way with God, little dove. . . ."

"Go your way, woman," the coppersmith creaked. Matryona went out again to the cow.

There stood Pyotr, thinking his gloomy thoughts. "And she is my love," he thought, turning to Matryona.

Pyotr was now thinking of Katya (the light streaks of

clouds were burning out in love); but no, like those clouds, Katya was far beyond him now; Katya was not for him; and his heart felt pinched.

"Oy," Matryona sighed, "I'm getting sleepy."

They had nothing to talk about.

"Listen, Matryona, if you like, we'll run away from here," Pyotr ventured. "I'll take you far away from here and hide you from the carpenter; we shall have a life of our own, our own life, a free and easy life (then he remembered he had said the same words to Katya); let us run away from here, Matryona."

"Don't talk like that. He'll hear us, maybe. . . ."

"He won't hear us: let's run away, Matryona!"

"Stop talking. He hears everything, sees everything; he'll be able to find us anywhere; I won't go away from him anywhere; and you won't go away either."

"I'll get away from you all, Matryona."

"Back to Katenka, that Frenchie, that's where you'll go. She'll chase you, that Frenchie will."

"I'm suffering, Matryona!"

"Stop tickling with your tongue!"

Pyotr thought of Katya, thought of her, and put his thoughts aside; Katya, like those clouds, was far beyond him now; Katya was not for him, and he felt his heart pinched.

The light-winged clouds, like the wings of love, were burning out, turning into celestial ashes and embers; menacing mounds of ash poured from the East, which had still been so luminous a short while ago; very soon all this gloom, all this airy bonfire, would turn blue and black like the face of a corpse, blacking out the surrounding country until next morning—just as a corpse's face may have been fresh and rosy only yesterday, smiling in greeting and words of welcome; the day like a ripened apple had rotted in the evening, and already the evening damp was breaking in through the windows, pouring in upon those standing outside the hut, making their faces blue and black like those of a corpse.

"Do you know, the carpenter is scheming to destroy me?"

"Stop that. He hears everything."

"And he'll destroy you too."

But Matryona, hanging her head treading over the manure, led off the reddish cow.

"How many good people has that carpenter destroyed!"

Matryona entered the hut; none of the lights had been lit. There was only the sound of whispering in a dark corner: *shu-shu-shu—shu-shu-shu.*

"Mitry Mironich, ah, Mitry Mironich!"

"*Shu* . . ."

"Mitry Mironich!"

"*Shu-shu-shu* . . ."

Matryona, as though accidentally, let drop a jug.

"Asenka?" the carpenter suddenly responded from the corner as sweetly as if he were a young rooster.

"What are you muttering about there?"

"We're creating prayers. . . ."

"Yes, we're creating prayers," the creaking cart wheel replied.

They lit the kerosene lamps.

"And so . . . he's her object, is he?" the coppersmith from Likhov asked, prodding now Pyotr, now Matryona with his finger. Matryona blushed and stared down at her belly.

"That's so, Sidor Semeonich, that's so," the carpenter replied. "They're two little doves together, they entertain each other with kisses and . . ."

"He-he-he: the little doves," the coppersmith creaked like a rusty cart wheel.

"Well then, let them be lovey-dovey!"

"Agreed, Sidor Semeonich, let them, let them; I tell them that too . . ."

"Pfff!" Matryona snorted, blushing with shame, and she stuffed herself into a corner.

Pyotr also felt ashamed and nauseous. He went out, banging the door; very soon after, the guest turned his cup upside down and with his host, left the vicinity of the hut.

There was still a glimmer in the distance: the five-fingered pillar over the village had not yet lost its luminosity.

About What Happened in the
〰 Tavern 〰

Soot, smoke, fumes, noise, puddles on the floor—that is
what confronted Pyotr in the tavern; Pyotr ordered tea and
sat down at a table covered with a tablecloth all spattered
with yellow stains; here and there people turned to stare at
him, some nudged each other, others whispered "the red
gent!"; some cleared their throats, others swore; the
drunken village constable frowned; and with that the matter ended.

Pyotr noticed nothing of all that: with his elbows on the
table he sat frozen in thought.

Intensely Pyotr pondered on his destiny: he found no
way of explaining his strange love affair, those wild ritual
sessions, and his job at the carpenter's: he had the impression that something vast and heavy had fallen upon him and
was stifling him, that a sweet sensation of sinfulness was
squeezing him by the throat—or was he being choked?—he
was not sure which, a feeling of unbelievable exaltation or
the endless torments of the soul and spirit; strange as it may
seem, whenever there were no ritual sessions, this sensation
of heaviness was transformed into sweet joy: doomed to
pain and crucifixion, which there was no way of avoiding
now, yet he strove to bless this crucifixion; and like a man
suffering from toothache, he was ready to batter his jaw
against a stone to heighten the pain; and in that poison of his
pain lay all the joy and sensuality; and that is how Pyotr
felt: in a state of sweet expectation he awaited the ritual

sessions: and in that state of sweet expectation, amid the light of day, he seemed to be confronted with enigmas and mysteries; and strangest thing of all: on those days he began to love his Russia more than ever: it was a sensual love, a cruel love; and on those days Matryona became all in all for him; and with Matryona he waited for the carpenter to satisfy his, Pyotr's, expectation; and then a new, clear world seemed to open before him, a world in which Mitry Mironich the carpenter awaited him with a goblet of sweet wine in his hand, offering that wine to all men.

But no sooner had he tasted of that wine than he began to imagine the strangest things; and he could not tell whether it was in reality or in dream that he experienced strange adventures: after those ritual sessions he used to get up with a dull pain in his head, a feeling of nausea and spiritual satiety, and everything that had happened to him on the previous evening now appeared to him nasty, shameful and terrifying; in fear in full daylight he was startled by bushes, empty corners, and he constantly had the impression that someone was dogging his footsteps; he felt someone's invisible stifling hand on his chest; and he feared that choking feeling; and ashamed of it, he would look straight at people, horses or cattle; and it seemed to him as if cattle and people pointed to him with their eyes; he felt that incredible rumors were circulating about him, and he felt ashamed of his disgrace.

He started just then and began to look round him: soot, fumes, noise, peasants: and in the midst of it all a manifest voice, saying: "Look, good people: there's the red gent sitting over there."

"And the *prilliants*, it seems, were not found," a voice could be heard saying distinctly at the next table, and two peasants stared reproachfully at Daryalsky. But, thank God, he did not understand all those insinuations, and many of them he did not even hear: "the red gent" rang in his ears; but these words were not what the peasants had uttered; and Daryalsky once again stared down at the tablecloth.

And there was Matryona too: in the last few days she had no longer impressed him as that love for whom it was right to sacrifice his soul; no, Matryona no longer seemed to be that love: rather, he saw her as an untidy, stupid wench and one, moreover, far too greedy for coarse caresses; all that held him perhaps to her was their mutually forged sensuality; and what held him even more were the carpenter's eyes; for, dear man, if the carpenter happened to look at you, you would become tied to him like a dog by the chain.

Mechanically Daryalsky had ordered some vodka, sausage and a packet of cigarettes (called "Lion," five kopecks for ten); he poured himself vodka from the teapot and emptied the burning liquid into his mouth; his throat was already tickling and the fire spread over his chest, and a pleasant buzz began in his head, when he suddenly perceived a drunken little man with gray side-whiskers, dressed all in gray, who had taken off his cap and was wiping his tearful eyes with a red handkerchief.

"Yevseich!"

"O master Pyotr, how thin you've grown, how black you look with your beard . . . O Lord, master mine!"

"Sit down with me, old man: let's drink some vodka. . . ."

Yevseich respectfully sat down at his table.

"Our young lady, with her grandma and with Pavel Pavlovich, have all gone to town. Ah, Pyotr Petrovich, my good master: what have you done to us all; the young lady was killing herself—a good young lady she is: God's child, Katenka . . . And isn't it a sin for you to torment her, a young child; for she's a child still, our young lady Katenka . . . Ah, Pyotr Petrovich!"

"Let's drink, old man."

"Your health, sir . . ."

"There's no need to remember the past: what's been, has gone."

"Come back to us, sir, come back; all the servants remember you; they don't like that here officer."

"What officer?"

"That here Cornet Lavrovsky . . ."

"Who is he, that Cornet?"

"A relative of the lady's: he's been a guest at the house since the Third Savior holiday. He came from Petersburg or Sarany, their village."

"Let's drink, old man."

"Your health, sir!"

"And do you remember, sir, how I ran after you and you, sir, ran away from me, an old man, jumping like a hare. A day didn't pass but my lady Katenka sent me down to the village with letters for you; we thought you were staying with your gentleman friend, Schmidt, but it turned out differently, it did," the old man said frowning and looking at Pyotr from under his brows. "It turned out differently, it did: badly, very badly. . . ."

Like a knife, those words stabbed Pyotr.

"And you've grown thin," the old man went on, "thin and dark, and you've let your beard grow, that's what . . ."

But Pyotr was no longer listening: his attention was distracted: he suddenly noticed the carpenter and the coppersmith making their way past the tables and sitting down, but when they noticed Pyotr in the company of Yevseich, they pretended for some reason not to see them. Yevseich was drunk by now; sobbing now, his speech was quite inaudible; but Pyotr now could tear his eyes away from that distant table where the carpenter and coppersmith had settled down to drink: he saw vodka was already being served them: "What could have brought them here?" Pyotr asked himself. "It must be sinister business," he concluded for some reason: and the familiar shiver ran down his spine; but the carpenter and the coppersmith concentrated on their own affairs: they lowered their faces toward each other and stared at each other with their dull eyes, with a sort of tenderness and even nostalgia, as though they could not be apart even for a minute without each other.

"So then you did put in some powder for that merchant?"

"Wasn't I. Anka did it . . ."

"Then you must have brought Anka the powder?"

"That I did. I brought Anka a small portion of powder . . ."

"And the merchant, he . . ."

"The merchant's as good as dead now."

"Lost his speech?"

"Lost his speech."

"And all else?"

"And all else."

"Well, well, Sidor Semeonich!"

"All we Sukhorukovs are of the same metal . . ."

"A hard people!"

"That's certain!"

"Ah, master, master: what company you've got mixed up with? With the lowest of the lowest, a wanton wench; and aren't you ashamed? Why, for lack of sleep for your young lady, I've tossed so many nights, I felt so sorry for her!"

"How is it, Sidor Semeonovich, you were so careless: you should have given him more powder. . . ."

"Don't teach me: I have never met a smarter man than myself—in *palitics:* if I'd put in more powder, it would have been too obvious—people would say he'd been poisoned. . . ."

"I am not teaching you, but listen . . ."

"No, wait: I must, you strange client, report to you that the merchant won't last another month. . . ."

"*Tili-tili-bim-bom,*" tinkled a triangle in the corner; three peasants were sipping tea from saucers and there was a crowd around them; they were outside peasants here for autumn work: they were corn threshers, a learned lot; each autumn they turned up in our locality; one of them kept explaining which star was a *planid* and which not; another peasant had thought up a machine, which could keep turning endlessly* of itself; a third peasant was banging away strongly on his triangle. It was autumn; and with autumn in the village appeared three autumn peasants: one peasant promised to show his machine: the other peasant explained which star was a *planid* and which not; and the third peasant played strongly on his triangle; no fourth peasant was present.

"*Tili-tili-bim-bom* . . ."

Daryalsky felt like a wolf with bared fangs, cornered by the hunt and ready to do battle with the despicable hounds: propping himself on his elbow, he eagerly tried amid the noise, shouting and riot, to catch what the pair over there was whispering about; but all he could hear was the tinkling of the triangle and an imposing voice saying:

"The earth, my brethren, is a sphere; and we, it turns out, dwell on that sphere. . . ."

"And I assume," a voice leapt out, "that we live *in* a sphere."

"You're loony! How could we live in a sphere without air? D'ye think there are windows in that sphere to let in the fresh air?"

That is all Daryalsky heard: thoughts again occupied his soul: he remembered that on days following the prayer meetings he had the very real impression of someone engaging him in conversation, someone whom neither ear, eye, or nose, could detect; whether he was carpentering in the hut or having a midday meal with the Kudeyarovs—that is what he experienced: there would be the three of them planing wood; but no: there seemed to be four when he lowered his eyes; and who was that *fourth?* When he raised his eyes, he could only see three: he would lower his eyes again and

---

* I assume this talk refers to *perpetuum mobile*. (Author's note.)

once more it would seem to him as though the carpenter were exchanging whispers with a *fourth* person; and that *fourth* was pointing a finger at Pyotr and sniggering, setting the carpenter against Pyotr: "You should let him have it, I'd let him have it, we should let him have it!" The carpenter would lay aside his plane, blow his nose, and even appear confused as he would wipe his mallet-like nose and, while listening, feel apologetic:

"As it is, I'm—why should I? We all—better you do it . . ."

"No, no, no: do it without me, you've got whiskers," the *fourth* insinuated and they all laughed together, and even Matryona put her head around the door to have a look at the sort of person the *fourth* was; then Pyotr could bear it no longer and, throwing his saw aside, he would stare at the *fourth;* and there would be no *fourth:* he'd stare at an empty corner and, as usual, he would see that there were only three of them in the working room as there had been three originally. Remembering all this, Pyotr, like a growling wolf cornered by hounds and ready to give battle, stretched himself out toward the coppersmith.

"And you think the earth is a ball or something of the sort, dangling on a string from the sky?"

"And I tell you: the earth is spherical. . . ."

"As it is, I'm—this is more than I can—all of us, we're—and you yourself . . ." the carpenter muttered, moving away from the coppersmith.

"No, no, no; leave me out, you've got whiskers yourself. . . ."

"That means that we're flying through space . . ."

"Of course!"

"But then if the earth is a sphere, in the likeness of a ball, let's say, and we're sitting on that ball, let's say, and the devils are tossing us about between them; and depending on that, you have the movement of the *planids*."

"The earth's a devil's ball," Daryalsky thought and plunged back into his reflections. . . .

Or, for instance, when they started to leave the hut: looking, you'd think they were still inside; and yet there they were already outside in the street on their way to the village; and there were *four* of them, not three; Pyotr would stop then and begin to count: and again he would count only three of them; the *fourth* had vanished into thin air.

That was the state he was in all these days, but not a word of his mental state did he broach to the carpenter: instead, he talked with Matryona. . . .

"Matryona love," he would ask her, "how many of us are there in the hut?"

"What do you mean, how many? Myself, you and Mironich."

"But who is the fourth?"

But the stupid girl went off and told the carpenter about this. The carpenter said nothing: he merely smiled into his mustaches.

All this raced rapidly through Pyotr's head as he scrutinized the coppersmith from afar; he was the man he had always been expecting; that's who it was, that *fourth* man; only what was his bond with the carpenter? And, besides, he did not at all resemble the *fourth* man: he looked much too insignificant—a zero of a figure.

Pyotr burst out laughing wildly and raised the teapot:

"Let's drink, Yevseich!"

"Your health, sir!"

"God sees that this fellow of yours, as far as the merchant is concerned, has done our church a service."

"That's no way to talk: what church do you mean!"

A yellow fly appeared and alighted on the carpenter's nose.

"That's the way things are, it's sinful without a church . . ."

"If it's like that, without a church, it's sinful, but it's sinful in every way. . . ."

The carpenter chased the fly: it described a circle and settled down in a lethargic way on the tablecloth, rubbing its legs together and displaying its polluted yellow belly.

"There you go: a fine comparison you've found: death and murder . . ."

"But isn't that murder? Don't sigh; there's no sin in it."

"How d'you figure that?"

"It's simple: it's an old wives' tale that; but you'd better squash that fly; it's been feeding on a corpse."

"What is there then, if there's no sin?"

The corpse-fed fly took off and flew away.

"There just isn't anything . . ."

"What about Him, Who metes out justice in the Heavens?"

"What's that?"

The fly now settled on Daryalsky's finger.

"It's not for you to teach me: I haven't met anyone smarter than myself; you'd better believe me: if there's sin, then, as concerns the poisoning of Luka Silitch, you're an obvious adversary; this I am revealing to you in the way of friendship; and don't cover yourself up in the church; it's clear there's no sin; there's nothing—no church and no supreme judge in the heavens."

"Hey, wait a minute!"

"Why should I wait? When I gave him that powder, I understood at once there was nothing; it's all as smooth as a ball; just emptiness; a chicken or a human being—it's all one flesh . . . inexorable. . . ."

"So it turns out we walk upside down?"

"The Americans do, not us."

"I wouldn't go to that America for anything in the world!"

Fumes, smoke, vapor, noise, peasants; voices were raised at the other end of the shop:

"What I'm saying, Mitryukha, saying is—yes: the stake, I say, sharpen it, I say: he'll set you on it, I say, for your vile, I say, scribble . . ."

"Go on, go on . . ."

"They're rousing up the people!"

"The ruffians!"

"The *skubents**!"

"Well, and what did he do?" the constable questioned.

"He said: we're standing up, he said, for a just cause . . . But I said to him, I said: it's a yiddish business that, I said; you're spoiling the people, I said, you damned fellows."

And so the peasants carried on, each in his turn, spitting and climbing out of their skin to please the constable; the tipsy constable; the tipsy constable was having a spree that day in the company of the snub-nosed lads on the occasion of the festival eve; and a loose, full-fleshed wench was drinking with him too.

Fumes, smoke, vapor, noise, peasants: Pyotr flung open the window and let in the chill air; Yevseich, already completely drunk, was sawing at a neighboring table:

"You'd better shut up about those *prilliants*, old man," a peasant was saying. "You'd better keep quiet about those *prilliants;* they disappeared, they did, those *prilliants* . . ."

"I swear on the cross, the *prilliants* were found!"

"Tell me another one!"

"Shall I take you to the constable?"

Pyotr, immersed in reverie, heard nothing of this; he was turning over in his mind that, of late, he had felt the carpenter's frowning eyes watching him, those same frowning eyes from which, as the folk said, hens dropped dead; increasingly the carpenter had frowned on Pyotr, keeping a

* Another variation on students.

ceaseless watch over him; and Pyotr watched the carpenter too, making note of his ever new subterfuges; and so they kept watch over each other.

The carpenter developed a dislike for Pyotr both because he did not execute his will over Matryona in the way he wanted, and also because Pyotr seemed to lack that strength on which the carpenter had counted; and it was upon that strength, as on a percentage of real capital placed in the bank, that the carpenter based his speeches about the *Child;* and it turned out that he was delving into the subject in vain: and if Pyotr did not love Matryona to the depths of his soul was *a fact of no importance;* it was just a matter of everyday shame: and that is why there were ill-omened *happenings with the luminous Child,* which was being formed from the exhalations of four human breaths.

But, most of all, the carpenter had taken a dislike to Pyotr because Matryona had become strongly attached to him: it would be difficult now to tear the stupid woman away from him, and it was necessary to tear her away from him and no second thoughts about it!

While they followed each other about, peeping out of corners, bushes, and looking down from their plank beds, Pyotr guessed that there was a *fourth man* walking about among them, whispering his terrifying speeches, watching them, stalking them, threatening them, yet firmly, very firmly binding them all together in one fatal, shameful and terrifying mystery.

Pyotr remembered how not so long ago he had fallen quite asleep stretched out on a bench (Matryona had just left him and gone back to her own bed)—Pyotr remembered how it had seemed to him as if a rope had been tightly pulled round his neck and a knee had pressed hard on his chest while the rope was pulled tighter; Pyotr had groaned and opened his eyes; and he had seen the carpenter standing over him thoughtfully, plucking at his beard and attentively staring at his bared chest; and Pyotr had leapt up from the bench. Mironich, observing his alarm, had turned away and stretched out his hand toward the jug, as if he wanted a drink of water: having drunk some water, he had coughed in a pitiful way and then gone off to bed without a word, good or bad. Pyotr could not calm down for a long time; he remained sitting on the bench squashing cock-roaches until the yellow eye of the dawn peeped through the window, lighting up the dust and crumbs on the floor; since that time Pyotr had taken to sleeping in the hayloft: he felt stifled in the hut from the breathing of four human bodies all emanating heat; he began to have tremors.

God knows why, but all this now flashed through his mind as he watched the coppersmith from a distance: "There they are sitting now," he thought, "the carpenter and the *fourth* man: but was it the *fourth?* Perhaps it was just *nobody*, a *zero?* There they sit, egging each other on; and if one were to say to anyone: 'Good folk, haven't you got an eye for all this?'—they'd only laugh and not believe a word of it."

While he was thinking this, in the opposite corner whis-pers continued and furtive glances were cast at Pyotr: but the smoke, the tea, the smart peasants and the constable all drowned that whispering.

"And, brethren mine, I saw a dream: it was as if I had three heads and each of them a different one: one was a dog's head, the second a carp's; and only the third was my own; and those heads were all defending themselves; and that made my brains crackle—yes, very much. . . ."

"Go on with you, you chump!"

"Why, what's wrong?"

"You ought to have your head ducked. . . ."

"The devil take him; but we must make a decision about it; just think it over, Sidor Semeonich; we can't let him wander off to the four quarters of the globe; you'll understand that yourself; and yet why should I hold on to him—a mouth too many—if there is no profit from him; it only means feeding him free."

When Pyotr passed them on the way out, having unconsciously made a firm resolution, the carpenter hailed him affectionately:

"Come here, come here . . ."

"Well?" Pyotr asked, turning toward them in a way that startled them both: challengingly, proudly, head held high; at that minute the gentleman in him was revealed, even though his tufted beard (only a month old) and his cap of uncombed hair, and the holes in his shirt elbows showed little evidence of the gentleman.

"Listen, sir," the carpenter sidled up to him as sweet as sugar, "there's business here for you: Sidor, here, Sidor Semeonich, is going back in the morning; you'd better go with him; there Yeropegina, the merchant's wife, will give you an order for me for some furniture. . . ."

"All right, I'll do it!"

"Try and get away early: we'll set off as soon as it's light," Sukhorukov said very politely, turning to him.

Like lightning a thought flashed through Pyotr's head, and he almost smiled joyfully, but, with some aim in view, he thought it necessary to hesitate.

"Ach!" Pyotr said, deliberately scratching his head. . . .

"Now, friend, you must do this for me," the carpenter said, putting his hand on Pyotr's shoulder. And, strangely enough, that dignified face with its long, hanging-down beard (a mixture of pig-writing with icon-writing) still suggested respect and fear in Pyotr; and the fact that the carpenter was drunk (it was the first time Pyotr had seen the carpenter drunk) and agitated—all this suggested through the hatred he felt for him also a sort of tenderness. "How is it I didn't notice before," he thought, "that *pig-writing* is blended with *icon-writing* in this face?" He had just invented the word "pig-writing" and it seemed he had coined the right word.

"All right, I'll go."

"Your health," the coppersmith said, offering him a glass of vodka.

They drank.

Then Pyotr went out: the dark evening still striped with sunset threw itself at him; and that evening wrapped him up in darkness until dawn. Pyotr set out toward the dawn.

Noise, thumping, shouts, smoke-laden air: the tables were being served carp, herrings and vodka in large teapots, and every sort of carcass, and "Lion" cigarettes in red boxes (five kopecks for ten); not everyone could afford "Lion," but they smoked them *for show;* around the tipsy constable pressed a crowd of tipsy peasants:

"You catch them and chuck them into the water."

"Why I . . ."

"We'll . . ."

"It's the real truth, may I say: that is what they're up to, for sure."

"You log, that's why they're rousing the people. . . ."

"It's the real truth, your honor, if I may say so; therefore, it means . . ."

"Then catch them and throw them into the water."

And the constable, drawing his nail across the red packet, with his shaking fingers pulled out a "Lion" cigarette and lit it with pleasure.

"Well, and what about it?"

"About it? Why, I think he'll try and get away."

"And what if he does?"

"Then, Mironich, you can write 'we're done for.' "

The carpenter concentrated his thoughts.

"We can never let that happen," he said.

"On my Sukhorukov word, I tell you he'll run away."

"Why don't you give him some powder?"

"I'd give him some . . ."

Silence.

"But since you are suggesting this here to me, I must tell you that for a thing like that you'll owe me something."

"So that's it: I'll bow to you . . ."

"You'll bow to me with the Yeropegin thousands?"

"I'll bow at your feet with the Yeropegin thousands."

"Good, good: then bow to me with those thousands . . ."

"I'll bow to you . . ."

Silence.

"Only one thing . . ."

"I'll tell you straight: there's no sin here: there's nothing, just emptiness, a trifling matter . . ."

"All right, take him to town . . ."

"I'll take him."

"One can't cope with him here: you can't do it here: my woman's here, Matryona . . ."

Silence.

"And when will action be taken against them?"

"Action will be taken: don't doubt that . . . very shortly . . ."

"O Lord, O Lord! . . ."

"We Sukhorukovs, brother, whatever we undertake— just ask anyone what sort of people we are: a well-known species . . ."

"And he won't get away from you?"

"Just let him try!"

"I was just—"

"Get away? No one's yet got away from me!"

Silence.

"Just let me tell you this, and you listen carefully: a chicken or a man—it's all one flesh; and there's no sin in it; men or beasts or birds—they are all born the same way; and since I tell you this out of friendship, you ought to thank me for it. D'you understand?"

The accordion began to squeal; a yellow fly flew over to the constable's table and alighted; a drunken peasant woman began to dance; she kicked the dust up from under her skirts with style, compressed her lips in a dignified way, and held her arms akimbo:

"So I went
For to get married—
But my man
Turned out a scoundrel . . ."

The drunken constable roared with laughter, and the snub-nosed village lads tore their mouths open and bawled:

"This way and that,
That way and this:
In between
No way at all . . ."

The woman stamped her feet boisterously and shouted:

"Radishes they ate
And cabbage too—
They were awfully hungry
And their bellies empty . . ."

And the lads took her up:

"This way and that,
That way and this:
In between
No way at all . . ."

It was a new song, and much in fashion: before that they used to sing *socialist* songs in the district; but after the authorities had tied up Father Nicholas and dragged him off to prison, the people in the district had grown a little timid; the meetings stopped, the guns had been thrown away, denunciations began to reach the police; and people began to sing new songs:

"My in-law now teaches,
Plays with me:
From the cabbage
My belly's swollen . . .
And that's all
The story I can tell . . ."

And the lads took it up:

"That's enough from you—
Just drink kvas!"

It was a new song, now in fashion.

The crazy woman would have gone on stamping her feet for a long time, the constable would have gone on roaring with laughter and smoking his "Lion" cigarettes, and every kind of song would have been sung—joyful songs, obscene songs, and sorrowful songs, if an extraordinary event had not interrupted them: amid the fumes, soot, darkness and smoke rings, someone suddenly yelled:

"Brothers, fire!"

The silence was immediate: the woman stopped dancing, the lads froze with gaping mouths, and the constable with a lighted match in the smoke-laden darkness; shouts could be heard in the village; they stared at the windows and the windows glowed red.

"A fire, you don't say?" the coppersmith queried in surprise.

"It's a fire all right . . ."

They hadn't time yet to recover when the Tzelebeyevo belfry began to ring; the brass bells sounded unaccustomedly into the evening gloom: rapidly one peal followed another: and when the folk rushed out of the tavern, a black-purple gloom stood in the sky and in it crackled, spluttered and leapt a bright flame coiling hither and thither in a bright shower of sparks; it was as though myriads of red and gold wasps, which had been hidden in a hive, had now flown out into the obscurity of the night in order to sting people and cover them with mortal bites from their red stings—and the angry golden wasps swarmed, intertwined and shone, flying out of the hive; and like bloody hornets, glowing logs leapt up into the night; there, luminous snakes puffed smoke and quickly, quickly they crept from under corners, stretching out their necks, hissing, and crawled toward neighboring huts, now lighting up the

Tzelebeyevo common; slowly the austere black rings of smoke rolled low over the common, stumbling over the common and falling to the earth in a dark-red curtain, from beneath which two-legged shadows ran rapidly back and forth; their faces were invisible and their shouts inaudible; only their black outlines could be seen there awkwardly waving their hands, screaming and panicking; it seemed as if an ominous horde of shadows, flying from every part, had descended there to feast amid the red glitter of fires.

"They look like devils, not people," some joker remarked behind the coppersmith's back, when they stopped some distance from the fire among the grasses and flowers; the constable was the only one to react to this witticism as he stared through the darkness with drunken eyes and muttered to himself, "Damn this dark!"

"You've found a fine time for joking!" he exclaimed.

"They ought to be thrashed!" someone else growled.

"They're foreigners: lads from 'Mare's Meadow.' . . ."

In the dark, drunken voices nastily sang out:

"Rise ye starvelings from your slumbers . . ."

And they faded into the night.

The belfry bellowed with brass: forward and back—forward and back and forward: *don-don-don-don:* the stifling smoke rolled on, falling upon the earth in a red curtain, from beneath which two-legged shadows continued to run to and fro: hissing, crackling, screams, and the helpless weeping of a child could be heard; an old woman began to lament loudly; frightened housekeepers jumped out of the neighboring houses, and into the smoke flew boots, sarafans, pillows, sheets, skirts; a large sack of corn thrown up into the night flew through the air; it was not the shop that was on fire, but the barn next door.

"Haul, haul, haul, haul!" a powerful shouting burst forth, and a dozen arms from under the red curtain itself pulled at a long grappling hook; with a red-hot iron tooth the hook bit out a dazzling blazing beam from the wall of the barn: it collapsed dully, scorching the grass; a fire hose was pouring water here and there, drenching not the flames, but the neighboring houses, roofs, grass and people, who, roaring, rushed about beneath the very curtain of fire; in their excessive zeal they had just damaged the village fire hose and, if it had not been for Utkin who galloped up with another hose and grappling irons from the next village, there would soon have been only black chimney stacks left on the site of the village.

"Haul, haul, haul, haul!" came the loud shouts, and the crimson curtain, like tightly stretched satin, quivered amid the smoke; and—crash; the roof collapsed; a waterfall of sparks foamed up over the stinging blaze like the gold lace of an extremely precious goblet; and a clear crackling tongue of flame shot up into the sky in spiteful joy.

At that instant the common was unexpectedly lit up, as though it had flared so strongly that even the people standing a good way off felt the heat, while the men who were fussing near the fire screamed and took to their heels, covering their sooty faces with their sleeves; then, by the cranberry bushes, people caught sight of a gaunt little figure garbed all in white: that little figure could be seen from afar, praying with a cross held up high toward the fire: it was Father Vukol who, with wind-tossed curls, was entering the lists armed with Christian prayer against the fire; his eyes did not see the red hell; God knows what those eyes saw, filled as they were with grief.

Only for an instant was the surrounding country so lit up, and then everything began to grow dark again; the cranberry bushes were plunged into the night again; and again the outstretched cross and the priest's gaunt little figure were plunged into the night: the bright tongue of flame, momentarily tossed up into the sky, began rapidly to fall back: and finally fell; they saved the village; and they also saved the shop.

The alert shopkeeper bore himself in a swaggering way; his beard bristled like a bush, his collar open, and a blaze of fires in his eyes! He was surrounded by villagers while the half-sobered constable made out a report.

Rumors began to spread among the folk that the incendiaries had come from "Mare's Meadow"; they even pointed to one young lad in particular; but the shopkeeper only smiled ironically; and, strange thing, he tried to smother the talk about incendiarism.

About What the
<span>~~~></span> Sunset Told Him <span><~~~</span>

An autumn evening!

Do you remember well how peaceful such an evening can be? How all the sorrows of the soul can become ungrumblingly reconciled with misfortune on such a quiet autumn evening, when out of an ash-gray dusk the fields seem to float below the clouds, displaying their brief vacancy, and a noble quietude spreads through your limbs, when the fields stare at you with the lights of villages as if swimming with tears, they quietly chat from afar with wordless songs, when the fear that has been stifling you for many days now harmlessly smiles at the last glimmers of sunset: "I no longer exist . . ."

"No longer exist . . ."

But you don't believe in emptiness; over there an unreaped strip with drooping heads of grain has spread toward the wormwood; you stare into the emptiness, disbelieving in it, because here and there people stand waving their arms—from here, from there, calling you; they all stare at you from there, nodding their heads and muttering; and you don't believe in emptiness.

But answer the call, respond to the voice; you would only rub a gray bit of wormwood in the palms of your hands and see some small beastie scurrying away from you; you would drink deeply of the bitter perfume of wormwood and of the stale smell of the soil: of an autumn evening the field is empty; along its rim is the splash of the setting sun and along it a long line of ravens stretches, and out there, where the night is spreading its dark hues on the earth, the forest mutters its old tale, which is always the same: it is time for the forest to surrender its leaves; far off the forest is dropping its leaves like a waterfall, as though night, invading the earth, were drumming on it with sad rumbling dreams.

Who, in such moments, has not experienced the soul's illumination, in him the soul has died, for all men—all men—have wept in these instants for their spent years; who has not watered the empty fields with a single tear, who has not watched the yellow gems retreating from the fields with the receding sun, who has never felt the touch of light fingers on his breast, the tenderly quivering lips pressed against his own—you must leave, run away from such a person, men and beasts, and you, grasses, wither if that rude tread brushes against your slender stems: on such nights it is right to weep and take pride in the submissive sobbing which has surrendered itself to the fields: those are blessed tears, in them crime is washed away, in them the unsheltered soul faces itself.

Pyotr's soul was all bathed in tears: he walked over an empty field in the wake of the sunset, crushed the bitter-tasting grasses in his hands and watched the yellow gems abandoning the field with the setting sun; on his breast he felt the touch of invisible fingers, on his lips the kisses of tenderly quivering lips; and he strode ever further over the empty field; and the evening sunset, clothed in yellow gems, ran ever further away; at times he almost thought he was catching up with the departing sun, but it was only the harvest reaping, stretching under his feet, only the wordless songs sounding gently in his ears, and always the same voice—the long familiar, long-forgotten voice, sounding again: "Come to me, come, come."

And he strode on.

"I hear you, I am returning—don't go away, wait for me . . ." He heard the rustle of light fingers on his chest, he held out his hands to catch those dear hands; but through his cold embraces a breeze whistled; and the long familiar, long-forgotten voice, sounding again, crumbled unresponding into a gentle wordless song; yet that song had its own words; and here they were, those words, running far ahead over the dew:

"Ca-r-r-y m-y-y sor-r-row w-i-t-t-h y-o-u-u, ra-a-p-i-d r-i-v-e-r," came a response from the nearby crossroads and died away: there was the creak of a cart, the glow of a cigarette and'. . . nothing more.

"I'll rush all-all-all away: all-all-all-all-all," the stream muttered at his feet.

"I'll carry it myself . . ."

Deeply over the empty fields the sound of the tocsin chased after Pyotr; he swung around: a fiery pillar stood over Tzelebeyevo.

About How They
Drove to Likhov

The sun had not yet peeped out, and the early morning frost in the ruts had spread in thin crisp layers and the road, as though made of stone, showed pale in frosty pallor, when a cart pulled up at Schmidt's cottage. A whip dangling from his wrist, the belted coppersmith leapt down from the cart and decisively knocked on the window with the whip.

"Come out, will you!"

Waiting for Daryalsky, he stood listening by the window; truly a remarkable thing; Daryalsky had not returned from the fields to the carpenter's hut; from the fire he'd gone straight to Schmidt's; neither the coppersmith nor the carpenter could understand what Pyotr and Schmidt were chattering about, what business they had in common; all they could see, the both of them, were the lights in Schmidt's cottage that burnt all that long September night; and that made them both uneasy, and that's why the coppersmith hastened away in his cart earlier than expected.

Such were the thoughts racing through the coppersmith's mind as, smoking a rolled-up cigarette, he re-arranged the hay in the cart, moved the bottles, and stuffed a gray bundle in front; as he was thus engaged he stopped to think; and again he drummed on the window with his whip.

"Come out, will you!"

The door opened—and the devil take all! The coppersmith's narrow, spiteful eyes blinked and shifted uneasily, and his stubby fingers began to jerk; he almost grasped his cap, but restrained himself in time: the devil take them all!

The main cause of that extraordinary agitation was that the coppersmith had failed to recognize in Pyotr the lad he was accustomed to seeing, for Pyotr was now wearing a well-fitting, though somewhat crumpled jacket and a starched collar which supported his unshaven neck; a grayish overcoat blew in the breeze and a wide-brimmed hat was pulled over his forehead and—what agitated the coppersmith more than anything else—Pyotr's gloved hand grasped a heavy cane with an ivory head knob; and the coppersmith's puzzled, spiteful eyes writhed as Pyotr, after shaking hands with Schmidt, cried out in a haughty enough manner:

"Bring up the horses!"

"Get in, sir," the coppersmith could not help saying, unexpectedly dropping his local pride when confronted with such a miraculous transformation of a ragged fellow into a gentleman.

"You'll send on my things when needed," Pyotr said to Schmidt.

They got in. The cart gave a jerk, and the fine sheets of ice crackled, and the sun stared down over a wide expanse; the day promised to be cold, high and pale-azure.

Pyotr turned sharply round; he waved his handkerchief in farewell to Schmidt. Pyotr was rendering his last thanks to the friend who had not only helped to turn Pyotr's decision into action and to give him strength for the hard struggle that lay ahead of him, but who had also helped overnight to transform his shameful conduct and disaster into an inevitable temptation such as is common enough in life. In days to come, the strange adventures of these last few weeks would fall into perspective, seem to be a mere episode or some oppressive long-forgotten dream; no, he would give no more thought to this stupidly fatal pattern which he himself had unwittingly and with such care embroidered for himself.

He reviewed his past once more; but he must have perceived therein something he had better remain unaware of; because a sigh of regret, like a moan of repentance, suddenly burst from his breast; but he suppressed it.

What had he seen?

There, there, she stood by the pond with a yoke over her shoulders and stared after him under her red kerchief dotted with white apples; did she realize that they were exchanging their last glance? If she had known that, she would have thrown herself with her yoke on the grass, would have torn off her kerchief; and for a long long time she would have writhed on the ground, forgetting her honor and her womanly modesty; but she did not fall; no, she did not know; there she stood by the pond, with her yoke over her shoulder, shading her eyes and looking after him almost cheerfully; and her red kerchief fluttered in the breeze. Pyotr did not notice the carpenter at all. As soon as they ascended from the village, and the village lay stretched in the distance beneath them so that the huts and the orchards were completely drowned in the morning smoke, and only the large ornamental cross of Tzelebeyevo glittered, a wild joy gripped Daryalsky; it was as though all the inundations which had burst over his head in the last months—his courtship, Gugolevo, Tzelebeyevo, Kudeyarov, Matryona—as if all these were now being carried away from him in the mist, just as he himself was being borne away with the coppersmith from Tzelebeyevo; and the world, which had been still immeasurable for him the day before, was now concentrated there in the distance in a single woolly strand of smoke; and the cross on the Tzelebeyevo belfry beat against his eyes with its prickly sparks; he thought of the city, of the friends he had left there; and he also thought of Katya, of how he would return to her out of the new world, smiling—liberated from his previous deliriums.

A touch of the coppersmith's hand upon his neck made him jerk his shoulders with disgust:

"What do you want?"

"I'm feeling the cloth: it's not at all bad; good cloth . . ."

"What?"

"Out of good cloth, I was saying, your overcoat is made. How much did you pay for it?"

"Why did you feel it?"

"Your collar was raised: the cloth, I'm sure I'm right, is English . . ."

Daryalsky thrust his hand into his pocket: he had his revolver with him.

"You mustn't judge me so badly, my dear sir, on account of the way I treated you yesterday. Who can tell what sort of a man you are. I saw you were working for the carpenter, and so I thought you were a common fellow . . . But who are you?"

"A writer."

Silence . . . The cart creaked on: all around, empty fields . . .

"Don't think I have anything on my mind: I have no thoughts in particular. I have an independent point of view from the carpenter, don't confuse the two of us: I am a fully respectable man. You can ask anyone you like—we are coppersmiths. . . ."

Daryalsky began to feel disgusted at the presence of such a traveling companion; he moved away toward the very edge of the cart, but his disagreeable companion evinced an astonishing inclination to press unobservedly against him.

"Well, and what about that furniture order?"

"Oh, the furniture? I've been carpentering only because I wanted to get to know the people better."

"A spy!" the coppersmith said to himself and became more than ever agitated; his hands were trembling. "The carpenter put his foot in it. What do we *do* with him now? And do we must, can't leave him like that or we'll all perish for nothing."

"Then you're not off to Moscow?"

"No, I've no intention of going away; I shall return . . ."

But to himself he thought: "Why is he questioning me about Moscow? How does he know?"

Not without some stirring fear in his heart, Pyotr watched the coppersmith's hands and shifty eyes; for a time they sat near each other, breathing heavily. Suddenly Daryalsky felt a cold shiver go down his spine; and, pulling out of his overcoat pocket a small book with a fig leaf on the cover, he thrust it under the coppersmith's nose and almost shouted under his ear:

"That is a book of mine: I am a writer. Everyone knows me; if anyone touches me, they will write about it in the papers."

But the coppersmith must have deduced something uncomplimentary about himself from Daryalsky's shout: he stopped breathing at once and, pulling himself together, reassumed his former tone:

"From time immemorial, we Sukhorukovs have occupied ourselves with tinning; of course, I don't intend this about the gentry, but in a word: in Likhov there are none smarter than us."

Thus they drove on through the deserted fields, both of them flushed, excited and, God knows why, they kept shouting loudly, interrupting each other and boasting about themselves. . . .

When they had driven over ten miles from the village, Pyotr began to notice that a good distance in front of them on the road from Tzelebeyevo someone was urging a dark bay horse at full speed; the horse was harnessed to a light racing drozhky and in it a small dark figure was seated sideways; the figure kept whipping the horse on, enticing them, as it were, to follow and, as it were, talking to them in dumb show.

Very soon Daryalsky began to realize that the dark little figure in the drozhky seemed, as if on purpose, to be keeping at the same distance from them; if they slowed down, so did the drozhky; if they drove faster, so did the drozhky; sometimes the drozhky was lost sight of in the gullies and then not a soul was to be seen in the fields; and then again the drozhky dived out of a gully and, emerging into the open, ran at full speed uphill. Soon curiosity got the better of Daryalsky.

"Speed up there," he said to the coppersmith and seizing the reins from him, he began to belabor the horse, thinking to catch up with the racing drozhky; but the dark little figure merely whipped on the horse faster; and so they raced at full speed over the fields, and there was no one else in these fields; in the meantime Pyotr formed a certain secret intention; and he kept looking stealthily at his watch, thinking he might arrive in time for the train leaving for Moscow: "If only I could get into a compartment!" he thought; and he already imagined how, when he was settled in his seat, he would smoke without a care in the world his "Lion" cigarettes as he rocked to the iron thunder of the wheels: a wonderful song bearing him away from this place.

But the Likhov townsman had begun to grunt again behind Pyotr, and Pyotr cast a sideways glance at him: he clearly felt those unclean eyes staring at his back and that unclean hand with shaking fingers stretching out to seize his cane; then, imperceptibly transferring the reins from one hand to the other, he grasped with his free hand the other end of the stick; he now held the stick, but in such a way that the coppersmith did not notice it: with pounding heart Pyotr waited for what would come, but nothing came: they were already approaching Dead Top, and the Grachikha spire had long butted through the azure sky; already the dark little figure in the drozhky had dived below; and for some reason Pyotr began to hold in the reins, expecting the drozhky to start going up; but the drozhky, having dived down, did not come up again, and the dark little figure did not come up either, it must have got stuck in the gully and had no wish to come up again; and Pyotr clearly felt the coppersmith breathing behind his back: his neck felt hot from that breathing which went down his collar.

Over Dead Top Pyotr stopped the horse: there was no one below; turning around, he noticed how anxiously the coppersmith was scanning the gullies and the road in the depths that ran to Grachikha; he understood then that he and the coppersmith were intent upon one and the same thing; for one instant only their eyes met and were then hidden by their eyelashes.

"Does this road lead to the village?"

"To the village . . ."

For an instant only he'd met the coppersmith's eyes and yet he was able to decipher an anxiety and even a certain regret in those eyes.

Pyotr let the horse go downhill and when they had reached the most deep-lying part, the coppersmith's hot breath once more scorched his temples:

"Stop the horse, sir."

"What is it?"

"The horse collar's got loose, I think . . ."

The horse stopped: the end of the cane was in Pyotr's hand; which of them would descend first from the cart?

But the coppersmith did not descend; barely perceptibly Pyotr touched the cane; the cane did not yield; that could only signify that the coppersmith was holding the other end: "Now he will descend to tighten the collar, and I won't let go of the stick after that; we'll descend, and I'll find that all this is merely my imagination."

But the coppersmith had no intention of descending from the cart.

"What about the horse's collar?" Pyotr asked.

An awkward silence ensued: Pyotr turned around and their eyes met again.

At that instant Pyotr felt the coppersmith's hand tugging at the cane, but Pyotr did not let go; and for a moment the cane ceased moving; then Pyotr, in his turn, pulled it toward him; but the coppersmith's hand obviously would not let go.

All this happened in a brief instant, but in that instant, Pyotr's concentrated gaze, for an instant only, tried to swim into the colorlessly blinking eyes running away from him.

"God be with us, let's go on: I was mistaken—the horse collar is all right."

Pyotr understood that the coppersmith would neither step out of the cart nor release the cane: "Why does he need my cane?" He tried to ask himself that question and tried to persuade himself that this was a real question; but, in his unconscious depths, *all this* had for some time even ceased to be a question.

Then, with his free hand, Pyotr whacked the horse with all his might; they now flew out on top; he turned to the coppersmith; right in front of him he saw both the coppersmith's hand gripping the cane-head, and his whole shrunken figure shaking in the cart; but noticing Pyotr's eyes interrogatively watching his movements, the coppersmith assumed an innocent expression, as if he were merely admiring the ornamentation of the bone handle.

"A fine cane, isn't it?" Pyotr asked, with a wry smile.

"Not a bad cane," the coppersmith smiled wryly back. "I was just looking to see what sort of bone the cane-head was made of."

"Give it me, I'll show you."

"Wait a minute, there's a stamp here."

"No, it's here."

And after a slight, almost imperceptible tug of war, Pyotr forcibly snatched the cane from the coppersmith's hands. . . .

They had crossed over the Top and were now galloping again through the fields.

And when they were again far from the Top, Pyotr, glancing back, perceived the racing drozhky crossing the Top and the same dark little figure noiselessly whipping on the horse as if calling on him to halt, as if talking in dumb show; but what had happened in the gully had given Pyotr courage: "No, no, no, I just imagined it all," he persuaded himself: "Yes, yes, yes—it was all true," his heart beat back. . . . But now Pyotr would not let go of the cane.

The coppersmith, now sitting on the edge of the cart, did not sniffle or pant: he did not seem at all agitated; but his swollen lips looked more puffy, and his back was deliberately turned to Pyotr.

"Do you know these merchants, the Yeropegins?" Pyotr asked him casually.

"Everyone hereabouts knows them: ask any little boy in Likhov . . ."

"But do you know them well? Do you shine their pans?" Pyotr pursued.

"No. I haven't yet shined their pans: they have another coppersmith; and I don't even know that coppersmith . . ."

So that was it. Pyotr's doubts were reassured.

Pyotr plunged into thought; the morning gaiety had left him: now they were driving—to Likhov. "How can I get rid of him, and then get to the station? The coppersmith might stick to me like a leech and insist on taking me round to the Yeropegins."

No sooner had they entered Likhov than they began to bump up and down in the cart, so much so that it seemed as if the sharpest cobblestones had been deliberately laid on the roadway.

Then came a smoother stretch; they rounded the high fence of the jail by the side of which a profusion of chickweed had sprouted; in the distance a lone bayonet glistened; behind the barred prison windows Pyotr noticed the clean-shaven face of a man wearing a gray dressing gown. "It's probably one of the Fokins or Alexins," Pyotr thought; and while he scrutinized that clean-shaven face, the coppersmith leapt down from the cart, ran up to a low house, and exchanged urgent whispers with a fellow capped

like himself; the capped fellow nodded his head in agreement and, spitting out sunflower seeds, stared with curiosity
at Pyotr; all this happened almost imperceptibly; and when
Sukhorukov the coppersmith climbed back into the cart and
took over the reins, Pyotr was still looking at the clean-
shaven face smiling at him from behind the barred window;
they drove on further.

"Why is everything so quiet here?" Pyotr asked.

"See for yourself, the road's bad."

The fellow in the cap was following them; and now the
drozhky was driving up to the house where the coppersmith had held his whispered conversation; if Pyotr had
turned around, he would have seen the dark little figure
climb out of the drozhky, and he would also have seen two
other figures join him; and he was surprised when the
coppersmith stopped the horse at the entrance to the market
square under the signboard "SUKHORUKOV."

"Well, sir, good-bye; I've brought you here, and now
you had better use your own two feet; I've got to go about
my business."

"Thanks, many thanks!" And climbing out, Pyotr offered
him payment.

"No, wait: keep the money: we are the *Sukhorukovs:* we
don't accept money for such things (he now held himself
again in a dignified manner; and his language was more
familiar).

"Well, thanks then!" Pyotr said and, instead of payment,
held out his hand (true, the hand was gloved; and since the
previous day Pyotr was acting quite like a gentleman!).

Pyotr sighed with relief at the simple ending of his adven-
ture with the coppersmith; he reproached himself for his
shameful suspicions; and now he stepped quickly and freely
in the direction of the station; in a half-hour it would all be
over; his shameful connection with this place would be
ended forever. Thus he walked on swinging his cane, and
none of the townsmen he met on the way could have said
on seeing him that only yesterday this city man had been

wearing a red shirt with a ragged elbow; the townsmen passed him without turning round; but one townsman, who followed closely on his heels, did not take his eyes off his back; this townsman neither caught up with him nor lagged behind, as he followed him at an even pace.

"The devil take that coppersmith!"

Daryalsky, as he approached, noticed that the ticket office was closed.

"When does the train come in?" he inquired.

"Well, sir, the train's been gone this hour or more!"

"When is the next train to Moscow?"

"Not till tomorrow."

"Is there any train going anywhere?"

"To Lysichensk."

Through sheer obstinacy Daryalsky almost went off to Lysichensk, but thought better of it just in time: there was nothing to do in Lysichensk anyhow; and he only had enough cash to get him straight to Moscow.

And so he stayed.

Evening was creeping in. Pyotr was still sitting there, drinking beer, golden beer, its froth covering his mustaches.

What was he thinking about? But does one think at such a time? At such a time one merely counts the buzzing flies. At such a time that half of the soul which is mortally wounded keeps dully silent: in this way, whole days, weeks, years, can pass away.

Pyotr rolled pellets of bread, quaffed his beer, feeling only a warm pleasure and amazement at the easy way it had all ended, and at his being able so easily to burst out of the devilish trap set for him. A sweet excitement invaded him;

he gulped his beer, counted the flies, and listened to a portly army officer talking to another:

"Cornet Lavrovsky, do you still drink?"

"Yessir, I do . . ."

"Let's squeeze in another one then!"

They squeezed one in; and the portly officer was then pleased to exclaim contemptuously:

"Ah, you . . ."

"Where have I heard that before? I have experienced it all before, but where and when?" Pyotr thought. "Cornet Lavrovksy! I've even heard that name before."

What has been, is; what is, shall be. Everything happens; and everything passes.

The Likhov townsman who had been stalking Pyotr behind his back was now shuffling about the station platform alone.

ꞋꞋꞋ𝒮 About What Came of It 𝒮ꞋꞋꞋ

It was an azure day when he entered the station; the
day was—but no, when he began leaving the station, there
was no day; and no night either, so it seemed to him; there
was merely a dark void; and it was not even dark: there was
nothing at all in that place where only an hour before the
townsfolk had bustled about and the trees had rustled; now
there was nothing there but small houses—mere nothingness
impressed itself upon him or, rather, he impressed himself
upon it; there was not a sound, not a rustle, not a . . . ; it
seemed as if he had emerged from an azure world into a
station building; and then, leaving it, plunged into a city of
shadows; that town of Likhov through which he had driven
not so long ago and this present Likhov were separated by
at least a million miles: *that* Likhov had been a town full of
people; *this* Likhov was a city of shadows.

He managed to distinguish a few objects. It was as though
a hesitant hand had sketched here and there some black
blotches on the gray surface that was stuck to his eyes and,
in places had somehow photographically removed the
shade; he even began to feel both the black and the white
blotches; very soon he became convinced that the blotches
were no blotches but real, three dimensional objects; gradu-
ally, even at a distance, he identified the eye of a lantern,
still another lantern, and more lights; but they all looked
blurred as though draped in mourning crepe.

Where was he to turn now?

Why had he not gone in good time to Lysichensk? But how was he to know that everything would change so quickly and so irretrievably?

Staring around him, the only thing he could perceive was an altogether obscure little figure of a person detaching itself from the not altogether dark surroundings.

"Oh, I say, listen," he shouted at the figure. "How am I to find my way here?"

But the figure merely showed itself noiselessly against the background of the whitish wall: it was evidently incapable of making any reply to Pyotr's questions. Perhaps, it was no man at all, but merely a charcoal outline which some boy had traced there. Pyotr turned away and plunged again into the void.

But when he moved on, the figure moved after him.

Soon Pyotr was approaching the street lamps; dimly, the dead town began to take shape in front of him. Pyotr was even able to observe through an open window a dusty Likhov townsman, surrounded by dusty objects, sawing away in solitude on a fiddle close to a samovar.

"All the rooms are already taken!"

That was all the change he got from the only hotel in town. What a void! It was like having an empty belly: Likhov, the city of shadows!

Once more Pyotr set out into the void; very soon he had lost his bearings in the marketplace; and very soon again he stumbled against the whitish wall; and again, as before, on that wall he perceived the painted outlines of a figure; no doubt some practical joker had sketched in black the outlined shadows on the whitish walls: a human shadow had recorded its own shadow there. But when Pyotr moved away from the figure, it moved again after Pyotr.

Suddenly, right under his nose, he heard a familiar voice, a voice as creaky as an unoiled cart wheel; suddenly, at his very ear, he heard the sound of so recently familiar breathing: a mixture of shag and garlic.

"And so it's you, sir?"

He recognized the coppersmith before he could see him: He could only hear him and, for that matter, smell him too. But he was overjoyed!

"Oh sir, what a greenhorn you are, if I may be excused for saying so: here you are and all alone in the mist, at such an hour too, and bad people about."

Pyotr was on the point of answering, "All of you here are bad people," but stopped in time.

"I'm in a fix. I don't know where to spend the night," he replied instead. "Is there a stabling inn here?"

"You should spend the night at Mistress Yeropegin's, that's where."

That was a happy thought indeed. There he would have company too, for the town was full of shadows.

"But how shall I find my way there?" he asked.

"I'd take you there, but . . . Hey, fellow—you wouldn't be going down to Ganshina Street, would you?" he suddenly shouted to someone in the darkness.

"Down to Ganshina all right," a voice replied somewhere near Pyotr.

"Then show this gentleman the way to the Yeropegins'."

Pyotr swung around, amazed that the obscure figure, at which he had been staring not so long ago, had now become vocal.

"Let's go," the figure grunted.

It moved hugging the wall. Pyotr followed: by way of a warning, he made his cane whistle through the air in order to impress the "figure" as to the interesting nature of the object he held in his hands.

Then, when these minutes had flashed by and had become the past, when he was already seated among carpets over a cup of tea, Pyotr tried to picture what he had felt as he walked along in that darkness. It seemed to him that they had walked on for years and years, forging millions of years ahead of future generations; the road seemed to have no end, and it could have no end, just as it could have no returning: ahead lay infinity; infinity, too, lay behind; and there was even no infinity; and the fact that there was no infinity robbed everything of a simple explanation; there was nothing, neither the void nor simple explanation; there was only a whitish wall; and on that wall the shadow of a Likhov townsman. In vain Pyotr attempted to visualize the authentic features of this townsman in the hope of imparting some sort of logical sense to these features, even some commonsense justification, or some safety valve for human weakness; but evidently in the case of men who overstep the limits of a settled life, they are mercilessly deprived of the condescension which envelops their gaze with customary simplicity; and painful as it may be, we must repeat these words here, because the townsman sliding along at Pyotr's side was neither tall nor short, but rather noiseless and lean; and, besides, he clearly had a pair of horns . . .

"What?"

"H'm . . . Oh, nothing . . ."

"But it seemed to me, sir, you had been pleased to swear in black words. . . ."

"Is it far?"

"No, it's right there, their lodging . . . where the lamp is still blinking."

No, this was no devil, because the devil was walking behind them.

⚜ The Liberation ⚜

Pale, pale, pale faces—do you know them? With blue
rings under their eyes? These usually pleasant faces are not
at all beautiful, but it is this that attracts you to them: it's as
though those faces loom out of remote dreams and pass
through the whole of your life—not manifestly, not even in
dreams or in the imagination, but only by way of premonition; but, nevertheless, you behold them or, at least, you
wish to see them: these faces begin to loom before you
indistinctly (they always only begin to loom and never
assume a final shape) as women; in the case of women, they
only loom as fair-headed men and fade away stormlessly,
ironically, without ever producing an ultimate confron-
tation.

How surprised Pyotr was to see just such a face. And
where? In the entrance hall of Yeropegin's house. And
whose face was it? That of a plain-haired, rather dim-
looking maid who opened the door for him. A quiet person,
she did not seem surprised at his appearance, as though she
had been expecting him, this woman unknown to him till
now and so comforting for him to see—smiled at the sight
of him with a familiar sort of smile as if she could tell him
something about life or salvation; and the stearine candle
shook in her hand. It was as if she were saying, "I'll tell you
everything, everything."

But then a formless dumpling-like shape, in a chocolate-colored dress and with a wart on her chin, rolled into the hall.

"With whom have I the honor of speaking?"

"Daryalsky, a writer—I have the honor to introduce myself," Daryalsky replied.

"Very pleased. And what can I do for you?"

"Since I am personally acquainted with your husband and was invited to stay with you in June, I, having missed my train, decided to fall back on your hospitality. May I spend the night in your house?"

"But there is a hotel in town!" Fyokla Matveyevna evidently distrusted the strange and belated arrival of Pyotr.

"That's just it: the hotel is full up."

"But my husband has lost his speech . . ."

"You don't say so! But he was in good health when I saw him not so long ago."

"And where was it you met him?"

"At the Baroness Todrabe-Graaben's, where I was a guest this summer," he replied, uttering these last words with pride. Poor fellow, he was so afraid of being pushed back into that dark state of non-being where the fourth man was waiting for him near the house.

His last statement produced results:

"Annushka, prepare a bed in the wing for the gentleman."

Pyotr noticed the dripping candle quiver in the hand of the woman whom, because of a mysterious presentiment, he wished to call his sister and whose features reminded him of something. But what did they remind him of?

"This way, please, sir!" lisped the lumpy little woman, folding her hands over her belly and shuffling through the rooms past the plump vases, the armchairs and the mirrors.

And, as the minutes passed, during which he overcame the feeling of endlessness and had, with his strange companion, forged millions of years ahead of future generations, when he was already seated in the soft comfortable arm-chair over a cup of tea, a lump of sugar in his mouth, he then thought that Moscow already lay behind him and that even Likhov, the town of shadows, was also behind him. But where was he to go now? Feeling at ease now, he gave vent to his eloquence in front of the lumpy little woman with the good-natured face and modestly lowered eyes.

Thinking to prove himself a guest pleasing in all respects, he even suggested that they might play a game of cards; but she declined.

Only one phenomenon or, rather, a fleeting mirage broke this idyll, and it was a fleeting mirage, because. . . . What would you say, reader, if from that dark ambush, you were to see death being dragged past you, lit by funereal candles and surrounded by muttering old women? You are accustomed to read of such happenings in novels, but this is no novel, no fantasy, but . . . Pyotr saw the somber ambush of rooms suddenly fill with candles: two old crones were leading by the hand none other than the figure of garbed death itself in a black robe and wearing black glasses; there was death itself shuffling along, hardly able to drag its feet, its slippers dully flapping on the floor. Annushka, sidling up behind with a candle in her hand, smiled at Pyotr with a sisterly smile, and it seemed to him as if she were beckoning to him and talking to him mutely:

"Pardon me . . . it's my sick husband," the "dumpling" explained to Pyotr. "It's only a week since he began walk-ing again . . ."

"Yes . . . And his speech?"

"The doctors say that he may talk again . . ."

"Sometime?"

"Perhaps never," she replied, lowering her eyes.

Pyotr grew thoughtful; but what was it he was thinking about?

But does one think of anything in moments like that? In moments like that one counts the buzzing flies; in moments like that the mortally wounded half of the soul keeps sullen silence; it keeps sullen silence for days, weeks, years; and it is only after those days, weeks, and by-gone years that one slowly begins to realize what has happened to that stricken half of the soul, and whether the person who has lost half his soul can still claim to have a soul at all; and, in the meantime, one does not know whether one's soul has died or whether one has merely fainted and one's soul would be returned to one; but its first fruitful return to you is marked by a savage pain or takes the form of a physical sickness which brings misery; death has manifested itself to you—have you forgotten that? As to the half-soul, it still has something of the grave about it; and, rising from the dead, it must face the last judgment: it experiences anew all that which you have long experienced in order to re-create the confusion of former days into heavenly beauty; if your soul lacks such strength, then its infected parts rot away leaving no trace.

What could Pyotr be thinking about in those moments? All he knew was that millions of miles, millions of spent days, now separated him from yesterday.

"So your husband may never speak again?"

"Never. But it's time for you to rest. Annushka, will you show the gentleman to his room."

Pyotr had been gone a long time, and with her hair still undone, Fyokla Matveyevna was bowed down in prayer in her stuffy bedroom—to which only Annushka-the-Dovecot had access—amid the blood-red glitter of icon lamps, amid the sheets, the pillows and the bolsters, before an image of the Dove molded in heavy silver.

She was no longer afraid of her husband, for he was now speechless; if he happened to notice anything and understand it, he could not say anything about it; but, truth to tell, having lost his reason, he could not understand; and, besides, he was about to give up his soul to God. But Luka Silitch's soul was strongly attached to his body; for week after week he went on giving up his soul; and, strange to say, even though the doctors expected him to die any day, for over a week already Luka Silitch had regained a little control over his feet and hands; for the last few days he even muttered and moved his tongue and made attempts to get out of bed; he obliged them to help him to walk around the room; and ever since, the old women each day walked him around the room before he went to sleep; but the doctor kept insisting that these were Luka Silitch's last days.

It would be sinful to suggest that Fyokla Matveyevna wished her husband to die, but she did worry about what would happen if he regained his speech and said to her, "Well, old woman, what's been going on here? Is that true?"

But even if he had regained his speech, still his reason would have been impaired: Luka Silitch's brain had been shattered. Just consider what had happened the day before, for example; when Fyokla Matveyevna visited her husband's room he had with shaking hand drawn some incomprehensible signs for her benefit, while a flood of tears cascaded from his eyes. She had been obliged to take off his glasses and dry his eyes; and he had stared at her so pitifully, sobbing profusely like a small child. Fyokla Matveyevna had joined in the weeping; and she remembered the trembling signs made by her husband's affected hand: the letter *O* was often repeated, followed by the letters *T* and *R;* that made *OTR* . . . but Fyokla Matveyevna could not understand the rest. It occurred to her to complete the word, and the result was *Otriganiev* (she was an Otriganiev by birth); and she began to wonder whether it was her death that Luka Silitch was foretelling. Those frail of spirit, those with ailing minds, are sometimes capable of prophesying no worse than wise men.

"O Lord, O Lord!" the merchant's wife moaned in the red light of the icon lamps.

"O Lord!" she moaned.

And the heavy silver bird, the Dove, spread its wings over her.

Suddenly there was a knocking and a light patter of slippers in the empty room: it was the "dumpling" in a night-shirt running down the corridor and then peeping into the room; and there she saw, standing in the center of the room, none other than Luka Silitch himself, holding a candle in his trembling hand. He had got up in the middle of the night and, dragging his feet through the rooms, had mustered enough strength to take a candle with him (the woman watching over him had evidently fallen asleep, and so he got up and staggered on). But what sort of a Luka Silitch was this? Through the black windows of his glasses death stared at Fyokla Matveyevna: it caught sight of her and was stretching after her now, after the Otriganiev family: the hand with the candle was doing a dance, and the other, quivering too, was sketching in the air what looked like "*o-te-er*"; and Luka Silitch's lips were hanging loosely, his mouth gaped and his tongue moved ineffectively. Perhaps he was trying to snarl at the "dumpling."

The "dumpling" gave a gasp, squatted down with her hands over her breasts (she was undressed), and stared at her husband.

Luka Silitch, at the sound of her gasp, dropped the candle and darkness enveloped the married couple. All that could be heard was Fyokla Matveyevna's sobbing, the shuffling of light slippers approaching her in the dark, and the heavy thud of the candlestick as it rolled on the floor.

From under a pallid, very pallid face peering out of a black kerchief Annushka's large eyes gazed at Pyotr so thoughtfully, with such assurance, so peacefully; sternly she stood there holding a lantern in her raised hand, a lantern which cast a light, blood-red glimmer upon her waxen features; with her other hand she held open the door into the darkness beyond; and this pointed hand seemed to beckon him ineluctably to descend into those depths, where there was nothing but darkness and the rustling of leaves and gusts of wind beating against his face.

Annushka, his new-found "sister," was leading him into that dark region, and her eyes seemed to be saying word-lessly but distinctly, "I shall tell you everything—every-thing: everything—everything—everything . . ."

"But let me speak myself."

"No, you must leave it to us to tell you that."

But nothing of the sort was said between them: only their eyes spoke to each other; their lips made other speeches.

"What? Am I to go in *there*?"

"That's where. Your bed's made up in the wing."

"And where is the wing?"

"In the fruit orchard. Please come along, sir."

For a second it occurred to Pyotr that it would not hurt him to bring his overcoat with him; but he put the thought aside; after all, his quarters were close by.

He followed her through the door.

Strange that all that absence of light and the darkness, in which he had not so very long ago wandered through the Likhov streets, was now filled with a darkness that was alive and noisy, boisterous even, under the gusts of a cold wind that seemed to obey the motions of his guide's hand; the darkness rustled with a thousand leaves; beneath the lan-tern's circle of light the pear trees threw themselves at them, flowering green in the light; and the peaceful night spread overhead with unusual magnificence, displaying its worlds and constellations. It seemed to Pyotr as if they were journeying toward the stars, and he strode firmly in the wake of the blinking lantern.

Then he caught sight of the pavilion in the depths of the orchard and its already lighted lamps winking a welcome to them.

But when Annushka unlocked the door, Pyotr shuddered for a second.

"Is the pavilion . . . empty?" he asked.

"Empty," she replied.

"And I am to stay here? All alone?"

"I'll stay with you, I'll stay," she said, with a pleasant enough smile.

She stood there on the threshold with lantern aloft while she pushed the door open with the other hand; and it seemed as though this hand, which was pressing on the door, was authoritatively pointing to the new path he was to follow.

Pyotr turned round, unable to breathe enough of that boisterous wind beating against his mighty chest, unable to satiate himself sufficiently with those stars which the tranquil night revealed to him. How many times had he seen all that, but on this night it seemed he was seeing it all for the first time and he tried to remember it all forever.

Annushka stood there, beckoning to him through the door with her upraised lantern.

Pyotr passed beneath her lantern: a musty smell struck his nostrils; she closed the door behind them; they found themselves now face to face inside that stifling interior.

On his way to the room, which had been set aside for his night's rest, he noticed that the floors had been washed with *kvas* and were, as a result, sticky; the corridor turned right and then left; in the center of it was a door; through this door they entered; and Pyotr saw a clean white room, a bed with freshly prepared pillows, a mahogany dressing table, a night table, a washstand, and other bedroom objects—all in immaculate order: there were even paper, stamps and envelopes on the writing table; and he also saw a length of rope which had been thrown underneath the bed. A rotund little lamp lit up the scene.

"I haven't slept in such luxury for a long time," Pyotr thought.

He glanced round the room once more. Then he noticed an empty space above the door where the glass had been removed—a space large enough for someone, if he so

wished, to thrust his head through if standing on a stool on
the other side of the door. Unconsciously he took all this in,
like any absent-minded person whose eyes record only
momentarily such uninteresting trifles and miss the main
point.

For the last time he glanced at his new friend, who
seemed silently to understand him. "My dear, darling
sister," he wanted to say as his heart contracted with
emotion, and he was drawn to tell her everything, to speak
openly, to share everything, to kiss her fraternally on those
entirely bloodless lips of hers, and to whisper to her as one
whispers only after a long separation.

"Well?"

And he said:

"Well?"

But she merely made a low, solemn bow, as though she
were a young nun bowing before an icon in a church.

"Well?"

She closed the door firmly after her; she was now outside.
Pyotr was left alone.

He sat for a long time, stooped over the table. Feverishly,
hastily, he was writing a letter to Katya as if, in that one
letter, he wished to express all of himself, to explain to her
all these past days which had proved so incomprehensible
even to himself but had now suddenly become crystal clear;
and let us believe that Pyotr did find words to express all
this; he addressed the envelope, attached a stamp, and thrust
the letter into the pocket of his jacket. But he still remained
sitting at the table. "My dear sister, you opened my eyes:
you have given me back to myself . . ." he kept repeating.
Pyotr's soul was washed in tears: he was already in a state of
oblivion; and it seemed to him he had left Likhov far
behind, that he was walking through an empty field trampling on the bitter grasses, that he was watching yellow
diamonds fade with the sun beyond the fields; on his chest
he felt the pressure of invisible fingers, on his lips the kisses
of tenderly quivering lips; he walked on over the empty

field toward the wordless songs that sounded faintly in his
ears; and he seemed to hear that forever familiar, long-
forgotten, sisterly voice, "Come to me—come, come!"

"I hear. I am coming back. . . ."

And he came out of his forgetfulness; a noise must have
wakened him and, when he turned round, he found the
door to his room open.

"Well?"

In the doorway he saw Annushka's sad, slightly ironical
face swathed in white.

"Would you like me to bring you anything?" she asked.
"Well?"

She laughed challengingly. She seemed to have difficulty
in uttering the following rather formless words, which
grated on Pyotr's ears:

"I looked in to see if there was any service I could do for
the young gentleman. . . ."

"What service can I need?"

"Dunno, but perhaps something a young man might
need . . ."

"No, I don't want that," Pyotr interrupted her rudely.

Then he saw her hand moving toward the key which was
in the lock on his side of the door.

"Leave the key alone!" Pyotr exclaimed. "I'll lock the
door for the night."

But as Pyotr rushed quickly to the door, Annushka
swiftly shut it in his face, laughing quietly and teasingly in a
sort of unearthly way.

Pyotr was now locked in.

At once he understood everything: he extinguished the
lamp and remained in utter darkness. When he ran over to
the window in order to break the panes, he saw a man's face
staring insolently at him from the outside; he also caught
sight of several shadowy, rapidly running figures with
lanterns in their hands, and they were fussily waving their
arms at him. Then he rushed to the door and, with rising
horror, began to listen while watching the window at the

same time. The shadowy figures were still to be seen scurrying about, but everything appeared quiet behind the door,
although a glimmer of candlelight could be seen through
the open space above the door. In an instant, Pyotr had
placed a stool by the door and, leaping on it, thrust his head
through the opening: four dark backs and four caps were
all he saw wedged together and pressed against the door; he
could not distinguish the faces. Pyotr jumped down and
was about to pull out his revolver; and only then he remembered that he had left his revolver, his cane, and his gray
coat in the main house. He understood it was all over now.

"O Lord, what is this, what is this?"

He covered his face with his hands, turned away, and
wept like a lost child.

"What for?"

But the voice of the malign spirit replied:

"What about Katya?"

With his back to a corner, he concluded that it was use-
less to resist. Quick as lightning an only prayer flashed
through his mind: that they should act quickly and execute
painlessly that to which he did not dare as yet give a name;
for he still had faith, he still had hope.

"What? Shall I in an instant become . . . *that thing?*"

But those few, brief, remaining instants were prolonged
into eternity.

"Open the door, then, open it quickly!" he shouted,
beside himself, while everything within him trembled.

"Lord, what is happening to me? What is this?"

By shouting and inviting them to do their will upon him,
he was, as it were, signing his own "death warrant."

The key clicked in the lock, and they appeared. Until he
had shouted, *they* were still debating whether to cross the
fatal threshold. For *they* were men too; but now they had
made their decision.

Pyotr saw the door opening slowly, saw a large dark blur
with eight stamping feet moving into the room. He was able

to see this because a candle in the corridor was lighting their way: someone's trembling hand held that candle. But *they* had not spotted him as yet, though they were cautiously advancing straight toward him. They stopped. Then a face was staring down at him, an almost extraordinarily ordinary face, a frightened rather than an evil face, and a whisper passed from that face to the others. . . .

"What have you against me, brothers?"

Whack! A blinding blow knocked him off his feet; stumbling, he felt he was already squatting down. Whack! A second blow, even more blinding; and then nothing; he fell headlong, uprooted. . . .

"Here, catch hold of him! . . ."

"Ah?"

"Pull him along, pull! . . ."

"Clack-clack-clack," the trampling feet sounded in the darkness.

"Get the rope!"

"Where is it?"

"Squeeze harder . . ."

"Clack-clack-clack," the trampling feet sounded in the darkness. They stopped trampling; in the deep silence heavy sighs could be heard coming from four figures, merged shoulder to shoulder, stooping over some object. Then there was the sound of a chest being crushed; and silence again . . .

"Clack-clack-clack," the feet started trampling again . . .

Pyotr lived a billion years in ether; he beheld all the splendor hidden from mortal eyes; and it was only after this that he blessedly returned, blessedly half-opened his eyes, and blessedly saw . . . .
. . . .
a certain pale face bent over him, the head covered with a dark kerchief; and from that face tears fell on his chest, and

the upraised hands of that sorrowful-looking person, hands crossed in the form of a crucifix were lowering a weighty silver object.

"My own dear sister," a distant voice sounded.

"Peace, brother," came the reply from far away.

He was still alive when she closed his eyes; he moved away and did not come back. . . .

In the gray, barely perceptible dawn, the yellow flame of a candle danced on a table; grim, foreheadless men hung about in the small room, while Pyotr's body, breathing feverishly, still lay on the floor; with blank faces that had no expression of cruelty on them the men stood over Pyotr's body, staring curiously at their handiwork, at the blueish shade of death, and the rivulet of blood seeping from his lip, which had probably been bitten through in the heat of the struggle.

"Looks like he's still alive . . ."

"He's breathing!"

"Choke him a little more . . ."

The woman, prostrate, held the emblem of the Silver Dove over him.

"Let him be. He's our brother, isn't he!"

"No, he's a traitor," Sukhorukov called out from a corner, rolling a cigarette between his fingers.

But the woman turned on him reproachfully and said:

"You can't tell. Maybe he's a brother."

A whisper of sympathy ran round the room:

"Dear heart!"

"We didn't finish him off . . ."

"He's going!"

"Gone!"

"The Kingdom of Heaven be with him!"

"Are the spades handy?"

"They are."

"Where shall we put him?"

"Oh, in the orchard."

And again from the corner a clear voice said:

"I whacked with that cane of his, which he tried to pull away from me on the road."

It was a breezy morning: the trees were rustling.